P9-DFW-208

ALSO BY TOM CLANCY

The Hunt for Red October
Red Storm Rising
Patriot Games
The Cardinal of the Kremlin
Clear and Present Danger
The Sum of All Fears
Without Remorse
Debt of Honor
Executive Orders
Rainbow Six
The Bear and the Dragon
Red Rabbit
The Teeth of the Tiger
Dead or Alive (with Grant Blackwood)
Against All Enemies (with Peter Telep)
Locked On (with Mark Greaney)
Threat Vector (with Mark Greaney)
Command Authority (with Mark Greaney)
Tom Clancy Support and Defend (by Mark Greaney)
Tom Clancy Full Force and Effect (by Mark Greaney)
Tom Clancy Under Fire (by Grant Blackwood)
Tom Clancy Commander in Chief (by Mark Greaney)
Tom Clancy Duty and Honor (by Grant Blackwood)
Tom Clancy True Faith and Allegiance (by Mark Greaney)
Tom Clancy Point of Contact (by Mike Maden)
Tom Clancy Power and Empire (by Marc Cameron)
Tom Clancy Line of Sight (by Mike Maden)
Tom Clancy Oath of Office (by Marc Cameron)
Tom Clancy Enemy Contact (by Mike Maden)
Tom Clancy Code of Honor (by Marc Cameron)
Tom Clancy Firing Point (by Mike Maden)
Tom Clancy Shadow of the Dragon (by Marc Cameron)
Tom Clancy Target Acquired (by Don Bentley)
Tom Clancy Chain of Command (by Marc Cameron)
Tom Clancy Zero Hour (by Don Bentley)
Tom Clancy Red Winter (by Marc Cameron)

TOM CLANCY

RED WINTER

MARC CAMERON

BERKLEY
New York

BERKLEY

An imprint of Penguin Random House LLC

penguinrandomhouse.com

Copyright © 2022 by The Estate of Thomas L. Clancy, Jr.; Rubicon, Inc.; Jack Ryan
Enterprises, Ltd.; and Jack Ryan Limited Partnership

Penguin Random House supports copyright. Copyright fuels creativity, encourages
diverse voices, promotes free speech, and creates a vibrant culture. Thank you for buying
an authorized edition of this book and for complying with copyright laws by not
reproducing, scanning, or distributing any part of it in any form without permission.
You are supporting writers and allowing Penguin Random House to continue to
publish books for every reader.

BERKLEY and the BERKLEY & B colophon are registered
trademarks of Penguin Random House LLC.

ISBN: 9780593422779

G. P. Putnam's Sons hardcover edition / December 2022
Berkley premium edition / October 2023

Printed in the United States of America
1   3   5   7   9   10   8   6   4   2

Maps by Jeffrey L. Ward

Whenever they catch you, they will kill you. But first, they must catch you . . .

Richard Adams, *Watership Down*

Hell is empty
And all the devils are here.

William Shakespeare, *The Tempest*

It is not scientific thought that leads to victory in battle, but pure instinctive madness.

Unknown

PRINCIPAL CHARACTERS

Jack Ryan, Sr.: CIA liaison to MI6, London

Dr. Caroline "Cathy" Ryan: Jack's wife, ophthalmic surgeon

John Clark: CIA operations officer, Special Activities Division

Mary Pat Foley: CIA operations officer, Moscow

Daniel Murray: FBI legal attaché, London

Admiral James Greer: deputy director (Intelligence), CIA

Robert Ritter: deputy director (Operations), CIA

Betty Harris: FBI special agent, Washington, D.C., Field Office

Lane Buckley: assistant deputy director (Operations), CIA

Ed Foley: CIA chief of station, Moscow

Skip Hulse: CIA chief of West Berlin Base

Jen North: CIA operations officer, West Berlin Base

Billy Dunn: CIA operations officer, West Berlin Base

Carol Morandini: CIA cypher clerk, West Berlin Base

Jason Newell: CIA chief of East Berlin Station

Truly Bishop: CIA officer, East Berlin Station

Ruby Keller: State Department Foreign Service officer, USBER

Boden Lee: F-117 pilot, 4450th Tactical Group, Nellis Air Force Base, Tonopah

Klaus Schneider: Stasi officer/Romeo

Elke Hauptman: professional singer, East Berlin

Uwe Hauptman: physicist, Humboldt University, East Berlin

Hans Hauptman: Elke and Uwe's six-year-old son

Kurt Pfeiffer: Stasi major, East Berlin, Elke Hauptman's handler

Evgeni Zima: KGB colonel, East Berlin

Ivan Popov: KGB major, East Berlin

Vladimir Mikhailov: KGB junior officer, East Berlin

Garit Richter: Stasi HVA illegal in the United States

Heather Beasley: UFO watcher

Dieter Fuchs: former thief turned assassin

Felix Becker: former East German Olympic gymnast turned assassin

Selma Kraus: former East German Olympic swimmer turned assassin

Mitzi Graff: Stasi guard, Hohenschönhausen Prison

Gunter Wolfe: Stasi guard, Hohenschönhausen Prison

USEFUL TERMS

West Germany FRG/BRD: Federal Republic of
  Germany/Bundesrepublik Deutschland

East Germany GDR/DDR: German Democratic
  Republic/Deutsche Demokratische Republik

Ossi: East German resident

USBER: U.S. Diplomatic Mission, West Berlin

1

The McDonald's off Clayallee seemed an unlikely place for espionage. One might as well attempt to defect at Woolworths.

West Berlin, guarded by twelve thousand Allied troops and surrounded by half a million soldiers of the Warsaw Pact? A defection there would make sense. The dark and snowy hollows of Grunewald Forest, six miles from the Wall and a stone's throw from the Berlin Brigade headquarters? Certainly.

Twenty-nine and single, with a degree in public policy from the University of Maryland, Ruby Keller was a ground-floor Foreign Service officer. She was a newbie to the State Department, handling visa applications, lost passports, and any other piddling issue that confronted U.S. citizens visiting West Berlin. She never admitted it during the daily calls to her mother, but an inordinate amount of her workday was spent getting coffee for all the good old boys in this isolated outpost of the State Department.

Everyone told her she'd be under the microscope, watched by all kinds of alphabet-soup agencies, Russians trying to get her to spy, Americans making sure she didn't. Crazy stuff for an Indiana farm girl. The Clayallee McDonald's (the first restaurant in Germany with a drive-through window) seemed safe, like home, laughably far from all the international intrigue.

Keller stomped her feet when she came in from the cold and shook the snow off her jacket. It was late, after ten, but her internal clock was still jiggered toward the time in Washington, D.C., where she'd attended eighteen months of training, and her body thought it was about time to eat dinner.

She'd spent the last fifteen minutes walking from her apartment near the diplomatic mission and had to squint under the stark glare of phosphorescent lighting. It was hard to believe she was still in Germany. The whole place could have been teleported directly from her hometown of Evansville. She ordered a Hamburger Royal (a Quarter Pounder, but that didn't translate into the metric system) and fries. The shake machine was broken.

Ruby was accustomed to chilly winters and had contemplated eating outside during her walk over, but it turned out to be a little too cold for that much adventure. Instead, she found a table by the window and nibbled on her sandwich—just like the ones at home—and people-watched.

Dinner rush was well past, but Europeans eat late—

and GIs ate all the time. The kids behind the counter spoke English, as did ninety percent of the customers—most of whom were soldiers or civilian employees of the British or U.S. military. Ruby spoke German, very well in fact, but had hoped to be able to practice a lot more. The vast majority of Germans she'd met since her arrival spoke English. They just gave her a sort of blank stare if she even tried to *Deutsch sprechen*. With all the chatter among the patrons about new American movies and V-8 hotrods it was easy to forget they were sitting smack in the heart of communist Germany.

State Department Diplomatic Security agents had warned her before she left Washington. Hauptverwaltung Aufklärung—HVA, the counterintelligence operatives of the dreaded Stasi—assumed every single person at Mission Berlin was a spy. The CIA did nothing to dissuade the East Germans of this notion since it caused them to waste manpower. From what Keller had read, that mattered little. The Stasi enlisted pretty much everyone in the country to their cause, giving them an almost unlimited supply of personnel to spy—mostly on one another.

Surveillance was a foregone conclusion. It was prudent to assume every room and telephone outside the embassy was bugged—if not by HVA, then by West German intelligence—BND. A sheltered Indiana orchestra kid, Ruby found the whole thing fascinating.

People called what they were living in a Cold War, and, for the most part, that was right, but when it boiled over, it did so in a very big way. Tensions between East and West were at their worst since the Cuban Missile Crisis. Every month, that knot of war that Khrushchev warned Kennedy about pulled tighter and tighter until it seemed there would be no untying it without swords. Pershing II missiles bristling all over Europe, American overflights of disputed islands, not to mention the President's Strategic Defense Initiative, all had the Soviets feeling twitchy and worried about their future. The rubles that had been used to prop up satellite states were repurposed for missiles meant to counter the capitalist threat of the Main Enemy—the United States. That left East Germany with a dwindling treasury and few resources to replace the missing Soviet assistance. Everyone was on edge.

Two years earlier, a Sukhoi Su-15 fighter had shot down a KAL civilian airliner when it inadvertently veered into Soviet airspace on its way to Seoul from Anchorage, Alaska—murdering 269 people. Keller kept the *Life* magazine photograph of the victims' shoes that had washed ashore as a reminder of Russian brutality. Just months before, Soviet troops opened fire on a U.S. Army soldier for taking photos of a military installation near Potsdam, killing him. Both sides ran recon missions. In the East, it could be a capital offense.

Ruby's mother was horrified that her little girl had decided to venture into what the nightly news frequently referred to as Ground Zero. But for Ruby, that was the flame that drew her close.

The State Department travel office had flown her into Bonn for her initial briefing, then she'd taken the train across the East German countryside to reach Berlin. For the most part, the journey had been at night, but she'd been too excited to sleep. Ruby Keller, midwestern violin player, found herself living the stuff of spy novels, of impossible missions. A terrifyingly adventurous place with narrow, smoke-filled railcars and curt policemen who were apparently issued scowling frowns with their daily dose of communism.

The uniformed TraPo, or Transport Policeman, had looked the part in his high-crowned hat and blueberry uniform. He'd dashed her preconceived notions when he checked her diplomatic passport and refunded the twenty-five deutsche marks she'd originally paid to transit the GDR. Diplomats, he explained with an easy smile, were exempt from the fee.

Night had given way to morning and curtains of smudgy haze from East Germany's ubiquitous brown coal. This was, she'd been warned, the smell of the place—lignite and rot. You could get away from it in Bonn or the countryside of West Germany, but here in Berlin, surrounded on all sides, the abject desperation of the East assaulted the Wall like siege warfare—and the smell drifted across.

The McDonald's door opened, startling Ruby out of her thoughts with a gust of frigid air and a chattering group of American servicemen. She finished her sandwich and stood, pulling her purse over her shoulder. It was going to feel amazing to snuggle up in her government-issue quilts and read a book while the radiator ticked and rattled her to sleep.

Cold pinched her nose as she stepped from the bright lights of the restaurant and onto a quiet forested side street off the wider boulevard of Clayallee. Dozens of pedestrians, all of them heavily bundled against the cold, went to and from the surrounding military apartments, chatting, laughing. The Brits had such cool accents . . .

Keller had just passed beneath a streetlamp on her way to the main thoroughfare when she heard commotion in the parking lot to her left, a sudden hush, as if the crowd could not believe what they were seeing.

Something heavy slammed into her shoulder before she could turn and investigate. The pavement was slick with trampled snow and her feet shot out from under her, planting her flat on her back, all the wind driven from her lungs. She remembered reading somewhere that you were supposed to exhale sharply to start breathing again. Great in theory, but all she could manage was a wheezing croak.

The man who'd run into her had hit the ground beside her. He cursed in German and clambered to his feet—now with her purse in his hands.

Ruby rolled onto her side, feeling like a floundering seal on the ice. She tried to yell, managed a pitiful gasp, but that didn't matter. Several passersby saw what had happened and rushed the young man, bowling him over in a scrum of fists and feet. Attempting to steal a woman's purse in the middle of a bunch of homesick soldiers was doomed to fail before it began. Civilians joined in as well, men, women, even a couple of teenage girls. Someone yelled to call the police. A baby-faced Army buck sergeant retrieved her purse from the miscreant and brought it to her. He smiled, the kind of smile that said he would have tipped his hat if he'd had one, and asked if she was okay as he helped her to her feet.

"Embarrassed, more than anything," she said, brushing the snow off her coat and checking herself for breaks. "Everything bends the way it's supposed to."

It was something her grandfather always said.

The mugger hadn't really had time to take anything from her purse, but Ruby stepped under the streetlight to check anyway. She paused when she saw what was inside. Looked up at the crowd in disbelief and then back to the purse.

This couldn't be right. It was her bag, but instead of stealing anything, the kid, or someone, had put something inside it. A brown paper bag with a folded piece of typing paper and a black eight-inch floppy.

Ruby whistled to get the sergeant's attention as he returned to the group holding the mugger to the ground. She held up the purse when he turned. "You took this directly off of him?"

The sergeant shook his head. "No, ma'am," he said. "I helped to pin him down. That lady . . ." He turned to look at the group standing over the downed mugger. "I don't see her anymore, but I'm pretty sure she was German. She'd already picked it up, I guess. She handed it to me and I gave it back to you."

"Thanks," Ruby said, staring into her open purse at the computer disk. The paper had an address in Chantilly, Virginia, and a hastily scrawled note that read: *I*

wish to speak to someone in your Special Services. Instruc-
tions to proceed are on disk. You will find decryption code
at Virginia location. Involve no one stationed in Germany.

Ruby closed the purse, squeezing the clasp until her knuckles hurt. She looked over her shoulder. Someone had to be watching her. And who was the lady who'd given the sergeant the purse? Why not just give it back herself?

Wanting to "speak to Special Services" was a kind of shorthand in the diplomatic world.

Whoever this was wanted to defect.

This was big. The CIA at USBER, probably Army Intelligence, a gob of people would want to talk to this mugger kid, find out who he was, and what he knew, and the woman, too, if they could find her.

A murmur ran through the crowd.

Someone said, "Stand back."

"Give him some room," said another.

It was dark and snowing and the crowd was so large now that from her vantage point, Keller could just make out her assailant's head. His wool hat had come off in the scuffle. Long hair splayed over the snow. Then one of the sergeant's friends who'd been stooped over the motionless figure stood up and edged away.

"Whoa! I think this guy's dead."

2

Dr. Cathy Ryan tossed her dressing gown on a paisley Queen Anne chair and fell back on her pillows, giving an exaggerated bounce against the mattress. "He's down and out and it's not quite ten p.m.!" She sighed. "It's a miracle."

On the other side of the bed, thirty-four-year-old Jack Ryan lowered an open folder to peer over the top of his light bedtime reading, a British Secret Intelligence Service study titled *A Soviet View of the Threat Posed by American Pershing II Missiles Deployed in Europe*. The document was marked *Confidential* rather than *Secret*. It had to be checked out from the office, and Ryan was allowed to bring it home to study as long as he secured it in the home safe MI6 had graciously provided.

A colder-than-usual London November nipped at the windows, promising a hell of a winter—but the bedroom was what Ryan called "Cathy-warm," meaning she could sleep in a light silk gown instead of one of the flannel grannie ones she wore if he turned down the heat.

Not the pajama type, Jack wore a white T-shirt and jogging shorts to bed, making it easier to roll out and throw on some sweats before lacing up his Nikes and braving the snowy streets around their home as soon as he got up in the morning. He was built like a runner, six one and trim, with a full head of dark hair that framed a longish face. Jack Ryan was also a doctor, though as his eight-year-old daughter often pointed out, "not the useful kind." He held a Ph.D. in history.

Cathy sighed again, as if she wanted his attention, moving her feet just enough to draw his gaze downward toward her freshly manicured toes. Cathy was her own woman to be sure, but she generally yielded to Jack's preference that nail polish looked best when it was a color that would look good on a sports car. She'd gone with something called Misty Cinnamon this time—close enough to candy-apple red. Her gown had hiked up to mid-thigh, leaving gorgeous legs alluringly exposed.

He swung his feet over the edge of the bed and knelt to open the safe so he could put away the folder.

Cathy chuckled. "I knew I married a rule-keeper . . . but . . ."

He jumped back onto the bed with an exaggerated bounce, scooting closer.

"Sorry," he said. "I should have come in and helped with the hellion. I got carried away reading about this Soviet general secretary . . ."

"That's fine," Cathy said. "Honestly."

"How about Sally?" Ryan asked after their daughter.

"She's still out." Cathy nestled against her pillow with a long yawn. "Surrounded by stacks of books." She yawned again, fluttered her eyes. "I'm glad we named that boy Jack Junior. He's got my heart, like his father, but he can also drive me crazy—"

"Like his father?"

"You got that right, mister," she said. "Did you know he's already got a girlfriend? Can you imagine? Four years old."

Ryan grinned. "Who's the lucky girl?"

"Little Maeve Norwood."

"Daughter of the Right Honorable Member of Parliament Warren James Norwood?" Ryan feigned a British accent. "Good fellow, that one. A fine family. I heartily approve of the arrangement."

Cathy gave him a playful smack on the arm. "She'll probably just break his heart."

"He's four." Ryan took off his watch and leaned over to set it on his side table. "If I move his toy Corvette it breaks his heart. Anyway, we Ryan men have an eye for highly intelligent, extremely beautiful women."

Cathy rolled onto her side. A lock of blond hair fell across her baby blues. "You're briefing with your MI6 overlords tomorrow. I suppose you should get right to sleep."

Jack swallowed. "My meeting isn't until nine a.m."

"Good." Cathy kicked the sheets off the end of the bed. "Because . . . you know . . . a woman has knees . . ."

Jack opened his mouth to speak but the phone rang,

cutting him off. He cursed under his breath. It wasn't that late, but ten p.m. calls were rarely good news.

An ophthalmic surgeon, Cathy got far more calls than he did, so the phone was on her side of the bed. She picked it up before it woke Jack Junior, listened for a moment, and then passed it across to Jack, scooting up against the headboard so the cord didn't fall across her face.

The familiar resonance of Admiral James Greer's voice poured out of the receiver.

"Jack," the CIA deputy director of intelligence said. "I know it's late. Hope I didn't wake you."

Ryan's parents had been killed in a plane crash just a decade earlier and the savvy intelligence officer had become a sort of stand-in father over the years. If Ryan considered anyone his mentor, it was Jim Greer. He'd walk barefoot over broken glass for that man.

"No, Admiral," Ryan said. "Not at all." He shot a glance at Cathy. "Just catching up on some reading."

"Good," Greer said. "How's London treating you, Jack?"

"All good on this side of the pond, sir," Ryan said. "Excellent colleagues, Cathy's enjoying her work, kids have lots of friends . . ." His eyes narrowed. Greer knew exactly what time it was. Deputy directors at the CIA didn't call to chat at ten o'clock at night. "Why do you ask?"

As was his custom, the admiral circled the issue once, then got to his reason for the call . . . in his own enigmatic way. He spoke for just three minutes before saying, "Give my love to Cathy," and then hanging up as some other important matter drew him away.

"What was that all about?" Cathy asked after Jack cradled the phone and lay down to stare at the ceiling.

"He wants me to come to D.C.," Jack said.

"I know you probably can't talk about it," she said, clutching a pillow to her chest like a shield against bad news. "But is something up?"

"No," Jack said. ". . . And yes, maybe. I couldn't tell. He didn't mention a specific assignment, but I'll tell you what I think. I think he's considering me for another job."

She perked up at that. "At Langley?"

"I could be way off," Jack said, slightly dumbfounded. "But that's what I'm gleaning."

His brain was in overdrive, parsing through the admiral's every word and inflection.

"You analyze things for a living, sweetheart. Pretty sure you can read Jim Greer."

"He says there are some people I need to get to know . . . and that he 'wants to run some ideas by me.'"

"Well." Cathy let the pillow fall away, relaxing by degree. "I'm prejudiced, but I think that's a smart move on their part. It wouldn't hurt to have you over there helping make sure the Cold War doesn't boil over."

"And you're ready to leave London if it happens?"

"There's something visceral about this place," she said. "Something incredibly real. I mean, the bomb smoke and brick dust from World War II have barely even settled. I am supremely happy here, and I'm sure I'll be supremely happy back in the States as well."

"But the kids' schools," Jack said. "Your work, all the relationships we've built."

"True enough." Cathy rolled up on one elbow to face him. "But the whole world's a shitshow right now, Jack. South Africa, Eastern Europe. And don't get me started on the Soviets in Afghanistan."

"You're right," Ryan said. "But we look at all of that from our offices here. Keeping an eye on the shitshow is pretty much my exact job description."

For the past several years, Ryan had been assigned as the CIA liaison to the UK's Secret Intelligence Service—SIS, commonly called MI6. The Brits and the Yanks shared everything—mostly. They were the two "big brothers" in Five Eyes, an intelligence alliance consisting of the U.S., the UK, Australia, Canada, and New Zealand. Springing from World War II when British and American codebreakers had worked together at Bletchley to defeat the Nazis, the Five Eyes alliance took its name from the classification and releasability designation on intelligence cover sheets— *AUS/CAN/NZ/UK/U.S. EYES ONLY.*

As young as he was, Jack Ryan was a millionaire several times over, having made his fortune on several intelligent gambles in the stock market—some of which had impressed the father of the beautiful blonde beside him now. He didn't need this job—in England or in Virginia—but the job needed to be done, and he was good at it. Damned good.

"They've been asking me to come back to Wilmer," Cathy said, pulling him back to the present. She'd gone to med school at Johns Hopkins and naturally impressed the surgeons there at the Wilmer Eye Institute.

"Makes sense," Jack said. "It would be a no-brainer for them to take you back. I could be reading this all wrong. Greer might not ask me to stay."

Cathy shuffled her legs again, rubbing the top of one foot with the other. "Reading things is what you do, sweetheart."

"I do, don't I." Ryan's eyebrow shot upward. "It's my specialty."

"One of many," she said.

He pushed aside thoughts of D.C. and the often-internecine politics of Langley. "How about we see to those womanly knees you were talking—"

The bedroom suddenly flooded with light from the hall as the door creaked open. Ryan raised up to see the silhouette of his four-year-old son, Jack Junior, clutching his favorite toy Corvette.

"Mommy . . ."

3

The National Security Agency's listening post perched atop a hill deep in West Berlin's Grunewald Forest was monumentally indiscreet for a spy station. Teufelsberg, or Devil's Mountain, was actually no mountain at all, but an 80-meter pile of overgrown bricks stacked on top of a never-completed Nazi military-technical college by *Trümmerfrauen*. These "rubble women" dug out and piled the debris from some four hundred thousand German homes and buildings that had been destroyed during World War II. Allied personnel who staffed the surveillance post called it the Hill. The huge spherical radomes prompted the locals to dub the installation "Berlin's Balls." Visible but shrouded in secrecy, the shared British and U.S. installation was the subject of all sorts of rumors and conspiracy theories.

Some thought a secret shaft below the installation led to an underground submarine base or a hidden nuclear weapon. The Stasi even opened an investigation that hypothesized there was a secret tunnel leading into the East, used for the most sensitive escapes. In reality, the white globes and antennas simply gathered signals intelligence from the other side of the Berlin Wall and all over the Eastern Bloc. Soviets and East Germans openly groused that the West was able to "hear their farts."

Sergeant Dennis McCambridge, an Army Intel signals clerk with the Berlin Brigade, adjusted his headset and fiddled with the amplifier in front of him.

"What you got?" Staff Sergeant Ramirez asked from the workstation beside him.

"Another hit on FLEDERMAUS," Sergeant McCambridge said. He made a note in the time log at his workstation.

Ramirez flipped through the pages of his notepad. "Third mention in two weeks."

"And that's just the times we're picking up," McCambridge said. "Weird word to use so often in a sentence."

Warsaw Pact nations ran frequent training ops, but FLEDERMAUS didn't appear to be one of those. For one thing, it was German, not Russian. Worse yet, the word was often heard in conjunction with U.S. or British operations or weapons systems—at least so far as the coded messages could be understood. FLEDERMAUS was a person—and, from the sound of things, that person was substantiating bits of Western intel.

That was above Sergeant McCambridge's pay grade. He listened, made notes, and then sent those notes up the chain to someone who had the big picture. FLE-DERMAUS . . . He had to admit, that was a kickass code name.

The BAT.

"Note the time stamp on the tape when you heard it," Ramirez said. "Get some DAFL guys to give it a listen. See if we missed any idioms."

McCambridge chuckled.

"E-I-E-I-O," he said.

Ramirez loved to make up his own acronyms. In Ramirezese, DAFL meant Deutsch As a First Language. No matter what you called them, it was a good idea—and standard procedure. Sergeants Ramirez and Mc-Cambridge had both been to DLIFLC—a real acronym that stood for the Defense Language Institute Foreign Language Center in Monterey. Their German was very good, but it took a native speaker to catch the subtle nuances and idioms. *"Tote Oma"* tripped up most everyone the first time they heard it. Translated literally, it meant "dead grandma," but was in reality a mashed blood sausage. You had to grow up here to get that kind of thing on the fly.

"Maybe FLEDERMAUS is a spy," McCambridge mused. "Some East German infiltrator?"

"Maybe," Ramirez said. "Hell, *we're* spies, Weedhopper. Shouldn't surprise us that they're spying on us. The guys in ops are probably already hunting this one down.

Our lowly asses will never get to know a damn thing unless we hear chatter from the other side . . ." He glanced
at McCambridge. "And anyway, who says FLEDER-
MAUS has to be German?"

4

Greasy hair splayed like a halo in the snow around the mugger's head. He stared skyward, face pulled back into a terrifying grimace. But he wasn't dead. Not yet. White froth bubbled from the corners of his mouth. His body writhed and seethed like a rattlesnake Ruby's grandfather had once thrown into a campfire.

The resigned look on the paramedics' faces as they loaded him into the back of an ambulance said he would not likely make it to the hospital.

Ruby told the responding military and West German police what she knew—which was almost nothing—but kept the information about the cryptic note and computer disk to herself.

The puzzle of it all gave her a worse headache than the fall had. Why her? They were in the West. If someone wanted to defect, why hadn't they just walked into the U.S. Mission? She was new to State and West Berlin. Was she being turned into some kind of scapegoat?

"Crapola," she said under her breath, blowing a cloud of vapor in the cold. It was pretty much the strongest byword her mother had allowed in the house. They'd covered defections during her Foreign Service officer training, but the information was sparse. Essentially, refer everything to the CIA. Even so, Ruby had read enough Ludlum to know what to do.

This was going to be one of those stories she could tell her kids someday, how she helped some Russian or East German flee the repression of communism. She found a pay phone outside the McDonald's and called the US-BER switchboard. The mission was only a few blocks away, but this information wasn't something she could sit on, even for a few minutes. She had to let someone in charge know what she had.

The United States government was prickly about Germans getting their diplomatic mission in Berlin confused with an embassy, so Army military police were assigned security duties rather than the Marine Corps guards that embassies got.

Ruby barely mentioned receiving the mysterious computer disk before the soldier who answered the phone, an Army sergeant who'd flirted with her when she'd left, instructed her to return immediately to USBER without saying anything else over the telephone. He obviously had a lot more experience with this sort of thing than she did.

It took her fifteen minutes to walk back down Clay-allee, imagining Stasi operatives behind every tree and park bench the entire way. To her dismay, no one spoke to her or even looked in her direction. Still, she felt like she might pass out by the time she reached the flirtatious sergeant at the front doors. A local German woman from the cleaning staff was already buffing the tile floor.

A woman who identified herself as consular officer Jennifer "Jen" North was waiting in the lobby. Fifteen years Ruby's senior, North's high cheekbones and auburn hair gave her a Slavic look. She wore tan high-waisted gabardine slacks and a baby-blue cotton pinpoint blouse with the collar popped up, stylishly, as if she'd stepped away from a *Cosmo* photo shoot for a Virginia Slims cigarette ad.

Ruby had been around the woman only a couple times when they crossed paths at USBER, but to her, North seemed like someone out of a movie. She rattled off German like a native and didn't take shit from anyone. She worked in an out-of-bounds area that was not consular officer space and did absolutely no consular work.

In Ruby's eyes, North was the epitome of what a woman could do in the U.S. government. She wasn't some lowly cypher clerk or cleaning lady with a buffer. Jen North was CIA, she had to be. Everyone knew it, even the Germans. She had, as they said, come a long way, baby.

North ushered Ruby back to the inner sanctum,

nodding curtly to the soldier in the hallway as she punched a code into the mechanical cypher lock on the door.

Inside turned out not to be a look behind the curtain, only another hall with polished floors and three nondescript doors without any signage.

"We'll use number three," North said, pushing another cypher lock to open the first door past the entry.

Room number three was even more bland than the hall was. Ten by ten feet and windowless, the walls were covered in sculpted gray acoustic foam, like the rooms Ruby's high school orchestra ensemble had practiced in when she played violin. Industrial carpet, gray to match the foam walls and ceiling, seemed to absorb light as well as dampen sound.

North pitched a steno pad and pen on the small metal table and motioned for Keller to take a seat in one of the only two chairs in the room. She hung on to Ruby's purse, clutching it in her fist.

Ruby took the pen and looked around the little space. There were two cameras in opposite corners, visible but recessed into the ceiling. The foam padding on the back of the door was identical to the walls, causing it to blend and almost disappear.

"Am I in trouble?"

North cocked her head. She didn't smile. "What makes you say that?"

"This looks like one of those rooms where they interrogate people in the movies."

"Funny," North said, deadpan, like it was not funny at all. "This isn't the movies, sweetie."

"I know that," Ruby said, embarrassed to sound like such a weirdo in front of this woman.

North studied her for a moment, as if coming to a decision, then groaned. "It's Lisa, right?"

"Ruby. Ruby Keller."

"Right," North said, shaking her head, distracted. "Ruby. You're not being interrogated. I need you to write down exactly what happened. Start with what you were doing before. Everything. Yesterday. Today. Since you've been in Germany."

Ruby nodded.

"And I need a description of this mystery woman who had your purse."

"I never saw her," Ruby said. "You'll have to ask that sergeant about her. Newsome, I think his name was."

"We are." North folded her arms across her chest and stared down. "I gotta ask. Why you?"

"Honestly," Ruby said. "I have—"

The cypher lock on the door clicked behind them.

North leaned back against the edge of the table, arms still folded.

"Perfect," she said under her breath, and then put on a tight smile.

A sandy-haired man who looked like he was pushing sixty poked his head through the door. He wore a dark suit and had a winter coat draped over his arm.

"What's this I'm hearing about a walk-in?" he said to North as he stepped inside and shook Ruby's hand. "I'm

Skip Hulse." He didn't give his title, but she knew he was head of the CIA in West Berlin.

"Ms. Keller is telling us about a *potential* walk-in," North corrected. "I have it handled."

Hulse smiled, a more genuine expression than North's. Ruby decided that might actually make him more dangerous. She braced herself. He was probably the good cop.

"Jen's got you writing up everything you can remember?"

"Yes, sir."

"Very good," he said, then turned to North. "Can I see you for a sec?"

Ruby released a pent-up breath. That wasn't so bad.

Jen North cleared her throat, not quite concealing how much the interruption annoyed her. "Sure."

"We'll be right back," Hulse said, flashing that good-cop smile again. "The door locks from the outside . . . You know, security and all. But don't worry. Just wave if you need anything."

Ruby jumped when the door shut, vanishing into the acoustic foam wall with an audible *click*.

"Welcome to Mission Berlin, Ruby Keller," she whispered to herself. Hunched over the table, pen in hand, she began to hum the doleful notes of a tune her grandfather had taught her.

Jen North paused for a moment outside the interview room. She listened to the song coming out of the speaker, frowned, and then wheeled to follow Skip Hulse down the polished hallway. He moved swiftly, like he wanted to be done with this whole affair as quickly as possible, pausing only long enough to punch in the code to access CIA office space. Blue government carpet squares and slate-gray cubicles ruled the day. The sparse décor was limited to a couple potted plants— mother-in-law's tongue—and the smallish framed photographs that CIA officers carried with them around the world—connections to their normal life, as if there was such a thing as normal anymore.

Farrah Fawcett's iconic red swimsuit poster hung on the wall of the first cubicle. The caption, written in black Magic Marker, read: *If someone who looks like me approaches you, you are being recruited, comrade!*

Billy Dunn, pulling duty for the evening, sat at the desk beneath the poster of Officer Fawcett. He'd gone a little native during his previous posting in Tokyo and often affected a guttural samurai voice, which he thought was funny but North considered asinine. He busied himself folding an origami crane while he pretended to read an economic brief beside a well-worn copy of Miyamoto Musashi's *The Book of Five Rings.*

He looked up, innocently sliding the brief over the top of the book. "Hey, boss."

"Come with us," Hulse said and kept walking.

They went straight to Hulse's office, where he dumped the contents of Ruby Keller's purse onto a small side table. He took a pencil from the pocket of his wrinkled dress shirt and used it to flip over the computer disk. "You haven't looked at any of this yet?"

North shook her head. "I read the note, but I haven't had time to look at the disk. The Keller girl just got here. I'd no sooner gotten her started with the statement when you came in and got me."

"Good," Hulse said, nodding slowly, mulling his options. "Good, good . . . We got another cable warning us about computer worms last week. The disk could have something like that, and I don't want to wreck our machines."

Hulse had come aboard the agency in 1962 when computers were something used to crack codes in a big room at Langley. Of course, they had computers in the office now. The machines were a juggernaut that could not be avoided, but not something every desk had to bother with. He made no secret of his fervent belief that too much reliance on technology flew in the face of good tradecraft. Terminators. That's what he called them, after the new Schwarzenegger flick. The end of the world. To Skip Hulse, the IBM Selectric was still cutting-edge.

Dunn read the note aloud. "'Special Services' . . . " He looked up to meet Hulse's eye. "No locals. Sounds like he doesn't trust us."

"Or he's fishing," North said. "Looking to see who shows up to meet."

"Meet where?" Hulse asked.

"I presume that information is on the disk," North said.

"The coded disk," Dunn said. "And the cypher key is in the States . . . Pretty smart if he doesn't want any of us privy to who he is."

"Or she," Hulse said.

Dunn tapped the table with his fingers in thought. "Maybe this guy has information on FLEDER-MAUS . . ."

Hulse grimaced. "We don't even know if there is a FLEDERMAUS. For all we know the Stasi Imperium has an infestation of bats."

"You really believe that, boss?" Dunn asked.

"I do not," Hulse said. "I just want to make sure we're looking at this from all angles."

"Could be someone from BND," North said, giving a nod of her own.

"What makes you say that?" Hulse asked.

The Bundesnachrichtendienst, or BND, was the Federal Intelligence Service of the West German government.

"I don't know," she said. "Gut feeling, I guess."

"That's more like it," Hulse said. "Gut feelings can lead to valuable outcomes."

North leaned on the table, eyeing the disk. "We co-operate with the BND on pretty much everything, but we know the Stasi have infiltrated the West German government on so many levels. I'm just saying that this BAT could be someone who's burrowed in over there, then feeding the GDR our intel."

"Whether FLEDERMAUS exists or not," Hulse said, "whoever sent this believes *we* have a leak."

North turned over the disk with her own pen, hoping she'd missed some bit of instruction written on the black paper sleeve, then turned to Hulse. "Taylor's a tech guy," she said. "I can get him to—"

"Nope," Hulse said.

His phone rang, and he turned to answer it. Head down, he spoke in hushed tones for a moment before hanging up.

"Word from on high," he said. "This is going in a diplomatic pouch."

North came up off the table. "I can handle—"

"I said no, Jen," Hulse said, giving her a jaundiced eye. "Look, I know recruitment is a touchy subject, considering the way you were treated. We all know what a piece of shit Buckley is."

Dunn smirked. "You mean Assistant Deputy Director Buckley."

"Shut up, Billy," Hulse said. He put a hand on North's arm, the condescending bastard. "You'll still get credit for handling the walk-in if it gets to that point. And once we establish trust, you can roll in and take over. But for now, the note explicitly states no local operators. It's a moot point anyway. The key to decipher this is in Chantilly, Virginia. We couldn't read it if we wanted to. This whole package, including the paper bag it came in, is going by courier to Langley tonight."

North moved to gather the items, but Hulse shook his head. "I'll take care of it."

"I'm the one who accepted it," North said. "I should—"

"I said I'd take care of it," Hulse said.

———

Hulse took care of the package himself, sending North and Dunn to let Ruby Keller out of the interview room.

North stopped at her desk, pulling up the CCTV and sound feeds. "Hold up," she said. "Let's see what she's up to before we cut her loose."

The black-and-white image showed their guest sitting quietly, pen and paper on the table in front of her. She'd apparently finished her statement and now swayed a little, humming to herself while she looked around the room.

"Cool as a cucumber," Dunn said. "Let me guess. You don't trust her."

"Do you?" North scoffed. "With that story? I mean, this cryptic note and computer disk magically appear in her purse after she's mugged? Give me a break."

"The mugger died," Dunn said. "*Polizei* are saying some type of poison, probably injected. That tends to bolster her story."

"Maybe," North said. "For all we know, she's the one who injected him."

"Yeah, but she didn't have to bring in the disk."

"True," North said. "But I still don't like her."

"What's that she's saying?" Dunn asked. "I can't quite make it out."

North leaned closer to the speaker, teeth clenched so tight she thought they might shatter. "She's singing."

Dunn shot her a side-glance. "Singing what?"

"Beats me," North said, focusing to relax her jaw.

But she knew exactly what Keller was singing—the fourth movement of Mahler's *Kindertotenlieder*.

Songs on the Death of Children.

This little bitch was not who she said she was . . .

5

The Pentagon gave the program the top secret SCI code word: SENIOR TREND. The official designation was F-117 Nighthawk. To Air Force OG bean counters and command staff of the 4450th Tactical Group, it was "the asset."

The men who flew it called it the Black Jet.

The first time Major Boden "Slinky" Lee laid eyes on the spindle-legged otherworldly thing had been a gut punch. All angles and lines, the jet looked like someone had shattered it into hundreds of pieces and then glued them all back together. To top it off, it was covered with RAM—radar-absorbing material—that resembled reptile skin.

A Frankenstein's monster of airplanes.

It took six months in the program before Major Lee wasn't startled when he walked into the hangar and saw the bird. By then, it had gone from an oddity to something beautiful.

Although his call sign was "Slinky," tonight in the Black Jet, Major Lee was "Bandit 168" when he talked on the radio at all.

He'd once known a young pilot who'd tried to give himself his own call sign. That didn't go well. Not at all. The guy had washed out of the program, likely for the same faulty reasoning skills that made him think he could assign himself a nickname when that was clearly something that had to be earned—usually by doing something stupid. Lee had earned his during training at Sheppard, when he'd tumbled down the stairs in his flight suit, did a roll, and jumped to his feet like nothing at all had happened. Half the squadron had been there to witness his clumsiness and his amazing recovery. From the moment he'd stood up, it was written in stone that Boden "Slinky" Lee would be stenciled on every aircraft assigned to him beyond those first T-38 trainers.

And he'd flown a lot of them. He loved them all, but he'd never even heard of anything like the Nighthawk— let alone imagined he'd have the opportunity to fly one.

He learned later that you needed at least a thousand hours of flight time to be considered for a slot, though you had no idea you were being considered at all.

Outside of a very small group of engineers from Lockheed Martin Skunk Works and the squadron of pilots and maintainers here at Tonopah Test Range, the number of people who knew of the F-117's existence was absurdly small. Somehow, contrary to what Lee had seen during his eleven years of military service, the United States government had actually been able to keep a secret.

They flew the bird at night, obviously. This week, Slinky was assigned to what was known as the "Late-Go," or second flight. The birds in the Late-Go would take off a few minutes apart, running the same mission one after the other. Wheels-up for Bandit 168 would be at 0230, last in the line after the Early-Go flight returned. Civilians and military alike who had not been read in on SENIOR TREND had heard rumors about a stealthy aircraft that could avoid radar, but they'd never seen one. The Air Force aimed to keep it that way.

Prospective pilots didn't even know what they were getting into when they were tapped to fly the thing. As a British pilot who'd come out as part of a highly competitive exchange program said, "One did not *ask* to fly the Black Jet. One *was asked* to fly the Black Jet."

Program managers kept a keen eye open for possible candidates, picking from not only the best pilots, but the most taciturn. Those given to excessive no-shit-there-I-was tales of derring-do were sent to apply their skills in more conventional squadrons. The competition was fierce, but pilots didn't know the program existed. Major Lee, competitive to begin with, had no idea he was competing for anything—or that the application process began from the day he'd first mustered into the Air Force.

The briefing went quickly but professionally tonight. The pilots rotated the responsibility of putting together the targeting packages. It was Major Gary "Heeler" Dundee's turn. Lee found him to be an extremely capable aviator. Hell, they all were. They had to be to get here.

Major Lee took care not to tap his class ring against the Formica top of his desk in the ready room. Attending that little engineering college north of Colorado Springs was something to be proud of. But he was a ring-wearer, not a ring-knocker. If anyone took care to read that far back in his file, they would have seen he was on the superintendent's list for military, academic, and athletic excellence every semester. It was an oft-repeated (and true) adage that as far as degrees went, "poli-sci flies." The relatively less intense liberal arts academic course of study might allow for a higher GPA than a math-and-science-heavy degree like aeronautical engineering. A higher class standing gave graduates greater choice in career fields. Lee chose the latter anyway, graduated number nine in his class (two spots ahead of his future brother-in-law), and somehow found the time to earn his jump wings at Fort Benning, attend SERE School at Fairchild AFB, and receive his private pilot's license. He rounded out his C1C year serving as vice commander of the Cadet Wing. He'd wanted to attend the Marine Corps Bulldog course at Quantico, but, visiting Rita in Wyoming on the weekends at least every two months, he just hadn't had enough time.

Air Force Academy cadets had to remain single until graduation—a deficiency Lee was able to address at the Academy chapel three hours after he'd thrown his hat in the air and the Thunderbirds performed their flyover. He'd known Rita Anderson since her brother, a squadron mate, had invited him home to Jackson Hole for Thanksgiving their freshman year. They'd started dating exclusively almost at once. So, when he thought about it, Rita had as much tenure with the Air Force as he did.

The pilot pipeline had taken up a significant portion of his early career—T-38s at Sheppard, going on to fly F-4 Phantom IIs with the 56th Tactical Fighter Wing at MacDill, then transitioning to F-16s with the 388th at the Hill. Rita had blessed him with two beautiful kids by the time they got to Utah. The Lees loved Ogden, nestled in the beautiful Wasatch Mountains. Skiing, fly-fishing, river rafting, and blue-bird clear days to slice up the sky with the most advanced aircraft in the world.

Or so Lee believed until his commander, a crusty old colonel, had called him into his office after a long day of classroom training. His name was Spoon—too cool to screw with by giving him a fake nickname, so no one bothered to try.

"The 4450th Tactical Group out of Nellis is looking for A-7 pilots," Colonel Spoon had said, gunning straight to the point as per usual. "I hate to lose you, but there is a specific set of criteria they are looking for, and damn it, son, if you don't tick all the boxes."

"Nellis." Lee gave an involuntary shake of his head.

The A-7 Corsair II was a Vietnam bird, subsonic, out-gunned and outmaneuvered by the newer, more capable fighters like the F-15 and F-16. To Lee, flying one would be a step backward.

Colonel Spoon raised an open hand. "Now, don't turn it down until you've heard the particulars."

"Of course, sir," Lee said. "I didn't mean . . ."

"I get it," Spoon said. "You were thinking what a shitty trade cactus and creosote are for pine trees and mountains just to fly an older airframe."

"My wife's from Jackson Hole, sir," Lee said. "No place we move is going to match the Tetons. Those particulars . . . ?"

Spoon perused the paper in front of him, then slipped it in the folder on his desk and slid it aside. "Turns out I'm not authorized to give you any particulars at this time. I can tell you that while you'd be assigned to Nellis, you will be flying out of Tonopah Test Range."

"Tonopah," Lee mused. "You can't say anything more?"

"I cannot," Spoon said. "But I can tell you that, officially, you will be flying the A-7."

"'Officially'?"

And on the back of that mysterious introduction, Major Boden Lee attended three months of training in the Corsair II with the 152nd Fighter Squadron Air National Guard in Tucson and then moved his little family from the beautiful Wasatch Front to Nellis Air Force Base outside of Las Vegas, which was . . . not the beautiful Wasatch Front.

The week before the move, Lee's father, a retired Navy F-4 Phantom pilot, had come out to Utah on a visit from Seattle. Boden had never been prouder than when showing his old man around the flight line at the Hill. Later, when he'd come to visit the grandkids at Nellis, Lee had to break the news that a tour was out of the question. The old man had been around the block a few times and recognized a secret program when he heard it.

And secret it was. The United States government went to great lengths to keep SENIOR TREND under wraps. Aircraft were disassembled at Lockheed Martin Skunk Works facilities and moved via C-5 to Groom Lake—sometimes called Area 51. In June of 1981 a Lockheed Skunk Works test pilot lifted off the tarmac in the first test aircraft—at that point, code-named HAVE BLUE. Less than a year and a half later, a pilot from the 4450th TG lifted off from Groom Lake in the first operational F-117A.

Testing of each new aircraft was still conducted by the Baja Scorpions at Groom Lake before they were turned over for operational use. By the time Lee entered the program, the Air Force had decided to move the 4450th to Tonopah Test Range. Special hangars were built to keep the Nighthawks out of sight. The Corsairs were parked on the tarmac out front, giving Soviet satellites something to look at and a supposed reason for all the hangars.

SENIOR TREND was not the only secret program at Tonopah Test Range.

Pilots and support personnel took a chartered passenger plane from Nellis to Tonopah every Monday. Their families knew only that they were engaged in secret work. During the daylight hours each Monday through Thursday, pilots from a program called CONSTANT PEG flew aggressor training in Soviet MiG-17s, -21s, and -23s against Marine, Air Force, and Navy flyers. F-117 missions happened under the cover of darkness. Personnel from both projects returned to Las Vegas each Friday.

Stories of the secrecy surrounding the Black Jet were legendary.

The year before Lee arrived, the 4450th's P-Unit participated in "Team Spirit" at Kunsan Air Base in South Korea. Word was leaked that the 4450th Tactical Group's A-7s had been fitted with ultrasecret anti-radar cloaking devices. The planes were outfitted with old napalm canisters with radiation warning tags and a slot that read *Reactor Cooling Fill Port*. Air Police closed the base when the 4450th birds arrived, making all the runway personnel turn their backs. On departure, personnel were ordered to lie facedown on the deck with their eyes closed until the A-7s were away.

SENIOR TREND was, as they said, a secret worth keeping.

An engineer at heart, Lee was astounded that the big brains at Skunk Works had been able to pull off a design that had the radar cross section of a hummingbird with essentially slide rules and graph paper.

There were no tandem Black Jets, which meant that first flight in the F-117 was also a pilot's first solo. In fact, the first "flight" in the Nighthawk was not a flight at all, but a ride down the runway, getting up to speed, deploying the drag chute, and coming to a stop. It was heady stuff. The first time you actually left the ground, an instructor pilot flew off the wing in an A-7, but you were essentially alone. Fortunately, it was an easy aircraft to fly once you got it up to speed. The General Electric F404 turbofan engines were the same as those used by F-18s (minus afterburners). Designers utilized the flight controls and fly-by-wire system of an F-16, and F-15 hydraulics and landing gear. This added not only to the secrecy when ordering spare parts, but also to the ease of transition for the pilot.

To Lee, the best part of flying was the aloneness. The pilot and the aircraft were on their own.

A subsonic bomber, the Black Jet carried no air-to-air weapons, no defenses. No chaff, no guns, no radar, no radar warning. Over the test range or in a war zone, the transponder would be turned off and the radio antennas withdrawn inside the airframe. During flight, the pilots changed speed altitude and direction so often that the only radar that could possibly detect it didn't recognize it as the same blip by the time the scan came around again.

Though a day rarely went by without someone reminding the pilots that the Black Jet was neither invisible nor invincible, it was easy to feel like it was both.

On the Late-Go, Major Lee carried a small box from the ready room to his bird, Bandit 168. He wore a G-suit and survival vest, though the pilots often joked that in an aircraft as slow as the Black Jet, the suit's main purpose was to look cool walking out to the airplane. Once in the cockpit, Lee plugged in and downloaded the preplanned mission waypoints. Tonight was an off-range camera run with ten targets ranging from a residential address in a small town near Lake Mead to a big-box store in St. George, Utah. It was scheduled to take just under two hours—during most of which the autopilot would fly the plane while Lee handled targeting and camera operation, simulating weapons release. Out of all the time in the air, he would get no more than twenty minutes of stick time manually flying the jet himself—a good portion of that during takeoff and landing.

The cockpit was roomy and, to a former F-16 pilot, familiar. Visibility on the ground sucked. In the air, FLIR—forward-looking infrared—and DLIR—downward-looking infrared—cameras located and locked on to targets with the help of a laser that was linked to the nav system.

Someone had dubbed the Nighthawk the Wobblin' Goblin, but Lee thought that was BS. It was relatively unstable in pitch and yaw at low speeds, but as long as you kept the speed up, it flew like a heavy F-16.

Eager to get back before daylight, Lee got the airplane spun up quickly, releasing the brakes as soon as he got permission to take off. It wasn't exactly the bolt to

the back that he was accustomed to with the Falcon, but
it wasn't mild, either. The plane's arrowhead shape made
wingtip drag a danger on takeoff, so pilots were perpetually warned to watch their angle on rotation. Meters off
the runway, Lee established positive rate and retracted
the landing gear. He adjusted throttle and pitch, accelerating toward a best-climb speed of 340 knots. Moments
after the gear folded into place a loud *whoosh* and a metallic *clunk* rattled the left side of the aircraft. A full second later, an identical *whoosh-bang* shook the plane to
Lee's right.

The terrible noise had scared the shit out of Major Lee
the first time he'd heard it. What sounded like the airplane falling apart were the huge blow-in doors slamming shut over the engines.

The gaping hole of an engine intake made a beautiful
radar signature—something Skunk Works designers had
wanted to avoid. A metal grid pilots called the ice cube
maker covered each intake. The devices not only de-
flected radar waves, but airflow as well, airflow the GE
F404 engines especially needed on takeoff. They solved
the problem by fitting huge doors that would remain
open on takeoff and then automatically blow shut with
alarming effect once the Black Jet reached somewhere
around Mach .5.

The first two targets were uneventful, with Lee locat-
ing and lasing each perfectly. On average, pilots "shot"
ten targets per night, two to four nights per week, but
two misses put you out of the running for top gun of the

quarter. So, apart from "doing everything they had to do to not die," Black Jet pilots took great care to ensure their accuracy on target.

The third target was slightly more problematic, a horse shed behind a mobile home off Highway 160 north of Pahrump, Nevada—an area with three mobile homes and nearly identical horse sheds. "Hitting" the wrong shed was a miss. To make matters worse, he was in the gray zone, the time of night Late-Go pilots came to know well. Desert temps rose during the day and fell during the night, reaching a point of relative equilibrium where inanimate objects all took on a similar gray color in the infrared viewers. Lee took special care with the FLIR and DLIR images in the center of three cockpit displays to double- and triple-check his target.

There it was. His target was the only mobile home without a swing set.

"Bombs away," he said to himself as he lased the target and snapped a photograph to record the "hit."

The autopilot adjusted the heading on its own, taking the Black Jet well north to skirt Las Vegas and then turning east cruising at just over 400 knots on a dogleg course toward his next target, the big-box store in St. George, Utah.

The first indication that anything was wrong happened north of Lake Mead—a violent shudder. With no warning, the Black Jet veered right, tremendous G-forces shoving Lee's head downward toward the stick. He heard a loud crack to the right and the airplane rolled, then, pitching upward, threw Lee against his harness as it porpoised violently through the night sky. Another series of bangs shook the fuselage. Out of control, the plane went into a steep dive. Wind roared, engines white, and Lee worked furiously to try and regain control.

Somewhere in the blackness below, jagged mountains were rising up to meet him, and his airplane was coming apart.

6

WHITNEY POCKET, NEVADA

The two dozen sky watchers encamped in the desert wash among looming sandstone boulders hoped for another sighting. Garit Richter wanted the same thing, but for significantly different reasons.

Thirty-eight, with broad shoulders and sandy hair, Richter's tendency to grow a beard before lunchtime had been a source of constant trouble in the Army. Later, in East Germany's Ministry for State Security school in Kallinchen, the perpetual stubble had been considered an asset. His manners and elocution instructor, Hilda—Frau Battenberg to the rest of the class—had certainly been fine with it. Even after he'd graduated, he often wondered if their brief but torrid affair was merely another part of the curriculum. Richter tended to frighten people if he looked at them hard and make them fall in love with him if he did not. Americans liked rugged—as long as rugged was also handsome. Richter's mother had

often told him that he was both. He was not so sure that
was the best description, but his superiors in the Hauptverwaltung Aufklärung, or HVA—the Stasi's Main Directorate for Reconnaissance—apparently thought so
and gave him one of the extremely rare postings to the
United States.

Recent news reports, astoundingly unfiltered by the
government, had led him to this stretch of desolate sandstone and gravel in Nevada, eighty kilometers northeast
of Las Vegas. More important, it was less than two hundred and forty kilometers southeast of Tonopah Test
Range.

He gazed at the cathedral of stars and nestled under
the heavy quilts, closer to the fleshy redhead. He'd been
coming here for two weeks, watching, waiting, listening
to stories of flying saucers and strange aircraft that the
others swore they'd seen. Some were crazy, the machin-
ation of madness from bad genetics or too much LSD.
But some stories had promise, even if the tellers had no
idea what they were talking about. The redhead provided
a pleasant distraction.

Growing up in postwar Berlin, he'd believed the
American desert to be like American women, incessantly
hot year-round. But now, in the dark of night in November, he found himself glad to have the quilts. He'd been
right about the women, though, at least where the redhead was concerned.

There had been three very specific "black triangle"
sightings in the last forty days. One only a week earlier—
brief, but significant, flying over the Virgin Mountains

east to west from Arizona to Nevada and then turning abruptly northwest. Conventional wisdom among the UFO watchers wrapped in blankets with their eyeballs glued to telescopes and binoculars, the craft was either returning to some star base, or, if it was "earthbound," returning to Groom Lake, the top secret Air Force base officially known as Homey Airport but that the rest of the world knew as Area 51. These sightings just had to be the rumored alien spacecraft the United States government was hiding. Hushed talk of abductions and lost time ran rampant among the campers. Dog-eared photographs of mutilated cattle and drawings of strange, triangular craft were shared and copied.

Richter thought differently. There were secrets at Groom Lake, but the ones he was interested in appeared to be operating out of Tonopah.

Richter wrote off all the alien stories as nonsense, but some nights, the more he listened the more his schoolboy imagination got carried away by it all. Then someone would start in with the foolishness about anal probes and any shred of belief evaporated. The notion that beings sophisticated enough to fly light-years away could find nothing better to do with their time than inspect human assholes was a dealbreaker for him.

Richter suspected something far more sinister than extraterrestrial visits or even little green men locked away somewhere in an Air Force bunker. He was a great believer in conspiracies, especially those that said the United States intelligence apparatus would stoop to any evil in order to crush socialism. That's what had brought him here. A place that to him, a born and bred Berliner, looked like the surface of the moon. At home, he would have called such a far-flung spot JWD—*janz weit draussen*. As the Americans who were so fond of their cinema might say—he wasn't in Kansas anymore, Toto . . .

Absent the garish lights that polluted the skies of Las Vegas or even the streetlights along Interstate 15, Whitney Pocket made the perfect spot to look upward and actually see something. The Milky Way, the stars, Venus, Mars, and Saturn all looked close enough to touch—overwhelmingly beautiful. A fire would have murdered everyone's night vision. Tiny red lights danced here and there as people checked telescopes or star charts. Queen's "Crazy Little Thing Called Love" blared on someone's cassette player. The glow of cigarettes floated in the darkness on disembodied shadows. Along Whitney Pass Road, someone touched his brake pedal, blasting the night with a sudden splash of red light and igniting a flurry of angry curses from the crowd.

"Dumbass," the redhead grumbled, cuddling even closer on the foam mattress that she'd dragged out of her battered pickup truck before it got dark. "Igmo should have known better than that."

On his back, Richter took his eyes off the sky for a scant moment and let his head fall sideways, his nose just inches from hers. Her hair was braided tight and tucked under a ragged wool Nepalese hat. "Igmo . . ." His English held no trace of an accent, but the idioms sometimes perplexed him.

She gave a whispered laugh—almost reverent. "You're funny," she said. "Ig-mo . . . You know, ignorant moron. You never heard that before?" She shrugged. "Maybe my mom made it up."

He hid behind a passive smile and gave her a kiss on the tip of her nose. Heather Beasley was three parts hippie and one part self-professed expert on the night sky. She'd been camping on this secluded gravel road for the better part of the week, eating canned Beanee Weenees and rationing her water with not-quite-frequent-enough spit baths. During the days, she explored on her three-wheeler. At night, she watched the stars in the hopes of glimpsing an alien craft. Like most of the people camped at Whitney Pocket, she'd had her own experience with a UFO. She promised to tell it to Richter when the time was right.

She'd apparently just been abandoned by the boyfriend she'd come in with when he was befriended by a pair of obviously wealthy English women with a group from BUFORA—the British UFO Research Association. It wasn't a big deal, she said. It was her truck, her trike. She'd been supporting him, the swine. Richter had yet to be impressed by any of the American males he'd come across.

He kissed her again, then returned his attention to the skies, scanning from left to right, moving his head along with his eyes so he didn't miss something, looking for anything out of the ordinary. The U-2 had flown out of Groom Lake in the days before satellite imagery, and faster, higher-flying SR-71 reconnaissance aircraft had rendered the ungainly spy plane obsolete. There were rumors of a stealth aircraft operating out of both Groom Lake and Tonopah—something that could evade radar. Black triangles. It made sense that the American CIA would be flying their secret aircraft in these very skies. Richter's job was to watch and take notes, to get a photograph if possible. If he had to do it in the arms of a fleshy redhead who smelled of sweat and juniper and campfire smoke, well, that was not bad duty. Not bad at all.

Behind them, a wall of sandstone blotted out the stars, a giant black hole in the night. But the darkness was palpable even where there were no sandstone hills. It was heavy enough that Richter could feel it against his teeth—or maybe that was just the musky smell of the redhead on the chilly night air. There were voices, too, whispers by the lumpy black shadows of parked cars scattered along the desert wash. A few yards to his left an avuncular man droned on to two women, intoxicating them with pontifications about the galaxy. A group of three youths Richter judged to be university dropouts, huddled around a Ouija board, banking on the notion that the alien spacecraft and demons of the underworld were somehow related. Stifled squeals came from the jumble of sandstone boulders and hills behind them, where a couple wandered before dark to share their blankets with the snakes and lizards and whatever else might be crawling around in the night.

A flash of light creased the sky, quick and white-hot. Richter threw a large pair of binoculars to his eyes, but the light fizzled out almost as quickly as it had appeared. A wave of awed murmurs rippled through the watchers. Everyone there recognized it was a meteorite the moment they saw it, or some piece of space junk burning up as it entered the atmosphere. Just months before, a four-meter chunk of metal from a Soviet satellite launch had lit up the sky over the eastern United States. While beautiful, that wasn't what they were looking for.

"How come you never let me use those?" Heather said, reaching for the hefty binoculars.

He didn't tell her that he was extra-careful with them because they concealed an infrared camera and were specially manufactured for the Soviet military. Instead, he pushed them to her.

"Go ahead," he said. "But they are a little heavy."

She held them to her eyes for a few seconds, grunting dramatically at their weight, before handing them back.

"Yeah," she said. "I'll stick with my little ones." Resting on one elbow, she gazed up into the night sky and sighed. "What's your favorite?"

Richter blew a cloud of vapor into the air. The Stasi had taught him to be a student of human nature. After only a few hours with this woman he knew she did not expect him to answer.

She proved him right by saying, "Mine's the Seven Sisters. The Pleiades."

"Ah," Richter said, to show in the darkness that he was listening.

Heather bucked her hips, rolling onto her back. "You know how to find them in the sky?"

"How?" He snuggled closer, expecting to be taught.

What child did not know how to find the Pleiades? But if his training had taught him anything, it was the art of social engineering. Give people what made them happy, and they give things to you in return. This woman was a teacher. She enjoyed imparting her wisdom to others far more than she liked to be taught.

She leaned in, mashing her breast against his arm as she pointed skyward. "Orion's super-easy to locate, right . . ." More leaning and mashing, then, "Now go to the right using his belt as a pointer . . . through his bow . . . and then on through Taurus . . ."

"And there they are," Richter said, acting impressed. Now he would teach her something to demonstrate his worth as a student.

"Did you know some people believe that in the story of Snow White and the seven dwarves, Snow White represents the sun, and the seven dwarves are the Pleiades? After the winter solstice the moon eclipses the Pleiades three times, the same number of times the evil stepmother visits the dwarves' house."

He neglected to tell her that in German folklore, seven was a number steeped in magic.

"I had no—"

Her body jolted, as if overcome with a sudden chill. Then a whispered hiss: "See that? Almost due north . . . Holy shit!"

He saw it, too, a flash of light shooting west to east, perhaps five miles away. He raised the binoculars but didn't put them to his eyes. That would have been useless.

A half-breath later, another, smaller flash arced up and away from the larger one, also moving west to east, fizzling out in the blackness.

Whispers of surprise and awe crackled up and down the wash. Even the amorous couple heard the change in mood and stumbled out of the rocks.

"Another meteorite?" someone mused.

"That was a solid three seconds," one of the Brit women said. "An eternity in the life of a meteorite. I think not."

"More debris," another voice offered amid hushed conjecture, all eyes pressed futilely to telescopes and binoculars.

Then someone spoke the words Richter was thinking.

"A crash!"

One of the nearby pontificators explained to his small group of acolyte shadows that the second flame was in all likelihood a bit of the spacecraft flying away from the main body as its propulsion system ignited.

Richter was already up. He knew exactly what that second light was.

The booster rockets of an aircraft ejection seat.

A fervor spread through the encampment like a sudden grassfire. Headlamps and flashlights now flicked on with abandon. People grabbed chairs and blankets and threw them into vehicles. Some tossed expensive telescopes in the back of pickups and Subarus, so eager to reach the site of a UFO crash that they didn't care about the replacement cost.

This was beyond big.

Richter looked left and right, making a plan. Even if

this turned out to be a civilian plane, the proximity of the crash to secret bases and restricted airspace meant the site could be crawling with military personnel within the hour. But there had been no navigation lights prior to the event, just a sudden bright fireball streaking across the starry sky. No, this was not a civilian plane, which meant not only rescue, but an impenetrable wall of security forces, probably within minutes.

Richter started for his car. He'd done some exploring during the day and knew the gravel road continued east into Arizona a little over six miles away before cutting north toward Utah again along the eastern slopes of the Virgin Mountains.

Heather stayed rooted in place, calling out after him. "Where are you going?"

"The same place you are, I would assume," he said. A rush of adrenaline pulsed through his limbs at the prospect of getting a fragment of secret military aircraft. He would be decorated by the DDR and Moscow alike.

She didn't move. "I hope so."

"We must hurry!" Richter said.

"We must hurry," she said and laughed, mocking his tone. "Why are you all of a sudden talking like you have a stick up your ass?"

"I'm leaving," he said.

Now she stepped to him. "Okay," she said. "I'm sorry I poked fun at you. But where do you plan to leave to?" She grabbed his jacket, nearly earning a slap in the process. He didn't have time for this, but something about her earnestness made him stop and listen.

"What are you talking about?"

"Listen to me," she whispered. "You want to get to the ship, right?"

"Of course."

"Black Rock Mountain Road cuts north less than five miles east of us."

"This I know," he said, grimacing at his speech pattern.

"That's what I'm trying to tell you. We don't want to go that way."

"And why is that? Everyone else is."

Richter did not care if everyone here retrieved a piece of the mysterious aircraft, as long as he got one.

Cars and trucks were already starting. Backup lights cast monster shadows on the sandstone as drivers maneuvered out of the wash before roaring east, sending up rooster tails of sand and gravel.

She turned and gave a little nod to the northwest, muted so none of the few remaining UFO watchers could catch it.

"Here's what I'm thinking," she whispered, lips brushing his ear. "That thing was on a sixty-degree down-angle when we saw it. Virgin Peak rises to over eight thousand feet." She held up her hand, demonstrating the flight path in the glow of passing headlights.

Richter understood immediately. "So it never made it over the mountains . . ."

"I'd bet money on it," she said. "Everyone else is going that way because they know there's a road there. On a map it might look like it's the closest road, but there's a mountain in the way."

"So which way do we go?" Richter asked, growing frantic again.

"I've been all over these hills on my trike," she said. "We take my pickup north. Four miles up there's a—"

"Come, come," Richter said, starting for his car again. "Explain the rest of it to me on the way."

"Hey!" she barked. "My truck's this way."

"Be right there," he said. "There's something I need to get."

7

TWO MINUTES EARLIER...

The airplane pitched violently to the right, then abruptly nose-down. At least Boden Lee thought it was pointed down. It could have been up. Or sideways. He was so rattled he really had no idea.

Visibility from the F-117 cockpit was marginal in the best of times, but in the dark with the aircraft bucking and pitching and spinning like a child's top, it was impossible to tell up from down. Negative Gs had him struggling to reach the ejection handles on either side of his seat. Wind buffeted the plane, warning buzzers blared, lights flashed. With no forward thrust and no stability, the Black Jet had the glide ratio of a bowling pin.

He'd been heading over the mountains at around 400 knots; now he was heading directly for them. The instruments, the windscreen, everything in the cockpit blushed a hazy pink as extreme negative G-forces pooled blood in his head, giving him red-out. He cursed, straining, reaching with his fingers for the ejection handles.

The canopy blew and the rockets under the seat ignited, seemingly at the same moment. The cockpit fell away into the night and 1.4 seconds after he pulled the handles, Boden Lee found himself under a fully inflated parachute canopy.

The best and worst thing was the sudden silence . . . Like he was waking up from a nightmare—to find himself peacefully dead.

The calm after the bone-rattling commotion in the cockpit was instantaneous. The silence overwhelming.

Pilots are taught that in the event of an emergency they should aviate, navigate, and then communicate. But F-117 pilots practiced being "stealthed up." They rarely communicated unless they were taking on fuel or during landing and takeoff. Normally drawn in for missions, Lee's antennas were out since he'd been flying off-range. Even so, the sudden catastrophic failure of what felt like a section of the tail had left him no time to do anything but eject, let alone call in an emergency.

Now he had time to assess. He was whole. He still had his legs. He'd heard stories of pilots who'd had their legs sheared off when they'd punched out. The seat had done its job and he was now part of that elite club to whom the company sent a necktie for the honor of having their life saved by a Martin-Baker seat. His seat kit—the envelope of survival gear that he sat on during a flight—now dangled some fifteen feet below him on a tether attached to his harness.

The lights of Las Vegas twinkled against the blackness in the distance.

When flying off-range, Black Jets were fitted with two radar cross section enhancers, pucks resembling half footballs that bolted on either side of the fuselage, allowing their radar signature to match the information from their squawk. Right now, flight following would be cussing out the hotshot A-7 pilot who'd disappeared from the radar and turned off his transponder—while Bandit 168 burned into the rocks below.

Drifting on the cold wind, Lee watched his aircraft hit the ground, the remaining fuel onboard bursting into flames and a cloud of inky black smoke that was immediately enveloped by the equally inky black night. From his vantage point, the explosion and resulting fireball rivaled a Hollywood movie, but, stuck between mountain peaks, Lee wondered if anyone would even be able to see it. Rattled, he shook his head, trying to remember if there was another bird behind him in the Late-Go, someone who would fly his same course and see the heat from the explosion . . . But there wasn't. He was the caboose. Dead last.

He removed the small handheld radio from the vest over his G-suit and called it in.

"Mayday! Mayday! Mayday! Bandit 168 is down," he

said, astounded at how calm his voice was. "Mayday! Mayday! Mayday! Bandit 168 is down."

No response.

The radio had limited range and the best option was to make contact while he still had some altitude. There was an outside chance the aircraft ahead of him might pick up a transmission.

"Mayday! Mayday! Mayday! Bandit 168 is down. Pilot is out of the aircraft and under canopy. Activating ELT."

This time he got static, but no answer.

The ground was coming up to meet him fast. He secured the radio back on his vest moments before he landed, rolling with a flourish worthy of the name Slinky, and narrowly missing the only Joshua tree on the side of the mountain. A chorus of coyotes met him as he released his harness and staggered drunkenly to his feet. His back was killing him, and he was pretty sure he was an inch shorter from the rocket ride on the ejection seat, but nothing seemed to be broken.

Blackness surrounded him on all sides, and he realized he'd landed in a shallow gully. He took a deep breath, expecting a whiff of jet fuel, but got nothing but creosote and sunbaked sandstone—a testament to how easy it was to lose an airplane in the mountains.

He took a second to clear his head, baffled that he'd survived, got his bearings with the stars, and began hiking up the hill to the west. Hopefully the ridge would give him line of sight to Las Vegas and he'd be able to make contact on the radio. It would be daylight in a couple hours and his aircraft—or what was left of it—had to be protected. The seat kit had a small knife, a flashlight, along with food bars and water pouches—but no firearm.

He needed gunships and security, and he needed them fast.

8

Four-year-old John Patrick Ryan, Jr.—Jack Junior to the family—wrapped his little arms around his mother's neck like she might run away if he let her go. He was really too big for her to be holding like that, but he was her baby. Considering they'd almost lost him after an attack by ULA terrorists while Cathy was pregnant, the kid could get away with murder. Eight-year-old Sally sat at the bottom of the steps, drawing a picture of a Thanksgiving turkey in a little notebook, allowed to stay up to see her dad off on his business trip. Ryan stood by the front door beside his luggage—a hanging two-suiter and one medium hard-side he'd had since he was a freshman at Boston College. He tore his eyes away from his little family to check out the window for the cab that would take him to Heathrow.

It was late, well past the kids' bedtime, but the boy had refused to eat his dinner and was only now deciding he was hungry. Ryan couldn't blame him. Their cook had made fish and chips with mushy peas. The fish and chips were fine, but the frothy green mess had been enough to put the kid off the whole shebang. For all their years stationed in the UK, Ryan still hadn't managed to get his head wrapped around mushy peas.

He'd considered driving himself to the airport, but Cathy had replaced her Porsche 911 with a new Porsche 911 Turbo (Type 930). The BMW E28 was roomier and kept the kids from fighting quite as much in the backseat. He could have driven the Porsche, but it seemed wrong to leave such a powerful beast parked idly at the airport while he was gone. And anyway, Cathy's car was her car. His car was *their* car.

First-world problems, to be sure.

Ryan's stock investments had seen to it that they did not hurt for money. Far from it. But on a month-to-month basis, his GS-14 salary with the CIA paled to that of an ophthalmic surgeon, even early in her career. If she wanted an astonishingly fast German sportscar in British Racing Green, then she bought one. When Ryan pointed out that the Lamborghini was faster, she batted her eyes and said she didn't want to be ostentatious.

"Want me to call the taxi company again?" Cathy asked, swaying back and forth to soothe Jack Junior.

Ryan yawned, then checked his watch. "I've still got a couple minutes. I'd rather spend the time watching you dance."

Cathy hugged their son, kissed the top of his head, then looked up so suddenly it caught Ryan off guard.

"No secrets, Jack," she said.

"Okay . . ."

"I'm serious. I know you've been in some . . . difficult situations, things you don't talk about, but . . ."

"This trip is one hundred percent meetings," Ryan said. "Greer just wants me to get a feel for things, that's all. 'Try the job on for size,' he says. But, honey, we are talking about the CIA. There are bound to be secrets."

"I know that," Cathy said. She stepped closer and, repositioning little Jack, ran the fingers of her free hand along Ryan's jaw. "You've had some awful experiences—"

"As have you," Ryan said.

"That's true," Cathy said. "But I've got you to talk to. You have the 'Official Secrets Act' nonsense over here and . . . the . . . Top Secret Brotherhood or whatever the hell they call it in the U.S. If there is one thing I know, Jack, it is that every secret is a weight, a burden that you shouldn't have to carry alone."

"You've got plenty of burdens of your own, Cath," Ryan said. "I'm not the kind of guy who wants to add to them."

"I don't care." Cathy put on her surgeon's voice— stern, no-nonsense. "We share our burdens. My biggest fear is that we'll move back to Langley and the secrets will pile up and grind you to dust, age you before your time." She toyed with the hair above his ear. "Don't get me wrong. I like a man with a little gray at the temples— but I want to be your partner. Some things you can't tell me because of national security and all, I get that. I'm talking about the secrets you choose not to tell me because you want to protect me."

The cab squeaked to a stop out front, rescuing Ryan.

"Look at the time," he said.

Sally heard it, too, and jumped up from her coloring. Ryan kissed his little family good-bye, saving Cathy for last.

"I'm serious, Jack!" she whispered. "No secrets."

"So . . . some secrets."

"Jack . . ."

"Don't worry," Ryan said, opening the door to let the cabbie know he was on the way out. "Besides, I'm an analyst. Greer wants me there to analyze stuff. This trip is all paperwork. What could be so secret about that?"

9

Heather Beasley slid her pickup to a dusty stop alongside the gravel road eight minutes after they'd rolled out of Whitney Pocket. As disheveled as she appeared, Richter found the woman to be extremely efficient when she wanted to be. She had her balloon-tired Honda 250 three-wheeler down a folding ramp from the truck bed before the dust had even settled.

She shouldered a small daypack and, silhouetted by the glow of the cab lamp, squatted down to let some air out of the front tire.

"This should keep us from bouncing all over hell and back," she said, patting the Honda's fuel tank. "This is a good machine. Only a year old. It's taken me all over these mountains and canyons. But . . ." She caught his eye, brow raised in warning. "The front wheel has a tendency to bounce up. With both of us on board, it's going to try very hard to rear up and tump over backward."

"Gotcha," Richter said. It was one of the colloquial words they taught in language school to help foreign operatives blend in.

She swung a leg over and scooted back to the luggage rack, giving the seat a pat between her thighs. "You ride here in front and steer. I'll give directions. That way we keep more weight forward. Careful, the gas tank can be a bit of a ball-buster if the going gets too rough—which it will if we want to get there fast."

The reflection of the headlight off yellow desert showed her cheeks were rosy with excitement. She genuinely believed they were on their way to see an alien crash site.

A two-stroke, the Honda's engine smelled of oil and buzzed like a boat motor—and, Richter had to admit, like many of the cars in the DDR.

Heather navigated with a compass she kept on a leather cord around her neck. The blazing headlamp had done away with their night vision the moment it came on, but Richter could still make out the faint outline of black mountain against black sky with his peripheral vision as they sped east and up onto the Virgin Mountain bench.

"Should be coming up to the mouth of a valley anytime," she shouted above the growling engine five minutes later.

Richter looked at his watch, then scanned the sky, missing thousands of stars now that he'd been exposed to the glare of the headlight. Impact minus fifteen. No sign of any security personnel as of yet.

The black maw of a mountain valley opened up in

front of them a few seconds later. Sure of her location now, Heather gave him a squeeze.

"We're gonna start climbing pretty soon," she said. "This is where we have to be careful not to flip over backward and kill ourselves."

Richter nodded. "This gap continues straight?"

"Almost due east," she yelled. "We have to skirt a big sandstone buttress in a little less than a mile, but yeah, after that it's a pretty straight shot up the valley . . . 'Course, the ship could have gone down anywhere on this side. I'm just saying it didn't make it over the ridge."

"Understood." Richter kept his speed up as much as he dared over the boulder-strewn sandstone, unwilling to push the reach of the handlamp. It would do no one any good if he broke his neck driving into a ravine.

There was no real road, only the faint signs of previous off-road vehicles—probably Heather's trike. Great slabs of rock rose on either side of them. Barrel cacti and Joshua trees lurked in the shadows like bandits. The turn came out of nowhere and Richter had to crank the handlebars hard over to keep from crashing into a rock wall. Heather yelped, tossed violently to one side, clinging to his waist to keep from flying off. He let off the throttle immediately, cursed, and then moved forward, stopping only when they'd made it around the corner and were pointed east again along a narrow trail that fell away to their right.

"Why are we stopping?" Heather said a little too loudly in his ear.

"Hand me my bag," he said, laser-focused on the black wall of the Virgin Mountains ahead.

She climbed off the bike first, hugging the rock on the left side of the trike. Richter followed, leaving it idling so they'd have light.

"I asked you why are we stopping?" She hugged herself, rocking back and forth against nervousness and the cold. "You're creeping me out."

He wondered what he'd done to rouse her suspicions. Women could be so intuitive.

"As you said, the aircraft could be in any of these valleys. We can't just ride around blindly."

"Okay . . ." she said. "You got some kind of Ouija board in there like those idiots back at Whitney Pocket?"

He chuckled in spite of the situation. "Much better," he said, taking the black box from his bag and lifting it to his eyes.

"You brought a magic toaster to look at the mountain?"

"A thermal camera," he said.

This one was more powerful than the binoculars, but too unique to use in front of the crowds.

Heat signatures showed up white against the black background of cooler rock. He saw the bloom immediately.

He looped the camera lanyard over his neck and gestured to their left. "Come on, it's just over that hill."

She leaned in close when they got going again, shaking with excitement. "Sorry about that back there."

"It's fine," Richter said over the whining engine.

"You're funny," she said, nuzzling past the collar of his coat to press her cold nose against his neck. "Did you know you curse in German?"

Richter's heart sank.

"This trail really scares me, that's all. Wouldn't take much to go over the edge."

The incline grew steeper the closer they got to the top, and Richter had to lean far over the handlebars to keep the front down. Heather opted to get off and walk the last fifteen yards, unwilling to chance tumbling over the side as the trail skirted a bulging escarpment.

He topped the ridge before her, greeted by hundreds of small fires and the pungent odor of burned metal. He steered the three-wheeler a little to the right so Heather would have to squeeze past on the narrow trail.

"Oh my," she said, hustling along the mountainside, breathless at the sight of what she thought was surely the wreckage of an alien spacecraft.

"Oh, *mein Schatz* . . ." he said, taking her firmly around the shoulders.

She looked up at him in awe, smiling—as he pushed her over the edge.

"Forgive me, *mein Liebling*," he said, and tore himself away from the awful moment and got to work. He'd not wanted to kill the girl, surely not. She was much too vibrant and kind and funny to die so young and in such a horrible way at the hands of someone who really did care for her, but this, this opportunity, it was bigger than either one of them.

He shook off the melancholy and grabbed the Leica SLR camera from his bag. Military security teams were bound to show up at any time, so he needed to work fast. It was more important that he record what he could and then get away cleanly than get too greedy and find himself captured. As his grandmother had always said, "Pigs got fed, hogs got slaughtered."

The aircraft had burned in hard, leaving most of it obliterated beyond any recognition. He found it impossible to tell the actual shape of the aircraft. It was angular, he could tell that much from what pieces were left, some of them no larger than dinner plates. At first glance he thought every bit and piece was covered in thick black soot, but closer inspection revealed that the entire craft had apparently been sheathed with some kind of rubberized skin.

He adjusted the flash for a clearer photograph and squatted to get a close-up.

A voice in the darkness behind him nearly sent him into shock.

"Hey!" It was a male voice. Friendly . . . so far. He thought at first it was the pilot.

"Can you believe this shit?" the voice asked.

Not the pilot.

"It is amazing," Richter said. He let the camera fall against the strap around his neck and stood to face the oncoming visitor.

"Y'all got here quick," the man said. Richter recognized him as one of the UFO watchers. A nice enough man who always wore a Clark County volunteer firefighter hat that lent him an air of authority. Everyone called him Firefighter Steve. "What do you think it is?"

He clicked on a flashlight and played it around the area.

"I'm not sure," Richter said honestly. "A classified aircraft, maybe."

"Did the pilot get out okay?"

"I don't know," Richter said. "I don't see him with the wreckage, but he could be under it. Or he could have ejected and drifted into Arizona."

Firefighter Steve continued to search the area with the flashlight. "Where'd Heather run off to?"

Richter feigned surprise, though he doubted the man could see it in the dark.

"She's not with the three-wheeler?" he asked.

Richter strode forward as if to go check on her.

"I didn't see her," the man said. "Maybe she had to—"

Richter held the kitchen knife so the blade was sideways, parallel to the ground. Slightly curved, seven inches long, and razor sharp, it slipped easily between Steve's ribs before he knew what was happening. At first he thought Richter had bumped into him.

"Watch it!" he snapped. "You're gonna knock me . . . over . . . the . . ."

The last words came on the back of a soft hiss.

Richter worked the blade back and forth, effectively severing the heart.

Steve clutched at him harder now, eyes wide in the long shadows cast from the flashlight he'd dropped on the ground.

The distant drone of an airplane hummed to the west.

Richter wiped the blade on the man's shoulder before he shoved the body over the side. It wasn't as steep here, so it slid only a few dozen yards instead of falling away like Heather had. It would be visible when the sun came up, but that couldn't be helped.

Richter picked up Firefighter Steve's flashlight and returned to the smoldering wreckage long enough to pick out an intact piece roughly thirty by thirty centimeters. The edges were burned and melted, but much of the mysterious rubberized skin material that covered it remained intact. Richter found it to be incredibly fragile and had to wrap it in his undershirt so it didn't rub off.

He stuffed it down the front of his shirt, figuring if he did get stopped by approaching security, they might take his bag, but they wouldn't be likely to search him personally. Americans were incredibly stupid that way.

It took him just seconds to get the three-wheeler turned around and pointed downhill. He adjusted the piece of wreckage so the jagged edges didn't cut into his belly and started down the trail toward his car.

In his haste to get away, he completely missed the lone figure of the pilot looking down on him from high on the eastern ridge.

WHITNEY POCKET
AND VIRGIN PEAK, NEVADA

N

Virgin Peak
✗
Crash site

Black Rock Mountain Road

NEVADA
UTAH

Whitney Pocket •
Whitney Pass Road

© 2022 Jeffrey L. Ward

10

The sun was still below the horizon, but more stars were starting to wink out as the sky turned from indigo to silver blue.

Excitement from his find and nerves at the prospect of getting caught at once warmed and chilled Richter. He saw the half-dozen dirt bikes and off-road vehicles heading toward him as soon as he came around the east-west draw and started south toward his car. He thought of avoiding them, but was unsure of the terrain if he left the established trail.

An American C-12 Huron flew overhead, checking on the group about the time Richter reached them. They all stopped and looked up. One of the women who sat behind the handlebars of a three-wheeler like Heather Beasley's stood on the pegs and shook her fist at the aircraft.

The twin-engine Beechcraft banked to the left and circled back, as if annoyed at the woman's defiant behavior. The others, including Richter, all raised their fists in solidarity. The pilot made a low pass that could have been a strafing run not too many years earlier, and then climbed on toward the crash site.

Moments later, the thump of a helicopter carried across the valley floor and a green Sikorsky HH-3 the Americans called Jolly Green Giant hove into view, bearing down on them. A large part of Richter's HVA training had been to recognize American military aircraft and vessels. The HH-3, called the Sea King by the Navy, was meant to counter the threat of Soviet submarines. The Air Force and Coast Guard both used the HH-3 for search and rescue—the mission this one was on now. It made sense that a base housing classified aircraft would have a divert team of SAR and security aircraft at their disposal. The C-12 pilot had obviously sent the chopper to investigate this rowdy group.

The bird settled onto the desert floor some thirty meters away from the knot of all-terrain vehicles, close enough to pelt them with dust and pebbles. Richter had no doubt that was their intention. It was what he would have done.

A man in suit pants and a white shirt and tie jumped out of the helicopter first, followed by three uniformed men in helmets, each carrying M16 rifles. They all trotted over to the group.

The three in uniform fanned out, weapons down but eyes up in that uniquely American cowboy way that looked as if they would relish the opportunity for a gunfight.

It was no surprise that the one in civilian clothes was

the apparent leader of the team. He was stocky, like he lifted a lot of weights, and his hair was long enough to blow in the downwash of the waiting helicopter. "This entire valley from the highway to the Arizona border has been declared a National Defense Area."

As was his habit, Richter sized up the man, noting the semiautomatic pistol in a well-worn leather holster on his hip.

The original fist-raiser pushed her floppy hat back and wagged her head. "So? What does National Defense Area even mean?"

"In a nutshell," the civilian said, "it means this is a temporary no-trespassing zone. You all have to leave."

"Why?" one of the British ufologists asked. "What are you hiding up there?"

"A military jet has crashed, rendering the area unsafe." The man spoke as if he'd memorized a speech his superiors had given him.

"What sort of jet?" Richter asked.

Deadpan and dead-eyed: "I'm not at liberty to say."

An elderly woman who could have been from a Tweety Bird cartoon lifted a camera from around her neck. "I don't have to get very close." She pointed at the mountains to the north, where Richter had come from. "May I go up there and shoot from a distance?"

"No, ma'am," the man said. "Photography isn't permitted in a National Defense Area."

A murmur ran through the group.

"That's against the Constitution," the first woman said.

"We'll work it out in court," the man said. "Now, turn your vehicles around and leave."

The elderly woman puffed up like she was going to spit.

"And may I ask who you are?"

"Nope," the man said. "I'm giving you fair warning. You're going to see military aircraft all over the place. If you are caught in this area after being told to leave, you will be dealt with appropriately by Air Force security personnel."

The man waved his hand in a circle over his head and turned to trot back to the Sikorsky. The uniforms stood for a moment longer, punctuating his point with their glares before wheeling to follow him.

Richter thumbed the throttle, complying with the man's orders and, more important, riding away before the others had a chance to ask him about Heather.

He rode the bouncing three-wheeler south as fast as he could, cutting east when he reached the road to Whitney Pocket. The piece of wreckage under his shirt dug into his belly, turning it into what he was sure was a bloody mess. That couldn't be helped. The sun was up now, and he needed to get back to his car. At any moment the authorities would find the bodies and any interaction with stone-faced men in helicopters would become much more of a problem.

While the desert was on fire with morning light, the rock formations of Whitney Pocket were still bathed in shadows. The glow of lights against sandstone alerted Richter to other vehicles and he pulled up short, skidding to a stop. He cursed, spat the grit out of his teeth, and inched forward, headlight off. As he suspected, the parking area was a hive of activity. While most of the UFO watchers from before had headed into the hills to find their crashed alien craft, more had arrived hoping to set up a base camp. The authorities had anticipated this. Marked units from the Clark County Sheriff's Office and the Nevada Highway Patrol lined the gravel road while uniformed deputies and officers dealt with the angry crowd. Richter started to roll forward and retrieve his car until he realized the police were in the process of checking everyone's identification—and not allowing anyone to leave.

A Pave Hawk helicopter gunship prowled the rocky fringe between Whitney Pocket and the trails leading to the downed aircraft. A man in uniform had spread what looked to be a large paper map on the hood of Richter's sedan. He and a man in a dark blue windbreaker hunched over it with flashlights, making plans.

Richter turned the three-wheeler around, heading toward the highway and Mesquite. Fortunately, no one had zeroed in on him—yet. He racked his brain, trying to recall anything incriminating he might have left in his car. He'd had enough sense to bring the duffel with his communication gear and night-vision device. The pistol he'd hidden beneath the spare tire in his trunk would have been nice, but kitchen knives were easy to come by and did not arouse suspicion. He had six hundred dollars cash in his wallet—not enough for a car, but he could always steal one.

The authorities would eventually get around to figuring out that poor sweet Heather and the unlucky Firefighter Steve had been murdered, but the crash site was the immediate priority. The military would go to great lengths to secure their secret aircraft and, likely as not, withhold precious information about the dead from the plodding locals who would be tasked with solving the murders. With luck, Richter would be hundreds of miles away by the time any semblance of a manhunt began.

But if anyone suspected he'd ended up with a piece of that aircraft, they would stop at nothing in their pursuit. He needed to move fast—and to do that he needed something besides a motorized tricycle.

His father, who'd fought with the Nazi Wehrmacht's 9th Infantry Division at the Ardennes Offensive, had described American GIs as not particularly smart or skilled. According to the elder Richter, the Allies had won the war only because they were rich. Richter suspected the words were salve to help heal the wounds of defeat. From what he'd seen, the Americans were smart, and, worse yet, they were relentless.

Garit Richter leaned forward, rolling on the throttle. So was he.

11

FBI Special Agent Daniel Murray never slept well the first few nights away from his wife. Now two days into his trip, jet lag was sure to crash down around him anytime, but for the time being his circadian clock was still on London time—12:30 p.m.—and he didn't mind the 7:30 a.m. report time to the outdoor ranges at Quantico. The Bureau loved its in-service agent training, even if they had to pull agents away from important work and fly them halfway around the world to complete it. Some agents used the periodic rehash of policy and defensive tactics as an opportunity to get away from mundane assignments or to take a vacation from an unhappy marriage. Murray habitually put it off for as long as the brass would let him. He was glad to be reunited with a few old friends, but he had important shit to do at home.

His law degree had given his career a little extra push

and he'd been promoted through the ranks to become the FBI legal attaché three years earlier, working with UK law enforcement and intelligence services. The job of legat normally entailed a great deal of hobnobbing with ambassadors and chief superintendents, but terror was back on the front pages in Europe. Murray found himself in the middle of massive, multiyear investigations into transnational criminal enterprises, "the Lord's Work," his counterpart at MI6 called it. Even so, the bean counters and policy wonks at the Bureau thought it wise to pull him away from said work and drag him across the pond to tick a little box in his training file.

His favorite part of the curriculum was weapons qualification—Remington 870 pump shotgun, Heckler & Koch MP5 submachine gun, and sidearm. In Murray's case, this was a Smith & Wesson Model 13 .357 Magnum revolver. Sixteen others, from brick agents to supervisors, were on the line this frosty morning. Four firearms instructors peered over the shooters' shoulders, ensuring safety and adding a measure of stress. Hailing from Baltimore to Billings, between them they'd racked up more than a century and a half of experience with the Bureau. A couple, like Murray, came from assignments overseas.

The outdoor range allowed for quals on both long guns and pistols. They'd just finished with the MP5, a firearm that Murray found particularly satisfying to shoot. He'd never considered himself a "barrel sucker" like some of the gun aficionados he worked with, but he had to admit the little black H&K was damned sexy. The

Bureau had adopted it not long after it was introduced in the sixties, supplanting old tommy guns as the shoulder weapon of choice. The still nascent FBI Hostage Rescue Team made the little black SMG their primary weapon. (Operators knew pistols were always secondary, used to fight your way back to the primary weapon, or if that primary failed.) It was easy to see why. Firearms instructors liked to say that the MP5 made poor shooters look good, good shooters look great, and great shooters look fantastic. Murray had shot clean, a tight group, small enough to cover with a closed fist. More important, he'd shot it fast.

Fantastic.

Handguns were next. The vast majority of agents and all the instructors on the line had made the switch to the new Smith & Wesson 459 semiauto in nine-millimeter parabellum. They were having trouble prying Murray's fingers off his venerable Model 13, a three-inch bull-barreled wheel gun he'd been issued along with his first set of creds at Quantico. Firearms instructors especially liked to make fun of the speed loaders he had to snatch from his coat pocket in order to reload. As they were fond of pointing out, his revolver went *click, click, click* after six shots, while the shiny black semiautos still had nine more bangs left to throw downrange.

"Mark my words," the lead firearms instructor said. "Revolvers are going the way of the dodo." His name was Tanner, but a bristle-brush mustache and his other paunchy attributes made him the spitting image of Mr. Potato Head. Instructors at the FBI Academy were supervisory special agents, or SSAs. In Murray's experience, Potato Head didn't know dick about being a leader in the field, but he was a hell of a shot. The Academy was just the place for him. The guy had nothing less than a superpower when it came to passing on that skill to others, rain or shine . . . or bone-numbingly cold.

Frost covered the grass that lined the range sidewalks, and most agents put their gloves back on while they topped off magazines, and, in Murray's case, HKS Speedloaders and a rubber Bianchi Speed Strip he kept in his shirt pocket for six extra rounds. A little Beretta .25 in his coat pocket served as his last-ditch get-off-me gun, but he kept that to himself. One, it was outside Bureau policy, and two, he didn't want to admit that he'd gone over to the dark side of semiautos.

"Leave it to a Southie boy to hang on to a dinosaur," Tanner said. A die-hard Yankees fan, he never missed an opportunity to dig at Murray's Boston roots.

Murray chuckled. The heady odor of gunfire and Hoppes #9 made him happy and immune to a little teasing. "I suppose I'm just old-school—"

The pager on his belt began to buzz. He unclipped it. It was a 202 number. D.C. Not exactly out of the ordinary as far as pages went.

Tanner glared at the offending piece of electronics and gave a shake of his head. "That's a big nope, Special Agent."

Murray chuckled at that. FBI agents almost universally addressed colleagues and subordinates by their last names—unless they happened to be pissed about something. Then they added the "Special Agent" title in the way angry mothers used a child's middle name to show they meant serious business.

"It's your range. You're the boss." Murray turned the digital LCD readout on his pager so Tanner could see it. "Unless this happens to be *the* boss. Recognize the number?"

Tanner shook his head. "I do not."

"It looks familiar. I'm thinking it's the Hoover Building."

Tanner rolled his eyes. "Make it quick. We have paper to punch."

Murray turned toward the classroom hut at the back of the range, where he knew there was a telephone.

Tanner called after him. "Where the hell are you going?"

Murray held up the pager. Wasn't it obvious?

"To make the call."

Tanner pushed a heavy Motorola DynaTAC brick phone across the ammo table. "You need to hop on the future bus, Big Iron. Go ahead and make your call on this and then get your ass back on the firing line."

It was the Hoover Building, all right. Potato Head looked on quizzically while Murray responded with "Yes, sir" a half-dozen times in less than a minute, and then pushed the bulky cell phone toward him.

"It's the deputy director," Murray said, grimacing for effect. "He wants to talk to *you*."

Tanner stood tall, saying "Yes, sir" almost as many times as Murray before he ended the call and held out the phone.

"I'm supposed to give you this."

"The brick?"

"Yeah. I guess you're going to need it where you're going. They're sending a—"

The thump of an approaching helicopter drowned him out, and a moment later, a green Bell UH-1N Iroquois, better known as the Twin Huey, settled onto a grassy field adjacent to the handgun range. Marine Corps helicopter squadron HMX-1, home of the birds that became Marine One when the President of the United States was on board, was within spitting distance of the FBI Academy. Those were all Sikorsky White Hawks and VH-3D Sea Kings utilized for frequent presidential lifts between the South Lawn of the White House and Andrews, where Air Force One was hangared. Murray had seen a couple visiting Hueys behind the fence when he'd driven over to visit an old Marine buddy the evening before. But he was surprised as hell to see one coming for him.

The chopper had barely touched down when the door slid open and a uniformed crew chief leaned out, waving him over.

The other agents on the range secured empty boxes and paper targets to keep them from blowing away in the frigid downwash.

"I want to be you when I grow up, Murray," Tanner muttered. "Shit like this only ever happens to you and Arnold Schwarzenegger."

The deputy director hadn't provided any details beyond an order to get on the helicopter when it arrived. Murray made certain his revolver was loaded—all too easy to overlook when a helicopter came to pick you up on the firing line—and then stuffed what scant gear he had into his range bag. Tanner, who was notorious for guarding ammunition like it was coming out of his own paycheck, pushed two boxes of Winchester 145-grain Silvertip duty ammo across the wooden table.

"I don't know where you're headed," he said. "But an exit of this nature means you're liable to need more bullets."

"I could just be going to headquarters," Murray said.

"In that case, I should give you another box."

The pilot kept the rotors going, ready to turn and burn. Though he didn't need to, Murray ducked instinctively, hand on top of his head as he trotted across the field. The crew chief leaned farther out and lifted one of his earphones, yelling over the Huey's engine whine.

"Are you our FBI guy, sir?"

"Special Agent Daniel Murray!" he shouted.

"You're the one we're looking for!" The Marine handed him a headset that was wired to the intercom and waved his gloved hand at the otherwise empty interior, offering a choice of seats.

Murray sat on the left side of the aircraft, securing himself to a forward-facing seat next to the window. It was hard as a board, reminding Murray just how spartan military aircraft could be. He kept the range bag in his lap and pulled on the headset, ready to find out what was going on.

The crew chief gave the pilots the go signal, and the bird lifted off immediately. He turned back around and, realizing Murray was trying to talk to him, shook his head and tapped his earphone, pantomiming putting the little boom mic right up next to his mouth. Murray tried, nearly eating the damned thing, but nothing worked.

The Marine checked the connection, then took the headset to look it over. The interior of the chopper was incredibly loud, and apparently unwilling to sacrifice his hearing to explain what was going on to a suit, he grabbed Murray's hand and used a ballpoint pen from his flight suit to scribble a terse explanation on his palm.

PLANE CRASH NEVADA

Murray studied the meager words, chewing on their meaning. The NTSB handled plane crashes . . . unless there was a nexus to terrorism. Still, he was an FBI legal attaché who just happened to be stateside. He wasn't a pilot and didn't particularly care for planes. Why would anyone send him—

The corporal tapped him on the shoulder and handed him the headset again.

This time it worked and Murray gave him a thumbs-up.

"Outstanding," the Marine said.

"I'm going to a plane crash in Nevada?"

"That's the information I have, sir."

"A long way to fly in a Huey."

"Oh, you're not going with us, sir," the Marine said. "There's a C-21 on the flight line, fueled and ready to take off as soon as we deliver you to them."

"What kind of plane?" Murray asked.

"A C-21," the Marine said again, sounding earnest as the day was long. "It's the military version of a Learjet, sir."

Murray shook his head. "I mean what kind of plane crashed."

"Sorry," the Marine said. "I do not know the answer to that, sir. They're not saying type. Sounds like the crash occurred somewhere over the Virgin Mountains . . ." His eyes narrowed behind his goggles, and he gave a con-spiratorial nod, prodding Murray to make the leap in logic. "A little over a hundred and sixty miles southeast of Tonopah Test Range . . ."

"Ah," Murray said. "That kind of plane."

12

I'm surprised this isn't being handled in the field," Judge Arthur Moore said as soon as the oak door to the seventh-floor conference room clicked shut. He ran the CIA but still preferred *Judge* to *Director*. Like many who'd been appointed to the bench, Moore hung on to the title. He spoke with just a hint of a drawl, enough to demonstrate he was from West Texas but with a law degree from Harvard.

"Difficult to argue with that," Robert Ritter, CIA deputy director of operations and fellow Texan, said from Moore's right.

"Well, gentlemen," Deputy Director of Intelligence James Greer said. "Arguing is not the point of this meeting, so we should be good."

The DDI waved Jack Ryan to his seat at the table. Greer was a mustang, having served as an enlisted sailor before graduating from the United States Naval Academy at Annapolis and eventually being promoted to vice admiral. A submariner and intelligence specialist, the CIA had been a natural progression in his public service.

The only other person in the room, a muscular man Ryan didn't recognize, sat in the chair next to Ritter. He spun a black lacquer Montblanc fountain pen on top of the red-striped folder in front of him.

The conference room was what Ryan thought of as government chic, boasting polished oak paneling, a mahogany table, and high-backed leather chairs—real leather, not Naugahyde or the dusty, foam-padded cloth crap the minions downstairs got. Evidently, seventh-floor asses were much more discerning about where they parked themselves. It was a corollary Ryan had seen not only in government but on Wall Street as well: Those doing the most work got the worst places to sit while they did it.

Many people at Langley, including Ritter, thought John Patrick "Jack" Ryan was still little more than a boy, someone barely out of grad school. And for all practical purposes he was—chronologically. But he'd packed a lifetime of experience into his thirty-four years. He held an honorary knighthood from Her Majesty the Queen, a doctorate in history, and was the author of several books. He was a father of two impetuous but brilliant kiddos, husband of the most amazing woman on the planet, and a millionaire several times over. His books had garnered the attention of the CIA and he'd worked for the admiral off and on for more than four years. He didn't need the job, at least not financially. Though, if he were honest with himself, something inside him needed to be engaged in exactly this kind of work. He hated flying, but loved the sea, and, even more than that, had an insatiable appetite for social puzzles, sussing out what made people tick. Which, he supposed, was why he was in this particular conference room with these particular men.

Something had happened during his flight from Heathrow that added an air of immediacy to his visit with Admiral Greer.

The hours in the air left him dry-mouthed and in need of a shave. His pager had blown up with repeated messages as soon as he landed. Greer had a car waiting for him at Dulles, so he came straight in without stopping off at his hotel. Few people at Langley had ever seen him in a suit that he hadn't slept in. Ryan draped his overcoat across an empty chair and rubbed a hand over his face.

Framed photographs of past CIA directors and American intelligence community heroes flanked larger, color portraits of the President and Judge Moore. Ryan took a seat under a black-and-white photograph of William J. "Wild Bill" Donovan, head of the famed OSS during World War II and founding father of the Central Intelligence Agency.

"Dr. Jack Ryan," Greer said, smiling with what appeared to Ryan to be the only honest eyes in the room. "Meet Lane Buckley, assistant deputy director of operations, formerly the chief of station in Bonn."

Ryan stood at the introduction and reached across the

table to shake hands—like his father had taught him. Buckley extended his hand without getting up. He gave a smug grunt, the kind of grunt Ryan sometimes got from folks on the operations side of the CIA house. Not quite condescending . . . but . . . . hell, it was all kinds of condescending. Ryan didn't care. He didn't exactly need Lane Buckley's approval. They'd been the ones to call him.

"No offense, Dr. Ryan," Ritter said, staring at his own red-striped folder as he spoke, deadpan. "I'd expected Jim to bring in someone with a little more time in grade for this one."

"Time in grade?" Admiral Greer didn't even try to stifle a belly laugh as he poured himself a cup of coffee from the pitcher on the table. "Are we talking years or experience, Bob? I can name a dozen in this building, hell, on this very floor, who have one year of experience twenty times. Last I checked, Ryan has proven himself out there on the bricks. I'm seriously thinking of luring him back from London full-time."

Ritter gave a slow nod and waved his hand in a little let's-get-on-with-it-then flourish.

Assistant Deputy Director Buckley fiddled with the cap of his fountain pen. Ryan imagined how fun it would be to play poker with this guy.

"So," Moore said, returning Ritter's flourish with one of his own. "Tell us about CALISTO. *Who is who?* as that prick Erich Mielke likes to say."

Mielke ran the East German Ministry for State Security. The secret police, or Stasi.

Ritter gestured to his right. "Lane has the wheres and wherefores, Judge. Insofar as we know them at this point."

Like everyone else at the conference table, Admiral Greer wore a dark business suit, but his bearing and composure left no room for doubt that he was a military man. He leaned back in his chair, both hands resting on his belly, and looked at Ryan, who was expertly masking his confusion. "My intention was to ease you into a few things," he said. "But there's been a development while you were over the Atlantic."

Ryan nodded to show he was listening, but said nothing. The windup was Jim Greer being Jim Greer.

"We've lost a very particular kind of aircraft," the admiral continued. "An F-117 Nighthawk."

Ryan had never heard of that aircraft designation, but leaned forward instinctively, waiting for the rest of the story. "Lost?"

"Catastrophic failure on a training run over the Virgin Mountains. The FBI and Air Force Security Forces are on-site now."

"And the pilot?" Ryan asked.

"He punched out," Buckley said. "Banged up but doing well."

"Hold on," Ryan said. "The Bureau is involved?"

"There's a chance someone on the ground ended up with a sample of debris," Greer said.

"Cathy and I spent some time on Lake Mead a year or so ago," Ryan said, picturing a map in his head. "You can see the Virgin Mountains from there. Awfully bleak terrain. What was anyone doing up there when the plane went down?"

Buckley scoffed. "UFO watchers, if you can believe it. They're hanging out there most nights, looking for black triangles and little green men."

"The Air Force found two bodies, Jack," Greer said. "An adult female and an adult male, who appears to be a volunteer firefighter—"

"Who was probably another nutjob out looking for flying saucers," Buckley said.

"Buckley's not wrong about that," Greer said. "The bodies are less than fifty yards from one another. The Nighthawk pilot was up on a ridge, but he feels sure he saw a man push the female victim to her death. They're still trying to retrieve the body from a crevice in the rocks. The firefighter was just off the trail. He was apparently stabbed. According to the AF OSI guy who was first on the scene, it looks like the killer knew exactly what he was doing with the blade. Clean. The work of a professional."

"Pilot is pretty banged up from punching out," Buckley said. "But he's adamant about what he saw."

Greer slid a sheet of paper sideways to Jack. It was a pencil sketch of a man with shaggy hair sticking out from beneath a wool cap.

"Not a great drawing," Ryan said.

"That's an understatement," Greer said.

"What could this person have taken from the crash site?" Ryan asked. "It's not like he could carry out any secret avionics—"

"RAM," Buckley said, as if it should have been obvious. "Radar-absorbing material. Too early to say, but their tracks indicate someone was shuffling around in the dirt by a portion of the tail section. It's possible he got a piece of a component called . . ." Buckley consulted his notes. "The Platypus."

Ritter piped up. "The Platypus is a kind of shield that extends below the rear of the engines, blocking the heat signature from beneath."

"Exactly," Buckley said. "Our engineers spent a hell of a lot of time and energy developing the components to make this airplane invisible."

"Nearly invisible," Greer corrected.

"Of course," Buckley said. "Anyway, the East Germans wouldn't have the capability or the money to manufacture an aircraft like this, but if they don't have to spend their own time and treasure figuring out and testing the angles, and then they reverse-engineer our RAM, the Soviets will throw money at it and get it built. Any tactical edge we have now would evaporate."

"Why are we jumping straight to East Germany as the culprit?" Ryan asked.

"We'll get to that," Greer said.

"A divert team from Nellis cordoned off the area relatively quickly," Ritter said. "The Air Force has designated it a National Defense Area so they can use the same rules of engagement as they would on a military installation."

Ryan grimaced. "But would they want to?"

Ritter shook his head, likely chalking Ryan's naïveté

up to age. "The area will remain closed to the public for some time. In the event anyone does slip through, the Air Force is seeding the area with F-101 wreckage they're bringing in from a hangar at Groom Lake. The official line is that a Voodoo went down on a night flight. A press release is going out tomorrow morning. If we give the public a story too soon, they'll think we have it prepared already and are hiding something."

Ryan gave a low groan. *No wonder there are so many conspiracy theories,* he thought, but kept it to himself.

Instead, he asked, "What now?"

"I need to read you in on SENIOR TREND," Greer said.

"SENIOR TREND . . ." Ryan tried the code name on for size. As usual, it was completely unrelated to the project it stood for.

"Buckley's already mentioned the Platypus and the RAM," Greer said. "You'll get the full briefing packet for review, but here's the skinny . . ."

Greer gave Ryan the rundown of the top secret Lockheed Martin Skunk Works project that began as HAVE BLUE and matured into SENIOR TREND. "For comparison's sake, an F-16 Falcon has the radar cross section of approximately four square meters. The F-117 Nighthawk has a radar cross section about the size of a hummingbird."

"F-117," Ryan mused. "A fighter?"

"Don't get me started," Greer said. "No. The F-117 doesn't have air-to-air capabilities. Any exterior weapons would add to the radar signature. Its mission is ground attack. A stealth bomber. And it's very good at its job."

"I've read rumors of a so-called F-19," Ryan said. "Conspiracy buffs refer to it as a flying Frisbee."

"They're not far off," Greer said.

Buckley spoke up. "Some pilots call this one the Wobblin' Goblin."

"They do," Greer said. "Most of them report that the name isn't warranted. It's been a very effective aircraft during the three years it's been in service. So far, we've been able to keep the project secret." He glanced up at Ryan. "You know the Bureau agent who'll be running the manhunt. Daniel Murray."

"He's in London," Ryan said, genuinely surprised. "I talked to him last month in the embassy dining hall."

"The Bureau detailed him to Quantico for retread training a couple days ago," Greer said. "I think they have him teaching a couple courses in counterterrorism to a class of new agent trainees while he's there as well."

"Dan Murray's a really solid guy," Ryan said. "My dad was a Baltimore homicide detective. Murray has the same dogged investigative determination I saw in my old man."

Ryan didn't mention it, but everyone at the table knew he'd foiled a plot by the Ulster Liberation Army to assassinate members of the British Royal Family—an action that nearly got his entire family murdered. Dan Murray had taken a leadership role in the investigation and became a good friend to the Ryans during the aftermath.

"I beg your pardon, Admiral," Ryan said. "But I'm still not catching what this has to do with me."

"Greer suggested we ask the Bureau for someone you know to run the Nighthawk fugitive operation," Judge Moore said. "There is a strong probability that it could be related to another matter."

"Another matter?"

"The reason I called you here straight off the plane, Jack," Greer said. "TRUE WIND."

He gave Buckley a nod to move forward.

"A possible defector," Buckley said. "Bottom line up front, someone in West Berlin handed off a note and a coded computer disk to a low-level Foreign Service officer assigned to the U.S. Mission there. This possible defector has been assigned the code name CALISTO."

He briefed the room with the details of Ruby Keller's mugging. Ryan took notes.

"There's always a possibility that this is a dangle," Moore suggested.

"Possibly." Buckley started fiddling with his pen again. "KGB and Stasi HVA agents are constantly probing embassy and mission personnel to ascertain who is who. But if CALISTO is a dangle, it's odd he wouldn't want to meet someone who's stationed there in West Berlin. The identity of the operations officers running our assets would be a valuable intelligence coup for both the East Germans and the Soviets. But the note specifically stated no local officers should be involved with the initial meeting. For whatever reason, CALISTO doesn't trust our guys on the ground in Berlin."

"He's aware of a mole . . ." Judge Moore pounded the table, looking like he wanted to shoot something . . . or someone.

"That's the thought," Buckley said. "I'd venture to guess that ninety-nine percent of the traitors we catch are given up by defectors who come over to our side. Our moles rat out their moles. Their moles rat out our moles . . . and the dance goes on . . ."

"Hell of a dance," Ritter said. "Since the Russians' dance partners get three hots and a cot in federal prison, while ours get their fingernails pulled out and a Soviet bullet in the back of the head."

"True enough," Buckley said, cavalier, though he'd surely had assets die while working for him. Several moles in the past decade had outed dozens of CIA assets, most of whom had been shot. There was no doubt the U.S. intelligence apparatus still had traitors in their ranks. Ryan wasn't read into everything, not by a long shot, but he was around Langley enough to read between the lines and see the massive investigations under way to locate these leaks who were still at large, possibly at the neighboring desk . . . or at this table. They lost agents in place every year, the volunteers who agreed to remain in their jobs in the Soviet Union for a time in order to glean more intelligence—all at great peril to themselves and their families. It made Ryan at once sick to his stomach and immensely proud to know a few such brave men and women.

Buckley continued. "The disk was coded, but CAL-ISTO mailed a onetime cypher key to a P.O. box in

Chantilly, Virginia. Most everyone in the West has moved to five-and-a-quarter-inch disks, but I saw plenty of Robotrons in the GDR while I was running the show in Bonn. Those older units are dinosaurs, still using eight-inch floppies . . . or even cassette tapes to store data."

The assistant DDO was quiet for a beat, allowing the information he'd shared to sink in, then said, "But here's the deal. The contents of the disk were a very interesting taste of what CALISTO has to offer." He paused again, glancing to Ritter for guidance on whether or not to continue.

Greer glanced up from his folio, looked at the two men, and then said, "We talked about this. Consider Dr. Ryan read in."

Buckley gave an if-you-say-so shrug.

"A series of mathematical formulas," he said. "Some trigonometry and physics that's light-years beyond me. Suffice it to say it looks like the DDR or the Soviets, maybe both, are conducting research on radar bounce and stealth technology."

"SENIOR TREND," Ryan mused. "The F-117."

Moore darkened. "Are we thinking they've gotten hold of our tech?"

"No," Ritter said. "Looking at the data on the disk, we believe their research is well behind where we're at. Their program appears to still be in nascent stages, but they're definitely on the right track."

Moore bounced his fist on the table, clearly agitated. "So the Russians or East Germans have somehow gotten this same technology . . ."

"We're not sure," Ritter said. "I had a contact at Lockheed Martin review the numbers for me. He believes this is a parallel development."

"That makes sense," Ryan said. "I remember reading about a Soviet scientist who wrote a paper on radar and low observability."

"Right," Greer said. "HAVE BLUE/SENIOR TREND expanded on that scientist's original hypothesis."

"So they're doing some expanding of their own," Moore said.

"Research," Buckley said. "The calculations and designs CALISTO provided are basic, but spot-on. They'd still need to conduct myriad tests, not to mention the fact that they're missing a major component." He paused, looking to Ritter again.

Greer took a sip of coffee. "Which they could have gotten from the crash last night."

"So, what do we know about this CALISTO?" Judge Moore asked.

"Nothing," Buckley said. "Or next to nothing, anyway. The person who mugged the Keller girl is dead. Cyanide."

"In front of a hamburger joint, no less," Moore scoffed. "Why did CALISTO choose this particular girl . . . Keller?"

"She's a consular officer for State," Buckley said. "Only been in Berlin a couple weeks. Can't quite break free of her McDonald's habit. She goes there almost every day."

"So CALISTO follows her from the embassy, makes his plan, and then executes it," Ryan said. "Do we want a defector who murders his accomplices? I mean, whoever this is, they killed the mugger."

"Maybe," Ritter said. "Maybe not. Some Stasi agent who was following the kid killed him and then fled. The streets were crowded."

"Could the mugger have been CALISTO?"

"We ruled that out first thing," Buckley said. "The deceased was a West German punk rocker with a criminal record as long as my arm."

Ritter leaned forward, resting both elbows on the table, eyes locked on Ryan as if to gauge his reaction. "I want to go back and touch on your previous question, Dr. Ryan. The short and brutal answer is yes. We'll take a murdering son of a bitch who wants to defect if that murdering son of a bitch gives us viable intelligence from behind the Iron Curtain. You'd be naïve to think otherwise. A man with your years of experience has to be aware of how blind we are over there."

"It's the sad truth of intelligence work, Jack," Greer said. "Our bedfellows are often riddled with moral maladies we don't like to talk about in the daylight." He groaned. "At any rate, that's the guts of what we know."

"We do know one other thing," Ryan pointed out.

All eyes turned to him.

"What's that, son?" Moore asked.

"CALISTO has information from the East, but he made the approach in the West. That means he not only has access to information. He has the ability to travel outside the GDR."

"Or he gave the information to someone who did," Buckley said.

"Maybe," Ryan said. "But would you give evidence that could get you shot to a third party to carry out?"

"Every damned day while I was in Bonn," Buckley said.

"At any rate," Moore said, "CALISTO's message is adamant that the initial meeting be with someone who's not from Bonn or Berlin. He alludes to the possibility of a leak in our security."

Buckley patted his folder but didn't say anything.

"FLEDERMAUS," Greer said.

"Bat?" Ryan said.

Buckley nodded, now that Greer had put it out there. "SIGINT shows repeated references to something or someone called FLEDERMAUS in conjunction with American ops and assets in Germany. Prevailing wisdom is that's the code name they use for their asset—our mole—or at least one of them."

Greer reached across the table and grabbed the coffee pitcher off the silver tray, pouring Ryan a cup. A bad sign.

"That's where you come in, Jack. We'd like you to ascertain if CALISTO should be brought into the fold, or, as they say, left out in the cold."

"Just a minute, sir," Ryan said. "You want me to go to West Berlin?"

Buckley shook his head. "East Berlin. CALISTO's

coded message gives us a drop location where we'll get further instructions."

"And by 'we,' you mean Ryan," Moore said.

"I'm familiar with the terrain, sir," Buckley said. "And I'm not a local anymore. It makes sense that I be the one to go with him."

"I beg to differ," Greer said. "No offense, Lane, but you were chief of Bonn Station for three years. You don't think the Stasi and the KGB have files on you two feet thick? Good Lord, man, you developed Chernenko as a volunteer and kept him in Line PR for what, the better part of two years? That had to throw a wrench in their apparatus."

Buckley beamed at the buttering. *Yep*, Ryan thought. He'd be a blast to get at the poker table.

"He's right," Moore said. "Greer's got a plan. Let's have his shop run this one."

Ritter started to protest, but the director raised an open hand. "Not because I don't trust you, Bob. I do. But we don't need multiple people making decisions. Committee-think is killing the Soviets. They never seem to get anything done."

Ritter raised a hand as if in surrender. He paused, then looked up at Ryan with a narrow eye.

"Can I ask how old you are?"

"I'm thirty-four," Ryan said. Robert Ritter knew full well about the classified work he'd done securing Soviet ballistic missile submarine *Red October*—and his actions in London against Irish terrorists—but to some, the blush of youth cast a shadow over any past success, making them seem like flukes.

"Thirty-four?" Buckley said. "Holy shit, Ryan! No offense, but we're talking about East Germany. The honest-to-God Iron Curtain police state of all police states. The Berlin Wall . . . what do they call it, the Anti-Fascist Protection Rampart. Some people over there actually believe this stuff and will happily riddle your spine with lead if you screw up operating over there."

Greer ignored Buckley and looked at Ritter. "I'm not blind to the fact that Dr. Ryan is an analyst. We'll need to send someone with significant expertise in hostile area tradecraft."

"Agreed," Ritter said.

"I've taken the liberty . . ." Greer slid a sheet of paper across the table to Judge Moore. Typed in OCR font, it would be fed into the Optical Character Reader by a cypher clerk, encrypted, then disbursed as Eyes Only to CIA stations and bases in Bonn and both sides of the Wall in Berlin.

Buckley, who'd yet to learn what was on the paper, leaned back in his chair, tapping his pen on his front teeth. "I have some ideas about who we could send with him."

Moore slid the paper draft cable to Ritter, who read it, thought for a moment, then said, "Evidently, so does Admiral Greer."

"Very well," Moore said. "Get it rolling."

Ryan glanced up from his notebook. "Who's the chief in East Berlin?"

"Jason Newell," Ritter said. "Steady man. Been there

two years—a lifetime in Eastern Europe. He was deputy chief of station in Paris before landing that job. Ambo's a female. Lois Simon. Career diplomat. Relatively effective . . . as far as diplomats go. You'll fly in to West Berlin. Skip Hulse is in charge of the base there. He's also good. I've been in some rough patches with him. I have and would continue to trust him with my life."

Ryan committed the names to memory without writing them down. "I'll get with the travel office as soon as I leave here."

"Time is of the essence in this one, Jack," Greer said. "Did Cathy come with you?"

"She's still in London with the kids."

"Good," Greer said.

It went without saying that Jack shouldn't mention anything about the assignment to Cathy. Buckley mentioned it anyway, just to show the intel weenie who the operational experts were.

"You'll want to play this one close to the vest, Ryan. Don't tell anyone where you're heading, even your wife."

"There is something else we have to consider," Ritter said. "CALISTO is offering intelligence that stands to thwart significant East German and Soviet defense initiatives. If the Stasi or KGB get wind of this—and if there is a leak they already have—then they are going to be working overtime to find out who CALISTO is so they can plug the leak." He stabbed the table with his index finger to make his point. "And they will not hesitate to put a bullet in the base of your skull if they believe it will help plug it."

"True," Greer said. "If you could provide us with some fresh faces for countersurveillance."

Ritter nodded to Buckley, who finally used his pen to write something down.

"I'll get a team in from Helsinki."

Moore pushed his leather chair away from the table and stood, prompting the others to do the same.

"Thank you, gentlemen," he said. "Keep me in the loop."

"I'm sending someone else as well," Greer said to Ritter.

"Fine," Buckley said. "Just have him link up with the team in Berlin."

Greer shook his head. "I'm not talking countersurveillance. This guy will be for the more hands-on matters, if it comes to that. He can be a bit of a blunt instrument . . ."

Judge Moore raised his hand to stop the discussion until he left the room, happy not to be quite that much in the loop, especially when it came to the messy stuff.

13

A female agent with frizzy auburn hair tied up into a loose bun met Murray at the base of the Learjet's boarding stairs. She introduced herself as Special Agent Betty Harris from the Washington Field Office. She held a canvas duffel in each hand and had a black ballistic nylon briefcase slung over her shoulder. Her dark blue FBI raid jacket hung open enough to reveal one of the new Smith & Wesson 459s on her hip. Ten years Murray's junior, it made sense she'd have made the switch to the Bureau's new firearm.

She looked about seventeen, with a healthy crop of freckles splashed over rosy cheeks. Murray decided she couldn't have been out of the Academy for more than five minutes.

He paused at the bottom step, eyeing the duffels.

"Dan Murray," he said. "For me?"

She nodded. "Sounds like a rural assignment. I was told to bring you a change of clothes, boots, socks, toiletries." She grimaced. "Hope boxers are okay. I figured a briefs guy would be fine with boxers, but if you happened not to like tighty whities . . ."

Murray held up an open hand. "Boxers are swell."

"Did you know they keep our sizes at the Hoover Building?"

"Yeah, for the issue stuff," Murray said, taking the bag. "Thanks for doing this." He reached for the other duffel, but she pulled it away.

"Oh, no, sir," she said. "These are for me. I'm to come with you."

Still trying to get his head wrapped around what was happening, Murray gave her a polite smile and decided not to worry about things over which he had no control. If the big brains at the J. Edgar Hoover Building wanted to send a teenager to assist him on . . . whatever this was, that was their issue.

Her baby face notwithstanding, Special Agent Harris was tall, nearly six feet, and had to stoop as much as Murray as they climbed onto the plane. Sleek and fast, the C-21 was well appointed with leather and teak, but it was not particularly roomy. Seating was configured business-jet-style, vis-à-vis, with small tables that folded up from below the windows. Murray sat with his back to the cockpit. To her credit, Harris took a forward-facing seat on the other side of the plane so they could talk but didn't have to battle for legroom.

She unzipped her briefcase and took out a leather folio

and a yellow legal pad. "I've never been on a plane that smells this good," she said. "It's like a saddle shop."

"I was going to say new car," Murray said. "You spend a lot of time in saddle shops?"

"Yes, sir," Harris said. "My family has an Arabian horse ranch in southern Utah, not too far from Mesquite, Nevada."

"Ah," Murray said. Now he understood why she was here. "You must be coming along to provide knowledge of the local terrain."

"I imagine you wanted someone older to partner on this," Harris said. "Someone with more experience."

"To tell you the truth, Harris," he said, "I'm not even sure what 'this' is. Please fill me in."

"I'm so sorry," she said. "I assumed you'd been briefed. We're looking for a fugitive."

She passed him a folded USGS topographic map that she'd stuck between the pages of her legal pad. An area below Virgin Peak was marked with a red *X*. Judging from the topo lines, it was near vertical.

"At a crash site? What'd he do, shoot down the plane?" Murray wasn't joking. CIA provided Stinger missiles to the mujahideen to use against the Russians in Afghanistan. The Bureau was on constant alert that some version of a man-portable antiaircraft device would find its way into the hands of a terrorist in the United States.

"No," Harris said. "Theft of some super-classified tech from the crash. They wouldn't tell me exactly which piece of tech. I'm assuming we'll get the rest when we get there. The special agent in charge had an Air Force four-star in his office when I came in to work out this morning. Next thing I know, I'm told to take my winter go-bag, get one for you from HQ, and then meet you here."

"We have a name for this fugitive?" Murray asked. "A description?"

Harris opened the folio to reveal the beginnings of a very sparse case file. A sheet of flimsy thermal paper bearing a black-and-white facsimile of a police sketch was on top, still curling from rolling off the fax machine.

"Not sure how much good this will do us," she said. "But it's all we have until we get there."

Judging from this specimen, fax image quality had taken a giant step backward since 1924 when a photo of Calvin Coolidge was transmitted to London via wireless radio signal. This one looked more like a Rorschach test than a drawing of anyone in particular. It depicted a male, white, Murray thought, with a wide face, a mustache, and a pageboy haircut.

"According to this, we're looking for Captain Kangaroo."

"Yeah," Harris said. "I think that's supposed to be a wool hat, not bangs. We'll need to meet with the witnesses ourselves once we get there."

Murray leaned back and closed his eyes. He folded his arms across his chest, trying hard to keep from gritting his teeth. "This isn't going to work."

"I'm no Betty Bureau Blue Suit," she assured him.

Murray's eyes flicked open, but the rest of his body stayed completely still. "I'm not talking about you."

"Maybe not," she said. "But you need to know I'll pull my weight and then some. I guarantee you'll find me a valuable asset to the team if you give me a chance."

He raised an eyebrow.

"We have a team?"

She slumped in her seat.

"So far it's just you and me."

Murray closed his eyes again.

"Do you work hard?"

"Absolutely."

"Are you smart?"

She paused.

He prodded. "Don't be modest."

"Then yes," she said. "I'm extremely curious, which, I believe, has made me smart."

"Okay, then." Murray leaned forward and rubbed his hands together, ready to roll up his sleeves and get started. "That's all I ask of anyone who works with me." He was quiet for a beat, then added, "Oh, and can you shoot?"

"What? Yes. I'm a decent shot."

"Shooting skill is far less important than brains," Murray said. "Until it's not."

An Air Force major in a green Nomex flight suit bounded up the air stairs and leaned in to the cabin. A female aviator stood behind him.

"Major Buck Smith, 458th Airlift Squadron," he said, left hand flat on his chest while he hung on to the teak bulkhead with the right. "I'm your pilot in command today, and this is Captain Donna Everette, one of the first female graduates of the United States Air Force Academy." He glanced over his shoulder at her. "Class of . . ."

"1980," she said, smiling modestly.

Special Agent Harris gave the captain a vigorous thumbs-up in solidarity—both successful women in jobs that were steeped in testosterone.

"And she's a hell of a pilot," Major Smith said.

One of the downsides of being the first female at anything was the fact that it became etched into every introduction, sometimes overshadowing more pertinent things.

Smith gave a quick preflight briefing on emergency procedures and the important things, like the location of the coffee and the whereabouts of the potty—which was hidden under one of the seats. It could be closed off if the need arose, a strong possibility on cross-country flights. Like most pilots, his voice grew especially animated when he began to describe his aircraft.

"This C-21A is a brand-new airplane, fresh off the line at Lear. We were supposed to be taking her to her new home at Scott Air Force Base with a couple three-stars when we were diverted to pick you up. Y'all must have a heck of a lot of juice to bounce not one but two lieutenant generals."

"Someone does, I guess," Harris said, looking at Murray.

"Anyway," Smith continued, "the Lear 35 shares enough in common with the Swiss P-16 ground attack fighter to be its kissing cousin—with a few extra seats. Her two Garrett turbofan engines will, excuse my French, kick us in the ass. I give you that warning because I have received word from on high that Captain Everette and I are not to spare the horses." He winked. "So buckle up. Should be a straight shot to Nellis, where another chopper will transport you from there."

Smith and Everette went forward to the cockpit, which was open to the rest of the cabin, and began their preflight procedures.

Murray leaned sideways, holding the Motorola's rubberized antenna against the plane's window to get a signal, and then punched in the phone number scrawled across the bottom of the atrocious police sketch.

"Trooper Stone," the man on the other end snapped, as if he were in the middle of something far more important than a phone call. His voice was distant, like he was at the bottom of a well.

Murray introduced himself and ran down a quick list of orders, couched as requests to make them more palatable. The FBI didn't outrank a local officer or trooper by any means, but they did have fifteen thousand agents and a shitload of resources. Someone had to be in charge, and that duty often fell to the FBI, who sometimes led by what Murray's Navy grandfather had called "right of way by tonnage."

Instead of arguing or even putting up a fight, the trooper said, "Hang on. I've got one of your guys right here."

Murray listened to a muffled game of telephone hot potato on the other end before a tentative voice came on the line.

"This is Pritchard."

The engine whine grew louder. The pilots released the brakes and the little jet shuddered, throwing Murray against his lap belt as they began to roll to the taxiway.

"Where you from, Special Agent Pritchard?"

"RA in St. George."

Murray established his bona fides with the fact that he was being sent by the director. Pritchard could call his SAC in Salt Lake if he had any questions. He wasn't one to name-drop, but in fugitive cases time was of the essence. The proverbial dragnet needed to be set up right damn now, not after Pritchard got permission or Murray arrived on scene to make his case in person. You couldn't spell *bureaucracy* without *Bureau*, and sometimes the wheels needed a little grease.

Pritchard explained that the special agent in charge of the Salt Lake field office was out with emergency gallbladder surgery.

"Right now, it's me, some locals, and a bunch of Air Force OSI agents and security forces. The military guys are keeping the locals on the perimeter before they get clearance from their brass. This whole shitshow is classified SCI code word clearance. We have roadblocks set up fifteen and thirty miles out on the main roads and Bureau of Land Management four-wheeler trails. It's about two hours until daylight. The Air Force has two helicopter gunships in the air now with FLIR capability. The OSI guys seem squared away, but I'm not sure these security forces have ever faced a homicide suspect before—"

"Hang on, now," Murray said. "What do you mean 'homicide'?"

"*Double* homicide," Pritchard said. "The pilot saw our guy push a woman into a deep crevice. It's, like, forty-something feet down and she's wedged in there pretty good. They're going to wait until it gets light to get the body."

"Double?"

"One of the UFO watchers," Pritchard said. "Looks like he may have confronted our guy when he was on his way off the mountain. Caught a knife in the chest for his trouble."

Murray ran a hand over the top of his head. "Shit. That adds a new wrinkle to things."

Harris looked up at him, interested.

"I'm sorry," Pritchard said. "I thought you were already aware."

"First I'm hearing of it," Murray said. "Sounds as though you're doing things right, though. What county is that?"

"Clark."

"Any Clark County sheriff's deputies barking about whose homicide cases these are?"

"Only that the Air Force isn't letting them near anyhow," Pritchard said. "To be honest, I don't think their bosses want the headache. It's federal land anyway, so we have no issues regarding jurisdiction."

"Sounds like you've got it handled," Murray said.

"Thank you, sir," Pritchard said. "But I'm not sure we're going to be very effective. This area is awfully porous. Lots of old mines and hidey-holes to get lost in. Even worse, you can't throw a rock in these mountains without hitting a lookie-loo or UFO hunter. Security forces are keeping them back from the actual crash site, but they're digging in around the perimeter like some kind of siege army. The SAC from Vegas should be here anytime."

"Good," Murray said. "I know Jimmy McCoy. He's a hell of a fugitive hunter. What about all the UFO watchers you mentioned?"

"I'm not sure we can just kick people off public land."

"We don't want to," Murray said. "In fact, you need to keep the witnesses on-site until we get there."

"Roger that," Pritchard said. "What's your ETA?"

Murray covered the receiver and leaned around the bulkhead to look over his shoulder and check with the pilots before relaying the information to Pritchard.

"Five hours, give or take," he said.

"What am I supposed to do if they decide to leave? I'm telling you, Murray, these people are out of their minds. They're already spinning all kinds of conspiracy stories about secret government programs—you know, cover-ups and shit like that."

"Are they wrong?"

"Well, no," Pritchard said. "But they're nuts."

"McCoy will know what to do," Murray said. "But I suggest you buy them breakfast courtesy of the FBI. Even nutjobs gotta eat." He started to end the call but glanced down at the fax in his lap. "Oh, and find me another sketch artist."

Murray pressed the button to end the call and then tapped the phone against his open hand, thinking.

The pilots began their takeoff roll, accelerating the Lear to over 140 knots in a matter of seconds. A moment later, the little plane leaped off the tarmac in a steep and rapid climb. Murray, facing aft, was shoved into his lap belt, almost hanging down above Special Agent Harris.

"Impressive," Harris said as the landing gear thumped, folding into the body of the aircraft once the pilots established a positive rate of climb. "They are definitely not sparing the horses."

Murray leaned over, handing her the Motorola. "You have room for this in your bag?"

"Sure."

"Good. You can be the bearer of the brick. I'm too much of a dinosaur."

He relayed what he'd learned about the murders, which wasn't much, except that they had happened. Then, seized with a sudden idea, he picked up the topographic map and studied the terrain surrounding the *X*, Virgin Peak. He tapped a cheap Bic pen against his teeth while he thought.

"You've spent time in these mountains?" he asked, speaking above the engine whine.

"I have," Harris said. "Been riding horses and dirt bikes all over those rocks since I was five. My family's been there for three generations."

"Okay." Murray held out the map and the pen. "I want you to take a look at this and tell me where you would go if you took something from the crash site and wanted to run with it. Then note your top three educated guesses on where someone who was unfamiliar

with the area would run. Natural flow of terrain, ob-
structions like canyons, that kind of thing."

"On it," she said.

"After that, as the local expert, I want you to make an
operational plan on how you would catch this guy if you
were in charge of the operation. Then write down the
five things you'd do immediately after we land in order
to implement your plan."

"Got it," she said. She glanced up at him, head to one
side. "What are you going to do?"

Murray reclined the soft leather seat and nestled in,
stretching out his legs in front of him.

"I am going to close my eyes for a minute and think
about how fortunate I am to have someone who knows
the area so we can capture this murdering son of a bitch."

The airplane continued to climb, banking slowly as
the pilots took it to thirty-six thousand feet. The low
winter sun fell in behind, chasing them west.

14

The shrill ring of the telephone shattered the tranquility of the warm kitchen, chilling Elke Hauptman and giving her an instant headache. Unnerved and filled with overwhelming dread, she dropped the glass she'd been washing into the sink and sliced her little finger to the bone. Blood arced across the porcelain as if sprayed from a tiny hose. Trapped between the ringing phone and the fear that her husband might notice her panic, she wrapped the throbbing pinkie in the nearest dish towel and snatched up the phone on the second ring.

"Hauptman, guten Abend." She answered politely as always, though she knew all too well who was on the other end of the line. Her husband would have become suspicious had she screamed into the phone like she wanted to. She steadied the phone against her ear, nearly retching from nerves and the odor of rosewater dish soap

on her hand. Her husband, sitting on the sofa reading a book to their six-year-old son, looked up and then returned his attention to Hansie.

Elke pushed a sandy curl out of her eyes with a forearm, doing her best not to smudge her face with the bloody towel. She still wore her makeup from a lunchtime performance. Most of her shows were in the evening, but the Imperial Club where she often sang had sponsored this one, giving her the night off with her little family.

The bastard had to pick tonight.

She nodded as she listened to the other end of the conversation.

In a way it was lucky that she had cut herself. It would explain to her husband why she'd suddenly grown so pale.

"Okay . . . Yes . . ." She glanced at the clock above the stove. It was seven-thirty. "Of course, my dear . . . I can be there in one hour . . ." She gave a smile so forced she thought her face would split. ". . . Me as well . . . I will see you soon. Ciao."

Hauptman replaced the receiver with a trembling hand, imagining the damage the sturdy Bakelite telephone could do if swung with force against a skull—

"Who was that?" her husband asked, startling her almost as much as the phone call. He didn't bother to look up from Hansie's book, but remained nonchalant. It was not uncommon for her to receive calls late into the evening. "Scheduling another show? I would like to attend."

"It was Gisselle," Elke said. Lying turned her mouth

into a desert and made her tongue click absurdly when she spoke. "I am sorry, Uwe." She pronounced his name *Ooo-vey.* As always, the lies came easier by degree with each word she spoke. "But she needs me. It sounds as though she is quite ill."

He gave a slow nod. "Sisters must look after one another."

"Yes, we must . . ." Elke got herself a glass of water from the tap and drank it down as if it were the antidote to some deadly poison. Dribbles ran down either side of her mouth and she wiped them with the back of her arm.

Hans smacked the couch cushion. "I don't want you to go!"

"Not to worry, my love." Uwe patted their son on the arm. "Go and get ready for bed. You and I will read more books until Mama returns."

Uwe joined her in the kitchen once the boy had disappeared into the bathroom, shocked to discover her wounded hand.

He helped bandage it and then clean up the broken pieces of glass. Finished with that, he kissed her lightly on the forehead.

"I think you have lost a lot of blood," he said. "Do you think it is wise to go out?"

"It was not that much," she said, then added, "I am fine. Gisselle needs me."

He took her by the hand and pulled her closer. Slippers shuffled on the kitchen tile as they began to dance.

She shuddered, a trembling bird in his arms.

Though he was a scientist now, he'd done his bit as a

soldier, and kept himself in excellent physical shape. He had a temper, too, and though he would never hurt her, his powerful hands were capable of doing great harm. She dreamed about it, even thought of telling him everything—but he would do something rash and get himself thrown in prison or worse.

"I am sorry," she whispered.

"*I* am the one who should be sorry." His lips buzzed in her ear so the microphones they both knew were there could not pick up their words. "This is my fault. It is beginning to make me crazy. Gray men outside our home at all hours. Listening devices on our telephone. I am certain most of our neighbors have been recruited to keep notes on our comings and goings. It is troublesome—"

"It is the price we pay for your work," she said. "It is important."

Dr. Uwe Hauptman was an aeronautical physicist conducting research at the prestigious Humboldt University—alma mater of the likes of Einstein, Schrödinger, and Planck. She, too, was a scientist by training, but now made a living with her voice, singing at clubs and shows, sometimes even in the West—a bright and shiny thing for the DDR to show off.

"I suppose," he whispered. "But this scrutiny is maddening. You very nearly jumped out of your skin when your sister called."

She buried her face in his chest.

"What you do is good for Germany," she said. "So it is good for us."

"Still," he said. "How am I supposed to concentrate

with Dr. Galkin watching my every move? And questioning it as well, mind you. It's impossible to keep a coherent train of thought."

Her mouth fell open. "Galkin is here?"

He nodded, craning lower to kiss her neck. "I received permission to meet with a colleague on the other side last week. They came as my minders."

Elke pulled away. "You went to the West? Why didn't you tell me?"

"I didn't want you to worry," he said. "It was just a day trip."

She knew his tells, the way one corner of his mouth twitched when he held something back—which he was doing now. She didn't press too hard. After all, the list of things she wasn't telling her husband was a long one.

He leaned closer, taking advantage of the listening devices to nibble on her ear. "Galkin's foul KGB minder, Comrade Colonel Zima, is with him."

She pulled away enough to look him in the face, then back to his ear. "KGB?" She pronounced it *kah geh beh*, breathy, quieter than a whisper.

"Science and Technology division," Uwe said. "Still, KGB is KGB. They suspect all of my ilk of being part of some Doctors' plot. Spies have never trusted scientists. We are highly dangerous because we prioritize truth over politics."

"Not all scientists," Elke said.

"Those who do not," Uwe said, perhaps a little too loudly, "are not scientists at all, but pawns of the government. I shouldn't be telling you this. Comrade Zima used our trip to the West as an opportunity to check in with his merry band of cigarette smugglers."

"That's dangerous," Elke said. "Being associated with the black market."

"I did not mind," Uwe said. "His business gave me a precious few minutes in the West without him and Galkin breathing down my neck."

"You should have stayed," Elke whispered.

Uwe scoffed. "You never stay!" He lowered his voice again. "That is precisely why they do not let us travel together. I would rather die than leave you and Hansie."

His fingers traveled slowly down her back past the knot of her apron, burrowing skillfully beneath the waistband of her skirt. He had a moment of fluster getting past the elastic rampart of her tights, but found his way under to caress the hollow at the base of her spine.

She shuddered again.

The water was still running in the bathroom, so they were momentarily safe from Hansie's inquisitive gaze.

Uwe pulled her closer, tracing a soft circle on her tailbone with the tip of his finger.

"Gisselle needs your help. I know this." He groaned. "But perhaps we might dance a little more when you return."

Her breath quickened. "Yes," she said, her mouth now even more parched than before. "Yes. That is a good idea."

"Hurry home, my sweet." His breath fluttered moist and warm against her throat. "You are the only one in the world I can trust."

———

The maples along Auguststrasse had lost their leaves by late October, turning them stark and skeletal in the November darkness. A bitter wind made the concrete prefab apartments known as *Plattenbauten* even grayer and more oppressive than they already felt.

Elke Hauptman snugged a woolen scarf up over her ears and stretched on a pair of hand-knit mittens, taking care not to bump her injured finger. An obedient East German, she pretended not to notice the man in the heavy coat across the street and halfway up the block, ignoring the glow of his cigarette in the shadows beyond the feeble streetlamp. Others described her as having the voice of a nightingale, but she was a scientist by training and personality, habitually analyzing paradoxes and trends. Spies always seemed to smoke, an odd habit, since they did not want to be noticed, but completely under-standable considering the soul-crushing weight of their actions.

Elke understood this all too well. She lit a cigarette of her own and took a deep drag in solidarity with the ass-hole lurking up the street. Smoke blossomed around her face in the cold as she fumbled with the chain on her scooter, a ten-year-old Simson Schwalbe KR 51/2, or Swallow, that was locked to a metal rack in front of the apartment building. It was similar to a Vespa—if a Vespa had a homely baby with a Honda Super Cub and that baby tumbled down a hill and was then pounded back into serviceable condition with a hammer. Uwe described the Schwalbe's color as baby-shit yellow, and he was not wrong.

Stowing the chain under her seat, Elke hitched up her heavy wool skirt high enough to kick-start the little motor, and then, happy to be wearing the thick tights, swung a leg over the chilly faux-leather seat. The coal at the end of the cigarette between her lips glowed like a forge. Dead maple leaves fluttered in her wake as the little Schwalbe buzzed southeast down the grimy brick streets toward the café near Alexanderplatz—nowhere near her sister's house.

D r. Uwe Hauptman leaned against the kitchen counter, staring at the telephone, breathing hard through his nose. Little Hans sat on the sofa singing along to good-night songs with Our Sandman, a bearded puppet on the television. Gritting his teeth, Hauptman snatched up the receiver and dialed his sister-in-law.

"*Hallo?*" a tentative voice said on the other end of the line.

"*Hallo*, Gisselle?"

"Yes," she said, recognizing the voice. "*Hallo*, Uwe. How are you?"

"I need to speak with Elke when she arrives," Uwe said.

"Okay . . ." Gisselle said.

Uwe paused for a beat, then said, "I . . . I hope you feel better soon."

"Thank you," she said. "I will tell Elke to ring you back."

He stared at the phone. Any number of questions would tell him more, test Gisselle to see if she was truly ill, if Elke was indeed on her way over, or if this was something else entirely.

"Uwe?" Gisselle said. "Are you still—"

"Good," he said. "Thank you, my dear."

He cradled the phone and buried his face in his hands. Some things were better left unknown.

15

Elke Hauptman saw the man through the café window when she rode up, the top of his balding head anyway, and the gray fedora hanging on the end of the booth.

She planted her feet firmly on the pavement and killed the Schwalbe's engine, taking a moment to steel herself before going inside.

Major Kurt Pfeiffer of the MfS—Ministerium für Staatssicherheit—more commonly known as the Stasi, was a piece of dogshit, but he was a smart piece of dogshit. Worse, he had near total power over Elke Hauptman's life. Elke locked the scooter to a post and tucked the key into her coat pocket. Her hair was a tangled nest of straw curls from the ride. The wind chapped her cheeks and made her nose run, but she didn't bother to primp before going in. Pfeiffer didn't care about things like that. Her fear was what aroused him—that and the information in her pocket.

Elke felt certain everyone in the café was Stasi. It was a small place with six booths running along the wall and as many tables that seemed strategically placed to force her to zigzag to get to the back, where Pfeiffer waited. The food smelled delicious. It could have been cozy, but the lighting was dull and decorations cold, giving it all the intimacy of a linen closet. Worse, it was stiflingly hot. The same half-dozen people were present on each of her visits, as if actors hired to play the role of café patrons—or, Elke thought, perhaps everyone who came here was just so incredibly dull they all looked alike.

Elke caught two new faces as she walked past the line of booths, a young couple, seated across from each other, leaning across their booth, speaking in hushed whispers. Like Elke, both wore heavy woolen coats.

Major Pfeiffer leaned out of the rearmost booth when he heard the door chime.

A round woman wiping down one of the tables leaned on her rag and gave Elke a hard stare. "I have heard you sing before," the woman said. It sounded more like a threat than a compliment. Two men in wrinkled suits sat at a table some ten feet away from the young couple. Both looked up momentarily from their beers, as if to see what insect had flown into the web, before returning to their conversation.

Pfeiffer stood as Elke approached, not because he was chivalrous or even moderately polite. At six feet three he was taller than Elke Hauptman by almost a foot and he enjoyed demonstrating this fact to her. He stepped out of the booth and waved her inside. It was always this way. He liked to have her trapped against the wall.

He was about her age, forty-three, maybe even a year or two younger. She suspected he'd started to lose his hair when he was young—or at least long enough ago that it didn't bother him now unless she called attention to it. He was athletic, and if he could be believed, an expert rifleman who spent a good deal of each week at his gun club. He carried a pistol under the tail of his coat or tucked into the nightstand beside the bed. She'd never gotten a close look at the thing, nor did she want to.

A blood-red pack of Roth-Händle cigarettes lay on the table in front of him. A fresh one hung lit from his bottom-feeder lips. He held it out to her. From the West, it was much stronger than her brand. She took it, grateful for the extra nicotine bump to make it through what she knew lay ahead.

It was late, but Pfeiffer's tie was still pulled tight to the collar button of his immaculate white shirt. Elke suspected he made a complete change of wardrobe at least once a day, more than that if he had to break a sweat. A Burberry overcoat that surely cost more than she made in three months hung on a peg beneath the fedora at the end of the booth.

He studied the bandage on her finger, just beginning to tinge with red, but said nothing about it. Instead, he waved a hand over the table and then picked a bit of tobacco off his lip.

"I ordered for us."

She slid into the booth, answering automatically. "Thank you, but I have eaten."

"Well, you have not eaten enough." Pfeiffer wagged his head, brimming with the usual gusto. "Just look at you, my dear." Brow raised, he turned sideways to leer, eyes crawling up and down her body. "Don't they feed you at those shows you do? Besides, they have actual Wiener schnitzel here, not the breadcrumbs and pig ass-holes that they serve down the street."

He eyed her for a reaction to his little talk of treason. Surely it was a crime against the state to call East German food anything other than delicious.

"Did you bring it?"

Elke closed her eyes, thinking briefly of climbing over the table and fleeing out the way she'd come in. The fat woman would probably shoot her in the back of the head.

She'd sat down without removing her coat and had to lean sideways, pressing against his body, in order to fish a plain brown envelope from her inside pocket. She pushed it to him like it was on fire.

The food came a moment later, two plates of schnitzel and two beers. As promised, breaded cutlets of actual fried veal, served with a slice of real lemon on top.

"I know this is difficult." Pfeiffer slid the envelope to the side of the table and tucked into his schnitzel with a knife and fork.

"You have no idea," she said, catching a sob before it left her throat. She didn't want to give him the satisfaction.

He gestured to her plate with the piece of cutlet impaled on the tines of his fork. "Eat up. I insist."

She ate, choking down every morsel.

"You provide a great service." Pfeiffer took a long drink of beer and then held the stein aloft. "Did you know this is the same stuff they serve to Honecker?" He leaned forward, lowering his voice to a conspiratorial whisper. "If we gave him the swill most comrades have to drink, perhaps he would be more aware of reality of life in the DDR."

This talk was surely a trap. In the Deutsche Demokratische Republik—the DDR—one could end up in prison for writing a poem decrying the growing number of concrete apartment buildings. If a few lines of poetry were "public vilification of an organ of state" worthy of two years behind bars, then speaking of Erich Honecker's beer must surely be a capital offense.

Pfeiffer did not seem to care. He took another drink. "Very patriotic of you to help, considering the circumstances."

"You make it sound as if I have a choice," Elke hissed. "Is that not the motto of State Security—'Come to us or we will come to you.'"

The major gave a little shrug but didn't deny it. If anything, he always appeared to be amused when she got her back up.

He dabbed at his mouth with a napkin. "You and your husband have a charmed life," he said. "But do not begin to think such niceties are without cost."

He gave a curt nod to the woman who'd brought the

beers, then leaned sideways and whispered to Elke, "There is something I want you to watch."

At his signal, the woman made her way to the young couple, looking furtively over her shoulder as she whispered something to the young man. Elke could only see the back of his head, but he sat up straighter in the booth. The young woman across the table flushed red over whatever the heavy woman told them, and then she, too, stiffened.

Major Pfeiffer gave a quiet play-by-play.

"These two traitors have no idea where they are."

"Traitors?" Elke said, loud enough to earn a stern elbow from Pfeiffer.

"See for yourself, my dear." Pfeiffer took a small earpiece from his pocket and handed it to Elke. "Listen," he said. "I insist."

The small rubber nipple barely fit inside her ear, but she wedged it in anyway. It was connected to a wire that disappeared inside Pfeiffer's suit coat. He slipped in an adjoining earpiece, both of which were connected to the receiver for a listening device somewhere near the young couple.

". . . *how dangerous it is?*" The girl was tremulous, verging on panic.

"*Nothing is foolproof,*" a wheezing voice said—the heavy woman. "*There are always risks. You can still turn back now if you want to.*"

"*No!*" the boy said, audible without the earpiece. Then, more quietly, "*We cannot stay in this place any longer.*"

Elke estimated he wasn't much over twenty. The girl probably still in her teens.

"Did you hear that?" Pfeiffer asked. "Even now, after all his treason, she gave him another opportunity to change his mind." Pfeiffer shook his head. "And people accuse us of being heartless . . ."

"Border guards are everywhere," the heavy woman said. *"Are you prepared to deal with it if we encounter one?"*

The girl stammered. *"You . . . mean . . . ?"*

"Yes," the boy said. *"I will do whatever I need to."*

"Even kill?" the woman asked.

"Whatever it takes," the boy said. *"They are pigs!"*

Pfeiffer leaned sideways, confiding in Elke. "That will make his trial easy."

"Very well," the heavy woman said. *"You leave to-night."*

"Wait!" The girl said, stunned. *"Tonight?"*

"A tunnel?" the boy asked.

"Of a sort," the heavy woman said. She stepped away from the table. *"We should leave this place the back way."*

The boy scooted out of the booth and stood, but the girl stayed put, looking wistfully toward the front door. Had she smelled a trap? Or was she part of this? In the DDR, it was impossible to know.

Elke wanted to scream.

Pfeiffer felt the shift in her posture and grabbed her leg, squeezing hard. A warning. He nodded to the men in wrinkled suits who sat at a nearby table.

Elke shuddered as they moved in quickly behind the startled young man and gave him the tap on the shoulder, barking the terse words that were the stuff of East German nightmares:

Staatssicherheit. Komm mit uns!

"State Security. Come with us!"

The girl collapsed against the table, racked with sobs. One of the men grabbed her by the arm to haul her out of the booth. Infuriated, her boyfriend took a swing, landing a lucky elbow on one of the Stasi men's nose. The injured man roared and slammed a black leather slapjack hard against the boy's ear. The sound of the impact caused Elke to gag—not merely a crack of lead-filled leather sap impacting human skin but of bursting flesh and shattering bone. The Stasi man struck again and again, blinded by rage, pulverizing the unconscious boy's face and nearly ripping off his ear. Pfeiffer had surely choreographed the arrest to keep Elke in line . . . and for his own amusement.

The heavy woman grabbed the girl from the booth while the two men dragged the boy out the back by his feet, mopping the tiled floor with a bloody smear.

Elke pounded the table with both fists, sending waves of pain through her injured finger.

"That was . . ." She wanted to scream. "You did not have to . . . Why would you . . ."

Pfeiffer shrugged, maddeningly calm. "I protect the socialist state from those who would betray us. Of course, I hate that we had to resort to physical violence. We prefer—"

"I know what you prefer!" She cut him off. "You prefer what you are doing to me! Decomposition!"

Zersetzung was indeed the Ministry for State Security's prime method of political repression. Literally to decompose or disrupt, Stasi officers used all sorts of methods to isolate anyone they believed was subversive and make them believe they were going insane—resetting clocks, spreading rumors, sending letters from fictional illegitimate children.

Pfeiffer shrugged. "That is absurd, my dear," he said. "You help me in this great work of your own free will. Any anomalies you may think you notice are nothing but your overactive imagination. I assure you."

Elke leaned forward, twisting at her forelock as she was prone to do when unnerved. "I don't understand why you need me. You already watch us at every turn. Steaming open our mail—"

The major gave a dry chuckle. "Do not count the Hauptman family as anything special in that regard, my dear," he said. "We steam open everyone's mail—all to benefit the state."

"Uwe does important work for the benefit of the DDR, and still, you place microphones in our house."

Pfeiffer shot a glance at the other diners, who'd continued with their meals through the horrific arrest, and then back to Elke. "Lower your voice, my dear," he said. "It would serve you well to remember that for all practical purposes you are speaking of *my* house. I allow your little family to live there so long as you continue to do your part and keep your husband productive at his work."

She imagined stabbing him in the eye with her fork, but pushed the thought out of her mind. For now.

"Anyway," Pfeiffer said, eating again. "You and your husband bear increased scrutiny. You both make periodic trips to the West."

"As do you," Elke snapped, sounding more defensive than challenging. She groaned. "What more could you possibly want? Dr. Galkin and his KGB minder dog him constantly. They w—"

"KGB?" Pfeiffer mused.

"You did not know?" She smiled inside, but did not show it. Gloating to a Stasi officer was a good way to end up underneath the prison.

"KGB," the major said again, nodding, as if deciding what to say next. He sighed. "The Soviets are growing tired, I think. Every day I read this report or that about their new glasnost and perestroika. Soon we in the DDR may have to manage on our own. I will tell you that much."

"I wish they would let my husband manage on his own," Elke said. "You all must see he is working for the good of the state, and still you—"

"Evgeni Zima," Pfeiffer muttered, as if he'd not listened to anything else she'd just said. He turned his nose as if the words tasted bitter. "You think I am cruel . . . That KGB asshole is an enemy of the people. A criminal who makes his fortune on the black market."

The major sounded more jealous than indignant.

She almost mentioned the Russian's trip to the West but sensed the danger of entanglement if caught between two powerful men. It turned out not to matter. Pfeiffer seemed to know already, making her wonder just how many people had been following her husband on his most recent trip outside the DDR.

Unable to contain herself, she prodded the bear. "I find it strange that Comrade Zima has open access to my husband's notes and yet he has not shared them with you."

"You are correct," Pfeiffer said, turning inward, mulling deeply over the issue. "You should be careful of that man. He is a criminal."

Her envelope delivered, Elke nodded to the door. "I should not be hearing this. May I please go? I'd like to return to my husband."

Beneath the table, Pfeiffer's hand traveled to the inside of her knee. It happened at least every other meeting. Places with adjoining Stasi apartments were especially problematic—safe houses that were anything but safe.

The proprietor of this restaurant was designated an IMK—Inoffizieller Mitarbeiter, or unofficial collaborator. The *K* meant they assisted with logistical matters like safe houses—and apartments where state operatives had liaisons with those under their thumb.

It took all Elke's will to keep from vomiting on the table. Her family's apartment, her position at the university, Hansie's schools, his affiliation with the best sports teams, clubs, even the spot where she chained her scooter in front of the apartment—all these things were controlled by this man. And now he wanted this.

She was not only Kurt Pfeiffer's spy, but his whore.

He lit another cigarette and stuffed the lighter into his

pocket, standing to let her out of the booth. He seemed somewhere else in thought, and for a fleeting moment, she thought he was letting her go. No such luck.

"I am going to finish my meal," he said, his voice heavy with anticipation, his breath vile enough to curdle milk. "Go upstairs and have a hot bath. And put a new bandage on that horrible finger wound of yours. I left you a gift on the bed. A small token for your work. Perhaps you will like it enough to sing me a song later . . ."

She gave an exhausted nod that he surely took for a smile.

"Oh," he said, sitting down in the booth again and picking up his fork. "I almost forgot. Your husband made a telephone call to your sister shortly after you left your apartment."

Elke grabbed the edge of the table to keep from falling.

"What?"

"He would like you to ring him back." Pfeiffer took a bite of schnitzel and spoke while he chewed. "She covered nicely for you, by the way, your sister."

"You should have told—"

Pfeiffer shrugged. "I am telling you now. Use the phone upstairs."

"What if he suspects?"

He leaned sideways, exposing his neck. Elke clenched her fists, ignoring the pain in her injured finger. If she were only stronger . . .

"Let me tell you a secret, my dear," he said. "I have listened to thousands of husbands, and they *all* suspect.

Every. Last. One." He took another bite of veal, scraping it off the fork with his teeth. "But suspecting and knowing are two vastly different animals."

Deaf and numb, hardly able to breathe, Elke started for the door that led to the back staircase.

The kernel of an idea had taken root in her mind at their meeting the month before. He'd climbed on top of her then, too. Her plans were already in play, but Pfeiffer's cruel little farce of the evening only steeled her resolve. It would be dangerous, but at least she would be done with all this.

It would either save her family or earn her a Stasi bullet.

16

During her more philosophical moments, especially in the wee hours of the morning, CIA Berlin Base cypher clerk Carol Morandini imagined that incoming cable traffic was like a wrapped Christmas present. It could be something bitchin', like keys to a new car or the latest George Strait album.

Today, it was just boring socks and underwear.

Visitors.

Rarely a week went by that some politician or staffer wasn't boots on the ground in Berlin so they'd be able to tell their grandkids they were in the trenches during the Cold War.

The dot matrix printer on the counter in front of Morandini buzzed back and forth, spitting out coded traffic from Langley, giving times and dates for the imminent arrival of two guests the following day.

CIA bases were subordinate to stations, meaning Skip

Hulse, chief of base West Berlin, reported to the chief of station in Bonn, West Germany. The cable was addressed to the chief of station, Bonn and chief of base, W. Berlin/ Eyes Only. No one liked to admit it out loud, but "Eyes Only" also included the lowly communicator. Someone had to tear the cables off the machine, determine who they were for, stick them in an envelope, and deliver them to the "only" eyes that were supposed to see them.

It was an ironic truth that the person in any CIA station or base with access to virtually every jot and tittle of sensitive information that came or went over the cable was also the most poorly paid and underappreciated. The communicator, often called the comms or cypher clerk, made about sixteen thousand a year, well below any case officer or most other administrative personnel. The depth and breadth of their knowledge was so great that they were not allowed to travel outside the embassy without an escort, being too ripe for recruitment by the other side.

Morandini used a straightedge to tear the message into a manageable piece of paper and stuffed it in an envelope for the boss.

> **EYES ONLY COS BONN/COB USBER**
> **IDEN CABLE**
> **1: PETER CRANE (P) . . . IDEN**
> **2: GWENDOLYNE WRIGHT (P) . . . IDEN**

For travel purposes, CIA officers' and analysts' arrival plans were often announced to the chief of receiving stations and bases using a pseudonym (P) so as to keep their true name and travel alias out of cable traffic. Care was taken to search the Agency phone book so the true names of actual personnel were not used.

To ensure operational security, the pseudonyms were used with travel times and details. A second cable would follow, hours later. Again, it would be read and delivered by a cypher clerk.

EYES ONLY—COS BONN, COB USBER
IDEN CABLE 2
1: IDEN IS—JOHN PATRICK RYAN
2: IDEN IS—MARY PAT FOLEY

17

ary Pat . . ." Ryan read the name on the iden
cable later, once they were in Greer's office.
He'd had a chance to get a bowl of soup from
the CIA cafeteria and grab a quick shave, which helped
to clear his head after the long flight. "We've crossed
paths a couple times here at Langley. She any relation to
Ed Foley, the chief of station in Moscow?"

"His wife," Greer said. "Ed's the best. I'd ask for both
of them if I could. But he's got his hands full in Moscow."

"Mary Pat," Ryan said again. "Good Irish name."

"Née Kaminsky." Greer leaned back in his chair. He
obviously didn't need the briefing paper to talk about
Mary Pat Foley. "She grew up speaking Russian and can
easily pass for a native. Hell, as I understand it, her
grandfather taught riding lessons to Tsar Nicholas II's
son. She's done tremendous work for the agency." Greer

peered over the top of his glasses. "I can see her going places, Jack. Like you."

"Ritter seems convinced you're sending some kind of cowboy."

"Bob Ritter is a narrow thinker," Greer said. "There are times, my boy, as you will come to learn, that a cowboy is exactly what we need in this war. Remember what Lincoln said about General Grant."

"He fights."

"Precisely," Greer said. "Fortunately, Mary Pat Foley isn't a hard drinker perpetually surrounded by cigar smoke. Yes, she can be a little unorthodox in her methods, some might say aggressive, but I've not known her to be cavalier about anything in this business. In my experience, anytime she resorts to . . . creative methods, she's already ruled out a half-dozen other scenarios. I trust her and you should, too. She'll provide you with the operational guidance you need and then some. The two of you think the same way—which is good, considering I'm about to drop you in the grease, so to speak."

"We'll be fine," Ryan said with the certitude of a thirty-four-year-old who'd seen bad things and made it out the other side. Not quite invincible, but nearly so.

"Of course you will."

Greer's phone intercom buzzed, and his secretary announced the arrival of Lane Buckley. The ADDO opened the door and poked his head in a half-second later.

"Admiral," he acknowledged Greer and ignored Ryan.

Greer gave him a nod. "What can we do for you, Lane?"

"Helsinki team is getting set up as we speak. They should arrive in Berlin well ahead of Riley."

"Ryan," Greer said.

"Right. Sorry about that." Buckley looked at Ryan, not sorry at all, but genuinely mistaken. Ryan pictured him as an elementary school bully tripping the new kid in the lunch line. Buckley changed gears and smirked at Ryan now. "You're going to get a kick out of Mary Pat. She's a real piece of work, if you know what I mean . . ."

"No idea," Ryan said, deadpan.

"She's got the assets." He raised his eyebrows up and down, Groucho Marx style. "She can shake a tail by shaking her tail. Comes in handy on a surveillance-detection run. The guys and I called her the Purple Peril," he said. "You know, like the fishing fly."

Ryan raised an eyebrow. "Okay . . ."

"No shit, one time she wore this lavender skirt on an op in Warsaw . . . That thing was something of beauty, let me tell you. So tight you could have bounced a quarter off that girl's ass. Turned the KGB hit team into a bunch of hardened killers, if you know what I—"

Greer let his chair rock forward, both hands flat on his desk. "Anything else, Lane?"

"No," Buckley said, failing to register the dyspeptic look on the admiral's face. "Just letting you know our boy's Helsinki team is good to go and en route."

He gave Ryan a mischievous wink as he pulled the door closed behind him.

Greer leaned back with a low groan and rested his

hands on his chest, interlacing his fingers. Ryan's father had done that when he was about to impart some tidbit of wisdom.

"Listen here, Jack, I want you to be wary of that shit-head."

"I gathered that."

Ryan almost chuckled. James Greer was normally an icon of civility, and Ryan found it refreshing to hear the man speak his mind.

"Not because he's a skirt-chaser. Foley would turn him into a eunuch if he ever crossed the line with her. I'm talking about operationally. Bonn is a super-station, a springboard in the Agency career path, and that asshole leveraged the hell out of it. I'm certain he stepped none-too-gently on the heads and shoulders of many a subordinate to get here."

Ryan gave an understanding nod. Government service was a noble endeavor, but unfortunately there were far too many ruthless self-promoters who clawed their way up through the ranks. "Assistant deputy director operations is a hell of a step."

Greer sighed. "To hear him tell it, he single-handedly recruited an asset named Chernenko from KGB PR Line. The guy came over with a trove of information on strategy and active measures."

"Single-handed, eh?"

"Hmmmf," Greer scoffed. "RUMINT says one of Buckley's case officers did the lion's share of the development and recruiting."

There was HUMINT (human-sourced intelligence),

SIGINT (signals-sourced intelligence), etc. RUMINT
was rumor intel—gossip—a mainstay of any organiza-
tion.

"I'll bet he's pissed."

"She," Greer said. "Jennifer North, a unilateral stationed at West Berlin Base."

A unilateral was a CIA officer under official cover, not
declared to the host nation.

"They let her stay in Germany and go to Berlin after
Bonn?" Ryan asked. "That's rare."

"Recompense for having to work with Lane Buckley,"
Greer said. "And reward for developing Chernenko. She
ran him in place as a volunteer for the better part of
eighteen months. Buckley showed up at just enough
meetings to ingratiate himself and make it look as though
he was doing the big favor when they finally pulled
Chernenko out."

"I can see where she might be upset at the guy," Ryan
said. "But you're the one running me. Buckley's only
setting up the Helsinki team and giving me the prelim-
inary briefings."

"There's the rub," Greer said. "The shadow of a mole
hunt has fallen over USBER Base and East Berlin Station. Odds are every last one of our people over there are
salt-of-the-earth patriots keeping heads down and doing
their jobs, often at great personal sacrifice to them and
their families. Now some faceless defector has made it
loud and clear that he does not trust a single one of
them. I'd imagine that's a hell of a gut punch. In the
midst of all this, the seventh floor is shoving you, an

analyst, down their throats to do a job that would normally be handled up the ops side of the house. Lane Buckley works on the seventh floor, down the hall from your office."

"Wait," Ryan said. "My what?"

"We'll talk about that after this is over. In the meantime, just remember, you'll be tarnished by association before you even set foot in Berlin."

"I'll keep that in mind," Ryan said. He yawned, apologized, then moved on. "You have a *deckname* assigned for me, sir?"

He pronounced it *deck-nama*.

"A what?"

Ryan gave an exhausted chuckle. "Sorry, sir, I'm a bit loopy. It's German for *pseudonym*. It sounds like THE BAT is taken, damn it."

"You are an interesting soul, Jack Ryan," Greer said. "Most people speak fewer languages when they're loopy . . . As you can see, for iden purposes, you are Peter Crane." He slid a folder across his desk.

Ryan opened it to find an alias packet. While the pseudonym was only to announce his intention to visit, an alias was the name he would use on the street. His "legend." A black diplomatic passport, Virginia driver's license, and a Visa credit card (with a fourteen-hundred-dollar balance on the five-thousand-dollar limit) all under the name of Jack Avery. Hard experience had taught that, with aliases, it was preferable for operatives to use their actual given name if possible. It could save the mission in the event you bumped into someone you knew and they shouted your name from across the mall or parking lot.

A paperclip in the corner of the folder held a library card, a dry-cleaning ticket, and a well-worn receipt from a mechanic shop for a new transmission on a 1981 Plymouth Reliant. The dry-cleaning ticket had only a number, no name. The garage receipt was torn in half, bearing only the first few letters of the last name. When establishing a legend, trying too hard with pocket litter could be as bad as not trying at all.

"Seriously?" Ryan held up the garage receipt. "A Plymouth K car? Are you trying to make me the most boring man in the world?"

Greer ignored the jibe. "I'll make the call to Andrews. They'll be waiting for you."

"So, not commercial travel?"

"No," Greer said. "We need you across the pond sooner rather than later."

"And this person you're sending over to watch our backs?"

"You'll never even know he's there," Greer said. "With any luck, neither will the Stasi."

"And absent luck?"

"Let's just say it would be better for the Stasi if he never has to introduce himself. The fact is, you'll probably never get to meet or get to know him. He's not really the 'getting to know people' kind of guy."

18

The fish ran, stripping a hundred feet of line in an instant. Gears screamed. A stolid grunt came from the man in the fighting chair as he snapped himself in for battle. Strong arms, heavily tattooed with carp and long-nosed demons and cherry blossoms, kept the thick graphite rod bowed. The size of a large grapefruit, the beefy PENN Senator 118 reel held one thousand yards of 130-pound test—and it was fast running out.

John Clark stood behind him, arms loose, watching, calculating.

The throb of the thirty-one-foot Innovator's twin Cummins diesels dropped in pitch. Cursed orders from above on the flying bridge and the two deckhands reeled furiously to clear those lines from the spread.

A tall Asian woman poked her head out of the cabin, sleepily asking what all the fuss was about and earning a guttural rebuke in Japanese from the man in the chair.

Fish on!

At the other end of the Dacron line, a magnificent Pacific blue marlin shot from the indigo water like a sub-launched missile, dancing on the surface, thrashing, shaking her powerful head. The big ones—this one likely topped eight hundred pounds—were always female. They cruised the deep waters off the western shores of the Big Island to drop their enormous skein of eggs. But that didn't happen until spring. Now, in November, the big fish was chasing mahi-mahi and yellowfin. Some of the tuna topped a hundred pounds, but in the fish hierarchy off the Kona coast there were only two types of fish—Pacific blue marlin . . . and bait.

Playing the part of deckhand for the moment, Clark encouraged the man to reel.

When it came to getting cooperation, the Agency preferred to play nice if at all possible. This trip to Hawaii, a cushy room at Mauna Kea Resort, the boat, the fishing charter, had all been meant as a carrot to entice Sato Ichiro into cooperating. The Yakuza underboss and sometimes spy was known to chop up his competitors and feed them to the fishes in Tokyo Bay. Tokyo Metropolitan Police had him on tape bragging about doing the same to his two previous wives, but so far they hadn't been able to make a case their prosecutors would accept. They were the same the world over, Clark thought.

Here was a man who would probably respond more readily to a stick.

To that end, the powers that be decided to send John Clark.

By law, Agency personnel were not supposed to engage in operations within the United States. The FBI took the lead on American soil. But this event was more of a debriefing, a friendly chat so long as Sato kept up his end of the deal. And if he did not, well, the nearest FBI guy was on Oahu. It would take him a while to get here.

Sato had known from the outset he would be meeting with Agency folks at some point during this trip. He just hadn't been aware it was today, now, on the boat, in more than three hundred fathoms of water and three miles offshore. Now that he understood, he continued to stall, explaining in great detail all the reasons he might lose his head, or worse, his reputation, when he gave them what they wanted to know. Oh, he would, he promised. He just needed to make a few adjustments to their agreement. Certain conditions he'd only recently considered needed to be met first. Then, in time, he could give them the information.

Clark had other plans for how this was going to play out. One way or another, Sato was spilling what he knew before he got off the boat. Whatever else he spilled depended on his attitude.

Like many of his former teammates with the Navy SEALs, John Clark had gone the commercial diver route after he separated from the service. That had been a lifetime ago, when he was something else . . . someone else. He was almost forty, the time Duffy Hugo called "the old age of youth." He intended to meet it head-on. The year before he'd done the 1984 Ironman, finishing the 2.4-mile swim, 112-mile bike ride, and subsequent marathon in just under twelve hours. For someone over six foot with a fighting weight of 220, it was a hell of an accomplishment. It had impressed Sandy, which, in the end, was all that really mattered to Clark. His daughters remained unimpressed about pretty much everything.

The sea was in Clark's blood, and he still enjoyed all things in and on the water. When he wasn't working, he had one rule: Life was too short to get in a boat with an idiot. Today was a workday.

Sato had brought his mistress along—not uncommon for fishing charters on this leeward side of the island where the shadow of the Mauna Kea volcano blocked the lion's share of storms, providing consistent sunny days and smooth seas. *Hula Girl* boasted a comfortable cabin, where Sato's friend, Takako, a girl of nineteen, was able to stretch out and rest while the men fished and talked shop. In this case, that meant information on a Soviet electronics company stealing sensitive computer technology from a Japanese firm, which it had stolen from a defense contractor in Texas. In their infinite wisdom some political wizard in Washington had decided the names and methods the organized crime boss had in his head were worth a new life and identity in the United States.

There were two other men on Clark's team.

The *Hula Girl*'s skipper for the day was a man named Greg Armstrong. Captain Greg was tall and lean, with shaggy blond hair and a silver goatee that contrasted with a deep mahogany tan. Like Clark, he wore a ball cap, board shorts, and a long-sleeve T-shirt for protection against the sun. A tattoo of a leaping blue marlin graced his left calf. It was as if central casting had found him for the part of marlin boat skipper.

In a way, that was exactly what had happened. Not an actual CIA operations officer, Captain Greg was an "agent," a contractor chosen for his particular set of skills. In this case, that meant his exemplary time with Golf Company 2nd Battalion, 5th Marines, during the Battle of Hue City in Vietnam—and, of course, his ability to skipper a gamefish boat. He and Clark understood each other, and apart from the usual good-natured jibes between Navy man and Marine, they got along well.

Dave, the muscular twentysomething deckhand, was from Alabama. He was new to the Agency, with no field experience beyond the halls and cubicles of Langley. He'd been chosen for his offshore fishing experience. Young enough to be unconcerned by the idea of his own mortality, he wore no shirt, daring the sun to burn him.

"Reel! Reel! Reel!" he yelled.

They all wanted to make Sato comfortable, and though none of them were really there to catch fish, it was impossible not to get caught up in the moment. It went against Clark's grain, but he had to admit, landing a big marlin might cajole the gangster into spilling more than he would with more aggressive methods.

And then Takako stepped up to get a better look at the dancing fish. Annoyed that she was crowding him when he'd ordered her to stay out of his way, Sato let go of the rod with his right hand and punched her square in the face.

Stunned, she swayed on deck for a moment, before a swell sent her staggering forward into a second wicked punch.

Dave shot a knowing look at Clark and forgot about the marlin, helping the bleeding woman to her feet.

Calmly, as if he were buttoning a shirt, Clark stepped in close to the fighting chair and deftly pierced the web of Sato Ichiro's hand with a heavy-gauge stainless-steel hook attached to an eight-inch marlin lure—about the size of a can of frozen orange juice. The hook was almost as large as the palm of the man's hand, nearly as thick as a number-two pencil. Clark moved quickly but took care to thread the barb between the bones of the thumb and the forefinger so it grabbed plenty of meat. Once in, it wasn't going anywhere. A second hook, also attached to the molded resin lure, Clark fed through the bones of the startled man's wrist. Five feet of heavy leader ran from the bug-eyed bullet lure, ending in a snap swivel. This Clark hooked to an eye on the heavy-duty PENN reel, effectively attaching the man to eight hundred pounds of blue marlin via the hooks through his flesh.

Sato let go of the rod, then grabbed it again, realizing almost too late that if the marlin took it, he was not far behind. He growled at Clark, cursing vehemently, but the growl soon faded to a shuddering whimper.

Clark stood by with his head canted to one side, not saying a word.

"Help me!" Sato yowled.

"*Help* me help you," Clark said, calm, almost whispering.

"I will . . . I cannot give you what you want . . . if . . ."

Captain Greg kept *Hula Girl*'s speed slow but steady forward, helping the fish peel line. The drag whirred like an electric motor, ticking off the seconds Sato had before he was jerked over the side with the rig.

Clark thought of reminding him of the fifteen-foot tiger shark they'd seen departing the harbor, but saw in the man's eyes that there was no need.

Deckhand Dave comforted a battered and bleeding Takako.

Clark pulled a black knife from his pocket and flicked it open with the push of a button.

"Please!" Sato said. "I will tell you what you want."

"I know," Clark said, and cut the leader near where it connected to the reel, leaving the hooks in, threaded between Sato San's bones.

Dave gave the girl's shoulder a comforting pat and sprang to grab the rod as a terrified Sato struggled to detach himself from it with his good hand.

"This goes against my grain," the deckhand muttered as he gave the marlin slack and flicked the rod a few times, dislodging the lure. He shook his head sadly as he spun the crank, reeling in the excess line.

Sato held his mangled hand aloft. "What about this?" he screamed, spit flying from his lips, anger overtaking fear now that he wasn't connected to the fleeing fish. He dabbed gingerly at the hooks with his free hand. Blood dripped from his elbow, spattering the deck. He threw back his head and bellowed.

"Get these things out of me!"

"In time," Clark said. "After we've had our talk."

Sato grimaced in disbelief. "All of this," he stammered, his voice cracking with emotion. "Because I hit my own bitch?"

Clark gave a wry shake of his head and then sent a lightning-fast right crashing into the man's jaw.

"No," he said. "*This* was for hitting her. The hooks are for wasting my time . . ."

I didn't want to bug you in the heat of the moment," Greg Armstrong said when they were all inside the air-conditioned cabin and Sato was writing up his statement and nursing a tall tumbler of whiskey against the pain in his injured hand.

Clark looked up from a bill-fishing magazine. "Why? Whatcha got?"

"No idea," Armstrong said. "But you left your beeper on the flying bridge."

"You mean my pager," Clark said.

"Right," Armstrong said. "Your beeper."

"Pager," Clark said.

"Does it go *beep, beep, beep*, or *page, page, page*? Anyway, somebody sure as hell wants to talk to you."

"Marines . . ." Clark muttered, looking at the little black box. Pager or beeper, it was more of a leash than anything. It was a 703 number. Virginia—and not the area where he lived. The other part . . . where Langley was. He checked to make sure Sato was still writing and then nodded toward land. "Guess we better head in and find a pay phone."

"I thought you guys all got one of those phones that talk to satellites," Armstrong said.

"We do," Clark said. "I just didn't feel like carrying a suitcase on a fishing boat." He looked west, toward the endless horizon. "Besides, there are a hell of a lot worse things than being unreachable."

19

The USAF C-21A (Lear 35) carrying Special Agents Dan Murray and Betty Harris landed at Nellis Air Force Base in the northeast corner of Las Vegas at five minutes to ten local time. An Air Force HH-3E helicopter was on the ground waiting to take them to a place called Whitney Pocket, a few miles south of the F-117 crash site. FBI Special Agent Pritchard was there to meet them, along with Special Agent Nathan Gillum of the Air Force Office of Special Investigations.

Many if not most OSI agents were active-duty military. Gillum was a civilian agent, which helped bridge the gap of posse comitatus, which prohibited members of the United States military from engaging in law enforcement duties on American soil except under specific circumstances, e.g., service members involved in criminal activity or a declaration of martial law. A former Air Force captain, Gillum understood the ins and outs of the military but was not bound by their constraints once the case left the newly designated National Defense Area. Murray folded him into the task force immediately.

Clark County sheriff's deputies had brought sandwiches for the group of thirteen witnesses, most of them sitting on blankets in the shade of the sandstone cliffs.

Pritchard handed Murray a new pencil sketch of the unidentified subject—the UNSUB. It was better than the Captain Kangaroo version, but still pretty basic.

"Bureau artist is supposed to be flying in from Denver," Pritchard said by way of apology. "I held off distributing anything until then. Seems like he'd be here by now, since you guys made it all the way out from D.C."

"We had a little help greasing the transportation skids," Harris said before Murray had to.

He wanted to catch this guy, but the last thing he planned to do was drop in from HQ and start barking orders and throwing his weight around. That did no good at all. If he needed to turn up the heat he would, but until then, he listened a lot and spoke a little.

First things first, he needed to get a picture of what Pritchard had done before he got here.

A Nevada Highway Patrol trooper sergeant named Allred came up to join the conversation.

Murray acknowledged him, then asked, "What do we have up at this moment in the way of a net?"

"The state and county guys are helping out," Pritchard said. "In addition to Bureau assets, we have agents from

U.S. Customs, some Marshals Service deputies, and a couple ATF guys who were working in St. George."

"That's good," Murray said, genuinely impressed.

Pritchard grimaced. "Sounds like a lot, but they're coming in in onesies and twosies and we have a lot of ground to cover."

He smoothed out a map on the hood of a maroon Chevrolet Caprice—the quintessential Bureau sedan—and traced the road from Whitney Pocket with the tip of his finger. "The guy we suspect is our UNSUB was last seen heading toward the highway on a three-wheeler believed to belong to the female vic. He won't get far on the ATV. Little town of Bunkerville is first, but Mesquite's not far past that and a bit bigger. A couple casinos, that sort of thing. Easier to slip in and get a better vehicle without being noticed. I've got people in both and every wide spot on the road for a hundred and fifty miles."

Sergeant Allred tapped the map with a hand that looked like it had changed a lot of irrigation pipe. "Our troopers are working I-15 all the way to Vegas and east to the Utah border. Troopers from Arizona and Utah are working their ends."

"Good to hear," Murray said. "So, we have a witness that actually saw him?"

"A couple," Pritchard said. "UNSUB is thought to be white male, late thirties, early forties. Shaggy blond hair. Six feet, a buck ninety. According to the victim's ex-boyfriend, our guy was chummy with her for the last couple of days."

"Her ex is here?" Harris asked.

"Yep," Pritchard said. "I guess they split the sheets after he got cozied up with some other UFO freaks. It's like a commune out here." He glanced over his shoulder at the group. "Anyway, our UNSUB rode off with our female victim after the crash, was gone for a couple hours, and then reappeared later on her three-wheeler without her."

"Very well," Murray said, looking at the map and then up at Harris. "Can you think of anything we're missing?"

"Hell of a lot of back roads and trails," she said. "Snowbirds come down here to get away from northern weather. That would give him more than a few vehicles to choose from—or a place to hide out and regroup."

Murray looked at Pritchard again. "What about our air assets?"

"Other than the military? Bureau has a Cessna 207 in Vegas. It's cruising the I-15 corridor now, looking for any sign of the three-wheeler."

Allred raised a hand. "I've got something you might want to hear."

"What's that?" Pritchard said, annoyed at being surprised in front of the boss.

The trooper looked at the group of witnesses and then pointed at a middle-aged man who looked like a lumberjack turned college professor—heavy red beard, hornrimmed glasses, wool sweater with leather patches on the elbows. He trotted up when the trooper pointed to him, eager to be of service.

"Tell them what you just told me," Allred said.

"Sure," Lumberjack said. "I think the guy hanging out with Heather might have been German."

"What makes you say that?" Betty Harris asked.

"For one thing," Lumberjack said, "he cursed in German. And not the normal *Scheisse* that American grand-dads brought back from the war. This was pretty colorful stuff even for a German."

"Interesting," Harris said, prodding. "You said 'for one thing.' What else?"

"Well," Lumberjack said. "You might think it's odd, but I heard him talking to Heather about Snow White and the Pleiades."

"Like the stars?" Murray asked.

"Yes," Lumberjack said. "My great-grandma was from Steinau. She used to tell me a similar story—about the stars representing the dwarves, that kind of thing. It's not much, but I thought you'd want to know."

"Would you mind writing that up?" Harris asked.

"So our UNSUB is German," Special Agent Pritchard mused to the others while Sergeant Allred took the man to his patrol car and got him outfitted with paper and pen.

"Or someone with a German great-grandma," Harris said.

"Let's not get so focused on one thing that we miss something that doesn't fit our narrative," Murray said. "But it makes sense." He looked at Gillum. "Are the bodies still at the crash site?"

"They are," Agent Gillum said. "To be honest, sir, the main priority of the Air Force is to secure the site from further incursion."

Murray tipped his head toward the mountains. "You've been to the scene?"

"I have," Gillum said.

Pritchard nodded. "Yes."

"Well, then you would both know better than I," Murray said, "but if we catch this UNSUB we may well stop an incursion that's already happened."

"True enough," Gillum said. "Are we calling it an espionage or a homicide case?"

"Tomato, tomahto," Murray said. "The mechanics of the investigation will be the same. That said, Washington throws buckets of money at espionage cases. West Germany is our ally. If East Germany is involved, then the Soviets will be up to their necks in this."

"Our victims won't care what we call it," Harris said.

Gillum gave a low groan, slightly embarrassed. "Roger that. Anyway, did you want to go up? I'd have to escort you."

"Seriously? We wouldn't be able to get in on our own?" Harris said. "We were both flown out here from Washington by the Air Force."

Gillum gave a little shrug. "I hear you," he said. "But right now, we've got a ring of young guys with loaded M16 rifles surrounding the crash site. We've instructed them not to let *anyone* in—and they take their job seriously. A National Defense Area is about the closest thing to martial law that you'll see in the United States. I hope, anyway . . ."

"That's fine," Murray said. "You seem like a savvy investigator. Anything jump out at you about the bodies?"

FBI cases were routinely broken up among squads. Murray was accustomed to piecing together witness interviews and surveillance reports done by a veritable army of agents to make a single case that was presentable to the U.S. Attorney. That was the beauty of the Bureau. Agents could move independently or as one giant organism, covering a hell of a lot of ground.

Gillum thought for a minute. "No. Other than what I mentioned to Pritchard. The female appears to have been pushed. No defensive wounds or apparent flesh under the nails to indicate she fought her killer—which meshes with what we're hearing from the pilot. And the male was stabbed. Also with no defensive wounds like you see sometimes with a knife. He probably never saw—"

Sergeant Allred's radio broke squelch. A Nevada Highway Patrol trooper in Mesquite came through on the static.

"*Sarge,*" the trooper said. "*I got a kid here who says his mother is missing.*"

Murray stepped around the hood of the car, closer to the radio.

"Stand by," Allred said. "I'm passing you over to the FBI."

"Dan Murray, FBI. What kind of car?"

"*Kid's not even three years old,*" the trooper said. "*And he's awful shaken up. It's hard to understand him.*"

"What can he tell you?" Murray asked.

"*His name is Noah Peterson,*" the trooper said. "*Got

that much. From the looks of things, his mom pulled over to use the restroom at the truck stop west of Mesquite a few minutes before seven this morning. The clerk remembers seeing her with the little kid but didn't catch what kind of car she was driving. No cameras. Mama bought a Dr Pepper and some Fritos but paid with cash. Not sure what happened, but Mama's gone and the little boy is unharmed, physically at least."

"Peterson," Allred muttered under his breath. "Like that's not a common name around these parts. I'll bet there's fifty of 'em in St. George alone . . ."

"The clerk saw her at seven o'clock?" Murray said. "The kid's been alone there since then?"

"Looks like he cried himself to sleep," the trooper said. *"The clerk went out to smoke about ten minutes ago and found him curled up under a picnic table. Gave him some ice cream and then he called us."*

Murray lowered the radio for a moment. "That gives our guy a four-hour head start."

The radio broke squelch again. *"Stand by,"* the trooper said. *"Noah remembers something else . . ."* Then, *"Kid says he was going to visit Grandma in Salt Lake."*

Betty Harris gave a little fist pump.

Murray winked at her. It was not much, but it was good news.

"Keep assets checking things toward Vegas, but let's make sure we're looking north on the route to Salt Lake City as well." He leaned over the Caprice to study the map. "I'd like to get eyes on as many of these side roads as possible. Move the net out to, say . . . two hundred and fifty miles, but include I-70 and these smaller highways going west as well."

"He's got a four-hour head start," Pritchard said. "This is going to be a—"

Murray put a hand on the younger agent's shoulder. "Try."

20

Garit Richter did not kill children. Not if he didn't have to.

He'd ridden the three-wheeler straight out of the desert without looking back, the sun coming up behind him and chasing him all the way to the little town of Mesquite. Like most places in Nevada, it oozed the decadence of capitalism. As far as Richter could tell, the economy of Mesquite revolved around two roadside casinos and a couple truck stops along Interstate 15.

He found a likely one on the west side of town and rode the little three-wheeler around back, parking it in the shadow of a filthy dumpster. They would be looking for a man on a trike, if they were not already.

Planes and helicopters roared and thundered overhead with greater and greater frequency. Dark sedans screamed by in the silver light of dawn, paying no attention to anything or anyone in the little burg.

For now.

Richter desperately needed to make a phone call to his control, but the most important thing to do now was escape—and to do that, he had to put as much distance between himself and the crash site as possible. The phone call had to wait.

The walkway along the outskirts of the fuel station/convenience store was landscaped with juniper shrubs and other hardy desert plants and lined with chunks of decorative red lava rock. Richter found a piece the size of a grapefruit and walked toward the gray Toyota sedan parked in the shade on the west side of the building and hit the woman bending over the trunk in the back of the head.

The little boy asleep in his child booster in the backseat had been blissfully unaware.

There was a reason a rabbit punch was against the rules in boxing. A blow to the base of the skull was as brutally effective as it was bloodless. The only sound was the woman's body falling across the spare tire. Richter shut the trunk lid, dropped the lava rock on the pavement, and opened the back door to retrieve the little boy.

He'd noted on his approach that the keys still dangled from the ignition.

The child stirred, whimpering a little.

He thought of saying something, trying to comfort him, but decided the sound of a stranger's voice would only startle him, and if he woke up and made noise . . .

He set the boy gently under the edge of a picnic table just around the corner at the rear of the store, with a beautiful view of the red rock desert. He draped the child's blanket over the edge of the table to keep the sun out of his eyes, and left him there, sleeping, while Richter sped away with the mother in the trunk.

The vehicle, a newer-model Toyota Cressida, was almost full of fuel. He took the north ramp onto I-15, reasoning that the authorities would assume he'd head for Las Vegas, the nearest large city.

It was light enough that they would have found the bodies by now. And the idiots on the motorcycles had seen him coming out. None of them knew his name or where he was from, but they would be able to describe him. It was a problem, but not an insurmountable one.

He kept the speedometer at a steady sixty miles an hour, fast enough to make good time, but not so fast as to arouse suspicion of any troopers he happened to meet. He hoped they'd be responding to the crash of a secret airplane and not fret over the death of a couple of insignificant citizens.

He passed through the little town of Beaver, Utah, two hours after leaving Mesquite, still encountering no resistance from law enforcement. He saw several helicopters, but they were all heading south and paying no attention to him.

His bladder finally got the best of him a little over an hour later and he pulled off the interstate and cut around an overpass outside a town called Nephi. He pissed on the road, hidden behind the car door. The wind was horrific, buffeting the car and nearly blowing the door shut on top of him. He didn't feel comfortable stopping long enough to get fuel until he was closer to the city, where he'd have more surface roads to cut down and avoid interaction with the police. He got back on the interstate quickly, still getting knocked around, but happy to be out of the wind.

A half-hour later, at nearly eleven o'clock in the morning, he turned off the interstate into a fuel station two blocks off the highway in the farming community of Payson. It looked like a fertile place, snowy fields surrounded by mountains, the close ones low and round, the far ones tall and magnificent, shrouded in white.

He circled the parking lot once, looking for any CCTV cameras like he'd seen in American department stores. Finding none, he filled up the tank and paid with cash and then used the restroom again. He added a large Coca-Cola from the fountain and two Baby Ruth candy bars to his purchase. He'd never get out of this cursed country if he passed out from lack of food.

He ate one of the Baby Ruth bars while he was still in the store, wolfing it down with half the Coke. No one approached the Toyota. A good sign.

The phone booth was at the far end of the parking lot, inexplicably beside an extremely loud air compressor for inflating tires. Richter parked beside the booth and then retrieved the TI SR-52 calculator from his bag. He used a needle to switch the function, and then typed in a quick message. He was in physical possession of valuable photographs and a sample of the actual technology. He needed egress and he needed it now. He would call in again in two hours for instructions.

He punched in the calling card number, the country code to Switzerland—which would raise far fewer eyebrows than East Berlin or Potsdam—and then asked to speak to his grandmother.

"Oh, ja, ja," the voice on the other end said. *"Einen Moment, bitte."*

Richter waited for the tone signifying his contact had connected the audio coupler and then he pushed the enter key on the calculator, holding it to the reciever. The coded message was sent as a series of electronic chirps and squeals that would be deciphered by the device on the other end, and then transmitted immediately to his controller in the DDR.

This done, he breathed a sigh of relief and dug the second Baby Ruth out of his coat pocket. The food made him feel less desperate, less like he might burst into flames at any given moment. He leaned against the phone booth and closed his eyes. He was actually going to make this work.

Then he opened his eyes and saw a dark liquid dripping to the pavement from beneath the Toyota's trunk. The grass around the parking lot was scabby with patches of snow, but the lot itself, darker and warmed by the sun, had melted off—so the growing pool of blood did not show.

He didn't think he'd struck the woman hard enough to open her up, but who could tell with a head wound. He knew from experience that the mouth and nose and even the ears often lost fluid when the body swelled. And the poor woman had been stuffed in the trunk for the past four hours. Heat from the interior of the car had no doubt made it to the trunk space.

He cursed, quickly running through his options. He could not drive around town dripping blood out the back of a stolen car.

The good citizens of Payson, Utah, mostly farmers and the children of farmers from the look of them, came and went from the store. None of them paid any attention to the gray Cressida. The evening news wouldn't be on for another few hours, and most people, including the woman behind the counter inside, were watching idiotic capitalist game shows.

A quick survey of the area revealed a small lane running behind the fuel station. He had to leave the parking lot and drive around the block to reach it, but what looked to be an abandoned grain silo rose up from behind a line of tall junipers that ran shoulder to shoulder along an irrigation ditch overgrown with winter-killed cattails. The trees had been planted as a windbreak for the two-hundred-meter driveway that led to the farmhouse and concrete silo beyond. The dense evergreens would shield him completely from prying eyes of passersby unless they drove down the lane right on top of him. At that point, he would see them coming. Even so close to town, the weedy ditch would provide the perfect spot to roll out the body.

Richter would be at least an hour away before anyone stumbled on the corpse. He checked up and down the lane one last time before inserting the key in the trunk.

With any luck, more snow would fall. It might be days
before—

His heart stopped when he raised the lid. The liquid
leaking out of the back came from an open can of motor
oil.

And the dead woman was not dead at all.

She was gone.

21

Mary Pat Foley identified the men surveilling her the moment her boots crunched on the driven snow outside the front door of her apartment. Picking them out from the other pedestrians hunched against the cold was not difficult. The trench coats and fedoras of just a few years before had given way to dark ski jackets and fur hats, but the men wearing them, the KGB, were just as easy to spot. To a man, they were marked by a bullish arrogance and paunchiness from standing around with no particular mission other than to watch and report.

It had snowed overnight, and was still snowing, adding another layer of something for the men to be grouchy about after spending the morning in the weather waiting for Foley to leave her apartment.

She tugged a heavy wool overcoat tighter against a bitter Moscow wind and waited for her husband to bring the car around. Her pedantic friends in the States corrected her when she said it was winter, pointing out that November was still technically autumn. Bullshit. Moscow winters didn't care what the date happened to be.

Little Eddie was staying with the wife of a State Department RSO while Foley was away. It took the sting out of Mom's absence, since they had a boy his age.

Ed knew the drill. He'd signed on for it when he married a CIA operations officer, but still, his worries came loud and clear in his silence on the way to the airport.

Moscow CIA chief of station was about as prestigious an overseas post as you could get in the Agency. But that prestige was tempered by danger to their young family—just another thing the Foleys signed on for with both eyes open. There were rules here, generally accepted by each side if not exactly codified. Operations officers were not to be harmed, at least not unless one side thought they could do it without getting their hands dirty. Ed had cover as a diplomat, but the KGB assumed he was a spy. They suspected everyone in the embassy was a spy—everyone except perhaps Mary Pat. She was a wife and a mother. Still, with seemingly endless supplies of agents, the Committee for State Security—Komitet Gosudarstvennoy Bezopasnosti—could afford to follow even a hockey mom when she decided to return to the United States for a short visit. After all, even hockey moms could be spies.

They were right, of course. Mary Pat was a career operations officer, and a damned good one, too. It was she who'd devised her egress out of this godforsaken deep freeze her family called home.

The Foleys' apartment was just off the inner ring road near the U.S. embassy. Winter weather snarled traffic and it took well over an hour to get to Sheremetyevo International Airport north of the city. The ski-jacket goons had no trouble following, especially since the listening devices inside the apartment let both the KGB and the GRU know exactly where they were going.

Ed pulled the little green Moskvich 2140 sedan to the curb in front of Terminal F. The driver's-side windshield wiper thumped away like crazy. The passenger's side had decided to move at half-speed, doing little but smear the slush other cars threw at them as they slogged by.

"You be careful of this Jack Ryan," Ed said, helping her with her bag. He kept his head turned and his voice low. The blowing wind would help defeat any directional or parabolic mics. The CIA used lip readers, so it stood to reason the Russkies did, too. "He's only an analyst, a bookworm who knows nothing about the street. That's liable to get him hurt, which could get you hurt. I've decided not to like him already—"

"I'll be fine." She gave his butt a playful pat. The Russians weren't big on PDA, but she was, as they said, on the next smokin' jet outta there.

She'd met Jack Ryan twice on trips to Langley and found him smart enough. But smart didn't necessarily translate to common sense in the field. Bag in hand, she tiptoed to give her husband a passionate kiss, their usual good-bye, despite the audience.

"Watch that beautiful ass of yours," he said and then drove into the gray, dragging the KGB surveillance goons behind him.

The two waiting inside were more discreet and Mary Pat didn't mark them until she had checked in and reached her gate. She breathed a sigh of relief to see that they were both men. That would make things a hell of a lot easier.

One of the goons was just a kid, not even thirty, with a boyish face and strawberry hair poking out from his wool stocking hat. He had one of those overly earnest looks that said he was either a serial killer or a lovestruck schoolboy. She called him Opie, like the kid from *The Andy Griffith Show*, and hoped for the latter. Either way, he was still KGB and would put a Makarov bullet in the back of her neck if it came to that, though he looked sweet enough that he might feel bad about it for a minute or two. His partner she called Floyd because of his mustache and fastidious nature. The look in his eyes said shooting her would be *nyet problem* as far as he was concerned.

Foley shrugged off her overcoat, revealing a high-waisted denim skirt—purposely tight across the hips—and a smart red silk blouse she'd unbuttoned enough to expose her collarbones. Dark hair hung loose around her shoulders. Opie and Floyd were new to her, and though they'd certainly studied photographs, they were not yet familiar with her quirks and habits. She wanted them focusing on her boobs and ass instead of her face. It would grease the skids for when they got to Amsterdam and she made things even more interesting.

Since the Soviet bastards had blown Korean Air Lines Flight 007 out of the sky near Alaska in 1983, Aeroflot planes were forbidden from landing in the United States. It made perfect sense to Foley's KGB minders that she'd booked her flight out of Moscow to Holland, where she would take British Airways to London before transferring to another flight bound for JFK. The KGB would probably follow her proposed itinerary all the way to the States, which was *bol'shaya problem*—a big problem—because she was going to Berlin.

She'd made a point of reminding Ed out loud of her itinerary to the U.S. three times the day before so those listening in could book the same flight if they chose to follow her.

She made two trips aft to the lavatory during the Amsterdam leg, her half-open blouse giving them an eyeful of pale décolletage as she slinked by. Ed called it her "happy to see me" blouse because of how much it exposed when it was chilly and she wore a sheer bra—which she made sure she did today. An elderly babushka hunched in the seat directly across the aisle curled her top lip and gave Foley a silent chiding, but that couldn't be helped. Back in her seat, Foley slipped off her shoe and let it dangle nonchalantly on the tip of her toe. The angle put it well within Opie's view. It pleased her to see him blushing when she passed him on her second trip to the lavatory.

The layover in Amsterdam was mercifully short. Opie and Floyd stuck with her, following her onto the British Airways flight.

They sat on the opposite side of the narrow-body Boeing 757 from Foley. Floyd, apparently wanting a better view than the one he'd had on the last flight, sat one row ahead of Opie, two and three rows behind her, respectively.

Flight time to Heathrow was less than ninety minutes. That gave her a very short window to do what needed to be done.

"Okay, Mary Pat," she whispered to herself. "Time to see what you got . . ."

She rose quickly as soon as the seat belt sign chimed off and made her way aft toward the lavatory. By this time, Opie and Floyd surely had to be thinking she had a very small bladder. A brunette flight attendant in the galley saw her coming and smiled before whispering something to her coworker and then ducking into the adjacent lavatory.

Foley worked fast, unbuttoning her blouse the moment she'd slid the door latch home. The tight quarters necessitated a good deal of acrobatics. Wriggling out of her skirt without falling over the toilet was especially tough. She'd had a terrible dream the night before about rolling into the aisle in nothing but her pantyhose and cringed every time her hips brushed the thin sheet of plastic and veneer that made up the door. The gray skirt and red-white-and-blue-striped blouse hidden under the sink fit her perfectly. A conservative navy-blue blazer finished her transformation into an attractive but matronly British Airways flight attendant. Her hair went up in a tight bun. A dab of blush here and lipstick there finished the process. She heard the telltale thump of Jane O'Keefe, the flight attendant who, in reality, worked for the British Secret Intelligence Service, slipping into her own denim skirt and silk blouse. She would deplane in Amsterdam and fly first class to New York while Foley served cocktails on the flight to Tegel in West Berlin. If things went to plan, Opie and Floyd would stick with O'Keefe.

Foley stashed her clothes under the sink and took a final look in the mirror. The silence on the other side of the bulkhead told her that her MI6 counterpart was doing the same thing. Though not exactly identical, the two women could easily have been sisters, and anyone not paying close attention should have been fooled.

At least that was the theory.

"Let's hope their primary focus is tits and ass," Mary Pat whispered to herself, touching up her lipstick one last time. "The resemblance in that department is uncanny . . ."

22

Jen North's reasons did not matter—but she'd confided them all anyway to the man on the bed in the apartment north of Tegel Airport in the French sector of West Berlin.

Confiding. The idea of it made her sick.

That's what had landed her here in the first place. She should have known better. It was her job to read people and sway them to her will—to social-engineer the hell out of them. And she was good. Very good. The problem was, Rolfe Schneider was better without even having to try. He was tall and blond and with shoulders that made him look like the biggest bull elk whenever he walked in the room. He was one of those rare guys who could be tough and still take care of his hands—powerful like a dockworker's, but absent the rough calluses. Most important, he was quiet. He let *her* do the talking.

Don't confide. If that wasn't the first rule of espionage, it should have been.

Schneider was her handler, but he seemed genuinely troubled by it, forever reminding her he wished he'd met her under different circumstances. His superiors with the HVA—the foreign intelligence side of the Stasi house— were heartless assholes, he said, always pestering him to get more information from her. It was out of his hands. After all, they had her file, the photos, the doctor's notes. It made her retch if she thought about it.

She confided in him now, spilling her worst fears.

"That bitch was humming *Kindertotenlieder*!" She felt his eyes on her as she sat at the dressing table, stretching a pair of pantyhose over long legs. "Songs on the Death of Children!" A sob caught in her throat. "It's like she knows."

They'd already discussed little miss Ruby Keller at length, but she didn't want him to forget to check her out.

He rolled up on his side, leaning on his hand like a blond Burt Reynolds. "Forgive me for saying so, but this is not healthy. You need to calm down. Maybe meditation . . ."

"So you're my yogi now? Maybe I should start smoking."

"If it relaxes you," Schneider said. "I would not mind it. I once made love to a woman who smoked two packs a day. I have to say, I found it pleasant enough." He gave her a wink. "Of course, I was seventeen at the time, so . . ."

"Seventeen!" she scoffed. "That woman could have been on fire and you would have found it pleasant."

Schneider was forever reminding her that he had been with other women before her, as if to say, *Of all the others, I have chosen you.* Either this guy was a really gifted liar or he was truly in love with her. North suspected a little of both.

"Must you hurry?" he asked tenderly, sticking out his bottom lip in a pout. "It seems as though you just got here and now you have to rush away."

"That's because I had to take so much time shaking your Stasi friends off my tail so I could meet you in the black. It seems like you could tell them to knock it off and just, I don't know, leave me the hell alone since I'm coming to see one of their own."

"You give me too much credit, *mein Liebling*," he chided. "I have no say in such things. Anyway, it is not only my people following you. You are American CIA, surrounded by legions of agents not only from HVA, but also KGB and GRU. The West is crawling with us, as you well know."

She rolled her eyes and stood, hopping up and down in place, pulling the pantyhose up all the way. "No shit . . . All of you who want to come over here and live the high life while extolling the virtues of the socialist utopia on the other side of the Wall."

If Schneider was upset he didn't show it. "There are indeed perks to working on this side of the Anti-Fascist Protection Rampart, time with you chief among them."

Yeah, he was gifted, all right.

"In any case," he continued, "you only just told me we have a leak. What would your side do if they learned from that leak that you are receiving special treatment from State Security and then—"

"I know," North said. "It's just . . ."

"No word on what sort of information was on this disk?"

She shook her head. "All coded. And your guy sent the key to a P.O. box near Langley."

"Is there no way for you to take a photograph of the disk? Even a look at the outside might be of help."

"Nope," she said. "My boss took it before I had the chance. Look, to be honest with you, I'm not even sure this attempted contact is real. That girl who brought it in knows more than she's letting on. *Kindertotenlieder* . . . I mean, what the hell . . ."

"You are under a great deal of pressure," Schneider said. "Perhaps you were mistaken."

She sat on the edge of the bed and glowered down, smacking him on the chest. "At no time in the history of history has a woman responded positively to being told she's hysterical! I don't trust her. This little computer disk has triggered a tornado of activity at the CIA. We're getting visitors from our headquarters to make contact with your defector in accordance with the instructions on the disk—whatever they are. I don't know who's coming or when they'll be here, but they're on their way. I know that much."

"Then it is simple," Schneider said. "You tell me who

they are when they arrive. My people will follow them to our traitor and identify him."

"What will you do when you figure out who he is?"

"Ah, *Liebling*," he said. "You do not want to know."

She shook her head. "You guys are medieval . . ."

"All for the good of the state." He patted the mattress beside him. "Come and lay by me for a while before you get dressed. I do not like to see you this worried."

She complied, grateful for the warmth and security of his body as she nestled into the crook of his arm. She turned slightly and looked him in the eye. "For all I know, this is an elaborate ruse—a trap so the CIA can catch their mole. And Ruby Keller is at the center of it."

He caressed her shoulder. "Okay. I will check out this Ruby woman and see what she is all about. Do not fret, my little *Fledermaus*."

23

John Clark sometimes felt like he'd spent more than half his life curled up on the floor of a military transport plane. He'd caught a commuter hop from Kona to Hickam, where he'd taken a C-141 to Aviano. The flight from Italy to Berlin was commercial so he could avoid drawing attention to himself by coming in on a military aircraft.

It hardly mattered.

He made the first member of his welcome committee as soon as he cleared customs and immigration with relative ease considering the fact that he was traveling on a fake Spanish passport. It was a good fake, manufactured from real blanks somehow procured by specialists at the CIA. He spoke Spanish like a native and was a good enough actor to speak English with a Castilian accent.

A stout man in his early thirties stood in the terminal looking at nothing. Cigarette dangling from his lips, he absentmindedly smacked a rolled newspaper against his thigh. A little shorter than Clark, he had a wide nose that looked as though it had been smeared across his face more than once in a brawl. There would be others, Clark was sure of that. This guy was the muscle, and nothing but.

Probably KGB . . . maybe. Stasi operatives were, by and large, a little less thuggish. Every bit as brutal, but slimy about it, less like a common gangster and more like the devil in a British movie.

The sheer number of spooks hanging out in the terminal was astounding. Clark made an American male-female team by the Avis car rental counter. Both with a healthy Midwest glow and earnest hunters' eyes. They would have the flight manifests and times and were likely here for someone specific. There would be others, too, on both sides, more seasoned and better at blending in. Berlin was, after all, behind enemy lines, the epicenter for intelligence work.

If Clark was honest with himself, he had to admit it felt good to be in the thick of things. It was the way he was built.

His British Airways flight from Venice touched down at Berlin Tegel Airport twenty minutes late at 1945 local time. He'd allowed himself time to think about Sandy and the girls during the flight. A commercial aircraft was a relative safe space, at least it used to be. Hezbollah terrorists had hijacked TWA 847 between Athens and Rome that summer. Using pistols and grenades they'd smuggled aboard, they terrorized passengers for days, eventually killing U.S. Navy diver Robert Stethem and dumping his body onto the tarmac. It turned Clark's stomach to think those shitheads were still in the wind, no doubt plotting new acts of terror. It was one of his most fervent hopes to run across them one day on a professional basis . . .

The world seemed in chaos with no shortage of evil—carried on the back of religious extremism, disputed lands, and natural disaster. Only a month earlier Palestinian terrorists had hijacked the passenger ship *Achille Lauro*, killing the wheelchair-bound Leon Klinghoffer. Soviets, getting their asses kicked in Afghanistan, were pissed about advances in U.S. military defense capabilities and now appeared bent on breaking their own economy in an attempt to catch up. South Africa—in their own very uncivil war over apartheid—had invaded Angola, and a devastating earthquake in Mexico City had killed almost ten thousand people. Now some twisted asshole or group of twisted assholes was sending random people package bombs in the U.S.

While the United States was not technically in a "hot" war, there was nothing cold about what they were doing. Men and women in John Clark's line of work—prosecuting all the "little" wars—never lacked for things to do.

The flat-nosed guy trundling along behind him proved it.

Dragging and dog-tired from nearly twenty-four hours of flying, Clark traveled light, just a carry-on duffel. The only thing he had resembling a weapon was the small folding knife he carried in his pocket. He'd learned early in his career as a Navy SEAL that the world around him was chock-full of things that could hurt people—including him if he didn't keep his eyes open. Still, his two principals would be arriving anytime and if he expected to protect them from the legion of Soviet and East German operatives or Baader-Meinhof wannabes who popped up like whack-a-moles on both sides of the Wall, he'd need a firearm.

An isolated island surrounded by Warsaw Pact barbed wire and bayonets, West Berlin wasn't exactly lacking in guns, but to get one (or two) he had to trust someone he'd never met—something he didn't do very often.

Clark had never been much of a clotheshorse, preferring function over form any day of the week. Sandy did her best, but he was really a lost cause. His time with the CIA had taught him to leverage the hell out of the clothing combinations he could get with a wrinkle-free navy blazer, a light blue oxford shirt, a pair of jeans, and a pair of khaki slacks. He wore the jeans for travel, and a black mock turtleneck that his wife said made him look like a sailor. A real turtleneck would have been slightly warmer—and would have made him look more seaman-like, but he hated the things; wearing one was like being strangled by a very weak man.

There was a pair of Norm Thompson cordovan chukka boots in his bag with his blazer and shaving gear in case he needed to dress up a bit. For now, he wore black Spot-bilt coaches shoes. They made him feel old, but the shoes were comfortable, and he could run in them if the need arose—which it often did. He'd shipped

his swim trunks and deck shoes home from Hawaii and
had just enough time on the layover in Italy to buy a decent ski parka from the Aviano base exchange—dark
gray, which worked well for urban camouflage. A wool
beanie rounded out his attire—and, as Sandy said, his
sailor look. It made sense; he'd left the Navy SEALs as a
chief petty officer.

Heading for the exit, Clark left the Americans to
whatever their mission of the moment was and kept his
eyes open for Russians and East Germans. Flat Nose followed like a puppy. It wasn't surprising. Even West German BND might put a tail on him. He was new meat, an
obvious military man, no matter how you sliced it. He
was worth tailing for a while just to see what he was up
to. Clark planned for it, but he wouldn't stand for it. Not
with what he had to do.

A scathing wind drove pellets of snow into his face
and ripped his breath away the moment he walked out
the doors. He shrugged the duffel over his shoulder and
zipped the ski jacket up to his chin, resolving to buy an
even heavier coat at his first opportunity. Garish lights
beat back the darkness, but the cold cut through his nylon jacket like it wasn't even there. Clark shook it off and
followed the sound and smell of idling diesel engines
toward the bus lanes.

A former Nazi rocket practice range (with unexploded
ordnance still periodically uncovered), Berlin Tegel Airport was built in the shape of a large hexagon. Taxiways
and aircraft gates were on the outer perimeter, while
buses and taxis queued up inside the hexagon—like the

park in the center of the Pentagon—but without the hot dog stand. Pure German efficiency, but to Clark's way of thinking, foolhardy. Walking into the Colosseum-like center, he felt like a fish in a barrel, and couldn't help but scan the surrounding roofline for gunmen. A couple well-placed bombs would block the vehicular escape— and emergency services response—leaving everyone in the middle vulnerable to sustained attack from above.

If you knew what to look for, the number of tails was staggering. Every third person going from the terminal to a taxi or a waiting private vehicle appeared to have someone following them. Soviet military intelligence— GRU, KGB goons with bad shoes and fur hats that they could not seem to give up, and Stasi men and women in slightly more fashionable overcoats.

Clark had come to Berlin in the black, i.e., without letting the local CIA chief or anyone else in the station make plans for his arrival. There was no one official to meet him and he had no official cover. He was very literally out in the cold, and without a safety net. He preferred it that way.

It was a universally accepted fact that taxi companies were either infiltrated by or owned outright by enemy intelligence organizations. Clark avoided them whenever possible, often walking blocks out of his way to catch a bus or train.

His contact lived near a street called Kurfürsten-strasse, a place known the world over for legal prostitu-tion. A single man heading straight there from the airport was not exactly uncommon. There was a more direct route, but Clark took the long way, using a combination of shoe leather, bus, and train, allowing him some semblance of a surveillance-detection run—rudimentary, since he was by himself, but it was better than nothing. If he couldn't shake them, at least he'd know who he was dealing with and make a decision when he reached his destination—before he approached his contact.

He boarded the bus that would take him almost due south, first along and then across the Spree River, part of which formed the border between East and West Berlin. The flat-nosed man got on the bus, too, and stood near the back, holding on to a strap, though there were a couple open seats.

Clark made the second guy when he transferred to an eastbound bus at Adenauerplatz. He considered jumping on the U-Bahn, which would take him on a nearly identical route, but decided that would show his hand and let the thugs know he was onto them. This new guy was good. He'd probably been with him from the beginning, just too smooth to be noticed. Obviously the brains of the team, he looked plenty capable and close to Clark's age, maybe a decade older and half a head shorter than his brawny, flat-nosed partner. Deceptively meek eyes overlooked a few days of blond scruff to go with his Robert Redford mustache. Clark was an unknown, a tourist who might be up to something . . . or might not. Worth checking out.

Russians were usually easy to spot. Though the Soviet Union dwarfed their socialist minions in the German

Democratic Republic, KGB personnel stationed in the GDR often lived under much more austere conditions than their Stasi counterparts. They were occupiers, living in a place they had brutalized in the months following their march into Nazi Berlin. Forty years was not enough time to erase the scars. There had been plenty of bad behavior from each conquering nation, but the Russians were particularly brutal. Resentment was so ingrained that German women referred to the Soviet War Memorial in Treptow as the Tomb of the Unknown Rapist.

Clark took the bus as far as Lützowplatz Park, a small triangle of shadows and winter-killed grass that, like most parks, took on a sinister feel after dark. Brains and Brawn, the KGB men, had given up any semblance of trying to hide their intentions. They'd stopped leapfrogging and simply plodded along after him, likely assuming he was a man looking for sex on the notorious hooker "strip" of Kurfürstenstrasse between Genthiner and Potsdamer.

Other than the streetwalkers, Berlin's red-light district was disappointingly normal. There were brothels nearby, hidden somewhere in the boxy buildings. But the girls who worked indoors were more high-end, not the sort who had to bother with freezing their asses off on Berlin's winter streets. That would come later, when men stopped choosing them for the evening and they moved down a rung on the social ladder.

Clark passed a sex shop and a shabby five-story hotsheet hotel. A gaggle of bored girls loitered out front, bathed in light from the windows. The bulk of the build-

ings were mundane stores ranging from stationery shops
to a bakery. Advertisements and graffiti tagged concrete
walls. A woman in a fake fur coat and mismatched winter
boots stood in front of a movie poster for *Footloose*. Sandy
had been on him to take her—which he had promised
to do when he got home. It was a thing they did. He
promised to do something when he came back. Ipso facto,
since he never broke a promise . . . he had to come back.

People who lived and shopped along Kurfürsten-
strasse came and went, staring at their feet. A dark-
skinned woman who looked to be in her fifties blew great
clouds of smoke into the cold night with her cigarillo and
whistled at a local businessman who loitered in front of a
dry cleaner's. He stomped his foot to show her he was
not interested, and she wandered off in search of someone who was.

Clark was stopped five times in the span of two blocks.
The going rate was a hundred and fifty deutsche marks—
around sixty bucks. A sallow-faced teenager standing
under a giant David Bowie poster unzipped a dingy
neon-green parka to flash ghost-pale breasts and skeletal
ribs. She whispered in a gravel voice that she'd be willing
to trade her body for some *schore*—meaning heroin. She
was so young and trampled it was heartbreaking. Clark's
thoughts flew back not too many years before, to a time
before Sandy and their own girls. A searing pain crawled
up his neck at the sight of the poor thing. He looked
away, fighting the urge to give her everything in his wallet. She'd have a pimp out there somewhere, watching her
every move. He'd take whatever she earned, just maybe

letting her hold on to enough to keep her strung out. She shrugged and returned to leaning against a smiling David Bowie. Clark walked on, brimming with anger and shame and pity.

Brains and Brawn stayed tight on his tail, hissing lewdly at any prostitute that ventured too close to them.

Clark's instructions were to call his contact from a pay phone in front of a particular drugstore a block off Potsdamer Strasse. He had no name or physical description, only the number and a pass phrase they would use to identify each other and the fact that he or she had served in the Special Operations branch of the Office of Strategic Services during the war. From that, Clark could infer at least two things: Even if the contact had started working for the OSS at twenty, he or she would now, forty years after the war, be at least sixty and change. Second, he knew this contact was a badass. The SO branch was modeled closely after Britain's Special Operations Executive, or SOE. Saboteurs and commandos from both groups worked behind enemy lines with resistance fighters to disrupt the enemy—at great personal risk. The vast majority did not come home alive. Many of those who did became the early clandestine officers of the newly formed CIA. Clark found himself wanting to hear what wisdom a person with such experience had to say before they all died off.

The two KGB thugs were fast becoming a nuisance.

Clark ducked into the underground car park of what looked to be a vacant office building, cutting around an orange-and-white construction barrier and a sawhorse with feeble flashing lights on top. Maybe they'd lose interest if he made himself too difficult to follow—without appearing to do it on purpose. Scant light from the streetlamps outside spilled beyond the concrete pillars at the front of the garage, not quite penetrating the farthest reaches. For all Brains and Brawn knew, he was going to meet a woman in one of the apartments on the other side. Many hookers in the GDR took men up to rented crash pads or even accompanied them home for the night if the price was right.

Clark picked up his pace when he entered the shadows, gaining distance while out of sight of his pursuers. This was the tricky part. If he'd been in a hostile environment, he could have more easily ruled out possible good guys just doing their job. He was ninety percent sure these were KGB thugs, but there was an outside chance they were West German intelligence, or *Sittenpolizei*—vice cops—following foreigners around. A brick to the head was out of the question—for now.

The rotten darkness of the parking garage smelled like a third-world country. Smoke and trash and shit. The poorest hookers, particularly the drug addicts, used the area not only as a hookup spot, but as their latrine. Clark swallowed his disgust and picked up the pace even more. This was one of those places he'd never tell Sandy about. Unlike him, his wife had a generally positive view of human nature, and he saw no point in bursting her bubble, however mistaken it might be.

He'd just popped out the other side into the numbingly

cold but relatively fresh air of a courtyard when he heard a pitiful noise behind him, like the keening of a bird looking for its chick. He kept going, thinking it was likely one of the prostitutes, dealing with a client or her pimp.

Houses and four- and five-story apartment buildings surrounded the courtyard at odd angles, giving it a confused zigzag shape. Barren linden trees added to the shadows. A lone streetlamp, squat and feeble, hid in a far corner of the courtyard, as if it were afraid to venture into the dark.

What little light there was came from curtainless windows in the apartments above. Clark looked up, scanning as he moved, feeling more exposed than he had in a very long time.

The keening came again, then a curse followed by a yelping scream.

Clark cut to his left, away from the streetlamp, blending into the darkness at the base of the tallest apartment building.

The girl in the neon-green coat scrambled out of the parking garage with surprising agility, moving like a frightened impala. Angry male voices poured from the darkness behind her as Brawn, the flat-nosed KGB thug, chased her out and grabbed her by the hood. Panicked, she kept running. Her feet ran out from under her, and she landed flat on her back. The bastard laughed and then dragged her backward toward the parking garage by the hood, a KGB caveman dragging her back to his cave.

She was not only a whore, but a drug addict. No one would come looking for her or believe her if she reported anything to the police.

Brains' mustached face appeared in the scant light, waving, calling for his friend to drag the girl over for a party. Clark remained motionless, watching. They'd forgotten about him completely. He could find the pay phone and call his contact while the two men who had been so intent on following him spent their time on the weeping girl in the neon coat.

They would be busy awhile. Clark was clear, free to slip away unhindered.

24

This girl . . . this child in the green coat had surely seen little justice in her short lifetime, but she got an eyeful when John Clark stepped out of the shadows and brained the flat-nosed boxer with a brick, knocking him off her. Clark had stopped caring whether the two thugs were KGB or BND—or even vice cops who were bent beyond repair. Their actions were proof enough that they were evil, worthy of whatever he meted out to them.

He knew full well the dangers of fighting three men—the girl's pimp would surely be along at any moment—but fighting wasn't on his menu. He worked methodically, forming his plan as he moved in, but keeping it loose and fluid. The flat-nosed bastard went down quickly, mewling like a baby, shuddering like spilled Jell-O, too injured to even clutch his broken skull. His partner's eyes flew wide at Clark's sudden appearance. He froze there, eyes bouncing from Clark to his injured partner, then back to Clark again. It took him a full two seconds to realize this was the man they'd been following. By that time, Clark had closed the distance.

Most of the KGB men he'd met were ruthless. Their special skill lay in shooting people in the back or overpowering them by sheer numbers and throwing them off balconies. They were rarely trained Spetsnaz troops. Few had been in a one-on-one fight for their lives.

Still, Comrade Brains was surprisingly quick and drew a lead-filled leather slapjack that KGB men seemed never to be without.

Clark moved in to finish the fight with another blow from the brick, but the girl hadn't gotten the memo. She sprang between them, seeing that Clark was her ally and trying to protect him from the oncoming slapjack.

"Get back!" Clark growled. He had to drop the brick in order to grab her by the coat and yank her out of the way. She landed on her knees with a sickening crack, skidding across the nasty concrete.

Brawn adjusted his aim with the weighted leather and dealt Clark a nauseating blow on the elbow. The Russian sprang to the side, spitting curses as he swung the sap again, this time aiming for Clark's head.

Clark shot forward, left shoulder first, head tucked, right hand up to his cheek, closing the distance to get inside the swing. His shoulder impacted the Russian's forearm, just above the wrist. The slapjack thudded against his back, robbed of its power. In virtually the same movement, Clark swiveled his hips, bringing his

right elbow across and slamming it into and through the
Russian's jaw. Without turning his back, Clark wrested
the slapjack from the stunned man's grasp and laid it
across his ear on the backswing. Knocking him cold. A
brutally effective boot to the temple saw that he stayed
there.

It was over before the girl could stand up.

Unsure of what to do, she zipped her coat tight to her
chin and looked dully at Clark. A gruff voice barked
something in German. Her pimp. Clark braced himself
for another attack, but the voice called out again without
venturing closer. The girl gave Clark a solemn nod, and
then turned to disappear into the putrid shadows of the
garage.

Clark slipped the slapjack into his coat pocket. He
found it surprising the pimp didn't confront him, until
he heard a shuffle of boots on the gravel path—and a
man with snow-white hair and a Remington 870 shotgun up and ready stepped out of the shadows.

"Fritz knows I live nearby," the man said in perfect
English. He nodded over his shoulder at the building
behind him, but kept the shotgun up and didn't take his
eyes off Clark. "I've warned him this area is off-limits.
Girls can come here. He's not welcome."

"I see," Clark said. "I'll be on my way, then."

"Suit yourself." The man's eyes narrowed over the top
of the shotgun. "But if I was to say 'five' to you . . ."

Clark gave a slow nod. "Then I'd say three."

The simple challenge/pass phrase was supposed to
have happened over the phone, prompting further in-

structions. Clark's contact could use whatever number he wished between zero and eight. Verification happened for this meeting if, one, the contact knew to give a number in the first place, and then the sum of that number when added to Clark's response added up to eight—"one" . . . "seven" . . . "two" . . . "six," and so on. Clark and his teammates had often used a similar challenge phrase as SEALs in Vietnam.

"Figured it was you when I saw you hit that bastard with a brick. Poetry in motion . . ."

"Not exactly Marquis of Queensberry," Clark said.

"Nobody ever won a fight by hitting the enemy in the head with a rule book." The man let the gun fall to his side, holding it by the action. "My name's Cobb."

Just as Clark had guessed, the man was in his sixties, most of those years difficult ones, judging from the stooped shoulders and the map of lines on his face. His movements were measured and precise, as if carrying the weight of the world—or some very heavy memories. Silver hair stuck out from under his tattered fedora.

A willow of a woman stepped into the scant light from behind a bony linden tree. She was about the old man's age, with the same world-weary presence. Clark did a double take when he caught a glimpse of the black Makarov pistol hanging in her hand. Scarecrow arms and legs stuck from her heavy coat like sticks from a bale of hay. Still, there was something powerful about this woman.

"Were they Russian?" she asked, peering through the darkness at Clark.

He nodded. "I believe so."

"I despise Russians!" the woman said to no one in particular, spitting onto the frozen ground. Her voice was soft but alarmingly hostile. Clouds of vapor formed around her face with each word. "A brick is too good for them." She moved as if to approach the downed KGB officers, but Cobb clucked at her and she stopped, seething.

"We were on our way down to help you, but . . ." Cobb nodded to the shadows where the bodies lay. "Looks like you finished before we got here. Speaking of that, we should go in before someone calls the *Polizei*."

Consider this your safe house," Cobb said when they were inside a simple and utilitarian home. "Be our guest."

The apartment was hypnotically warm, filled with the aroma of bread and spiced cabbage and pork, making it difficult for Clark to keep his eyes open.

"I don't want to put you out." He yawned and peeled off his wool hat, nodding to the lady of the house. He didn't ask her name. In this line of work, he often interacted with people for large swaths of time without ever getting to know much of anything about them. That was not to be the case with the Cobbs.

"Nonsense," Cobb said. "Lotte has made her *Lumpen und Flöh*. It means 'rags and fleas,' but don't let the name fool you. It's delicious."

Mr. and Mrs. Cobb were much more at ease once

inside the walls of their own home. Both appeared to be genuinely interested in Clark as they sat down at the table around steaming bowls of what looked suspiciously like Irish stew.

"I envy you what you're doing, son," Cobb said. "Whatever it is."

"I'd imagine you've done similar work, sir," Clark guessed. "And then some."

"Takes one to know one, I suppose," Cobb said. "Call me Richard if you want, or Rich, or Cobb. Doesn't matter." He lifted a spoonful of the stew and blew on it. Lotte chided him for blowing soup drops onto her tablecloth, while she sawed thick slices of brown bread from a fresh loaf. She held out a saucer with the first slice. "Sir?"

"Clark," he said. "John Clark. And yes, I would love some bread."

"She made it herself," Cobb said.

Lotte's hands fell to her lap.

"We watched you, you know, Mr. Clark," she said reverently, barely above a whisper. Her English was perfect, but held a noticeable German accent. "The screams drew us to the window and . . . I must say, it was glorious to see you leap out of the shadows."

Clark ate and Cobb talked, hinting at his time during the war, but providing no details. "Just a lot of drinking and foolin' around," he said, drawing a disbelieving side-eye from his wife.

Clark thanked Mrs. Cobb for the meal and pushed away from the table. "I should be on my way."

"Go if you want to," Cobb said. "But as I understand

it, you're not to go near USBER. The details of your assignment will come in here, to our machine." He rubbed a hand over silver hair, thinking, then said, "Hold up one second," before disappearing down the narrow hall.

Clark glanced at Lotte, who shrugged.

"Who can tell with him?"

Cobb returned a moment later. He pushed his bowl out of the way and set a black plastic box on the table. He peeled back the Tupperware-style plastic lid to reveal what looked like a toy pistol, the frame of which was also molded of black plastic. The slide was metal, locked open, showing an empty chamber. An empty magazine—also plastic—lay in the box beside it. Clark prided himself on keeping up with the firearms of the world. He'd yet to shoot one, but recognized this one as a Glock Model 17.

Clark nodded at the handgun. "May I?"

"It's yours," Cobb said.

Clark checked the chamber and then released the slide, but refrained from dry-firing someone else's gun. "Does it have a mag disconnect?"

Cobb shook his head. "Nope. I hear you, though. My only quibble about the Browning Hi-Power is that damned magazine disconnect. No, the Glock might be ugly as hell, but it's a fighting gun, pure and simple. If there's a round in the chamber, she'll go bang whether you have the magazine in or not."

Clark aimed the pistol at the floor. It was surprisingly light and didn't point the same as his 1911. Not worse, just different. He glanced up at Cobb, still holding the gun at arm's length. "So this is the pistol the Austrian military went with?"

Lotte Cobb nodded. "In '82."

"They call it the Pistole 80," Cobb said. "The Norwegians adopted it, too. Swedes are close to doing the same. This puppy beat out SIG, Heckler & Koch, Steyr . . . all the big boys."

"Obviously not in a beauty contest," Clark said. "It's no 1911."

"You got that right, son," Cobb said. "It's two 1911s and some change left over."

"I have to admit, the seventeen-round magazine could grow on me."

"You're right," Cobb said. "It's not much for looks, but I guarantee you, the way of the gun is changing. Revolvers and 1911s are giving way to the likes of Steyr, SIG Sauer, and this Austrian hunk of polymer." He slid two more empty magazines toward Clark and then got a box of rounds plus two loose singles out of a rolltop desk in the dining room. "Three times seventeen is fifty-one, plus one in the tube."

"A box of ammo in three mags," Clark said. "If I can't get it done with that . . ."

"Then you will have this." Cobb set a Fairbairn Sykes killing dagger on the table beside the Glock. "This old thing is getting rusty just sitting in my drawer."

Clark picked up the knife and drew it out of the simple leather sheath, admiring the seven-inch stiletto blade. "I can't be responsible for this. It looks like an heirloom."

"Blades should fulfill their purpose," Cobb said. "Not sit around in a desk and collect dust. No offense, but you seem a man who is not a stranger to that sort of work. This and the Glock should serve you well."

Lotte sat with her elbows on the table, resting her chin on her hands, studying Clark.

"Something old," she said. "Something new . . ."

He stifled another yawn.

"You are exhausted," Lotte said, raising her voice for the first time since they'd come inside. "I insist you stay here with us."

"Better let her show you to your room." Cobb leaned in, sotto voce. "She gets mean if you cross her."

Lotte waved him off, but then looked at Clark with a hard gaze common to junior high school English teachers and Prussian generals.

Clark sighed and gave up, dropping the empty Glock, magazines, and the box of ammo into his duffel before shuffling down the hall behind Lotte Cobb. He had to trust someone.

25

Dieter Fuchs stabbed the tip of his dagger over and over into the desk, gouging out large splinters of wood while he listened to the instructions coming from the other end of the crackling phone line. The desk was an antique, easily worth thousands of francs without the jagged fist-sized wound in the otherwise polished top. Fuchs didn't care. If felt good to destroy something so beautiful.

He was a slight man who looked as though he might blow away in a strong wind—with a high forehead and stubby ponytail. A quilted silk robe and plush slippers fended off the chill in the drafty farmhouse.

"I understand," Fuchs said. His words clipped, the verbal equivalent of snapping his heels together, demonstrating that he understood the gravity of the situation. "We leave tonight."

Fuchs hung up the phone and buried the point of his dagger in the desk, leaving it there when he turned.

A man standing at the dining table and a woman at the stove looked at him in anticipation. Both were about his age, tall, and muscular in counterpoint to his skeletal appearance. East German Olympians, Felix Becker was a gymnast known for his ability on the rings, and Selma Kraus a swimmer who excelled at the butterfly. Both had done well in the 1980 Moscow games, but that hardly mattered since half the world boycotted and did not show up. The '84 games were worse when their drug tests came back positive for anabolic steroids. Embarrassed by the revelation that their utopian athletes were doping, the East German sports federation did the sensible thing and swept those who were caught up in the scandal aside and went to work finding performance-enhancing drugs that were not so easily detectable.

Far from an Olympian, Dieter Fuchs saw exercise as something one did when chased by the authorities, not for a daily fitness routine. His father had been Ringvereine—Ring Club, a thief and a murderer—before Fuchs had put a dagger through the man's ear.

Selma Kraus brandished a large metal serving spoon. "Well?"

Felix Becker held a metal tray aloft. "We should eat these birds while they are hot."

Fuchs poured wine and Becker dished each of them three birds as they took their places at the table. They'd caught the ortolan buntings themselves that fall, with nets on their farm in southern France. Selma blinded each of the tiny songbirds with a quilting needle before putting them in a cage with all the millet they could eat. The blindness caused the buntings to gorge themselves, doubling their size to that of two thumbs instead of one. Felix took over when the birds were fat enough, drowning them in Armagnac and leaving them there to marinate. Eventually, they were roasted—Becker used a stopwatch to ensure exactly eight minutes—then plucked the little birds and served them whole on the plate, looking like little candied pears in their own juice. Traditionally, those who dined on ortolan bunting draped a cloth napkin over their faces, supposedly to hide their faces from God. Fuchs suspected the more likely reason was to hide their spitting the marinated bones and beaks into their dishes.

These three dispensed with the napkins. God knew them for what they were, napkin or no, and they'd done far worse than spit a few bones onto their plates. Besides, Selma crunched and swallowed everything save the beak.

"So," she said, holding a roasted bunting by its head, singed nubbins where its feet had once been, poised at her lips. A heavy jaw, one of the side effects of the performance-enhancing steroids, moved back and forth as if deciding when to strike. "Please tell me that was the colonel. All this idleness makes me fat."

She popped the bird into her mouth whole, turning it slowly with her tongue, eyes fluttering, head swaying on her powerful neck, cobra-like.

Fuchs inhaled the rich aroma of roasted bunting fat

and Armagnac. "Yes. A primary target and at least one additional. Perhaps more. He will leave instructions at the usual location."

The ortolan beak fell from Selma's lips, landing on the plate with a tiny clink.

"Is the primary a politician?"

"He's not been identified as of yet," Fuchs said.

"A defector, then," Felix mused.

"Schneider did not say." Fuchs picked up a bird, thumb and forefinger covering its mangled eyes. He was not a barbarian. "Enough of a troublemaker for the Stasi to want our services. We are to take care of whomever makes contact with this troublemaker."

"Americans?" Felix asked.

"Or Brits." Selma grunted, then licked the grease off the tips of her fingers. "I hate them both in equal measure."

"American," Fuchs said.

"Good." Selma wolfed down the last of her meal and rose from the table before the men even began. "I am going to see to my gear."

"Such a waste," Felix said after she'd gone. But he, too, rushed, spitting the bones of his last bird at the same time Fuchs bit into his first.

Incredibly rich, three buntings were more than plenty. Fuchs chewed slowly, alone at the table now, savoring the warm fat that made him think of roasted hazelnuts.

This new Soviet glasnost and perestroika were troubling. Too much openness was bad for business. Still, Fuchs supposed, as long as there was an East Germany, there would be room for people like him and his two friends. The Soviets—both GRU and KGB—had people within their ranks who took care of the wet-work, heavy-handed thugs who were capable of tossing people off balconies and knew their way around a crowbar but lacked the finesse to execute a seamless political assassination. The Americans were good, but they, too, preferred to handle such matters in-house, telling themselves blowing someone's brains out from a distance with a suppressed 7.62×51mm NATO projectile was just and patriotic for the cause of democracy. The East Germans were the Goldilocks of nations when it came to hiring contractors—brutal enough to have someone killed, sophisticated enough to want it done . . . just right, so long as their fingerprints were nowhere to be found.

Fuchs chewed slowly, cleaning each bone of meat with his tongue before spitting them one by one onto his plate. The Trinité would take care of the American contact—and anyone else who got in the way.

26

It wasn't like eligible men were at a premium or anything. As soon as she stepped off the train, Ruby Keller could see West Berlin was crawling with soldiers, staffers, and spies. Many of them single . . . some were what the girls in the office called "single beyond repair." Keller decided she could do a lot worse than Staff Sergeant Tony Peña on her first date since she'd arrived in Germany. She didn't admit it to Peña, but it was her first date in months.

He took her to a restaurant called Alter Kurg—the Old Jug—near Free University Berlin. It was an old place, and like many businesses in Berlin, looked as if it had been dropped in the middle of a neighborhood garden. The trees were bare now and the cobblestone walks covered with a skiff of fresh snow, but in the summer the place must have been a jungle.

The restaurant itself looked like something out of a

Grimms' fairy tale. Picket fence, whitewashed walls, and woodsy gingerbread trim.

Ruby's mouth began to water the moment they stepped inside, further warmed by the way Sergeant Peña's hand brushed the small of her back as the hostess showed them to their table.

It really had been a long time, and she promised herself this evening was going to be awesome.

Outside the restaurant, Colonel Rolfe Schneider of the East German Ministry for State Security stood in the shadows of trees and shrubs across König-Luise-Strasse. He watched Keller and her date go in. The Stasi man was patient if he was anything, and waited a full half-hour to allow the Rohypnol he'd paid the cooperative waitress to put into the girl's wine to take effect. The normal form of the powerful sedative turned drinks blue when mixed, making it imperative to mix it with a red wine or some other dark-colored beverage. Stasi chemists had come up with generic concoctions that were colorless and tasteless.

When Keller had time to be well into her cups, Schneider pointed a flashlight at a windowless van half a block down the street and flashed it on and off three times. The van's brake lights flashed twice.

At the same moment, a beat-up Mercedes sedan that had seen better days rolled to a stop in front of the garden center across the street from the restaurant. The driver, a young man with a balaclava covering his face, got out of the car. Smoke began to pour from under the hood as he trotted down the street, away from the van. The silhouette of a woman was visible in the passenger seat and a child's face pressed against the rear window.

Schneider flashed his light again, twice this time. A small explosive charge detonated in the bushes near the Mercedes, the blast strong enough to rattle the restaurant windows and get everyone's attention without destroying the car.

Patrons rushed from the building to investigate what they probably believed to be a car crash. Who, Schneider thought, did not become mesmerized by blood and mangled steel?

The windowless van disappeared around the block as Keller's date ran out to help. He was a soldier, after all, and surely wanted to play the hero in front of his girl.

Schneider's team had been careful not to set the Mercedes on fire. He wanted smoke, not flames—not because he cared about the welfare of the woman in the front seat, but because the rescuers needed to be able to save someone. A woman burning to death inside a car would not last nearly long enough to keep the crowd busy.

Inside Alter Kurg, Ruby Keller had to keep both hands flat on the table so she didn't slide out of her chair. She'd heard a noise. Glass breaking . . . and then Tony had run off. Just left her sitting there . . . Why had he done that? She swayed in place, squinting to make sense of her surroundings. Except for one old man in the back corner, every seat in the place was empty. They'd all run off . . . What in the hell was going on here?

Ruby tried to stand, wobbled, then the waitress appeared out of nowhere to help. At least she hadn't run off like Tony. That was good.

Then two men came in from the kitchen, beelining straight at her. Even groggy, she could tell something was off. She tried to stand, but one of the men grabbed her by the arms. The other man stooped low, grabbing her by the ankles. A hand snaked over her mouth, stifling a scream, clamping hard, a finger jammed against her nose so she couldn't breathe.

She threw her head back, like she'd been taught in church self-defense classes, but smashed against her own chair. One of the men laughed as they heaved her upward, one holding her under the arms, the other at her feet. The waitress got the doors. She wanted to fight, to rip these men's faces off with her fingernails, but her entire body felt impossibly heavy. Her arms refused to obey. Abject panic caused her to gag. The man at her arms cursed, jerking her shoulders sideways to twist her face away, trying and failing to steer clear of the eruption of vomit. She was vaguely aware of him ripping a cloth napkin off a nearby table as they passed and shoving it into her mouth.

"Choke on this!" he hissed.

The waitress protested. "You're going to kill her!"

The man shoved the cloth deeper. "If she dies, she dies . . ."

They took her straight out the kitchen doors and tossed her into the back of a waiting van.

The man covered in her vomit peeled off his sweater and threw it in the corner of the van. He loomed over the top of her, spewing curses and threats. Flat on her back, Ruby managed to work her jaw enough to spit out the napkin, gagging again.

"Oh, no you don't!" the man roared, red eyes glaring down at her—and then stomped her square in the face.

A cross the street, Colonel Schneider watched Ruby Keller's soldier date assist four others to rescue the drugged woman and her child from the smoke-filled Mercedes. The group cheered when the child sputtered and coughed.

She lived, Schneider thought. *That is good. Now they can all feel like heroes.*

The dark van emerged from the alley behind the restaurant and turned, speeding east.

27

The manager at the Imperial, a dinner club in the Mitte District not far from the Brandenburg Gate, provided Elke Hauptman with a chair when she sang, but she rarely used it. She had to be able to move. Dressed in faded high-waisted Levi's—her only pair, worth over two hundred American dollars—a white T-shirt, and a fake leather motorcycle jacket, Elke sang everything imaginable, from "Lili Marleen," a favorite of soldiers East and West, to Aretha Franklin's "Respect."

Despite living under a surveillance state, or maybe because of it, East Germans were a convivial lot when among people they knew well, given to fondue parties and socializing in groups. The Imperial was full of three such work clubs made up of a half-dozen or so couples each. There were more than a few unattached patrons, who'd come to drown their sorrow in watered-down alcohol or sour Berliner Weisse beer.

Most people paid little attention to the newspaper, knowing it was a propaganda arm of the DDR. Hollywood movies were deemed decadent in general, harmful to the well-being of the state. It was possible to get Western television—*Dallas* was a popular program. But you had to point your antennas in that direction, leading the Stasi to believe your heart and mind were pointed west as well.

It was much easier for couples to fill their time with card games and clubs, dancing, drinking—and coming to hear Elke Hauptman sing.

Some performers played to the audience, but Elke, caressing the mic, swaying her hips, sang for herself. For the most part, she ignored the crowds. Tonight, she forced herself to look at the others who were trapped in the East with her. The DDR liked to show off her talent and periodically sent her to sing in the West—always holding Uwe and Hans hostage so she wouldn't be tempted to stay. The money was good, but the people were too well dressed, too fat, too . . . happy.

Shared misery brought with it a perverse sense of peace. Swine going to slaughter were calmer when they went as a group.

Blinding stage lights made it impossible to see faces beyond a few tables away, but she finished her set with a cover of Pat Benatar's new single, "Invincible," for them, her fellow prisoners. Everyone in the club clapped or rapped feverishly on their tables with their knuckles, everyone, that is, except Kurt Pfeiffer, who slumped sullenly by himself at a table to the right of the stage, where he could see both the entrance and the exits. The gunman seat, he called it.

The stage lights dimmed, leaving her in the glare of Pfeiffer's hateful gaze. Elke shuddered when she saw him, as if an adder had slithered across her path.

She stripped off the faux-leather jacket and took a long drink of water from a glass on the stool beside her. The darkness of his approach was palpable and she had to will her hand not to shake.

Several audience members gathered around to greet her and compliment her on her singing. It didn't take long for them to recognize Pfeiffer for what he was and they parted like a biblical sea, scattering to give him a wide berth. Having a Stasi friend was akin to having the plague, and Elke wondered if anyone would ever come hear her sing again.

As always, Pfeiffer was dressed impeccably. A gold bar kept his tie and the collar of his starched shirt in perfect alignment. Matching gold cuff links glinted in the houselights as he clapped, slowly, bitterly, as if he were anything but amused.

Elke pulled a towel off the stool by her water glass and dabbed at her forehead. Her white T-shirt was soaked with sweat, rendering it virtually transparent. She regretted taking off the jacket but didn't want to give him the pleasure of seeing her put it back on.

She forced a smile. "What are you doing here?"

"The question," Pfeiffer said, menacing with his eyes, "is what are *you* doing here?"

Taken aback, she shrugged. "What does it look like I am doing here, Major? I am working."

"Is that so?" He sniffed the air, leering at her shirt. "Places of this nature often attract a vile sort of person—"

Elke nodded to a couple at a nearby table. "I will be sure to point that out to Herr Schuman, a general prosecutor for the Ministry of Justice. Herr Schuman is here with his wife, Christina. Or perhaps Herr Lutz, who is at the bar. I understand he is married to the general secretary's cousin."

Pfeiffer's lip began to twitch, but he regained his composure quickly. "Not the clientele," he said. "I'm speaking of those who prey on the clientele. Let me be blunt. HwG."

HwG was shorthand for *häufig wechselndem Geschlechtsverkehr*—roughly, one who has sex with frequently changing partners. A prostitute.

Pfeiffer licked his lips and then lit a cigarette. "How much money might a girl make while lying on her back, I wonder."

"You bastard," Elke said, unable to contain herself.

It was all she could do to keep from gouging his eyes out.

Pfeiffer took a drag from his cigarette, still eyeing her breasts through the T-shirt. "I have to say, your presence here, the whorish manner of your dress . . . It gives one pause—"

"You are the expert!" She leaned toward him, fuming,

spittle flying with each word. "If anyone has turned me into a whore it is you!"

"Be still!" Pfeiffer hissed. "I promise you—"

"Promise me what? That you'll ruin my family, my husband's career? It seems to me that the DDR needs my husband's work."

Several patrons looked up from their tables, unable to hear the conversation, but clearly aware there was a juicy altercation going on.

"You need to calm down," Pfeiffer whispered. He forced a smile, patting her on the shoulder to demonstrate to those around them that everything was all right. He took a beat to study her through a blossom of cigarette smoke, then, to show he was still in charge, said, "Your last song was shamefully subversive."

Elke folded her arms across her chest, disgusted and chilled by the clamminess of her T-shirt.

"The audience seemed to like it." She needed a drink of water but her hands shook too badly to lift the glass.

"Audiences love to wallow in Western bourgeois decadence. It is the instigator who bears the responsibility. I am telling you to stay away from that Benatar song." He blew smoke in her face. "The songs you sing make you sound like a whore."

She dug in. "'Invincible' is on the charts right here in the DDR! Your government has not stopped it."

A low growl rumbled from Pfeiffer's chest. "*My* government? Let me ask you, my dear. Just who is this enemy in the song? Who do you want to defy . . . to stand against? Is it me? The state?"

"It is a song, nothing more."

"And a joke is a joke," he said. "But jokes and songs tend to reveal one's true nature, they tend to, as they say, peel back the skin and show what is beneath."

She turned and grabbed her jacket off the edge of the stage. "I need to go home."

Pfeiffer leaned closer, pinning her. The cigarette dangled from his crooked lips. The French cologne he bathed himself in every morning pecked at her eyes like a stinking bird.

"I will ask you this one time," he said. "Are you following me?"

"What?"

He grabbed her brutally by the forearm, jerking her closer.

Elke yelped, tried to pull away, but his fingers dug in. The inevitable bruises would be difficult to explain to her husband.

The manager of the club started toward them, but she waved him off with her free hand.

"No," she said. "I am not following you. I told you. I am working. My performance here has been scheduled for months. Check with the office if you do not believe me."

"I will tell you what I think," he said. "I think all the applause and adoring fans have given you a counterfeit sense of your own power." He drew her to him as if to say good night. "If the Imperial is such a wholesome place, then why is sweet little Hansie not here to watch his mummy sing? I suppose it is past his bedtime. He must be asleep in his little wooden bed below the window with the latch that is not quite secure from the ledge of the fire escape . . ."

"Stop it!"

Pfeiffer put a hand flat over his heart. "Oh," he said, dripping with condescension. "I would never harm little Hans. We are such good friends. I often visit with him at his school. But I have to tell you, Elke Hauptman, there are many evil men in this world, horrible, depraved men who hunt for unlocked windows. So long as we are friends, then I simply offer you my protection. The safety of our sweet boy is entirely in your hands, my dear."

A tear rolled down her cheek, stopped by her quivering lip.

He frowned, mocking her. "Oh, my," he said. "We are not so invincible now, are we?" He stubbed his cigarette out on the edge of the stage. A malignant smile spread across his face. "Now, I have a room next door. Since you are already in the neighborhood, you may come up and sing to me."

28

Mary Pat Foley arrived at U.S. Mission Berlin off Clayallee well before she was supposed to meet Jack Ryan. A youthful CIA operations officer who introduced himself as Billy Dunn ushered her straight to the conference room. Case officers from the Agency station in Bonn had steered clear of USBER for this exercise, not wanting to alert the Germans that there was anything out of the ordinary going on.

Foley acknowledged Skip Hulse with a smile and a nod as she peeled off her coat and dropped it in a chair near the head of a long oval conference table. She and Ed had had Hulse and his wife to dinner many times over the years. Skip was a smart guy, the kind you wanted to have watching your back—even if he did look like he slept in his clothes. Other than Hulse, Foley counted seven others in the room, and she didn't really know any of them. She found herself marveling at how young the other case officers were. This new crop of college kids made her feel like part of the old guard, though she was still in her thirties.

"I'm glad they sent you," North said, mouth pinched, nose crinkled like she was on the perpetual verge of a sneeze.

"You don't look especially glad," Foley joked.

"Sorry," North said, shaking Foley's hand. "It's just that . . . I was the one who received this information. It gets old having Langley shove seventh-floor assholes down our throats when we are plenty capable of handling things ourselves."

"Ryan's stationed in London," Foley said. "Liaison to MI6."

"That's not exactly any better," North said, making a point Foley couldn't argue with. "They send a liaison analyst to show a base full of operations officers how we're supposed to get a read on a would-be defector."

"I hear you," Foley said. "I really do, loud and clear. But we all shoot where we're aimed. Believe me, I did some checking into the man's hall file as soon as I got the cable with this assignment."

A hall file was the watercooler talk, the down-low, the unofficial reputation that didn't go into a formal personnel record.

"And?" North asked. "What's the scoop?"

"Family man," Foley said. "I've met his wife. She's a

doc of some sort. Eyes, I think. Anyway, he doesn't strike me as a guy who has something to prove. Maybe a bit of a blue flamer, but I'm not sure that's his fault."

"We've known a few of those," North grumbled, arms folded so tightly across her chest her knuckles turned white. Foley was beginning to wonder if North knew something about Jack Ryan that she did not.

"Greer trusts him," Foley said. "That's enough for me."

Hulse rapped on the conference table with his coffee mug, getting everyone's attention. The six-person team from Helsinki had made it past the Army guards downstairs and were now filing in, still dressed for the winter weather in hats and scarves.

Hulse looked at his watch, shuffled his feet in place like an impatient horse in the gates before a big race, and then addressed the room.

"We're waiting on one more and then we'll start with introductions. I want everyone to know all the players before we begin. Too easy to start killing each other if this thing turns to shit."

A seventh man came through the door behind the Helsinki crowd and stood with them at the back of the room. He was tall, looked like he needed a shave. A wool coat was draped over one arm and he clutched a sable hat in his fist.

Billy Dunn, the youthful case officer who'd shown Foley in, leaned sideways. "I agree with Jen. We're busy enough here without another headquarters asshole dropping in to tell us how to hold our mouths right while we're doing our job."

Foley stifled a grin when the man with the sable hat took a half-step forward. "Please don't wait on the HQ asshole," Jack Ryan said. "He is present and accounted for."

Jen North rolled her eyes. Billy Dunn blanched ghost-white, attempting to shrink into the crowd.

Hulse didn't miss a beat.

"Welcome to Berlin," he said. "As you all know, we've had to bring in outside help for this operation. USBER case officers won't have direct involvement in making contact with CALISTO. East Berlin Station will be running the radio and monitoring station."

Ryan perked up, raising an eyebrow at the last. Foley gave a toss of her head, indicating that she would explain later.

At that same moment, the lights on the phone in the center of the conference table lit up and a military policeman escorted in a small man who hummed with so much energy he looked like he might at any moment burst into flames.

"That's Boone Grissom," Billy Dunn leaned sideways to explain to Foley. "Ranking official with the State Department. He wouldn't have clearance for this briefing."

"I apologize, Mr. Hulse," the MP said. "He wouldn't—"

Grissom flicked his hand, shooing the soldier away. "I told him he had to let me past or shoot me. You people need to answer your phones!"

"What can we do for you, Boone?" Hulse said.

"One of our FSOs has been taken."

Foley frowned. "Taken?"

"New girl by the name of Keller," Grissom said. "She's only been here a few weeks."

Jen North put a hand on the table to steady herself.

29

A Nevada highway patrolman trotted up to Sergeant Allred, hand on top of his Stetson campaign hat to keep it on in the stiff wind that barreled in from the red-rock desert. Pritchard, Murray, Harris, and the sergeant had all driven to the truck stop outside of Mesquite in hopes of finding any little detail from the abandoned child.

At any moment, a Utah Department of Public Safety chopper was supposed to pick up the agents and transport them to the FBI field office in Salt Lake, where they would set up a command center.

OSI Special Agent Gillum had returned to the site of the crash—and the homicides—to see if he could glean any further information that would help them find the UNSUB. At this point, even an entire footprint would be more than they had.

The abandoned rental car at Whitney Pocket came

back to a Bob Robertson out of Roswell, New Mexico. They'd found a pistol, reported stolen in California six years earlier, meaning it could have been in a dozen hands between the time of its theft and now. They had the UNSUB's clothing size. Large and tall. Basically, the same size Murray wore. This guy liked new socks and had a pile of them. Like two dozen. As if he just had to put a fresh pair on every day. To each their own. People were weird. He'd sent out a notice for agents to contact clerks at every department store between Las Vegas and the Canadian border to keep an eye out for a guy with a vague resemblance to Captain Kangaroo's handsome cousin who came in to buy a shitload of socks.

Cases had been broken on less.

The rest of the car's trunk was interesting, if not particularly helpful. Three hard-shell cases with foam cutouts—for a large pair of binoculars, a set of Soviet night-vision goggles, and a handheld thermal imager, also of Soviet manufacture, which meant it was the clunky tractor of thermal imagers.

Betty Harris, who was light-years ahead of Murray in the nurturing department, had bought the kid a milk-shake and now sat with him inside the store, drawing pictures in Harris's notebook.

Murray was on the pay phone briefing the deputy director when Sergeant Allred, having just spoken to his subordinate, wheeled in with a smile so large it looked like his cheeks might crack. He gave Murray a big thumbs-up and then pumped his fist, like an umpire might do to call an out on a base runner.

"Gotta go, sir," Murray said, and hung up the pay phone—checking for change out of habit as he folded open the door.

"What have you got?"

"You're not gonna believe it," Allred said. "The kid's mom is alive! Our numbnuts clunked her on the head and threw her in the back of her own car. Must have thought he'd killed her. Sounds like she used the metal spout on a can of oil she had in the trunk to jimmy open the lid and jump out when our guy stopped to take a leak."

"She get a good look at him?" Murray asked, feeling hope for the first time in hours.

"No," the sergeant said. "She was too busy crawling into the weeds."

"Smart," Murray said.

"But we got a plate and vehicle description. Gray 1984 Toyota Cressida. My office is putting out a BOLO now."

Murray glanced through the window at the little boy inside talking to Harris. "How bad is she hurt?"

"Pretty bad," Allred said. "She took a bad hit. Lot of swelling on the brain from what I understand. Lucky to be alive. They're prepping her for surgery now."

On the other side of the window, Harris brightened, and pointed behind Murray. He turned to see the approaching helicopter.

"Wonder if the kid's ever been on a chopper," he said. "Be nice to have him there when his mom wakes up."

30

Richter drove as fast as he dared, keeping to the interstate for a few miles before exiting to take surface streets.

The woman must have gotten out when he stopped to piss. It was brilliant using the oil can spout to pry open the latch. Just. Plain. Brilliant . . . And disastrous.

That was an hour ago, meaning the police could have all his information by now. They surely already had a description. Now they knew not only what he was driving, but his direction of travel. He began to hyperventilate, thinking he might as well go straight to the nearest office of the FBI and turn himself in.

He shook it off. *No.* This wasn't over. And he began to see that staying on the smaller streets was stupid. Traffic on the interstate was horrible, which was a good thing for him. Easier to get lost. He needed to disappear until transportation was arranged.

A police car passed him on the left, lights on, speeding toward some unknown emergency.

Gut churning, he got off the interstate again. It was time to part ways with the vehicle. He had his coat, his duffel, and a portion of an extremely secret American aircraft. From this point on, it would be safer to get out and walk. It was probably safe to take a taxi, as long as he did it quickly. It would take some time for the police to spread the word. He'd killed for this piece of metal, and he would kill again if he had to. Whatever it took to get it out of the country. Until then, he needed a place to hide, out of sight, where the authorities would not think to look.

31

Clark made it a habit not to sleep deeply when on an operation. Though dog-tired, his eyes flicked open to the sound of soft footfalls on creaking wood, moments before a knock at the bedroom door. The knock relaxed him. Threats rarely announced themselves on flimsy interior doors. Next came the smell of baking bread, which relaxed him even more. He glanced at his watch—four a.m.—and gave a long, groaning stretch, replaying the events of the previous night. He'd taken the time to brush his teeth and load the Glock, then passed out as soon as his head hit the pillow. Four hours of uninterrupted horizontal sleep in an actual bed was a godsend after the past few days.

Lotte Cobb's muffled voice carried into the room. "John, I am sorry to wake you, but we have cable traffic coming in."

Cold seeped in through a gap in the window frame,

so he'd slept in a T-shirt and sweats, allowing him to roll out of bed and open the door.

"Good to go, ma'am. What's up?"

With her silver hair braided and coiled into a tight bun, Lotte Cobb stood in the doorway drying her hands on a tea towel as if she'd just stepped away from the kitchen.

"We've received a standby order," she said. "Someone at the embassy has gone missing. There is a strong possibility that it is an abduction."

Lotte's light pink T-shirt, faded high-waisted Levi's, and a ruffled apron belied the troubling news. It was difficult to imagine that she'd lived through the horrors of World War II Berlin, until you looked at her eyes.

"Who?" Clark asked.

"No name was provided," Lotte said. "But the brief says it is one of the embassy staff. You are to await further instructions, which should be forthcoming within the next two hours."

It made sense. An abduction of someone at the embassy would throw a wrench into any plans Foley and Ryan had worked out. It was also unlikely to be a coincidence. The bosses at USBER and Bonn and D.C. and Langley were surely in a full-bore panic right now, rethinking strategy and getting ready to punt.

Clark's gut reaction was to rush to USBER to help track down the missing person—and deal with those responsible. But his mission parameters kept him on the outside of things, an unknown face in the crowd. Any attempt to contact officials at Berlin Mission directly would rob him of the anonymity he needed to protect Foley and Ryan.

"In the meantime," Lotte said. "I made you breakfast."

Clark checked his watch again. "You must have—"

"Sleep . . ." Her voice trailed off, punctuated by a little shrug. ". . . eludes me." She toyed with a lock of hair. "Come down and eat when you are dressed. That way you will be ready to go when the time comes."

Ten minutes later, with no further orders from Berlin Mission, Lotte Cobb sat Clark down to a table piled high with fresh rolls, assorted meats, and a platter of golden-brown potato pancakes.

Clark smiled, hand on his belly. "I'm not sure I—"

"Nonsense," Lotte said. "If I learned anything during the war it is to eat when there is food. You never know when you might be fed again."

She wiped her hands on a dish towel stuffed into the waist of her apron and began to fill Clark's plate.

"Where is Mr. Cobb?" he asked, taking her advice and slathering a roll with butter, suddenly hungrier than he'd imagined he would be.

"At the newsstand," she said. "We need the morning paper to unscramble any cable traffic that comes in after noon."

"Of course." Clark raised his coffee cup. "I really appreciate the hospitality, Mrs. Cobb. I am in your debt."

"Nonsense," Lotte said again. She turned to the same rolltop desk where her husband had retrieved the ammunition the night before and came out with a small wooden box. "I want to give you something else."

Clark wiped his mouth with a cloth napkin and pushed away from the table.

Lotte lifted the lid to reveal a small blue steel Browning Fabrique Nationale 1910 pistol in .32 ACP. Black Hand assassin Gavrilo Princip had used a similar gun chambered in .380 ACP to murder Archduke Ferdinand, kicking off the First World War.

She pushed the box toward Clark.

"Please," she said. "It is no fancy new Austrian Glock, but I believe it may be of some use to you if you find yourself in need of a pocket gun."

"I couldn't—"

"Please, John," she said. "It would make an old woman happy to see her pistol put to good use." She pulled her chair close to his and grabbed a potato pancake, holding it in both hands to nibble while she talked. "I killed many Nazis and more than a few Russian pigs with this."

Clark hefted the little gun, pulling back the slide to make sure it was unloaded. It was not.

She nodded, took the weapon, cleared it, and handed it back. "When I was a young girl, our guns were always loaded. We had to use them often."

"You were German resistance," Clark ventured, aiming the empty gun at the floor. The sights were minuscule, a needle-fine front almost impossible to see in the tiny rear notch. This was a weapon for close quarters, a get-back gun for fighting your way to something bigger. Though, even as a die-hard proponent of the venerable

.45, Clark had to admit a 60-grain .32 slug through the noggin could ruin someone's day.

"Yes," Lotte said. "I fought in the resistance alongside members of the British Special Operations Executive. Have you heard of them?"

Clark gave her a knowing smile. "SOE? Oh, yeah. Commandos and saboteurs working behind enemy lines."

"Just so," Lotte said. "That's how I met Richard. He was with the U.S. Office of Strategic Services, Special Operations."

"I can tell from the way he carries himself," Clark said.

The OSS had been extremely effective in gathering intelligence, breaking codes, and spreading disinformation and chaos throughout Axis powers during the war. To John Clark, operators like the Cobbs were giants, mythical gods.

He smiled. "So, the two of you worked together."

"For a short while," Lotte said. "I was only seventeen, but a war rears her young quickly. My time working alongside Richard was the finest two weeks and three days of my life up to that point. Then he was sent off by his commanders to fight some other battle. The war ended and I found myself a German woman in the smoldering ruins of a Berlin 'liberated' by Soviet troops. I assumed Richard Cobb had forgotten me."

"I see," Clark said, bracing himself for the rest of the story.

"You know," Lotte said, nibbling on the potato cake,

"the first group of soldiers who came through were brutal but professional. They simply lined up all our men and boys, shot them dead, and moved on. The second echelon . . ." Lotte looked as though she wanted to spit. "They were the monsters. Most were younger, less experienced in combat, cooks, logistics support, even women. I heard it said that no German female eight to eighty was safe . . . but even that is not right. Those dogs took anyone and everyone. If a girl resisted at all, she was shot in the neck . . . and then raped." Lotte gazed at nothing, reliving the horror. "Some girls' fathers hanged themselves out of shame. Mothers gave their raped daughters stones and told them to go drown themselves in the river . . . which many did. I knew my way around guns and knives, and I killed as many Russians as I could . . . Eleven that I am sure about. Three more who may have survived their wounds . . ."

Clark started to say something, but she raised her hand, needing to finish.

"Eventually," she said, "I ran out of ammunition and hid the gun. The assaults were so frequent that . . . I will spare you the details, but suffice it to say that I was forced to find a protector. Mine was a Soviet colonel named Andreyev, a pig who climbed on me only once a day and then pretended he was doing me a favor. He was, I suppose, because it kept me from being raped many times each day by roving gangs of soldiers."

Cobb's voice came from the front hallway. "Needless to say, I didn't much care for Colonel Andreyev. I gutted the bastard and left him to rot in a ditch as soon as I learned what was happening." Cobb dragged a chair across the dining room and sat down next to his wife. "No word?"

Lotte shook her head. "Not yet. But he is ready to go when we hear."

Cobb listed sideways, touching shoulders with his wife, then looked at Clark. "I'd been sent on assignment in Italy but came back as soon as I could to find Lotte."

"That was before the Wall," she said. "Richard took me with him to the American sector, where he had friends."

"And you stayed here," Clark said.

Cobb grabbed a potato pancake and a slice of beef, making a sandwich out of it.

"We did. I got out of the Army and started a lucrative trading business on the black market . . . not necessarily in that order. Turns out running a black-market operation gins up some useful information for the Agency— especially when over half my customers were Russians." He took a bite of his pancake sandwich, eyeing Clark while he chewed. "Ended up raising our boy here . . . How about you, son? The wife and I have pretty much vomited up our life stories. Don't tell us anything classified, but I deal with so many damned spooks, it's good to talk to another operator once in a while. Greer said we are to trust you completely. That's enough for us."

"You know Admiral Greer?"

Lotte gave a soft smile. "He has stayed many times in the same room where you slept last night. A good man."

"That is very true," Clark said. There were some

things he'd never divulge, like the fact that he'd grown up as John Kelly, but Jim Greer had seen enough potential in him to give him a new identity and let him start over.

Jim Greer never did anything without a reason. Sending Clark here, to these two particular contacts, had obviously been his idea of a reward . . . or therapy.

He considered telling them more about himself, but the habit of silence was just too ingrained. To their credit, they did not quiz him further, accepting him instead on Greer's word . . . and what they had seen firsthand.

Not one to sit idly for long, Clark rolled his neck, wincing at an old injury from when he was John Kelly.

Cobb saw it and gave him a tight smile. "Take it from me, someday you're going to look back and remember that scrap you had with the Russians last night in crimson detail and say to yourself, *So that moment is why this rib feels like shit . . .*"

A light above a door in the hallway illuminated and a soft chime sounded, indicating incoming traffic on the communication equipment in the closet.

Cobb stood with a groan, hand on his back, and hobbled to the door. "Speaking of ribs that feel like shit . . ."

Five minutes later, Clark was ready to go, outfitted with a heavy wool coat the Cobbs loaned him.

"We'll scan it for isotopes every time you come back," Lotte said.

"I'd appreciate that," Clark said. He was going to be operating on the other side of the Wall and Stasi agents were known to plant radioactive materials on clothing to make it easier for them to follow a target. The Glock came with a funky little plastic holster. Clark dismissed it as being a gimmick at first, but it turned out to be serviceable—and vastly superior to stuffing the pistol down his waistband. That looked cool in the movies, and might even work in a pinch, but there were few feelings more sickening than having a gun slide down the inside of your pant leg and hit the floor at an inopportune moment. The Glock was big, but so was Clark, and he was able to conceal it on his belt at four o'clock as long as he kept his sport coat on. Lotte's little FN .32 went in the pocket of his overcoat.

Cobb noted the Fairbairn Sykes. "Truth be told, you'll probably have more use for that than the handguns."

Lotte tucked a roll of East German twenty-pfennig coins into his pocket, along with a piece of yellow cloth she'd folded inside a small plastic sandwich bag. "I sprayed a handkerchief with Lysol," she said. "We fret about Stasi bullets, but the greatest danger in Germany at this moment may well be the filth that slimes the pay phones . . ."

earing pain jolted Ruby Keller awake, shooting from her jaw up the side of her ear. An odd clicking noise pecked at her senses, compounding the throbbing ache in her head and adding to the tumult in her belly. An unbearable weight pressed against her chest, making it difficult to breathe and impossible to move.

She caught the sound of gurgling water nearby. The smell of raw sewage overpowered a sweeter odor of freshly dug earth.

Memories of her abduction flooded back.

Moist earth . . . Dripping water! Had they buried her alive?

Above her a man gave a low chuckle, genuinely amused.

It took her a moment to realize her hands and feet were tied. She was strapped to something, a board or a gurney. She arched her back, screaming impotent threats against her gag, throwing her weight from side to side.

A sickening blow impacted the side of her skull, rattling her but not knocking her out.

"You'll kill her!" a female voice snapped. It was the waitress from the restaurant.

A man laughed, then coughed up a mouthful of phlegm and spat. "You gave her enough dope to kill a horse. She dies, that's not my problem."

A sense of doom crept in, overwhelming Keller's mind and body. The mumbled voices grew distant, the pain in her head suddenly more intense, and then all went black.

33

Ryan and Foley met privately with the six members of the Helsinki team—four men, two women. Foley did the lion's share of the talking, discussing plans and protocols. She was a known entity. Ryan was not even close. The team would travel as tourists, out to explore the East. Ryan and Foley would work to lose any tails they picked up on crossing, then link up with a case officer from the U.S. embassy in East Germany for the communications gear they would need. From that point on, any stop by the authorities and they would be identified as spies.

Foley cut the team loose after only ten minutes, with a plan to link up at a predetermined rally point once they were in the black, i.e., without any hangers-on, and they left to begin their SDRs—surveillance-detection routes.

CIA USBER staff waited in their cubicles and offices, fuming at being incommunicado until Ryan and Foley were gone and clear. State, military police, and the FBI were working the missing staffer case—further infuriating case officers, who felt they should have been involved. No one wanted to be told they were not trusted, and still, deep down, everyone there knew it was not only possible but probable that there was a traitor among them, maybe in the room, certainly in the country. The list of moles who'd infiltrated Western intelligence was pitifully long—names like Blake and Bennett, spies who'd done terrible damage to American and British intelligence operations and outed hundreds of Western assets, who were tortured and executed.

None of them had been told anything regarding the contents of the disk, but Foley was extra cautious, making certain no one was able to get word to compatriots on the outside. Phones, radios, even window shades were to be left untouched.

With the Helsinki team on their way, Ryan and Foley met privately with Skip Hulse in his office. Hulse all but fell into his squeaky office chair and leaned back to stare up at the ceiling, rubbing his face.

"I hope the intelligence CALISTO is offering up is juicy," Hulse said. "Because this is killing our morale."

"Look, Skip," Foley said. "We're not trying to—"

"You don't need to say anything." Hulse tugged at his collar. "I understand the need for secrecy and compartmented information. Hell, we all do, but that doesn't make it easier to swallow for any of us. Especially considering the situation with the Keller woman. I can't begin to—"

A knock at his door cut him off and Jen North peeked her head in.

"Sorry to intrude, Skipper." She smiled at Foley, surely looking for an ally. "But I wanted to give you my perspective before you head out."

Foley glanced at Ryan, then Hulse.

Hulse rocked forward in his chair, flicking a hand to wave her into the office. "She's okay," he said to Foley. Then, to North, "I'll give you two minutes, more than that and people will start forming a line. I don't have time to hear that many perspectives."

"Thank you," she said. "I've been in Germany long enough to have contacts on both sides of the Wall. Let me use them to try and find the girl—"

"Look, Jen," Hulse said. "I know you feel some level of kinship for this kid. You were the one who handled the walk-in. But law enforcement is handling that side of things. Whoever this defector turns out to be, we're not blowing the op over a girl who's probably at the bottom of the Spree River by now."

Foley grimaced. "That's a hell of a dark place to go from the jump, Skip."

"Oh, you think *that's* a dark place?" Hulse said. "You know what these bastards are like, Mary Pat. If they suspect Keller has even a shred of information about this mysterious defector that she has not shared, they will . . ." He shook his head. "Let's just say the bottom of the river would be a merciful end."

"There's another possibility," North said. "What if

she's gone to ground?" Her eyes flicked from Hulse to Foley to Ryan, studying them for a reaction.

"'To ground'?" Ryan mused.

"On the run."

Hulse scoffed. He started to say something, but Foley cleared her throat, getting his attention.

"Kidnapping a mother and child and setting their car on fire . . . That seems like an elaborate ruse. Why would she go to all that trouble when she could have slipped away in the night?"

"Because she wants us to think she's been taken," North said, still laser-focused on Foley's reactions, as if she were the one conducting an interrogation. "I have a suspicion that this girl is not who she says she is."

"Jen . . ." Hulse sighed, rubbing his face again. He rested his hand on top of his head as he spoke. "I thought you were going to give us some—"

"Listen," North said. "Langley is accusing us of having a mole in our midst—"

"No," Ryan said. "The *defector* said no locals. We're following instructions as a precaution. Nobody is accusing anyone of anything."

North scoffed. "Right. And we just take the shithead at his word. For all we know this keeper of oh-so-special East German secrets is no more than some lunchy diplomat who's been screwing his boss's wife. Now he wants us to rescue him before he ends up in prison for 'disparaging an organ of the State.'"

"Jen," Hulse said again.

"And anyway," North pushed ahead, "if this guy can get to the West so easy to drop off a computer disk, why didn't he just come to us then?"

"A question we're sure to ask him," Ryan said.

"I just think we're ignoring the possibility that Keller fabricated all of this and you guys are walking into a trap."

"We'll keep that in mind," Foley said.

"Thank you, Jen." Hulse nodded toward the door, the look on his face leaving no room for more of her theories.

"Don't say I didn't warn you," North said. "That bitch is going to get someone killed." She threw up her hands and left, slamming the door behind her.

"Damn," Foley said under her breath. "Seems like there's some kind of bad blood there. Did she know Ruby Keller before she was approached?"

"Not that she's admitting," Hulse said. "This is the first time she's voiced those concerns."

"Her theory could make sense," Ryan observed.

"You think?" Foley said. "Absent the bug-eyed ranting, this seems like it's something personal to her."

"I know," Hulse said. "Jen's just . . . Well, you know her background with Buckley. She's got trust issues with the higher-ups."

Ryan glanced at his watch.

"I know you need to go," Hulse said. "But I feel like it's my duty to let you know what you'll be facing on the other side. Mary Pat's been across before. But this is going to be new to you."

Ryan wasn't exactly a neophyte when it came to hairy situations, or the communist intelligence apparatus for that matter, but he kept that to himself.

"For instance," Hulse said, "it's estimated that there was at least one Gestapo agent per every two thousand citizens under the Third Reich." Hulse stabbed the top of his desk with his forefinger to make his point. "But in the GDR, we estimate that if you put ten people in a room, at least one of them would be a Stasi officer or a part-time Stasi cooperator. I'm guessing it's more than that. Kids rat out parents, students report professors, friends betray friends. Three short miles from where you are standing now is an honest-to-God Orwellian nightmare. Just thinking ill of Erich Honecker is a crime. As far as the East Germans are concerned, the Soviets have shit the bed entirely, spending every spare ruble in a race to beat us in defense spending—spare rubles that used to help prop up their utopia of the GDR. Everyone is afraid to tell him the great experiment is failing. Their currency is worthless anywhere else. They're keeping the country solvent by selling political prisoners back to the West or charging us to dump toxic waste inside their borders."

Ryan nodded. "And that weakness makes them dangerous."

"Absolutely," Hulse said. "Very dangerous. Jason Newell is the station chief on that side, he and his people will do their best to take care of you if things turn rodeo, but we'll have about as much chance as rescuing you from the surface of the moon if the Stasi picks you up."

Now Hulse looked at his watch. "I don't believe in

coincidences. Keller's disappearance means the other side knows CALISTO exists. They'll be going out of their minds trying to find out who he is. I know I don't need to say this, but I'm going to say it anyway. The easiest way to find their leak and put a hole in his head is to follow you to him."

"That's what the Helsinki team is for," Foley said.

"You ever do an SDR, Ryan?"

"Surveillance-detection route?" Ryan gave a somber nod. "Not many."

"Follow Mary Pat's lead, then," Hulse said.

"We'll be just fine," Foley said. "Speaking of backup, I need to borrow your secure phone and leave a message for the insurance Greer set up for us."

Hulse waved a hand at the bulky STU-II—the secure telephone unit in a dedicated cabinet beside his credenza—and handed Foley a small metallic card.

She inserted this key into a slot on the phone and made the call. The STU would encrypt her conversation, which would be decrypted by someone with a similar unit and similar key on the other end.

"Need me to step out?" Hulse asked.

Foley waited for the line to connect. "No need," she said. Then, into the handset, "Go secure." She turned a knob on the face of the machine and then, waiting a beat, said, "Let him know we are good to go. Checkpoint RAG-GEDY ANN at the time agreed . . . Yes . . . That is all."

Foley turned the knob back to "normal," replaced the handset, and then returned the key to Hulse.

"And away we go," she said.

Hulse rose from his desk and shook Foley's and Ryan's hands in turn before stepping to the door. He stopped, turning, like Detective Columbo with "Just one more thing."

"You want to leave a letter or anything for Ed? How about you, Ryan? Want to write a quick note I can get to your wife if things . . . don't go as planned?"

"What happened to you, Skipper?" Foley shook her head. "You've always been a deep thinker, but this Eeyore shit is starting to wear thin."

"The Cold War happened to me, Mary Pat," Hulse said.

"Skip," Foley said. "Would you mind—"

"Rest easy," he said. "We'll all hang out here long enough for you to get across. I'll keep everyone off the phones. If you pick up a tail, it won't come from this office."

Skip Hulse wasn't really surprised when he didn't find Jen North sitting peacefully at her desk. She was obviously pissed about this whole deal and probably in the break room bending someone else's ear. She wasn't one to keep quiet once she'd latched on to a pet theory.

He didn't find her in the break room, either, and was beginning to worry, when he stopped at Billy Dunn's cubicle.

"Is Jen in the head?"

Dunn looked from the file he was reading. "She's gone, boss."

"What?"

"Yeah," Dunn said. "I thought you knew. She told us you sent her on an urgent assignment. She didn't say it, but I inferred it was something to do with the missing Keller girl. I volunteered to go with her, but she was out the door before I could get any details."

A frown crept over Hulse's face.

"Hold the phone," Dunn said. "You didn't tell her she could go?"

"I did not," Hulse said.

"You don't think she's the—"

"No, Billy," Hulse said. "I don't. She's worried about that girl to the point where she's lost her mind and willing to risk her career, but no way she betrays her country." He scoffed, turning the possibilities over in his head. "Nah. No way. Not a chance."

"Due respect, boss," Dunn said. "But it sounds like you're trying to convince yourself."

"Come with me," Hulse said, striding quickly to North's desk. He opened the side drawer where she kept the Heckler & Koch P7 she favored for personal defense. He groaned when he saw the pistol was missing.

"Spread the word around the office. I'll cable East Berlin Station. I want her located and brought in. If the Helsinki team by chance calls in, let them know what's going on."

"I'm not even sure what is going on."

Hulse glowered. "Billy . . ."

"But, boss," Dunn said, "you told us all to stay here. She didn't. We should bring her in."

"Get everyone ready to go, but tell them to stand by until I give the go order."

"Should we take weapons?" Dunn asked.

The average CIA officer was not, as many believed, the James Bond type, armed beneath his tuxedo with a Beretta or Walther PPK in a slick chamois holster. Most would spend their entire careers wielding nothing more deadly than an encrypted radio. The idea of carrying a handgun set Dunn's chin twitching with anticipation.

"Seriously, Billy," Hulse said. "You think Jennifer North is going to shoot you?"

"She took her gun."

"For protection, I'm sure. Now go tell the rest of the team. I have calls to make."

As soon as Hulse turned around, Billy Dunn opened his desk drawer and retrieved a little five-shot Smith & Wesson .38 Special, opened the cylinder to make sure it was loaded, and then stuffed it into the pocket of his khakis. Jen North wasn't going to be the only one carrying protection.

Skip Hulse spoke over his shoulder as he walked away. "Careful, Billy. Carry it that way, you might blow your brains out."

34

North hit the ground at a steady trot as soon as she left the building, blowing vapor like a freight train. Cold air pinched her nose and burned her lungs, forcing her to slow to a ground-eating walk, zigging and zagging, toward the U-Bahn station at the Free University. Then, doubling back on herself, she walked a block out of the way to a pay phone.

In addition to her pistol, she'd grabbed a wig, a large pair of glasses, and a device that looked like a small calculator from her desk drawer before leaving the office.

Early on, when her relationship with Schneider had taken the insanely natural turn from lovers to mole and handler who muddled frequent sex with her treason, he'd written a phone number on a cocktail napkin beside the bed. He passed it to her, then let his fingers do the walking while she memorized it. Twenty minutes later, when her breathing grew frantic and her thoughts were otherwise deeply engaged, he stopped what he was doing and demanded she recite the telephone number back to him. Even now, two years in, he often quizzed her on the number at the most inopportune moments.

Someone needed to intercept Ryan and Foley at Checkpoint Charlie—East Germans called it the Friedrichstrasse Border Crossing Point. If there was ever a time to use the emergency phone number, it was now.

Any call from West Berlin to an East Berlin exchange required an 0372 prefix—the dialing of which would likely set off trip wires at half a dozen intelligence agencies that kept tabs on such calls. The East was cordoned off, but relatives called one another from either side of the Wall more and more every day, talking about everything from the weather to wish-list items from the West, like blue jeans or metal plumbing fixtures. North would keep her call quick and generic, hoping to get lost in the chatter.

The phone rang twice in that extra-urgent tone spy movies tended to get right before a woman answered with the last four of the extension. In typical German fashion, she used two sets of two-digit numbers. Instead of five-one-six-seven, she greeted North with *"Einundfünfzig, siebenundsechzig."* Fifty-one, sixty-seven.

"Dolly Dupont, guten Tag!" North said, introducing herself. *"Bitte sagen Sie ihm, dass die Leitung besetzt ist."*

Please tell him the line is busy.

It sounded perfectly normal to anyone who happened to be listening in on the call.

The lady on the other end asked North to hold for a moment. Then, approximately ten seconds later, told her to go ahead.

Before placing the call, North had inserted a sewing needle into an almost invisible hole on the side of a TI SR-52, converting it from a working calculator to a device capable of digitizing encoded messages if she simply held the device to the telephone receiver. The Stasi clerk on the other end of the call had placed her handset on an acoustic coupler that would decrypt the message. The Stasi's Technical Operations Sector nerds dubbed the device a *Schnellgeber*—or speed-giver.

The message was simple and concise.

"Ryan and Foley crossing on foot Friedrichstrasse as Jack and Mary Avery. 4M, 2F already there to greet/ backup . . ."

North followed with basic descriptions for the six members of the team from Helsinki.

With her message sent, North hung up, making certain she used the needle to switch the SR-52 back to calculator mode. She'd call and talk to Schneider in person as soon as she crossed—if she wasn't in a CIA holding cell by then.

Skip Hulse was more than a little naïve when it came to trusting people, but even he would be smart enough to call the guard shack at Checkpoint Charlie and have them stop her if she tried to cross. It was the entry point for all Allied nation personnel and non-German tourists who wanted to cross to the East. So, for today, she would just have to be German and cross at Friedrichstrasse station. Her German was impeccable and, though the travel documents Schneider provided said she was a citizen of the DDR, he'd added an innocuous annotation in the lower-left corner of her identity card so the Pass and Control units of the Border Police would know to let her cross unmolested.

North slowed in front of a shop selling designer shoes, using the reflection in the window to check her six o'clock on both sides of the street. CIA operations officers were creatures of habit—and she knew their habits. Oh, they all tried to be clever and creative, and some were better at it than others, but if they didn't see a tail, people tended to grow lazy after a few minutes of a surveillance-detection route. Even North, who was considered one of the best, fell back on the same techniques when tailing someone. Army CID, Air Force OSI, DIA, they all attended much of the same training. She would be able to spot them if by some long shot they'd been able to get spooled up in time to be looking for her already.

Of course, depending on what Skip Hulse believed about her now that she'd disobeyed his embargo on leaving the office, tailing her might be the last thing on his mind. He might well just put a bag over her head and drive her to some dark German forest or secret NATO bunker for a lengthy interrogation. She shivered at the notion. Truth be told, there were monsters in every agency, in every country—even good American patriots who would pull out a fingernail or two if the need arose. She should know . . .

North rubbed her eyes with a thumb and forefinger, trying in vain to pinch away the thumper of a headache. This shitstorm was still salvageable, maybe. It had to be. Everything depended on silencing CALISTO, and to do that, North had to know who he was. Ruby Keller was either very guilty or very innocent. And if she was guilty, she held the key. If she was innocent . . . North didn't want to think about that.

35

Keller woke to a musky antiseptic smell and the distant snap of boots walking across a hard floor. She tried to open her eyes, but they would not cooperate. The way her head felt, she would not have been surprised to find they were matted shut with blood. Every part of her body seemed to have clocked out. She was in a bed, her head was killing her, and this place stank. No, that wasn't quite right. The smell was annoying but not altogether ugly. It was like a barnyard . . . if all the animals were human, sweating, and crowded in together—

A whispered voice nearly sent Keller out of her skin.

"*Sehr gut*. You are awake."

The sudden sound broke the spell, and her eyes flicked open. It took her a moment to realize the young woman in the bed next to hers was speaking to her in English. Keller squinted, trying to focus her vision. The woman's face looked friendly as she slowly came into focus, but trying too hard made Ruby's head hurt worse. She could tell it was covered with freckles. It was enough to know that much for now.

Keller attempted to sit up, but the throbbing ache in her brain pressed her back against the pillow, the case obviously starched by someone who didn't realize that pillows were supposed to be comfortable. She tried to rub her eyes but found her right wrist was chained to the bedrail.

"What in the actual hell?"

Something was wrong with her neck, so she had to move her entire upper body to look around. The walls of the sorry little medical ward were covered with sickly yellow floral wallpaper, the floors busy linoleum. There were four beds, but she and the freckled woman beside her were the only two patients. There were no guards, but that mattered little since there were no windows, either.

"Jail, sweetie," the girl beside her said.

Keller had to keep her tongue away from her broken teeth, making her sound like she had a mouthful of marbles when she spoke. Only then did she realize that someone had taken her blouse and dressed her in a backless gown. The thought of strangers stripping off her clothes while she was unconscious made her want to throw up.

"But why . . . ? How did I . . . ?"

"You don't remember?"

Keller dabbed at her jaw with her left hand, sure it was

broken. "I don't. I had a drink . . . There was a fire and my date went outside . . ." She rattled the handcuffs, trying to cut through the fog of pain. "Was I drunk? I just . . . I need to call the consular office."

"Oh, me too," the girl said and grinned, almost but not quite mocking her. "My name is Mitzi, Mitzi Graff. Sadly, I know why I am in here."

"Why?"

"I chopped off my boyfriend's toe with an ax."

Keller shuddered. "That's awful."

"Do not feel sorry for him," Graff said. "It was the same toe he used to kick the shit out of me. Do not waste your tears. Anyway, the asshole has friends in the People's Police. They put their boots to my door and arrested me faster than you could say *eine, zwei, Polizei*." She put a hand on her belly and cocked her head. Auburn hair fell across the shoulder of her blue jumpsuit. "You know the counting game? *Eine, zwei, Polizei*?"

"My grandfather used to sing it with me when I was small. One, Two, Police. The kids at school . . ." Her voice trailed off when it dawned on her what Graff had said. "Friends with . . . Who did you say?"

"The People's Police," Graff said. "I'm pregnant, so they will be keeping me in here overnight to make sure—"

"You mean the Bundesgrenzschutz," Keller said. "The West German federal police."

"I wish that were the case," Graff said. "In the DDR it is the People's Police."

"I can't be . . . I'm not in East Berlin!"

"Tell that to the Stasi guards when they come for you," Graff said. "I'm sure they will see their mistake immediately and set you free."

Keller choked back a tear.

Graff shook her head, a freckled cheek pressed against the pillow. "I am sorry," she said. "I should not joke. It is not funny at all. I joke when I am frightened."

An awful hissing suddenly filled the room, harsh, like thousands of angry whispers.

Keller's eyes flew wide. She tugged against the chains. "What is that?"

Graff raised her head off the pillow for a moment and then lay back down again. "They are filling one of the wet cells."

"What"—she gulped—"is a wet cell?"

"Ugh . . . It is the most awful thing. But do not worry. They only make you believe you will die."

"What . . . Why? I haven't done any . . ." She paused.

"There." Graff stabbed the air with her index finger. "Whatever it was you were thinking about at the instant that made you go quiet. *That* is the reason you are in here."

"Are you an American?"

Graff glanced up at the camera in the corner of the ceiling, then shook her head again. "German. My mother was a translator after the war. She made me learn English. I speak Russian, too. I think that is why they don't kill me." She rolled up farther on her side, hand on her belly now. "Do you happen to speak Russian? That might help you stay alive."

"No," Keller said, incredulous. "I . . . No, I don't speak Russian. Why would they want to kill me?"

"Why does the Stasi do anything? Listen to me. A little advice. If they come into your cell, just make your mind go somewhere else. Somewhere . . . happier. What they do will be easier that way."

"Holy shit!" Keller began to hyperventilate. "What . . . What are you saying? Do you really think they would come to my cell and . . . do that to me?"

Graff nodded. "I am sorry. Listen, I think they will leave me here in the clinic all night. When it gets too bad, tell them—"

The metal door creaked open and slammed against the wall with a deafening clang.

A guard in a green uniform loomed at the opening, hands behind his back, out of sight.

"Sechsundneunzig!" he barked.

Keller could only lie there and stare at the horrible man. This couldn't be happening.

"Sechsundneunzig!"

"He wants you to sit up," Graff whispered.

"But he said—"

"Right. Ninety-six," Graff said. "That is your cell number. They will never call you by your name." She gave a noticeable shiver and said under her breath, "Your cell is in the U-boat."

"Submarine?" Keller jerked against the chains, searching futilely for any way out. She had to get away from these people. "What's the U-boat?"

"You will see," Graff whispered.

The guard stomped into the room.

"Du sprichst nicht!" No talking!

Keller pretended not to understand and whispered to Graff, "Tell them what?"

"Huh?"

Keller was frantic. She had to know what Graff had been trying to tell her. "If they try to rape me," Keller said, "you said I should—"

The guard brought a wooden rod down hard across the top of Keller's thighs.

The explosive pain snuffed out Keller's scream. She shot a terrified look at Graff, who pursed her lips and looked away.

A second guard strode through the door and assisted the first, releasing Keller from the bed and wrenching her hands behind her back to cuff them. Every screaming command was to Ninety-six, landing on Keller's ears like incoming artillery. The men had her cuffed and moving in no time. They dragged her out the door and down the hall toward a set of stairs leading into the shadows . . . to the windowless U-boat cells below Hohenschönhausen Prison.

36

The taller of the two guards who'd dragged Keller from the medical clinic removed her handcuffs at the door and gave her a shove in the small of the back, pushing her the rest of the way into cell 96, a ten-by-ten enclosure with sad-looking rust streaks dripping down the concrete walls. The light fixture in a metal cage in the center of the ten-foot ceiling was bright enough that she had to squint after coming from the dim halls. She wasn't sure, but she thought she'd heard the shorter guard call the tall one Wolfe, so to her, that became his name. It was something to hold on to, to wrap her mind around.

Wolfe was direct, even brutal in his application of discipline if Keller strayed out of line or spoke when she was supposed to be silent—which was all the time except when directly addressed by a guard. Wolfe seemed to believe he was just doing his job and did not appear to hold any personal grudge. The shorter, probably younger, guard was nothing less than a tyrant, intent, it seemed, on punishing Keller for the smallest infraction. His commands dripped with such derision that she began to believe he must have blamed her for every slight and injustice he'd experienced in his life. He had a tendency to rise up on his toes when he screamed at her, flecking her cheeks with spittle.

Together, the guards made it perfectly clear that there were rules in Hohenschönhausen Prison. Rules that had to be followed or the consequences would be severe.

She fell when they shoved her into the cell, scraping silver dollar sized wounds on her knees. Keller's grandfather had immigrated to the United States before the war. She'd grown up listening to him and spoke passable German, but the angry shouts from the guards were nothing but gibberish. A moment later, a shadow passed over the far wall as if someone else had walked up behind her. She chanced a quick look over her shoulder and got the point of a rubber truncheon jammed in her kidney.

The pain sent her sagging to her knees. She grabbed the edge of the wooden bed to keep on her feet. Out of the corner of her eye, she caught a glimpse of a female guard. The guard wore the same uniform as Wolfe and his partner, but where they were bareheaded, she wore a peaked hat pulled low over her eyes.

"Face the wall!" Wolfe screamed.

It slowly dawned on her that except for a few ranting threats, the guards rarely said more than three things. "Come!" "Stop!" "Face the wall!"

The female voice spoke next, quiet clicking words, far more terrifying than the screaming men. They could hurt her physically, even rape her, but it was apparent in just a few moments that this woman wanted to kill her soul.

Though the woman spoke German like the men, her orders were more precise, easier to understand, and far more chilling. If spiders could talk . . .

"Remove your clothes!"

Keller shuddered. Once more, she tried to look behind her, and once more felt the blunt force of the truncheon in her back.

"Face the wall!" a male voice barked. Wolfe.

The hospital gown slid easily off her shoulders. She placed it at the foot of the bed, next to a folded blue jumpsuit she'd not noticed until that moment. She picked up the suit to put it on, bringing another volley of orders and insults.

"Remove everything!" the female guard said.

Keller froze, earning another vicious blow from the truncheon. She gritted her teeth, trying to steel herself, but unable to keep her body from shaking. She could feel Wolfe and his partner still behind her, leering.

"Now!"

Jolted into action at the prospect of further beating, Keller scrambled out of her underwear and stood naked and trembling, her toes digging into the filthy concrete floor.

The female guard put her through a series of squats and coughs and turns, a strip search ostensibly to be certain she wasn't bringing contraband into the facility, but designed to maximize humiliation. Keller was forced to look at her feet throughout the process, avoiding eye contact with the guards.

"Face the wall!" the female guard barked when Keller finished her third complete turn.

Keller yelped when the truncheon brushed her at the base of the neck. It slid slowly down her back, then paused at the top of her hip. She stopped breathing.

Gruff voices carried down the hall, men's voices, followed by the snap of boots.

Keller felt a sharp pain on her buttock, like a sting or the jab of a hypodermic needle. This bitch had just pinched her, hard, as if she wanted to leave her mark.

"Get dressed!" the woman snapped.

Keller complied instantly, yearning for the relative safety of the coarse blue coveralls and flimsy slippers.

Wolfe took over issuing the commands, each given with an air of finality, as if a comprehensive exam was sure to follow.

"No sitting! No leaning on the wall! No touching the wall! Sleep at ten p.m. sharp!"

He listed off myriad other rules as if they were all obvious and she should already know them. She was to lie flat on her back at ten p.m. The single blanket would be used to cover her body, but her arms and hands were to remain by her sides and on top of the blanket when she was asleep. Wolfe did not explain in detail, but Ruby learned through experience that if she made the horrible error of rolling onto her side or pulling a hand under the blanket in the middle of the night a guard would awaken her and remind her of the correct sleeping position. The light stayed on, and strange, throbbing music played incessantly. Every hour, a guard would walk down the hall, visiting the cells one by one, lifting the peephole covers and shouting, "You are ordered to be asleep!"

It would have been laughable if it were not so cruel.

37

Elke Hauptman gave a pitiful yelp when her husband walked up behind her in the kitchen. She threw a hand to her chest, catching her breath, forcing a grin.

"Why do you sneak around like that?"

Uwe wore a Nordic ski sweater this morning, tan with lines of tiny evergreens. It was her favorite piece of his clothing—one that she had often worn to bed when they were younger and they did not have to deal with all the bullshit that weighed them down now. The sweater made him look like a woodsman, strong and virile like he actually was.

"Are you all right?" he asked. "I worry for you."

"I am fine," she said. "It is that upcoming trip. You know how singing in the West always makes me jumpy." She leaned forward, whispering so that bastard Pfeiffer's microphones would not pick her up. "I wish you and Hans could come with me."

"We'll come see your next show here. How about to-night?"

"I would like that." Her lip quivered when she lied, so she feigned a cough to cover it up. They had been married long enough that she doubted he bought it. She checked her wristwatch. "I'm sorry. I really must go." Then, louder for the listening ears, "There's a broiler bar beside the club. I'll pick us up some nice chicken for dinner."

Uwe touched her face, more tenderly than she felt she deserved. "Someone your age should not live on the perpetual verge of a heart attack."

Elke trapped her husband's hand and held it gently against her cheek, savoring the surety of it.

"I love you, Uwe Hauptman," she said. "I . . . I will see you tonight." Her lip began to quiver uncontrollably. She kissed him quickly, grabbed her purse from the cupboard, and hurried out the door.

Everything she was about to do, she was doing for him and their son.

Uwe Hauptman told Hans to put on his coat as soon as the door shut. Lorna Shuman, a twenty-year-old mother of a new baby from down the hall, had agreed to watch Hans so he could surprise his wife at work.

Hauptman couldn't tell if Elke was having an affair or

if she was ill—or both. Whatever the problem was, he aimed to get to the bottom of it this very day. To do that, he would have to follow her.

He put on his coat and boots and bolted out the door with Hans in tow, dropping him quickly at the Shumans' and reaching his own scooter seconds after Elke pulled into traffic on her baby-shit-yellow Schwalbe. He'd planned his departure in advance and hadn't secured his chain with a lock. In no time he'd started his scooter and fallen in behind his wife, far enough away that she would not notice him.

A bitter wind hit him in the face as they turned east and joined the steady flow of traffic on the divided boulevard Karl-Marx-Allee.

Half a block behind Uwe Hauptman, a thirty-year-old KGB junior officer named Vladimir Mikhailov wheeled his brown Lada sedan away from the curb. Dog farts were warmer than the air puffing out of the Lada's pitiful heater, but Mikhailov did not care. He was young, at the bottom of the pecking order in the office, and counted himself fortunate to have a vehicle at all. The posting in East Berlin was a plum, so he was lucky all around. He'd wanted to be KGB since he was a small boy and his father had introduced him to a friend in the intelligence field. The man's soft astrakhan wool hat and the keen look of adventure in his dark eyes entranced a twelve-year-old Vladimir, to the point of thinking of little else. One glimpse of the man's shiny black

Makarov pistol and Vladimir's future was all but written in stone.

"You can tell no one your goal is to be a spy," his father had told him. But he set the goal nonetheless and scored high enough on his exams and language-aptitude batteries that, with a whisper in the right ear from his father's friend, he gained acceptance to Moscow Academy, the KGB's elite spy school.

Today, Mikhailov's partner had eaten some bad fish, leaving Mikhailov working alone for the time being. Colonel Zima had assigned him to follow a physicist from Humboldt University. He was to note where the physicist went and report back via radio if anything out of the ordinary happened.

Mikhailov was prepared to be at it all day if he had to. His wife had made him a sandwich wrapped in wax paper. He had no idea what it was but figured that anything other than cucumber would be good if he was hungry enough—and she knew not to make him cucumber. Other than that, he didn't need much, a thermos of tea and a glass jar with a tight lid to piss in if he had to sit in the car for too long after drinking all the tea. A 9×18mm Makarov PM pistol and a dash-mounted radio rounded out his kit.

He keyed his radio as he drove, keeping the mic low and out of sight, as demonstrated in the academy.

"Subject on the move," he said.

"Received," a male voice he recognized as Evgeni Zima answered. *"Eyes wide open, Volodya."*

"Yes, Comrade Colonel."

Vladimir Mikhailov smiled that his boss would use the familiar form of his name on the radio. His wife and the boss's wife were getting to be good friends. Nonetheless, Mikhailov kept it professional. He'd be getting enough shit from the other guys about being the favorite.

Evgeni Zima knelt beside the Hauptmans' bed and reached underneath. He was not old—barely forty—but he felt old today. He'd somehow injured his back the week before and didn't want to lie all the way down for fear he wouldn't be able to stand again. In all his years in the KGB, he'd never known anyone to be quite so stupid as to hide incriminating evidence under a bed, but he looked anyway. He often found other interesting things.

The electronics technician on Zima's team set his leather briefcase on the bed and lifted the lid, revealing perfectly arrayed tools and assorted listening devices. Thick glasses and an easy smile made him look more like a university professor than a KGB expert in electronic surveillance measures.

"The phone line runs along the baseboard here," he said, nodding to a small bedside table. "I can tie into it without too much trouble. This stack of physics texts indicates Dr. Hauptman sleeps here."

"I agree," Zima said.

The table nearest him was surely Mrs. Hauptman's side—half a glass of water, the alarm clock, and a jar of perfumed hand cream. Zima marveled at how cavalierly people left items lying around to be tampered with.

Drinking water and lotions could both be poisoned. Zima's mentor during his early years with the KGB often spoke of spraying hallucinogens on the toothbrushes of dissidents in order to discredit them. Something stronger could be used to make them sick, or if a more permanent outcome was warranted.

His position put his nose level with the nightstand and the hand cream and Elke Hauptman's pillow . . . He'd heard her sing once and found her voice to be one of the singularly most beautiful things he had ever experienced—

The technician pulled him back into the moment.

"This side of the bed, Comrade Zima?"

"Go ahead," Zima said. "And the actual phone as well."

"Of course."

The technician removed a small glassine bag from his case, and from that took a tiny rectangle of metal with three wires protruding from one end, and held it gingerly between his fingertips. Less than two inches long and a quarter inch in diameter, the listening device was manufactured in the Socialist Republic of Romania. Ironically, the microphone component of this and many of the covert listening devices of Warsaw Pact secret police was manufactured by the U.S. company Knowles, which made hearing aid batteries. The technician set the device in a small plastic tray in his case, surveying the area, planning how to best perform the installation without leaving any evidence of the bug's existence.

The device would be powered by the existing phone line, which ran along the top of the baseboard. Though the baseboard was visible and easy to access, any bug tied to the line would need to be hidden in some way. The technician used a small spray bottle to loosen the wallpaper and peel it back above the phone line enough to cut a small divot in the Sheetrock and embed the bug after splicing it in. A few sprays of adhesive would tack the wallpaper down when he was finished.

"What do you hope to find?" Major Popov whined with a voice that sounded much too close to that of Zima's mother-in-law. He was fresh from Moscow, with only two weeks of experience in the DDR—and not much more than that in the KGB.

Zima looked over his shoulder, playing his hand back and forth under the bed. He found nothing for his trouble but cobwebs and a pair of black tights with a hole in the toe.

"There are two kinds of searches," Zima reminded his subordinate. "If we wanted to be sure of finding a specific thing, we would have brought it with us. We are looking for answers, not trying to make a case—"

"I have something," an agent said from the bathroom.

Zima rose with a low groan, using the bed to push himself up, then straightening the duvet to leave no trace. There would be tracks beneath the bed, if either of the Hauptmans decided to crawl under and look, but that did not appear to happen very often. He brushed the dust off his hands and made his way to the bathroom.

"What?"

Major Popov had beat him there and now looked at a

folder of documents the other agent had found taped behind the sink.

"Mathematical formulas and diagrams," Popov said. "He is copying items at work and bringing them home."

Zima spread the papers out on the counter beside the bathroom sink. The major was right, though he had no idea what he was right about. The drawings were geometric shapes, angles, and pyramids, each with accompanying formulas.

Zima scratched his chin. "But this is Dr. Hauptman's work. He could easily re-create it at home or anywhere. There is no reason for him to take it from work."

"And yet that is exactly what he appears to have done," Popov said. "You are the one who ordered the surveillance on the man. You must believe he is up to no good."

"I believe he is up to something," Zima said. "Just what, I do not know—"

The technician stuck his head in from the hallway. "Comrade," he said, looking directly at Zima. "I think you will want to see this."

"Just a moment—"

"There are other devices."

"What?"

"A *Holzwurm* in the door," the tech said. The woodworm was a tube about the size of a medium flashlight and powered by two 1.5-volt batteries. It was installed in a hole drilled in the door and concealed behind a thin wafer of matching wood.

"Two additional 31216s so far, but I would guess we will find more. I left them in place."

Developed by Stasi ITU, the 31216-1 RF devices were small enough that they could be covered with a thumb. Battery-powered, they were not dependent on a phone line for juice.

Zima mouthed the word *Where?*

The tech gave a flick of his hand, bidding the senior agent to follow to a tiny pinhole in the wall above the headboard.

"Nice work," Zima said, speaking in his normal voice. Whoever was on the other end of these had been listening to everything up to now anyway. "The others?"

"The likely spots," the tech said. "Dining room. The phone in the kitchen. I'm sure there's one in the bathroom. Were you aware of this?"

"I suppose I should have been," Zima said.

The Stasi was known to be more aggressive than the KGB when it came to technical surveillance. They bugged everyone and sorted out the innocents later, if they happened to find any.

The tech's eyes shifted to the bedroom. "And there is a camera."

Zima went silent again, whispering, "A camera in the bedroom?"

"Yes," the tech said.

Colonel Zima studied Dr. Hauptman's hidden diagrams for a moment and then glanced toward the bedroom.

"Very well," he whispered to his men. "Finish up with what you're doing here. Popov, make contact with the

Stasi unit on the other end of these devices so that we may merge their records with ours." Then louder, addressing the wall, the lamp, the phone on the kitchen counter, "Please prepare copies of all logs and tapes. I will send someone to you."

38

Ryan knew it was only his imagination, but it felt as if the already frigid temperature fell ten degrees when he reached the checkpoint. At home, the kids would be gearing up for Thanksgiving in a couple of weeks, but it felt like the middle of winter here.

The East German government required non-Germans and Allied forces entering the GDR to utilize the Friedrichstrasse crossing point. Known as Checkpoint Charlie, it was staffed by U.S. and British Army personnel and open twenty-four hours a day, seven days a week. Allied forces did not officially recognize East Germany as a separate country, and had only a small, temporary guard shack.

"Something you need to know about me," Foley said as they walked side by side down Friedrichstrasse. She kept her voice low, just loud enough for him to hear. "I do not intend to be captured."

"That's a good plan," Ryan said.

Foley pulled up short, stopping momentarily in the middle of the sidewalk. A couple walking behind them had to go around. "I'm not sure you understand what I mean."

"Maybe I don't," Ryan said. There was a look in this woman's eye that said she wasn't someone to suffer fools. "Listen. Jim let me know in no uncertain terms that you're the expert in operating in denied areas. You tell me what to do and I'll do it. I'm following your lead."

"That's the thing," she said. "When I say I don't intend to be captured, I mean I'm not going to be taken alive."

"Damn," Ryan said. "I forgot the cyanide pill I usually keep in my back molar."

"You won't need a pill," Foley said. "Just fight back. They'll do the heavy lifting. If we are approached and questioned on the street, that's one thing, but nobody's arresting me. I'll get away or die trying." She tapped the side of her head with her index finger. "Too much juicy stuff up here that I don't feel like sharing . . . Pull out enough teeth, pump in enough drugs . . . and sooner or later, interrogations work."

"Okay, then," Ryan said. "I guess I'm just a little more of an optimist."

"Must be nice," she said. "That whole Boy Scout, everything's-going-to-work-out-in-the-long-run mentality. Well, it's important for you to realize that, very often, things do not work out. Skip's right. The Keller girl is probably already dead—and we could be, too, before this is over. I just want to be sure you're realistic about it from the get-go."

She smiled, taking his hand so they looked like a couple as they started walking again. "I like to get that kind of thing out of the way with anyone I work with. Only fair for you to know what a crazy woman I am. Other than that, we should probably stay a little vague with each other regarding our personal information. If they do manage to capture and torture us, we don't want to give the bastards anything that they can use to pit us against one another." She slowed, looked up at him through the falling snow, and shrugged. "Sorry. There I go getting negative again."

Ryan thought about that. "Not getting captured and tortured is a good plan," he said. It hadn't been too many months since he'd been instrumental in the transfer of the Soviet ballistic missile submarine *Red October* into American hands by defector Captain Marko Ramius.

The Soviets would be sure to execute him twice for that.

They crossed Checkpoint Charlie on foot, using their travel names, Jack and Mary Avery. The Army sergeant inside the temporary shed, bundled up in a wool greatcoat and fake-fur uniform hat, handed their passports through the window with a polite shrug. As far as he or the United States government was concerned, they were as free to walk into East Germany as they were to cross the street in the West, but he took down their names in order to keep track and make sure they made it out.

Ryan read the verbiage on the white warning placard just past the shack before entering the strip of no-man's-land in the gap of the Wall.

The place they'd be shot in the back if they tried to make a run for it on the way back into West Berlin. From the sour look on the guards' faces, Ryan suspected some of them would be all too happy to shoot them in the front right now.

He read the sign out loud.

You are leaving the American Sector

"Chilling when you think of it for too long." Foley pulled her wool scarf down an inch. "For us, that marker might as well say *From this point forward, assume you are being hunted.*"

Unlike the simple temporary shack of the Allies, the East German point of entry consisted of not only the Wall, but a gun tower and search shed. Vehicles entering or exiting the GDR had to run a serpentine gauntlet of bollards guarded by dour men—some of them painfully young—clutching machine guns. Pedestrians like Ryan and Foley were greeted by uniformed Border Police, more than half of them incognito Stasi officers who examined their travel documents out of sight in another room and then returned to grill them on why in the world they would want to visit this socialist utopia, the irony of their questions seemingly lost on the guards. Ryan was surprised at the broken English of the guard who spoke with him. There was a moment when a senior man appeared from a back room to interview Foley—obviously bumping his subordinate out of the way to speak to an attractive young woman. He pointedly asked if she'd secreted any contraband on her person, intimating that she might need to be searched. Foley assured him she had nothing illegal and demonstrated the appropriate amount of subservient fear, which seemed to placate the man. He waved her through with a flick of his hand and retired through the door he'd come out of.

Ryan and Foley were each required to exchange twenty-five West German deutsche marks for twenty-five East German marks—though the latter was worth just a fifth of the former. It was another way the GDR kept money inside the country, since no East German currency could be taken out. It was worthless outside anyway.

Though he'd been warned ad nauseam about how different the GDR would be, stepping into East Germany was a gut punch. Somehow colder and grayer, the sky slouched over sad buildings and sullen streets. Slick BMW and Mercedes-Benz sedans gave way to rusted Ladas—the best thing about them was that they were rarely stolen—and two-stroke Trabants that used a gasoline-oil mix and sounded like a fleet of lawn mowers. The GDR seemed stripped of vibrancy, leaving only thin pastels and shades of gray.

Ryan was far from experienced at surveillance-detection routes, but he'd been pursued by enough evil men over the course of his short career to appreciate the concept. In their purest form, SDRs were planned routes with prearranged clearance locations along the way where countersurveillance team members could wait and watch, noting any possible tails. An SDR did not lose a tail, it only revealed it.

The trick was losing a tail without seeming to want to. In Eastern Bloc countries, the state assumed everyone to be a potential troublemaker or dissident. Any attempt to evade a KGB or Stasi surveillance team meant you had something to hide and was prima facie evidence of guilt. They did not need to build a criminal case or even follow you enough to find evidence. All that could be manufactured after you were in custody. They just needed to follow long enough to see if you were worth the trouble, or, as in this case, if you might lead them to a bigger fish.

A good SDR took time and, unless it went terribly wrong, was incredibly mundane. They needed to look like they were going somewhere specific, not simply wandering the streets trying to get lost. Foley had been to East Berlin before and knew the terrain. She'd planned the route.

They doubled back on themselves naturally, stopped to talk to a little boy in a parka twice his size walking an enormous dog, and looked in virtually every shop that contained anything that Foley found remotely interesting. After two hours, Mike Rogers from the Helsinki team met them coming the opposite way, took his hat off and smoothed what was left of his thinning hair to show that they were in the black—clear of surveillance . . . probably.

They walked three more blocks before Foley pointed

at a small bake shop tucked in the bottom of a sad, gray apartment building on Wattstrasse. Always in character—just in case they were not as clear as they thought—she turned to grab Ryan's arm with both hands, as if to drag him inside to show him something.

A bell clanged when Ryan opened the door and held it for her.

"Guten Tag," a small brunette woman behind a nearly empty glass display case said without much gusto. The sleeves of her turtleneck sweater were pushed up above sinewy forearms. Dark eyes said she was holding back bad news.

Foley perused the sparse pickings under the glass. It was late in the day, so only a half-dozen loaves and a broken strudel were left. Still looking down, Foley took off her wool gloves and held them both in her right hand. "I was hoping to find buckwheat," she said in German.

"No buckwheat," the woman behind the counter said. "But I will have a nice rye tomorrow."

An older woman in a white apron came out and took her place behind the counter.

"I'm Truly Bishop," the brunette said, extending her hand after she'd led Ryan and Foley through a swinging door into the tiny kitchen.

"Truly," Ryan said.

"Yeah," Bishop said. "My dad was in the business. Big Ian Fleming fan. I think he would have saddled me with Truly Scrumptious if my mom would have let him. There are worse Ian Fleming names, I suppose. Anyway, bad news. Skip Hulse called my boss. Sounds like Jennifer

North legged it as soon as you two left the building, even though Skip told everyone they had to stay until you were across."

"Where'd she go?" Ryan asked.

Bishop shot a furtive glance over each shoulder, then shrugged. "That's the issue. No one knows. Look, there's still a chance this can be explained away because she's worried about the missing girl. Just leaving the building doesn't prove she's a traitor."

"It doesn't help her case, either," Foley said.

"There's something else. Skip checked in the desk drawer where Jen keeps a handgun." Bishop gave a tight-lipped shake of her head. "Looks like she took it with her."

"She's not getting across the border with a gun," Foley said.

"Unless she's got friends in the East," Ryan observed, stating the hard truth.

"Do either of you want a gun?" Bishop asked.

"A gun would just give the Stasi a reason to shoot us if we're searched," Foley said. "It might come to that, but I don't think so. Not yet, anyway."

"Nah," Ryan said. "Doesn't really match our legend."

"Good answer." Bishop gave them a thumbs-up. "The chief made me ask. He wanted me to get a read on you both."

Foley frowned. "Because he's heard I'm a cowboy?"

"We've all heard that, ma'am," Bishop said. "But you passed."

"That's a relief." Foley darkened. "And what's this ma'am shit? I'm not that much older than you."

"You went through the Farm with Mary Cross, right?"

"Correct," Foley said. "The instructors called us the Queen Marys. We're the same age."

"My dad recruited her." Bishop grinned like the Cheshire cat. "She used to babysit me."

"Great . . ."

"For what it's worth," Bishop said, "everything I've ever heard about you is kick-ass. I want to be you when I grow up."

"Well . . ." Foley grinned. "Check your windage and elevation. You might want to set your sights a little higher than that."

The bell in front jingled and they all froze. Bishop pointed to the back door, then held up a fist, waiting. Just a customer who bought her loaf of rustic bread and left in stoic silence.

"Okay," Bishop said after the bell sounded the customer's departure. "We don't have a gob of time. The boss sent a couple of presents for you."

She reached behind a pile of flour sacks and retrieved a canvas satchel, out of which she removed a plastic box about the size of a deck of playing cards fastened to a three-inch-wide elastic belt.

Bishop handed the device to Foley, who explained it to Ryan.

"You'll wear this around your chest, hidden under your shirt. Truly and the chief of station will monitor known East German police and Soviet intelligence frequencies and triangulate their positions. Any of them get too close and this will give you a little shock."

"A shock?" Ryan said. "Seriously?"

"No." Foley grinned. "It just vibrates."

"It doesn't send a signal," Bishop said. "It only receives so they can't track it. The closer the buzzes are together, the closer East German authorities are to your location. Their presence could be completely unrelated to your operation, or they could be bearing down with a bunch of saps and sub-guns to scoop you up. If we start to believe it's the latter, I'll hit you with a constant SOS in Morse code. Really, consider any constant buzz a message meaning bad news. The Helsinki team will relay us updates when they're able—which will not likely be very often."

"So how will you know where we are?" he asked.

"That brings us to the other presents I have for you," Bishop said. "You'll need to provide the location of your initial meeting. The chief of station and I will be the only ones with that information. I know you can't trust us any more than the rest of the office, but this way your information is compartmentalized."

Foley smirked at Ryan. "Meaning Langley knows who to shoot if you and I wake up dead."

"Exactly," Bishop said. "Keeps us honest, I suppose."

Ryan gave her the address, but not the pass phrase that CALISTO had provided in his instructions. Only he and Foley had that.

Bishop shot a look over each shoulder again, clearly ready to go. "A couple of quick things," she said. "Our sources tell us the East German presidium is losing its shit over something right at the moment. We can't tell if they know about the defection or if this is just a blip in everyday paranoia. That said, they appear to be double- and triple-checking everything and everyone—and they have the manpower to do it, so be on your toes. It's not at all uncommon for some guys in suits to come up and demand 'your papers!' if he just doesn't like the smell of you."

"Understood," Ryan said.

Bishop reached in her satchel again and brought out what appeared to be a radio transmitter. Roughly six by six inches square, it was less than an inch thick. Closer inspection revealed it was modular, with a small remov- able keypad in one corner and a battery that made up a third of the unit.

Foley took the device and, already familiar with it, passed it to Ryan for his inspection.

"SRAC," she said. "Short-range agent communica- tions device. Keeps us from having to service dead drops quite as often."

Ryan nodded. "A radio . . ."

"A satellite transmitter, yes," Bishop said. "Use the keypad to type your message. It's automatically en- crypted as you go. Keep it concise. This handles a grand total of 1,579 characters. Shouldn't take that many to relay your second location."

Ryan glanced at Foley. "Second location?"

"If I were CALISTO," Bishop said, "I wouldn't meet you straight off, especially with the Stasi all running around at this moment like their hair is on fire. I'd leave you a note with further instructions at the first location, then watch from someplace safe to see if anyone who could hurt me was following you. If and only if you weren't being followed, I'd make myself known at the next location."

"Yep," Foley said. "That's the way I'd do it."

"That's when the SRAC comes into play. Type in the location, time, et cetera."

"What keeps Stasi or KGB techs from triangulating in on our signal?" Ryan said.

"It transmits the information in a short burst, four to twelve seconds. That doesn't give them long to get a fix. Even so, if it were me, I wouldn't hang out for too long in the spot I broadcast from. You just never know when the other side might have developed some slightly more advanced tech. Anyway, let us know where you'll be and we'll do the rest. Same drill. You'll get a buzz if we hear anyone closing in on your position. Now," Bishop continued, "how's your German?"

"I understand it," Ryan said. "But no one's going to mistake me for a local, if that's what you're getting at."

"I can pass for a Russian," Foley said.

"Even better. We like redundant measures here in the East. Murphy's Law and all." Bishop handed Foley a glossy guidebook extolling the wonders of East Berlin. "There is a one hundred percent chance any call from a pay phone will be monitored. If something happens to your SRAC, use the guidebook as your key. You remember how to use a book cypher?"

Foley gave her a good-natured glare. "Yes . . ."

"Keep it simple, nothing but when and where. Skew

the date and time by three on the later side of the true numbers."

"Got it," Foley said, repeating everything back, including the "hello" phone number at an off-site location away from the embassy. She patted Ryan on the arm. "Let's get this vibrator thingy on you while we're out of sight from the world. No telling if we'll have any place to put it on in the clear before our meeting."

"You'll forget it's there unless you feel a buzz," Bishop said. "Fair warning, though. It can startle the piss out of you when it goes off. I can bear witness to that . . ."

Foley chuckled. "Yep."

Ryan unbuttoned his shirt.

Bishop exhaled hard through her mouth. "I feel like I'm forgetting something, but we don't have time to hang out. Just remember this: East Berlin has a thousand eyes and ears on every block. The Stasi are the new Gestapo, some true believers but also a hell of a lot of evil bastards just taking advantage of the opportunity to become tyrant voyeurs. That said, it's easy to forget that not everyone here is a spy. There are tens of thousands of decent folks who just want to work and make babies and raise those babies and read whatever they choose without the state telling them otherwise. But don't you for one minute forget that every one of those people is living with a gun to their head. Even good guys can turn on you under the right set of circumstances."

Foley strapped the band snug around Ryan's midsection, centering the receiver over his sternum. "Noted," she said. She stepped back to take a look at the device and then gave Ryan a thumbs-up. "We're good to go if that feels okay."

Ryan lifted and lowered his arms. "Not the most comfortable feeling," he said.

Foley put her hands on her own chest and nodded. "Welcome to my world, Jackie Boy. You are good to go, sir."

Ryan chuckled, then straightened his shirt collar. He turned to Bishop as he shrugged on his overcoat. "Can I ask you something?"

"Go for it."

"Any intel from this side of the Wall about the missing State Department employee, Ruby Keller?"

"Maybe," she said. "The reports are still unsubstantiated, but I'm hearing a mysterious new prisoner arrived in Hohenschönhausen Prison last night . . ."

"That could be a good thing," Foley said. "If they're holding Keller as a political prisoner, she could be considered for a swap at some point."

"True," Bishop said. "These bastards make a shit ton of dough selling us our own people back, so one can hope. The chief's in constant communication with the Bureau, Diplomatic Security, Army CID, the alphabet soup of everybody working on her disappearance. I'm sure he's keeping Skip in the loop, too."

"Thanks," Ryan said. "Weird that her kidnapping happened to coincide with our visit."

"It has to be connected," Bishop said. "Just unsure

how at the moment. I'll keep my ear to the ground for anything more." She clapped her hands together. "Y'all ready to scoot?"

"Yep," Foley said.

Ryan nodded.

"Okay," Bishop said. "I'll give you fifteen minutes, then buzz you three times, five seconds apart, so you'll know what to expect. If I buzz you after that initial test, you should assume we're picking up East German official radio traffic moving toward the location."

Ryan touched the center of his chest. "What if it doesn't work?"

Foley reached and pulled his hand away. "Let's not get in the habit of doing that, Jack," she said. "You don't want to draw attention to the fancy spy gear you happen to be wearing."

Ryan blushed. "Right. Guess I wouldn't make a very good smuggler."

"The honest guys rarely do," Foley said. "You have to be just a teensy bit sociopathic to pull off some of this."

"And your partner here is a master." Bishop smirked. "Anyway, I tested it an hour ago, but if for some reason it goes tits-up and you don't get my planned signal in fifteen minutes . . . well, that's up to you. Either way, if the shit hits the fan, your best option is always to slip away. Quietly if you can, with force if you must. Your Helsinki team will do what they can to draw any threats away, but don't forget, we are deep in the belly of the beast on this side of the Wall. If things turn to shit, we'll do what we can to extract you, but there's no such thing as calling in the cavalry. There are only a handful of case officers on this side of the Wall, and none of us here are declared. No Agency liaison. No nothing. If you get nabbed by the KGB or GRU, or, God forbid, the Stasi . . . this rodeo turns political. It'll be out of my hands."

Outside, after Truly Bishop disappeared in a cloud of swirling snow, Ryan leaned toward Foley.

"You opted not to tell her about this mysterious guy who's watching our backs."

"You are correct," Foley said. "The fewer people who know the details about him, the better."

39

John Clark followed at a distance, keeping Mary Pat Foley's hat in view ninety percent of the time. He wasn't in contact with members of the Helsinki team to tell them what he was doing, but occasionally, to keep from being burned by any would-be countersurveillance, he fell back even farther and let them have the eye. Distance was less conspicuous, but it was also less sure. He'd never worked with any of this team. They were operations, clandestine officers who recruited and ran assets—agents from foreign nations. Clark was Special Activities. If he was in the field, someone needed either rescuing or redirecting, sometimes permanently.

Foley was still running SDRs, teaching the new guy how it was done. *Good for her,* Clark thought. They had no idea how good Truly Bishop's tradecraft was. For all Clark knew, she'd shown up at the meet with half of Stasi counterintelligence in tow. Clark had the location for the first meeting, which made it easier for him to anticipate. Foley was good, which meant she'd likely do the same thing he would do.

This Ryan character appeared to be bright enough. He wasn't gawking. Clark had once seen a new recruit in Prague that was so sure that a car packed full of KGB agents was going to jump out and get him that he eyeballed every passing Lada until the KGB grew suspicious and his fear came true. Ryan carried himself like he'd been around the block a time or two. Greer had told a couple hypothetical stories, which eased Clark's mind some. It was much easier to protect someone who could help with their own rescue if it came down to that. Clark customarily divided opponents into three categories: men he felt he could handle hand to hand, men he would face with a pistol, and men who he would just as soon take out with an M1 Garand from three hundred yards. Ryan wasn't a big guy, and there was little doubt in Clark's mind that he could best the guy in a fistfight. But there was something about him that made Clark think they could be friends—if Clark allowed himself the luxury of friends, which he did not.

Foley led them on a grand tour around East Berlin for two hours, visiting a Lutheran church that looked like it hadn't been used in decades, and several shops, many of them on the verge of closing for the day. Clark stomped his feet to stay warm and kept his eyes open. East Berlin was not a place to lose focus.

He watched from the window of a small café as Foley and Ryan came out of a cobbler, where it looked like

Ryan was having a shoe repaired. *Smart move,* Clark thought. A stop inside to warm up. Clark expected to see one of the Helsinki couples fall in behind. But nobody showed. For a fleeting moment, he thought maybe they were just getting better at their job, honing their surveillance skills enough to blend into the woodwork. Nope. Clark couldn't put his finger on it, but something was off.

He paid for his coffee and said good night to the hostess, who was surprisingly chipper. She wasn't talkative. It was dangerous to be too open with strangers, but she smiled when she gave him his change, and a smile in East Berlin went a hell of a long way.

Clark waited inside the café for a beat, giving the area one more scan through the window before venturing out into the cold. Across the street a couple did emerge from the shadows and fall in half a block behind Foley and Ryan. Like everyone else walking the streets on this snowy night, they were bundled head to toe in ski parkas, wool coats, and assorted hats. The woman was taller than either of the Helsinki team females. You could wear a wig, or glue on a fake mustache, but it was hard to change height. This woman had a slight limp.

They turned off a block later, but they'd followed with such predatory intensity that Clark was tempted to follow them just to see where they went. There was no question in his mind that this couple was dangerous. Whether or not they were dangerous to Foley remained to be seen.

Ahead, Foley and Ryan were swallowed up by blowing

snow. Clark crossed to the opposite side of the street and picked up his pace, peering down the alley where the tall woman with the limp and her partner had disappeared. He recognized a predator when he saw one—and his gut told him he would see this one again.

40

D an Murray had just laid his head on the conference table when a Salt Lake City agent named Green burst into the room, his voice buzzing with excitement.

"I think we've got him, boss."

Murray sat up, jittery from being yanked out of the first few moments of sleep. He rubbed his eyes with the heel of his hand and then gave a long, shuddering stretch.

"What . . . ? Where?"

Harris lay on the floor in the back of the room, using her rolled coat as a pillow, an extra sweater over her face. She lifted the sweater to see what was going on, then clamored to her feet when she saw Murray stand.

They'd been baiting hooks, as Murray called it, essentially setting out a large dragnet since they'd boarded the Lear 35 in Virginia. The UNSUB's last known point was on the I-15 corridor. Agents from the FBI and virtually every other alphabet agency had teamed up with local law enforcement to form an ad hoc task force. Every fuel stop, café, and motel along all conceivable routes north, east, and west got telephone calls and follow-up personal visits. U.S. Customs and Border Patrol officers on the Canadian border in Washington, Idaho, and Montana were all put on alert. Agents checked locations to the south as well, in the unlikely event the UNSUB turned back toward Las Vegas.

Had this not been a national security case, staffing would have been an issue. The Salt Lake City field office already supported two standing task forces at the moment, in addition to Murray's UNSUB—a squad investigating three recent bombings and another as part of a nationwide effort to apprehend the "Truck Stop Killer(s)" who preyed on prostitutes and hitchhikers.

It was a member of this task force who had apparently come up with the most recent lead.

"Salt Lake County's working the truck stop south of town near Point of the Mountain on I-15," Green said. "One of the deputies has a lot lizard who's a sort of unofficial informant. She's a hundred percent positive she saw our guy get in a blue Peterbilt parked third from the west end on the back row."

"An eighteen-wheeler," Murray mused. "Makes sense. Does this deputy still have eyes on the rig?"

"He does."

"Outstanding." Murray yawned, but he was fully awake now. "Who do we have out there now?"

"Just the Salt Lake County deputy for the moment.

The truckers are used to seeing him prowling the lot, but as soon as a few more marked units show up word will spread like crazy over the CB."

"Let's get whoever's close, then," Murray said, throwing on his coat. "Harris, you're with me. Let's go."

Harris had grown up on a horse ranch near Mesquite, Nevada, but she knew the Salt Lake Valley well enough that Murray put her behind the wheel of the boxy Crown Victoria Bu-car. (Other agencies called their government rides G-cars. FBI culture dictated the Bureau stand apart, so agents called their rides Bu-cars.)

Traffic in the wee hours of the morning was nonexistent and they made good time.

"As tired as I am," Murray said, "I love working this time of night. Nobody out but cops, paperboys, and assholes."

Harris turned sideways and grinned, her face glowing green from the dash lights.

"Which one are we?"

The radio mic hung by a plastic ring from the AM/FM knob. Murray had no sooner picked it up when the Salt Lake County deputy sheriff, whose name was LaRue, broke squelch.

"I've got movement from the truck," the deputy said. "Male, white, green flannel coat, wool hat . . . It could be your guy. I'm too far away to be sure . . . Well, shit . . . I think he made me."

"We're two minutes out," Murray said.

LaRue came over the radio again, clearly pissed now. "Subject running across the lot toward the main building.

I'm behind him. Any unit come in from the west side and we'll box him in."

He repeated the description.

Harris drifted the Crown Vic's rear tires as she turned into the parking lot. She shifted the car into park a half-second before it stopped rolling, causing the transmission to chatter in protest.

Murray bailed out, touching the butt of his revolver, but not drawing it just yet. Better to leave it in the holster until he needed it. Harris followed him inside to find Deputy LaRue, sidearm out, working his way slowly around an aisle of cough drops and Hostess Twinkies. Now Murray drew his revolver.

LaRue pointed to the back wall and mouthed something Murray didn't catch. The truck stop store was a dim and dusty place, more shadow than light, with a lingering smell somewhere between a well-worn tire and a used sock. The skeletal clerk hid behind displays of caffeine powder, Spanish fly, and locker room poppers. He made a half-hearted effort to raise his hands.

Harris fanned out to the left as two more agents followed them in, and another set hit the doors behind LaRue.

Harris made contact first.

"FBI! Don't move!"

Murray angled to his right to bring the man in the green flannel coat into view. He'd turned to flee at Harris's announcement, running headlong into the rack of glossy girly magazines, on top of which he now lay facedown, floundering.

Murray resisted the urge to give orders—or rush up and put the cuffs on. That job went to LaRue, who had the man restrained, patted down for weapons, and kneeling in a matter of seconds. The Bureau went after the big fish, but state and local officers made more arrests in a month than many FBI agents would make over the course of their careers.

Murray holstered his Smith & Wesson, deflating as soon as he got a good look at the suspect.

"Damn it!" Harris said, seeing it at the same time.

The man's hair was right, the mustache, the wool hat, but the top three buttons of his shirt were open, revealing a Stars and Bars Confederate flag tattooed over his heart.

Murray hunkered down in front of him.

"Mind if I ask where you're from?"

"Slidell, Louisiana," the man sniffed, chin quivering. "I swear, I didn't know pickin' up a hooker was a federal crime . . ."

Sorry about that," Deputy LaRue said once they were all outside. The cold air was a welcome relief from the essence of sweat sock inside the store. "Turns out he had a girl in the sleeper before we got here and was coming inside to get a snack when he saw me. Thought I was tagging him for the earlier rendezvous."

"Better safe than sorry," Harris said.

Murray gave a nodding grunt, too disappointed and tired to say much. Their UNSUB was somewhere out there. The truth was, they would likely do this again many times before they got their man . . . if they got their man. Murray had an army of FBI and other federal agents at his disposal, and he was no closer to catching this bastard than he had been fifteen hours ago.

A tractor-trailer rig thumped past on the interstate, whining north toward Salt Lake and beyond. Two more rolled south, amber trailer lights glowing in the darkness.

"Gotta add truck drivers," Harris said.

Murray tore his eyes off the interstate.

"Pardon?"

"The people out late at night," Harris said. "Cops, paperboys, assholes . . . and truck drivers."

41

Jen North trudged sullenly along Rosa-Luxemburg-Strasse, her coat pulled tight, shoulders humped up against cold and nerves. Schneider's black 1984 Volvo 240 GL pulled along the curb beside her, chattering the slushy snow in the gutter. The luxury sedan oozed capitalist extravagance when compared to the river of buzzy little Trabants and Wartburgs. It garnered a lot of disgruntled stares but only added to his cover as an officer from the West Berlin division of a refuse company that paid the DDR to dump waste in the East. He did not stop the car completely, but slowed enough for North to jump in.

Behind the wheel, Schneider hurriedly took something off his right hand and stuffed it into his pocket as she settled into the passenger seat beside him. North had long held suspicions that the bastard had a wife in the East. She took a breath and told herself the ring was just cover for one of his other operations. They would talk about this later.

Schneider shoulder-checked and then eased back into traffic. "This is not a good idea, my dear," he said. "Too many eyes and ears. You should not even be here."

"Well, I am here, Rolfe," North said. "My boss thinks I'm out looking for Ruby Keller."

Schneider glanced sideways. "Are you? I told you I have that handled."

"You could have followed her, but—" North raised her hands. "We've already been over this."

"We have indeed," Schneider said. He made a right turn, checked the rearview mirror, and then made another right. "I received your message. Thank you for taking that initiative. It will be handled as well."

"No Americans are to be harmed," North said, chewing on her thumbnail. She glanced up at him, locking eyes. "Do your people understand that?"

Still driving, Schneider reached across and gently pulled her hand away from her mouth. "Don't do that, my dear," he said. "You'll give yourself an infection."

She batted him away. "I'm serious, Rolfe!" she said. "Whoever you have on this, I want to know they understand. Our mission is to find CALISTO. Those people are my friends. Hurting them would be a bridge too far."

"Oh, my dearest Jennifer . . ." Schneider gave a soft sigh. "You have crossed that bridge so long ago." He put a hand on her thigh and gave her a reassuring squeeze. "But do not fret. My people know their mission."

The Volvo slowed and Schneider pulled to the curb

along the eerily quiet Genslerstrasse. Lined with trees and small, unassuming houses, it was impossible to imagine these cobblestone streets ran beside a horror show like Hohenschönhausen Prison.

"This is your stop," he said. "Call me in two hours. I will check with my sources in the West and make sure you are able to return home."

Hand on the door, North froze, the stark reality of her situation hitting her in the gut.

"And what if I can't?"

"Then we must make it so you can," Schneider said.

Five minutes after he dropped North off, Colonel Schneider turned down a side street beside Obersee Park. He backed the Volvo into a parking spot for quick egress and then checked his rearview and both outside mirrors out of habit. His father, a staff colonel for one of Hitler's "red generals," had often told him growing up about the German shoulder-check, which proceeded virtually every utterance that might remotely be construed as not in perfect alignment with the Führer's ever-changing plans.

"Things are not so different in the DDR, Papa," he said to himself as he dug the wedding band out of his pocket and slipped it back on his left ring finger. "But now I have to worry about my wife as well . . ."

HVA, the foreign intelligence service of the Stasi, employed hundreds of Romeo agents, men who were specially trained to mold themselves into the perfect man for a specific woman. If you spied on a woman long enough—read her mail, listened to her calls home, studied the books she read and the programs she watched on the television—it was a straightforward matter to become the man of her dreams and subtly insert yourself into her life.

But Rolfe Schneider had no such training. He'd simply been in the right place at the right moment to lend a listening ear to an attractive CIA case officer after she'd been tragically wronged.

The tall, sexy woman at the Königshof Hotel bar in Bonn had been crying—a look that he had always found attractive on women—and stared into her third Johnnie Walker of the evening.

He ordered two Rothaus Black Forest whiskeys and nodded at the barkeep to give one to her.

"Stick to good German single-malt," he said when she glared at him. "You will not be disappointed."

Then he kept his mouth shut and listened.

She said nothing about what she did for a living at first, just that her boss was a dickhead and was taking credit for months of her hard work. The conversation moved upstairs, where he surmised by the way she casually checked the room for surveillance equipment that she was an American intelligence officer.

That first night had been about the sex—the poor woman was starving—and a listening ear. She admitted to him she was CIA on their second liaison in a hotel that she chose, also in Bonn. She'd checked him out by then, and learned he really was an executive in Roth and Sons

Refuse and Waste Disposal. A job, he assured her, that, while extremely lucrative, few men would brag about to a beautiful woman. Again, he listened, and she, being human, filled the silence with talk, eventually letting it slip about her job. It was a foolish, rookie mistake, and she was embarrassed the moment she made it, but relieved, too, he could tell. Secrets were a burden and sharing them with others lightened the load . . . for a time.

She knew he went back and forth to East Berlin with his work and even joked that she should recruit him. He agreed and gave her a few observations about the East German economy, nothing damaging or important, but enough to whet her appetite. He didn't reveal that he was a Stasi officer for three months—long enough for her to get pregnant.

She was understandably beside herself. Many men in the CIA still viewed their female counterparts as glorified coffee-getters. They had their place, but men ran the show. Her dickhead boss, a man named Buckley, was a case in point. A male CIA officer might get a slap on the wrist for sleeping with an asset. He'd be transferred, certainly, but his reputation would remain intact, possibly even bolstered. But a woman in the exact same position would be forever branded and transferred to Langley to work in the mail room if she wasn't fired outright.

She begged him to help her save her career.

He agreed to help her go to the East and terminate the pregnancy. Abortions were technically illegal in the DDR, unless one sat in counsel with a state psychologist to discuss options. Colonel Schneider did not care to tell his wife that he had a love child with an American spy, so he used his position to hurry the process along with nothing more than a cursory talk with a Stasi psychologist posing as a health official, and a quick visit to the doctor's office. North took two weeks' leave from work, ostensibly to visit friends in Switzerland, but spent it recuperating in a prefab concrete apartment watching East German television and crying her eyes out. Schneider stayed away for an entire week, letting her stew. When he did visit, he broke the news that he was a Stasi officer and told her that though he'd fallen in love with her, his superiors demanded something in return.

And just like that, she realized she'd been his asset all along.

And now it looked as though her usefulness was coming to an end . . . It was sad, really. They had shared some enjoyable times . . .

S atisfied no one was about to bear down on him, Schneider opened the glove box and retrieved a blocky radio telephone that was wired to the vehicle.

He checked his watch. Fuchs would be calling at any moment. The phone was heavy but still a miracle of modern technology. If Schneider had wanted to, he could have unplugged the handset from the vehicle and had half an hour of battery to talk to any phone in the world, though the charges would certainly enrage the Stasi accountants—bean counters, the Americans called them.

The phone gave an electronic pulse, like something from a science fiction movie.

"Hallo," Schneider said, feeling as though he were holding a fireplace log to his ear as he hefted the heavy device.

"We have them," Fuchs said.

"And the primary?" Schneider asked, unwilling to use even code names over the air.

"Not yet," Fuchs said. "I'm looking at the two-plus-six you told us about. They are not aware at this point."

"To be clear," Schneider said. "I will need to have a short face-to-face meeting with the primary before we're finished with him."

"Understood," Fuchs said. "And the others?"

"Not required," Schneider said. "Their services are no longer needed."

"No notice or severance package?" Fuchs asked.

"No," Schneider said. "Terminate them all. Today."

42

Just as Truly Bishop had predicted, Ryan and Foley found a coded note at the first meeting spot, directing them to a ten-story apartment building across a narrow cobblestone street from the woods of Friedrichshain People's Park. The top three floors were under construction. They'd run yet another string of SDRs after the first location and it was after ten p.m. by the time they reached the building. The few people still out walking scurried along crumbling sidewalks in the grubby darkness, eager to get out of the numbing cold. Ryan understood how they felt. Hat and overcoat were working fine, but he made a mental note to bring a better pair of boots next time he trucked off to vet a potential East German defector in the middle of a mini ice age.

Ryan and Foley walked past the building without stopping, made a block, and then waited for five minutes across the street. Foley put a hand on top of her hat and leaned back, counting up seven floors. In Germany the ground floor was just that. The first floor was one flight up, making the top of a ten-story building the ninth floor.

"Looks like we're good," she said, nodding to the third window from the corner. A thin line of light escaped from behind a heavy drape, just enough to show the outline of a toolbox on the sill. CALISTO's signal that it was all clear to come up.

"Almost too good," Ryan observed. He was no field operative, but his old man had taught him to have a healthy dose of paranoia. The right kind of fear could keep you alive.

There'd been a couple intermittent buzzes on the chest rig, but so far, Stasi and KGB patrols were looking elsewhere—or observing radio silence.

An elderly man in a red velour tracksuit that made him look like a retired Russian gangster shuffled into the lobby from a side room, holding his mail in one hand and the leash of a little Benji dog in the other. He and the dog walked with Ryan and Foley to the elevator. He pushed the call button for the sixth floor. Foley leaned over and pushed the button for the fifth.

"Guess it would have been odd if we'd been going up to a vacant floor," Ryan said once the elevator doors had shut behind them and they were alone in the fifth-floor elevator alcove.

"Exactly," Foley said. "We'll take the stairs up to seven."

"That's why you make the big money," Ryan said.

"It's not a bad idea to check out the stairs anyway," Foley said. "Keep our eyes open for escape routes, that kind of thing. A hell of a lot of things could go wrong here. I haven't seen any sign of the Helsinki team in half an hour. We could have unwanted company at any time—or CALISTO could be some kind of trap designed to nab a couple American operatives."

"What are the odds of that?"

"Well, Jack." Foley gave him a grim smile. "They're not zero."

"Gotcha," Ryan said. "Let's hope it doesn't come to that."

Foley smiled and gave him a motherly pat on the arm. "One of the first things they teach us," she said, "is that hope does not constitute a plan."

43

Ruby Keller had no way of knowing what time it was when a guard opened the peephole cover and ordered her to stand up and make her bed. It could have been days, or mere hours. Her brain and muscles were frayed and knotted from standing for hours on end with nothing to do but ponder her sad fate.

The food slot in the door squeaked open and a plastic tray came through along with a barked order to take it.

Cold oatmeal mush and a cup of water.

The food slot slammed shut but the eye in the peephole remained, staring down at her, commanding her to eat. They didn't want her to starve and rob them of the opportunity to brutalize her for as long as they could.

She choked down the mush, salted, as if plain mush would have been too much of a luxury.

A metal bucket in the corner—in direct view of the peephole and an ancient ceiling-mounted CCTV camera—served as her toilet. She used it, despite the embarrassment, hovering over it until her legs shook, so she didn't have to touch the filthy thing. She'd no sooner stood and replaced the dented metal lid when she heard footsteps in the hall.

"Face the wall!"

The door swung open, squealing with the anguish of the hundreds of prisoners who'd occupied this basement cell before her.

A soapy antiseptic odor rolled in, pinching her nose. It was a welcome change from the outhouse stench of her cell. The guards—two men this time—handcuffed her behind her back and then ordered her into the hallway. Her entire body quaked, feeling like it might come unglued at any moment. She could barely put one foot in front of the other, she was so terrified. Using two guards to move her seemed like overkill. She found herself relieved to see Wolfe, looking stern as a boulder. Anyone had to be better than the crazy woman.

Dazed and exhausted, she still got a better look at the deserted hallways than she had when they'd brought her in.

The basement, or U-boat, was a long subterranean tunnel with exposed piping that ran along the concrete ceiling. Rusted metal cell doors with coat after coat of flaking paint lined both sides of the dim tunnel. Frenzied screams came from some. Others moaned, as if the cell itself was desperate. Most were silent tombs. Uneven yellow tiles covered portions of the floor; the rest was painted concrete. A sagging insulated wire was strung the length of each side of the hall at shoulder level, marked every few feet by plastic connectors linking shorter pieces into one continuous line. From what she knew about the fastidiousness of the German psyche, Ruby found it odd that they would leave electric wire exposed and cobbled together like that.

Officer Wolfe gave a curt nod forward. His shouted order to "Go!" rattled down the empty tunnel.

Ruby hadn't gone three steps before a series of strobing red lights illuminated along the ceiling.

A side door creaked open.

"Stop!" Wolfe barked, voice quavering slightly. The man was genuinely surprised. He barked again, ordering Ruby to face the wall.

Two more uniformed guards exited the door less than ten feet down the hall, flanking a male prisoner. The man was a foot taller than either guard, built like a bull, and older than Ruby by at least a decade. His head was shaved and his broad face covered by a dark, bushy beard that was matted with food—or something worse.

One of the guards was a female. Ruby nearly choked on her own breath when she saw her. The vile woman kept her hat pulled low over her eyes and her back turned, but she had to be the same one. Ruby's heart lodged in her throat when she caught a glimpse of the freckled face. She sobbed, ready to scream until she got another look. No . . . the nose was wrong. This wasn't Mitzi Graff. This woman was gaunt, barely filling out her baggy uniform—far from pregnant.

The prisoner, "Seventeen," was not walking fast

enough and the freckled female guard gave him a brutal pool-cue jab between the shoulders with her truncheon.

The man staggered and fell against the wall, mumbling something unintelligible before catching himself. He stood and stumbled toward the male guard, less of an attack than a reaction from bumping the concrete. The poor man hardly seemed in his right mind, but the guards took his behavior as aggression. The male guard reached up and yanked the exposed wire, pulling it apart at the nearest plastic connector. Lights began to strobe and a faint buzzing could be heard from the end of the hall. Of course. The wires were a simple alarm system. Break the circuit and the alarms went off, notifying other guards that their comrades needed assistance from an unruly prisoner.

The freckled guard cursed, derisively calling her partner a *Hosenscheisser*, a pants-shitting coward, and set about to demonstrate that *she* did not require any reinforcements.

She went berserk with the stick, cursing and striking the addled prisoner over and over. Her first blow took him across the side of his thigh, driving him to his knees. Cuffed behind his back, the poor man could do nothing but yowl in pain. He was down on her level now. Humming with rage, she swung the truncheon like a baseball bat. The hard rubber, essentially a club molded from the same material as a bowling ball, cracked against the man's temple.

Ruby whimpered at the cruelty of it all. Behind her, even Wolfe muttered something under his breath.

Prisoner Seventeen swayed in place, on his knees but out cold. The woman hit him twice more before he hit the tile floor, and then continued to rain down punishment even after he lay motionless. Blood flecked the walls and ran freely from the wound where the man's ear had once been, tracing the tile grout in a horrible mosaic around his battered face. The freckled guard stooped forward, hands resting on her knees, panting from her efforts.

Wolfe ushered Ruby back into her cell, considerably more passive this time when he ordered her to face the wall.

And there she stayed, unable to do anything but pace her tiny basement cell, count the rapid beats of her heart, and ponder the barbarity she'd just witnessed.

Outside in the hallway, she could hear the swish of brushes as someone, likely another prisoner, scrubbed the gore from the putrid yellow tile.

Interminable hours later, the door opened again and the wall-facing, handcuffing routine was repeated, this time by two guards Ruby had never seen before. Both were older, mossy and emotionless in their ill-fitting uniforms. Again, she found herself relieved to see strangers instead of the freckled female.

The guards ushered her up the stairs to a similar maze of cells and painted steel metal bars. Yellow tile gave way to ugly yellow linoleum, but the place was still haunted by the hanging odor of bleach and chemical disinfectant.

Natural light flowed in from an actual window at the far end, opaque so she couldn't see out. The guards prodded her through two sets of gates that unlocked with a metal *whir* at their approach. A final steel door led outside to a twenty-by-twenty-foot concrete box. Ruby was surprised to find it was late evening, getting dark, temperatures falling. She didn't care. Frigid, coal-laden air was better than the stench inside.

A light skiff of snow had sifted down through the chain-link covering above. It was like being walked into the bottom of an empty swimming pool. A guard on the wall fifteen feet above looked down with his Kalashnikov, eyes wide, as if he feared she might scramble up the wall. There was no wind, but at least there was light. Gray walls made it feel especially cold, and Ruby hunched forward.

The guard who had escorted her in removed her handcuffs and then nodded to the far end of the enclosure.

"Walk!"

Ruby didn't move. Was this the end of her? Was she to die by firing squad in some East German kill room? That's the way it happened in the spy books she read. Her belly roiled and burned. She sobbed, certain she was about to lose control of her bowels. Then the guard warned her that she had "fifteen minutes of fresh air" and went in through the door they'd come out, leaving her in the care of the one on the wall. They wanted her to exercise.

Tears of relief streamed down her cheeks. A coat

would have been nice, but she would have trudged through any storm for a breath of outside air.

Less than a minute later, Mitzi Graff sauntered in looking as pregnant and freckled as ever. Her blue jumpsuit was extra-large to accommodate the baby bump, requiring the legs to be rolled up to keep them from flapping. A neatly rolled wool blanket was tucked under her arm. They evidently treated you better here if you were pregnant. Graff stood while the guard removed her handcuffs. Once free, she draped the blanket over her shoulders and waddled across the tiny exercise yard. Ruby had never been pregnant, but the idea of being in that condition in this place made her want to vomit.

Ruby's mouth fell open when Graff came up beside her. "There is a guard in here that could be your sister."

Graff gave a little shrug. "I know," she said. "I suppose it is possible. My father was a . . . How do you say a man who is a whore in English?"

"A man," Ruby said, startled that she had the capacity to joke under these circumstances.

"You are funny," Graff said. "Anyway, my father probably sired many children all around Berlin. His behavior drove my mother to drown herself in the Spree River."

"That's terrible," Ruby said. "I'm so sorry."

"Don't be," Graff said. "I cut his head off with an ax. My boyfriend got off lucky when I only took his toe."

It was impossible to know if this girl was joking. She certainly looked as though she would cut off someone's head if they wronged her. Ruby didn't know what to say, so she said nothing. The intensity in Mitzi Graff's voice was terrifying, and the freckles . . . But she was pregnant, and her nose was all wrong. Wasn't it?

"They never do this, you know," Graff said. "Letting two prisoners exercise in the tiger cage at the same time. When last I was here we had no contact with any other prisoners."

"The tiger cage." Ruby repeated the phrase. "I feel more like a mouse than a tiger."

Graff grimaced like she had a bad case of indigestion. She turned her head to look at Ruby as they walked, and gestured to the blanket. "Want to warm up for a bit?"

"I couldn't," Ruby said. "I'd worry about the baby."

"Why are they letting us talk, do you think? Are you spying on me?"

"What? No. Of course not. I still haven't figured out why *I* am here."

"Sure you have," Graff said. "Everyone in this place knows what they have done. They may not agree with the state's assessment, but they know why they were taken into custody."

"Well, I don't," Keller said. "I mean, I assume it has to do with a computer disk I received." She leaned sideways, lowering her voice so the guard above could not hear. "I gave it to the CIA, but I have no idea what was on it."

"The CIA?" Graff said. "No wonder they picked you up. It sounds as though you are a spy."

The guard yelled for them to stop whispering, but his heart wasn't in the order and he turned away after he gave it to light a cigarette.

"I'm a lot of things, Mitzi," Keller said. "But I am not a spy. Do you mind if I call you Mitzi?"

"Please," Graff said, smiling more broadly.

"I . . . I just got caught up in the wrong place at the wrong time, I guess," Ruby said. "I'm probably the most boring person you'll ever meet."

"That sounds precisely like something a spy would say." Graff pulled the blanket tighter around her neck against the cold.

"Spies have to be brave," Ruby said. "I am not. I . . ."

"You what?"

Ruby shook her head. "Nothing."

"Your German is quite good," Graff said. "Better than my English."

"Nah." Ruby shivered, wishing Graff would offer her a few minutes with the blanket again. She did not. "Your English is great. My grandfather immigrated to the United States before the war. He lived next door to us, so we grew up speaking with him in German. He played the violin. Taught me to play it, too."

"Played?"

"He died last year," Ruby said, tearful with fear and despair. She put a hand to her chest and swallowed a sob. "Sorry. It's just . . . I don't know. All this has me . . . It's like all my emotions are right at the surface . . . Ya know?"

"So your grandfather was from where?" Graff asked.

"Munich," Keller said. "That's one of the reasons I wanted to come to Germany with my job. To learn more about his roots."

"Your job?"

"Nothing special," Ruby said. "Just a nobody with the State Department. I suppose that's why my government hasn't called to demand my return."

"Perhaps they have no idea that you are here," Graff said.

Ruby sniffed back a sob. "I've thought about that." She lowered her voice again, staring straight ahead while they walked, speaking like a ventriloquist. "I saw the guards kill a man today." Her body began to shake again, more from hopelessness than from the bitter cold.

"Kill?"

"Pretty sure." Her words caught like a jagged bone in her throat at the raw memory of it. "That woman, that one who could be your sister, she just kept hitting him and hitting him . . . Honestly, it was like she'd lost her mind. She hit that poor man so many times it tore his ear off. His face was all . . . I don't know, just gone . . . He has to be dead."

"Oh, ja," Graff said and chuckled. *"Er ist tot."*

"I shouldn't have told you," Ruby whispered. "I don't want to get you into troub—"

It took a moment to sink in that Graff had answered her in German, her voice suddenly lower in pitch and timbre, laughing. Ruby stopped walking and turned to her in horror.

Graff stood facing her, flecks of dried blood mingling with the freckles along her jaw.

44

Ruby gasped. "It . . . was you . . ."

Mitzi Graff peeled off the prosthetic nose, then gave her own belly—where the baby should have been—a hard punch with a closed fist before cuffing a stupefied Ruby on the side of the head.

"You idiotic bitch!" Graff's face flushed crimson. "Of course it is me." Her lips pulled back in a soulless grin as she grabbed Ruby's wrist. "Face the wall, Ninety-six!"

Stunned, Ruby did as she was told, catching a glimpse of the horrible black truncheon that must have been hidden beneath the blanket. Graff grabbed her right hand and shoved it palm-out against the concrete, giving a satisfied grunt as she swung the truncheon. Ruby screamed when it smashed into the back of her hand. Sick to her stomach from the sudden shock, Ruby looked away from her battered hand, horrified to see a severed thumb lying on the concrete at her feet.

Her thumb.

Graff had not been hiding her truncheon at all, but a small hand ax.

"Oh, do not cry," Graff whispered, pressing Keller against the wall with her full weight. The German was quieter now. Her sickeningly sweet breath fluttered against Ruby's ear, mocking her. "You may think me cruel," she said. "But you will think of me often—every day, in fact, when you attempt some simple task like picking up a cup and remember that, once upon a time, you used to have a pretty little thumb . . ."

O n the other side of the concrete wall, CIA operations officer Jennifer North stood with her arms folded tight across her chest, watching the events in the tiger cage unfold. Speakers in the wood paneling alongside the CCTV monitors broadcast the conversation.

"Are we recording this on video?" she asked the guard who was seated at the desk.

"Of course," he said with curt German efficiency.

North turned and began to pace the small surveillance room, gnawing on her thumbnail as she thought about her next move. This Ruby Keller kid was a poisoned pawn, a weak little nothing of a girl whose destruction threatened to galvanize everyone in USBER and Berlin Station. Every asset would be mobilized, every marker called in. The CIA was perpetually one step behind the Soviets and East Germans, but they would eventually find out where Keller was being held.

The door buzzed open and Mitzi Graff came in. She'd rolled her blue Smurf suit down to her waist, exposing a white T-shirt and muscular arms.

North was taller, physically stronger, with at least a decade more experience—but she'd never hacked off any-body's thumb. This bitch was insane. She was also in charge—at least until Rolfe Schneider got here. The way she carried herself nose-high made it clear that she knew it.

North hugged herself tighter, struggling to retain her composure.

"Why the masquerade?"

Graff took out a box of tissues from a drawer at the end of the cabinet and began to rub the blood off her hands and face. The guard at the monitors flinched when she got close. Mitzi Graff was a Stasi major, frequently called to ply her trade at Hohenschönhausen and other prisons around the country because of her expertise in interrogation and, though everyone called it by more flowery words, torture. In North's experience, other than the terrified dupes who just needed a job, there were three types of people in the Stasi—true believers who felt it was perfectly okay to destroy others to prop up the socialist utopia in the name of blind patriotism, politicians and apparatchiks who were drunk on the power of ruling others, and sociopaths who might have been voyeurs, rapists, or serial killers but now found legal outlets for their twisted passions under the guise of the secret police.

Graff was the kind of damaged human that would

have flourished within the Nazi regime, which meant she fit in splendidly among the Stasi.

She found a compact mirror in the same drawer where she'd gotten the tissues and used it to study her face, jutting out her chin to get a hard-to-reach bit of the dead man's blood.

"I was led to believe there was some urgency with this one. That it was time-sensitive."

"I suppose . . ."

Graff gave her face one last scan in the little mirror and then pitched the soiled tissue into a plastic trash bin before turning to North. She, too, folded her arms across her chest. When North let her hands fall by her sides, Graff did the same, mirroring her movements, toying with her.

"Sleep deprivation works extremely well to break down the mind," Graff said. "But it takes a considerable amount of time. Some people prove to be astoundingly resilient. Women especially, in my experience. Though some turn to jelly immediately, soiling their pants at the first set of questions." Graff cocked her head, eyeing North like a piece of meat. "Do you ever wonder how long you would be able to hold out?"

"May we focus?" North said, hiding a shudder.

"Ah," Graff said, shaking it off as if the spell had been broken. "Of course. Anyway, drugs, water treatment, any number of our methods would have worked eventually, but we did not have that luxury. One look at our pitiful little Ruby and I knew she merely needed a friend. Americans want so badly to see the good in people."

"Letting you see her as a guard was—"

"All part of the process, Jennifer," Graff said, wielding North's real name like a club. "Bending someone's mind is no different than forging steel. Both must be heated to a red-hot frenzy before they can be shaped. To put it another way, show someone they are drowning in insanity and then be there for them to grab when they find themselves sinking. Frankly, I am surprised the American spymasters do not teach you this basic tactic for interrogation."

Graff spoke as if she were discussing a recipe for roast beef instead of shattering the mind of an innocent girl.

"What is your opinion, then," North asked. "Is she part of some larger investigation?"

Graff threw up her hand at the notion. "She was chosen at random to deliver the message from your would-be defector," Graff said. "Nothing more. The question becomes, what do we do with her? No one knows she is here."

"Maybe"—North nodded to the guard at the panel—"we shouldn't even be speaking in front of him."

Graff gave a hearty belly laugh. "Jonas? He would not speak a word. Would you, Jonas?"

"*Nein,*" the man said, eyes glued to the cameras.

Graff darkened. "Because Jonas knows I would cut off his ball sack and use it to make a tiny leather case for my pocket mirror . . . Don't you, Jonas?"

His Adam's apple bobbed as he swallowed hard. Otherwise, he did not move.

"Anyway," Graff said, pitching the mirror back into the drawer. "I suggest a quiet end."

North began to gnaw at her thumbnail again. "You mean kill her?"

"Schneider said you wanted her arrested," Graff said. "What did you suppose would happen to her once we were finished? That we would set her on the Glienicke Bridge and shoo her across to the West with a pat on the bottom?"

"I did not want her arrested," North snapped. "I wanted to know if she was hunting me."

Graff gave a little shrug. "Well, she is ours to deal with now. And we took her off the street in the West. There is no going back from that. It would prove embarrassing if word got out."

North couldn't conceal her chuckle. "You give the DDR too much credit. No one in the West would be at all surprised to find out you snatched an innocent girl off the street and trundled her over the wall. They'll chalk it up to your inherently evil nature and be happy to get her back."

Graff studied her for a moment, as if deciding where to cut first.

"If we in the DDR are such monsters, then why do you work with us?"

Because I have no choice, North thought, but considering she was in the bowels of a Stasi prison, she kept it to herself.

"You and Rolfe are the . . . How do you say it? The deciders." Graff chuckled, a far-off look in her eyes. "Anyway, I am sorry to cut this conversation short." Hatchet in hand, she winked at her pun. "But our Ruby is not the only riddle that I have to solve here today."

The temperature in the sterile control room warmed appreciably when Graff walked out. Jonas, the guard, gave an audible sigh, apparently relieved that his ball sack was safe for the time being. He jumped when North moved up beside him and leaned on the counter with both hands.

"I need to make a telephone call."

Jonas nodded to the phone at the end of the long counter, but kept his attention focused on the screens like an automaton. This guy was a machine. He would listen and memorize everything she said, probably reporting it back to Graff if it wasn't recorded already. It didn't matter. She needed to speak with Schneider.

The telephone cord was just long enough that she could stand at the counter and turn slightly away, granting her at least the illusion of privacy.

The phone gave only a short ring, as if the woman had been waiting there and pounced to answer.

"*Einundfünfzig, siebenundsechzig.*" Fifty-one, sixty-seven.

"Dolly Dupont," North said. "*Guten Tag.*"

"*Einen Moment, bitte,*" the woman said. She knew exactly why North was calling.

There was a click, a momentary silence—probably a tape recorder being switched on—and then Schneider came on the line.

"*Hallo,* Dolly!" he said. "Tell me something happy!"

45

Elke Hauptman sat in the dark on an overturned paint bucket in the middle of the vacant room, waiting. A flashing sign above the café across the street cast eerie shadows on the wall. The entire seventh floor was under construction. Rolls of carpet were stacked against bare walls. Wood scraps and paint splashes littered the concrete floors. A roll of clear plastic sheeting lay at her feet, like in a kill room in a crime movie. One of the windows was missing a pane and cold air poured in, turning the room into a deep freeze. Still in her coat and hat, she huddled with her knees together, slumped forward on the bucket, resting her elbows on her thighs. A black revolver hung in her hand, loose, dangling, like she might drop it at any moment.

It was a horrible thing, the gun, but alarmingly easy to come by if one knew the right people. Berlin was crawling with soldiers on both sides of the wall. Most of

those soldiers, especially the ones in the service of Warsaw Pact nations, were poorly paid. They had access to
guns, which offered them access to money, giving rise to
a lucrative black-market weapons trade. The man in the
club who'd procured the revolver for her explained that
semiautomatic pistols—especially like the ones James
Bond carried—were all the rage now. An old Nagant
could be had for "an apple and an egg"—next to nothing. He pawed at her and offered to take his fee in trade,
the swine. She'd had far too much of that behavior from
Pfeiffer and insisted on paying cash. Disappointed, he'd
charged considerably more than an apple and an egg.

The Nagant came loaded with seven bullets already in
the cylinder. There was no extra ammunition, but that
was fine because Elke had no idea how to reload the
thing anyway. The man had given her a quick lesson.
Point it at what you want to destroy, cock the hammer,
squeeze the trigger. Simple enough, though at this moment, Elke was having trouble remembering to breathe.

A soft thud on the other side of the wall startled her
back to the present. She stood, gun in hand, and stared
at the door.

Had someone followed her? She'd been so careful. It
didn't matter. She had no choice but to see this through
to the end. People did insane things when they were
cornered. She would throw away everything to save her
family.

Ear to the door, she put a trembling hand on the knob
and listened to the approaching footsteps.

T he stairwell exited onto the seventh floor in a ten-by-ten-foot elevator alcove where two long and extremely dark hallways converged. Fortunately, Ryan and Foley's short foray onto the fifth floor when the old man and his dog had gotten on the elevator had offered them a look at the building's layout on a floor where there was enough light to see.

"You do this kind of stuff a lot?" Ryan whispered.

"You mean venture into dangerous situations in vacant apartment buildings with somebody I barely know?" Foley batted long lashes. "It's the number one reason I took this job . . ."

Ryan didn't have a comeback. There was something about Mary Pat Foley that made him trust her—a surety in the way she moved, completely void of the cockiness that usually went along with such certitude. She was careful, even a little bit afraid, but once she came to a decision, she marched on, committed to the end—wherever that might take her. There was a savvy there, as if she'd played this game before or was born to it. In many ways, she reminded him of Cathy, though with harder edges and something far darker behind her eyes. If Ryan was going to walk into a vacant building unarmed to meet a spy of unknown veracity in the middle of one of the most repressive countries on the planet, he couldn't imagine anyone he'd rather have by his side.

Unencumbered by OSHA rules and regulations, the

building's owners hadn't bothered with lighted exit signs. What little light there was came from the elevator alcove and a bank of windows at the far end of the hall. The floor was littered with dust and construction debris— half-used paint cans, wads of masking tape. Scattered Sheetrock nails were strewn everywhere, looking as if someone had thrown them there on purpose. The doors were white, making them stand out in stark contrast to the shadows.

"Up here on the left," Foley whispered. "Three from the corner." She glanced sideways at Ryan. "Take a couple steps to your right."

"Okay . . ." Ryan said. "Why? What's up?"

"Makes it a tad harder to shoot both of us at the same time if we're not bunched up . . ."

"Right . . ."

Ryan tensed as the door to his left opened a hair.

Foley paused, hands by her sides, unthreatening. "We're looking for the eighth floor," she said, giving the first part of the agreed-upon pass phrase.

The door opened wider. "The view is better on nine."

"We're more concerned with the neighbors," Foley said.

The door swung open and an arm, clad in a baby-blue dress shirt and gold cuff links, beckoned them inside.

A balding man with the most expensive-looking suit Ryan had seen during his short stay in East Berlin clicked his heels together and offered his outstretched hand. "I am Major Kurt Pfeiffer of DDR Ministry for State Security—the Stasi—and who might you—"

Foley raised a hand to shush him, then put a finger to her lips.

The Stasi man laughed out loud. "Do not worry, my dear. I performed a complete sweep of this entire room for cameras and listening devices long before your arrival." His English was near perfect as far as grammar went but held the clipped accent of someone who'd learned from a book. Ryan had to concentrate to keep from cringing. Every word was so painfully exaggerated, like a bad British actor attempting a German accent for a part on *Hogan's Heroes*.

"It is my job to be aware of such things, you know," Pfeiffer continued. "I am sure you know the reputation of the Stasi. Though we are not the monsters you make us out to be in the West, we are familiar with . . . bugs, as you call them." He clapped his hands together and heaved a deep sigh, ready to get down to business.

Foley edged to her right, toward the wall. Ryan moved with her, a silent dance to position their backs away from the door. The German was forced to turn to keep facing them. It was impressive the way Foley took subtle control, step by step, breath by breath.

Pfeiffer waved a hand around the dusty room. It was under construction like the rest of the floor, and there was a cot and neatly stacked blankets on the far wall, a small card table, two folding chairs. Several five-gallon paint cans rounded out the furnishings. A heavy tarp was nailed to the window, blacking out light from three battery-powered lanterns.

"In any case," he joked, "we are intelligent enough to

wait until construction was almost complete before installing our devices. I can assure you, this location is clean. Please feel free to speak . . . freely."

"This is your meeting, Colonel," Foley said.

"Major," Pfeiffer corrected.

"I apologize." Foley ducked her head a little, looking up from downcast eyes. She'd unbuttoned the heavy coat, revealing the form-fitting dress that showed off her figure and black tights underneath.

Ryan couldn't decide if it was just his imagination, or if this guy was giving Foley more than a normal once-over. Apparently liking what he saw, Pfeiffer smiled, and then turned to Ryan. "Now you know who I am . . ."

Ryan said, "You may call me Jack, and this is my friend, Mary."

Their given names weren't a secret. They were the same ones on their travel documents, including the visas the border guard had issued when they'd crossed into East Germany.

"Very well, Jack." The major overemphasized his name, as if he did not quite believe Ryan was telling the truth. Down to the business of the evening, he no longer bothered looking at Foley. "I am assuming you are a representative of the CIA."

"We are here to listen," Ryan said. "I understand you have a business proposal."

"What?" Pfeiffer said, confused. "Business? No. I need to know who you are."

Foley spoke next. "We are the people who can help

you. But as I said before, this is your meeting. Tell us what *you* want."

Pfeiffer snorted, eyes shifting between the door and Ryan. He tugged on the lapels of his suit jacket, purposely showing Ryan a glimpse of a holster. He hooked a thumb over his shoulder. "This one sounds like Stasi, laying a trap for me to incriminate myself."

"You sent the invitation," Ryan said. "We are here. It's your move. Otherwise, we're at an impasse."

Pfeiffer let his hands fall to his sides. "Very well," he blurted. "I wish to offer my services to the United States. I want to defect."

"That can be arranged," Foley said. "Provided you are who you say you are."

Pfeiffer shot her a quick glance, then turned again to Ryan. "You are here," he said. "So I assume your government is interested in the small taste of the radar-avoidance technology I have to offer."

"Maybe," Ryan said, in the understatement of the year. "But as my colleague has explained, we need to establish your bona fides."

"Listen to me," Pfeiffer said. "I speak with you at great risk to my own life. If we are caught, my people will put you in prison. Yes, there would be no small amount of torture, but we accept that when we undertake this line of work. Do we not? Perhaps a few of your bones will be broken, a tooth or two damaged, but in the end, the DDR would trade you back to your government for someone . . . something we need. I would be a different story altogether. I, too, would be tortured, even more brutally than you, for you see, we save our best for our own when they go astray. Your torture will be a means to extract information, but mine will focus on inflicting as much pain as possible for as long as possible. They must demonstrate to others in my position the dangers of betraying one's country. So yes, I am who I say I am—a dead man walking, if you decide not to help me."

I n the apartment next door, Elke Hauptman pressed a six-inch section of plastic pipe between the common wall and her ear. It worked well to focus the sound, better than the water glass people always used in the movies. Her mouth hung open in shock. She'd known Pfeiffer was here to meet someone, but she'd assumed it was a woman. He was a predator, a sociopathic bastard who fed on the misery of the women he forced to sleep with him. But never in her wildest dreams had she imagined him to be a traitor.

The possibilities that had suddenly been placed in front of her were enormous.

This. Changed. Everything.

The words were muffled, but East German walls were notoriously thin, and Elke heard enough to know that treason was unfolding mere inches away from her. She smiled, forcing herself to keep from jumping up and down. Pfeiffer had intruded into the most intimate aspects of her home with all manner of sophisticated electronic bugs and cameras—and now she listened to every word he said through a short length of plumbing pressed against the wall.

She froze, suddenly fearful that she might sneeze or make some tiny misstep that would reveal her presence. Surely the pounding of her heart would give her away.

She'd followed Kurt Pfeiffer to put a bullet in his head, but this was better. Oh, the ending would be the same for him, but if Elke played the right cards, she would not have to be the one who pulled the trigger.

That morning, she'd gone to the Stasi headquarters building directly after saying good-bye to Uwe. The poor man had no idea that she had been planning to commit murder for the past week—or that she'd been betraying him with this foul Stasi officer who was now droning on about his importance on the other side of the wall.

Known as the Round Corner from the curvature of its façade, the Berlin headquarters building of the Ministry for State Security, the Sword and Shield for sticking it to the people, was very close in color to the baby-shit-yellow Schwalbe scooter. Pfeiffer's office was on the second floor, as was his secretary, an attractive woman named Marta Wunch, with strong shoulders and large bosoms she proudly displayed beneath tight cashmere sweaters. She wore long golden locks in braids like the perfect Aryan woman from a Third Reich propaganda poster. Elke had never met her, but Pfeiffer had shown her photographs. He spoke of "his Marta" often, bragging incessantly of her abject devotion.

It was not bad enough that the pig forced Elke to

sleep with him, but he took perverse pleasure in bringing up his secretary at every turn, as if it were possible for Elke to be jealous over someone whom she did not want to be with in the first place. *Marta does it this way,* or *Marta is over the moon when I . . . Marta becomes so cross if I miss our date for coffee each and every morning . . .*

He would be at his office. Elke was certain of it.

It was almost lunchtime before he finally left the building, alone in his black Lada. He'd made half-hearted attempts to see if anyone was following him—doubling back, going around and around several blocks. Elke would have lost him had she not been on her Schwalbe. The little scooters were everywhere, but hardly noticed by anyone. Threats did not come on two wheels, which surely accounted for why so many of them were run off the road every year. She cut in and out of traffic to keep the Lada in view, careful to keep her distance. He stopped at several shops, all run by women over whom he apparently lorded some kind of control. Elke couldn't hear the conversations taking place through the shop windows, but she could tell by the look on the women's faces that they were all in the same predicament as she was.

He'd made other stops, too, one at an abandoned typewriter repair shop. She'd watched him drop off an envelope there, and thought of trying to read it, but she would have lost him.

Elke followed him here just after dark. He parked around the corner, casting a furtive but ineffective glance over each shoulder before grabbing a suit bag and a small insulated cooler from the trunk of his Lada before heading upstairs. It had made perfect sense when she first saw it. Kurt Pfeiffer was driven by three appetites—fine clothes, rich food, and women.

He planned to meet someone. Elke followed him, sprinting up the stairs just in time to see him disappear into the apartment. The entire floor was vacant, under construction. The door to the apartment next to his did not even lock. She'd slipped in and waited, working up the courage to burst through Pfeiffer's door, savoring the look she would see on his terrified face when he realized she had a gun. She could not have dreamed of a spot more perfect to kill someone . . . And still, as much as she loathed the man, shooting him . . . shooting anyone . . . was not as easy as she'd imagined it would be.

Then the Americans had arrived, and her options grew exponentially. She did not have to use the wretched black revolver to kill anyone. It was so simple. Finally, she could prove her loyalty to the state and convince them to leave her family alone. She would listen carefully and learn where the next meeting was to take place. Then, when they had all gone, she would return to the Round Corner and inform the Stasi of the traitor in their midst and the American spies who'd come to help him.

46

I must tell you," Pfeiffer said, his top lip quivering. "I had envisioned this as a much happier moment. Tell me, Jack, what must I do to establish my bona fides?"

"You can start with the dead boy on Clayallee," Foley said. She had far more experience at recruiting assets, and they'd established early on that she would ask the hard-ball questions, giving Ryan an opportunity to observe. Pfeiffer had made it easy for her to be the "bad cop," treating her from the moment they'd met as if she were Ryan's secretary.

The major got a pained look on his face, as if he had a case of indigestion.

"Who?"

"Freddie Heinrich," Foley said. "The nineteen-year-old punk rocker who you hired to steal Ruby Keller's purse and create the diversion."

"Ah, yes, him." Pfeiffer looked at her, licking his lips

like a reptile tasting the air. "That was an unfortunate turn of events. I did not know his name, nor the name of the girl, for that matter. Keller, you say? She was chosen at random because she left your consulate to go to that horrible little café every day for almost a week. I paid the boy five marks to take the purse and drop in my message."

"And then poisoned him?" Foley prodded.

"Not at all," Pfeiffer said. If being accused of murder bothered him, he showed no outward sign of it. If anything, he grew calmer. "You know as well as I do that the KGB and agents from my own HVA make a habit of following your diplomats. I believe they were following this Keller girl already. When they saw the mugging, they thought it was a brush-pass and moved to intercept."

"And the woman who returned the bag?" Ryan asked.

Pfeiffer shrugged and turned to peek around the edge of the heavy canvas tarp tacked to the window. "A Good Samaritan, perhaps? She was a stranger to me. I am just fortunate my message was not intercepted."

"Indeed," Ryan said.

He and Foley exchanged looks. Neither of them believed his story. Pfeiffer had silenced the kid to tie up a loose end. The "Good Samaritan" was probably lucky to be alive . . . if she still was.

Foley folded her arms, canting her head to study the man. "All right, Major Pfeiffer. Let us suppose just for a moment that this bullshit story of yours is true. Tell us why."

Pfeiffer spun away from the window, facing her.

"What do you mean, 'why'?" Ryan couldn't tell if he was getting nervous or just angry that they weren't welcoming him in with open arms.

"You had to come to the West to leave your message," Ryan said. "Why would you run the risk of having us meet you on this side of the wall? Forgive me, Major, but you could have approached anyone. West Berlin is crawling with soldiers and diplomats—"

"And moles," Pfeiffer said. "I am personally aware of at least one turncoat among you. I naturally assume there are more. My life would be cut short all too quickly if I happened to present myself to the wrong person."

"This mole," Ryan asked. "Do you have a name to give us? That would go a long way."

"In time," Pfeiffer said. "You do not quite trust me . . . Well, the feeling is mutual, I assure you."

Ryan looked the major up and down, getting a measure of the man. He carried himself with a haughty confidence, nose up, chin out. His suit looked like something off Savile Row and surely cost more than a Stasi major would make in one month. Ryan's homicide detective father had taught him early on to pay attention to a man's footwear—both the type and the way he took care of them.

Pfeiffer's cap-toe oxfords were polished to a high sheen. Expensive, possibly even bespoke like his suit, but they were far from new. This was a man who put a good many miles on his shoe leather. Not a boss or a desk jockey, he was a worker bee who enjoyed the finer things in life. Stasi majors were likely the same as majors stationed at the Pentagon—field-grade officers getting coffee for a bunch of colonels and generals.

Pfeiffer exhaled quickly through his nose, the verbal equivalent of stomping his foot. "I am here offering you troves of information, intelligence treasures you can only dream of."

A soft smile spread over Foley's face, surprisingly demure from the Mary Pat she'd been displaying over the past ten minutes. Pfeiffer was a big fish that needed to be played gently but firmly.

"You and I are in the intelligence business, Major," she said. "If the situations were reversed and I showed up under exactly these circumstances, with exactly this kind of information, would you take my word for it out of hand?"

He shook his head. "If vital intelligence fell into my lap, I'd be happy to get it."

"You know as well as we do that there are only a handful of reasons people switch sides. To put it bluntly, our bosses want to know your reasons before they trust you."

Pfeiffer waved her off like a bothersome fly and addressed Ryan directly. "This information regarding radar cloaking . . . I am talking about invisibility here. Is not that kind of knowledge appealing? It could make your career!"

"I will admit it looks promising," Ryan said. "But, as my colleague asked, if the shoe were on the other foot, would it be enough for you?"

Pfeiffer's face screwed into a tight grimace, a pouting child in an expensive suit. "I suppose not . . ."

Both Ryan and Foley were silent, letting Pfeiffer stew. He paced the length of the room twice, peeked through the thin gap between the tarp and the window again, and then turned abruptly with a long sigh, completely resigned.

"There is a story, my dear," he said. "A joke, really, but it illustrates my point. It seems that Erich Honecker, the general secretary of the DDR, took a trip to Moscow. Khrushchev wined him and dined him and provided a harem of beautiful Russian women to see to his every carnal need." Pfeiffer eyed Foley with a lascivious grin. When she didn't respond, he continued.

"At the end of the visit, Khrushchev gifted Honecker a fine new ZiL-4104. Beautiful and glossy black, the limousine was luxurious, fitting, he said, of the leader of the Deutsche Demokratische Republik. But when it was time to leave, Honecker found that the shiny ZiL had no motor. He complained, of course, but Khrushchev explained, 'You do not need a motor when you are only going downhill.'"

"So," Foley said. "You believe East Germany is failing—"

"To use your words, my dear, you, too, are in the intelligence business. How long do you Americans think the DDR can continue as a viable nation? One month? Ten years? Those Soviet bastards have troubles of their own. They have all but abandoned us. Even now, our utopian society is little more than flaking paint and rust. If you had any intelligence apparatus at all, you would see that this country is held together with nothing but coal dust and the tears of Erich Honecker. Not too many years will pass before there will be no DDR left for me to betray. I, and men like me, have at times been forced to take drastic measures to protect and shield the state. As I feel certain you would have under similar circumstances. And what will we have to show for our decades of service when this great experiment ends? We will fade into the shadows—if we are not hunted down for some Nuremberg show trial and hanged for imagined offenses . . . or shot by a vengeful comrade's bullet who boo-hoos about how badly he has been treated." His eyes narrowed. "I have seen a good deal of death in my time, Jack and Mary, or whatever your names are. I do not choose to have my brains spattered against a wall because I happened to be good at my job."

Ryan shot a glance at Foley. Time to add a little pressure—carefully, though; they *were* still in his backyard. "What is the saying? A police state is not so bad if you're the state police."

Pfeiffer raised a brow, eyeing him, dead serious. "Precisely."

"How do you see this playing out?" Foley asked.

"That is simple," the major said. "I give you what you're looking for. You provide me with resettlement and a reasonably comfortable life in the United States. Somewhere warm, if it's all the same to you. Oh, and I would rather retire. I am too old and set in my ways to stomach any of the vocational retraining I have heard you offer. There will be no need to spirit me out of the DDR as you people are always attempting to do. I am free to travel. I will come to your diplomatic mission on Clayallee and walk in as soon as you can assure my safety. You can fly me out of the country from West Berlin."

"That could be arranged," Foley said. "As long as our superiors think your information is valuable enough."

Pfeiffer fished a bright red pack of cigarettes from his pocket. His movements were precise, choreographed. Ryan and Foley braced, thinking for a moment this might be a signal for anyone watching on hidden cameras to swoop in and arrest them.

He lit a cigarette, then picked a bit of tobacco off his lip and flicked it toward Foley.

"Valuable enough? Who do you think you are talking to? I am a Stasi major. The information I possess would make you piss your panties, my dear." He took a deep drag off the cigarette and turned to Ryan. "What I have to offer is—"

"Look at *me*, Major," Foley snapped, dispensing with the sweetheart act completely. "Not him. We can meet your demands, but you must be vetted."

As Ryan suspected, they had the stronger hand.

Pfeiffer held the cigarette to one side while he weighed his options. Then he looked directly at Foley and tried to sweeten the pot.

"I will provide you with the name of the mole."

Foley kept her game face, but Ryan knew this had piqued her interest.

"That would go a long way to prove veracity," she said. "But, again, we can't just take you at your word."

Pfeiffer's face began to twitch, and he looked like he

was about to boil over. "So I am to sit in the DDR and twist in the wind while you stir a hornets' nest in the West?"

Foley frowned. "I didn't say that. You could accuse anyone of being a mole and then watch from the sidelines as we devour our young. It is a favorite tactic of the KGB."

Pfeiffer smoked in silence, the wheels turning in his head.

Ryan extended a hand toward the cigarette, catching the major's eye and shooting a sidelong glance at Foley, as if to say, *Hey, I have to work with this battle-ax.*

Pfeiffer took out the pack of Roth-Händles and shook out a cigarette. He put it between his lips next to his own, lit it, and then handed the half-smoked one to Ryan. Ryan pretended to be grateful. A real piece of work, this guy.

"HVA is the part of the Stasi that handles foreign intelligence," Ryan said. He pushed thoughts of what Cathy would say about him smoking again out of his mind.

"That is correct." Pfeiffer eyed him as if unsure about where this was going. "You would call HVA our Directorate for Reconnaissance."

"And what do you run?"

Pfeiffer twitched again. "I . . . Various programs. Many, actually."

"I see," Ryan said. "But you are stationed in the DDR, while most HVA agents are overseas."

"Correct again, or in West Germany. But some must

remain here. I oversee Division A, military technology. Even so, I am kept apprised of the names of many operatives and operations. I will be happy to provide them once we have come to an accord. I will tell you now, though, we've never had much luck infiltrating institutions in the United States. We tend to leave that to the KGB." He scoffed and blew a smoke ring. "You have no idea . . ."

"What can you tell us about Nevada?" Ryan asked.

Pfeiffer's eyes flashed. A smile perked at the corners of his lips, as if he'd won. He calmed himself with a long drag off his cigarette.

"Nevada?"

"Yes."

Pfeiffer nodded slowly. "Nevada is a very large place."

"Yes, it is," Ryan said. "Tell me what you know about HVA there."

"Oh, my friend, the things I know about events in Nevada would astound you. But I need assurances before I give you that. For now, I will tell you the name of your mole. That should let your superiors at Langley see that I am a serious man with serious information. You can only imagine the importance we place on an asset deep in the bowels of the American CIA. She is vital."

Neither Ryan nor Foley were shocked when he named Jen North. In fact, it seemed inevitable.

The receiver in the center of Ryan's chest buzzed once and stopped. It was the first time he'd gotten any kind of signal in half an hour and he jumped, drawing a side-eye from Pfeiffer. The notifications had come periodically, even before they'd arrived at the meeting spot—a vibration here, two there, as Truly Bishop and her boss triangulated radio signals that were moving closer to their given location. The city was teeming with police—secret and otherwise. Complete radio silence would have been cause for concern.

Ryan went to the window now, staying well back as he pulled aside the tarp a hair to peek outside. Though not crowded, the sidewalks had a steady flow of pedestrians, many of them coming from a small bar on the corner to Ryan's right. At the opposite end of the block, near the corner on the left, a lone man stood beside the driver's-side door of a brown Lada. He wore a heavy coat and a fur hat. It was difficult to be sure from that far away, but Ryan thought he held a radio microphone in his hand. He scanned the block, checking out the buildings from roofline to street level. It was much too far away for Ryan to read his lips, but it was obvious he'd said something into the mic.

Moments later, the device on Ryan's chest buzzed again. Berlin Station had picked up the transmission near his location.

Nice to know it worked.

Ryan bladed and stepped back, making himself slightly less visible.

"You need to take a look at this."

Foley switched places with him at the window, leaving Ryan to keep an eye on the major. If there were a raid, the quickest way for Pfeiffer to save himself would be to shoot both American spies before anyone had a chance to hear their side of the story. His supervisors would have questions, but he might even come away as a hero.

Hand on the window covering, Foley turned and glanced over her shoulder. "There's a man sitting in his car down the street. Are you expecting someone?"

"Probably just a routine Volkspolizei patrol." He pushed away from the wall. "Even so, we have been in this place far too long. There is no need to meet face-to-face again."

He pulled a bright green stocking cap down low over his ears and then shrugged into a heavy wool sweater. With the addition of a pair of dark-rimmed glasses, he'd completely changed his look from when he'd arrived. His overcoat and fedora went into a large paper sack he carried as if he'd been to the market. Ready to go, he took a cube of pool-cue chalk from his pocket and handed it to Ryan.

Pfeiffer gave them the address of a phone box.

"Speak with your people. Tell them what I told you. If they want more and agree to the terms as I have explained them to you, then put a mark at the top of the sign on the door of the phone box. You can do it as you step inside. The sign is white. The chalk is white. No one will be able to see it unless they specifically look for it. Any Stasi who are following you will be far more interested in what call you are making. So, make one. Telephone someplace innocuous and not attributable to your government. Once I see the chalk mark . . . If I see the chalk mark . . . I will assume that Jennifer North has been arrested, and that the gods who decide such things have agreed to my terms. I will present myself to the U.S. Mission in West Berlin."

Ryan shot a glance at Foley.

"No," he said.

All the color drained from Pfeiffer's face.

"What do you mean, 'no'?"

"We're going home," Foley said. "You're right in that there is no need for another face-to-face meeting, or any sort of meeting, for that matter."

"What—"

"Look, Major," Foley said. "I'm ready to sign off if you check out. Don't come to the Mission first, though. Your people are watching that place twenty-four/seven. Once you go in, there'll be no changing your mind."

"I don't intend to change my mind," Pfeiffer snapped.

"Better you meet us at the McDonald's near Grunewald Forest tomorrow at noon. You know where it is."

"I do," Pfeiffer said. "But I am not prepared to come over until—"

"The information you gave us on Jennifer North is old news," Foley said. "She fled the U.S. Mission earlier. As a matter of fact, we believe she's already crossed into East Berlin."

Ryan shrugged. "You'll be safer in the West."

The major twisted his wool scarf in a tight knot. "I will think on it."

"Just be there," Foley said.

Pfeiffer left quickly, turning back at the door just long

enough to give a slight dip of his head, agreeing to the terms. With that, he wheeled and slunk down the hall like the vermin that he was.

There was never any question that the CIA would accept Pfeiffer's relatively inexpensive demands *if* he turned out to be a legitimate walk-in. He appeared to be a horrible human being, feckless and irredeemable, but just like in the federal Witness Protection Program, angels who betrayed their own people were at a premium. More often than not, it was merely the first pig to the trough who got the best deal. It was a dirty little secret in the CIA—one of many, Ryan was learning. A staggeringly high percentage of the people they recruited were tyrants, murderers, and rapists in their previous lives. If those rapists, murderers, and tyrants had something of value to the United States, they received a get-out-of-jail-free visa, a new life, and some money to live it. They were of course required to behave themselves from that point forward, a task that most people of that ilk found impossible. But there were other ways to deal with that—after the intelligence had been gathered.

"Looks like the Lada is leaving," Ryan said, peering out the window. The driver down the block was back in his vehicle, headlights on. A cloud of exhaust said the engine was running. "That was interesting."

"We need to get on the road." Foley was already in her coat and now used her thumbs to punch a message in the SRAC. "First things first, though. We need to confirm with Berlin Station that Jen North has possibly turned."

"Possibly?" Ryan asked. "You said it, she's bent."

"Yep," Foley said. "But I've had those KGB assholes name too many innocent friends of mine just to watch the Agency crucify them out of an abundance of caution."

"She ran, Mary Pat," Ryan said. "Occam's razor . . ."

Foley groaned, finished her missive, and then walked to the window and peeked out. "I know. It just sucks to hear that one of your own . . ."

"Are you sending that from up here?" Ryan asked, getting her mind back on task.

"When we're ready to walk out the door," she said. "We'll get coverage if we're a little higher out of the building's shadow. The signal goes out in something like an eight-second burst. Supposedly that makes it harder to triangulate, but I want to be on the move the moment I broadcast."

"I'm ready when you are."

She spoke without turning around. "Just watching the street for a minute, getting a feel for what we're going to be walking into. Hey, did you see Pfeiffer about shit himself when you asked about Nevada?"

"What do you think that means?"

"Either he knows something he doesn't want to tell us," Foley said, "or he's worried he doesn't know enough to be worth anything to us. If I was a betting woman, I'd say it's the latter. His government tit is drying up and he's rooting around for something new."

"And wants to make sure he has enough to trade."

"That's my assessment, too." Foley gave a resigned

sigh. "He's an asshole, but he'll have loads of useful insight. Most of it I doubt he even knows he knows. I'm going to recommend the director PL 110 him."

Public Law 110 allowed the director of the CIA to grant asylum to a given number of assets every year and use public monies for their maintenance and support.

"The man's shrewd," Foley said. "I'll give him that much. He knows exactly what he's doing. He just exited the building down the block right on top of the Lada, but . . . That's weird. The guy was in or beside his car last time you looked. Right?"

Ryan joined her at the window. "What's weird?"

"The Lada's still there," she said. "Lights still on, engine running . . . but I'm not seeing the driver." She shoved the SRAC into her coat pocket. "We'll wait to send this until we're clear. Too much danger of getting captured." She darkened. "And I already told you how that would go down."

Ryan resisted the urge to pull back the tarp for a better look. The buzzer went off again. Once . . . then three times. Then a constant humming vibration—*S . . . O . . . S . . . O . . . S-O-S-O-SOSOSOSOS*—until the signals melded together like a swarm of angry bees.

"You're right," he said. "We should go now!"

47

On the other side of the wall in the apartment next door, Elke Hauptman popped her neck from side to side, cramped from leaning sideways with one ear pressed against the length of plastic pipe. She'd listened to the entire conversation, warmed by each treasonous word Pfeiffer had spoken. She had the edge now, the power she needed to be clear of him. She just needed to figure out how to use it.

Pfeiffer's footsteps clicked down the hall as he left the apartment, and for a fleeting moment she trembled at the thought that he might burst through her unlocked door and confront her for spying on him—as he'd done in the Imperial Club. She relaxed by degree as the footfalls grew distant. The Americans were still talking. They seemed to understand that Pfeiffer was a pig, and yet they were still going to help him! It made Elke want to scream.

She chanced a look out the window. Pfeiffer was on the street below now, crossing in the shadows, foolishly thinking he was invisible because he'd taken off his fedora and put on a different hat. It worked, but only because the agent behind the wheel of the Lada was young and too focused on the building.

She'd pegged the Lada driver as KGB as soon as she got a good look at him. Shabby coat, fur hat, and an oafish, plodding manner as if he were fresh from the collective and this was his first trip to the big city.

Curiously, he left his car running and trotted down the sidewalk. Elke's heart raced when he turned and crossed diagonally toward the building. He was alone now, but he wouldn't be alone for long. KGB always traveled in wolf packs. Elke had planned to wait until she heard the Americans leave, but there was no time for that. She gave a fleeting thought to warning them, but they were spies. Who could trust a spy?

She grabbed her coat and ran into the hallway without putting it on, nearly running into the two Americans as they came out of the next apartment.

All three of them froze, staring at one another. Elke kept her hands open and out to her sides. She knew from Western television that Americans were trigger-happy cowboys, and she didn't want them to shoot her.

"Guten Abend," the American man said, nodding slightly as if to show he wasn't a threat. The woman's lips pulled back in a feral growl, looking like she might rip Elke's head off at the slightest provocation—or no provocation at all.

"No time to explain." Elke racked her brain to be certain she used the correct English. "Pfeiffer . . . he plays games with you. KGB, Stasi . . ." She pointed to the wall and the street beyond. "I do not know which, but they are here."

Ryan was surprised to hear this new mystery woman spoke English.

Foley bladed, one hand raised to ward off an attack, the other drawn back, ready to swing.

"And you are?"

"*Ich bin* . . . My name . . . is Elke Hauptman," the woman said. She shook her head, out of breath, hands shaking. "We must go now! I got the gist of who you are through the wall." She nodded to the elevator alcove just three apartments away. "They will come out there. We should go to the far end of the hall and take the other set of stairs."

"We know where the stairs are," Foley said.

"Good for you," the woman snapped. "That KGB thug is alone—which gives us a moment to flee. They are known more for prudence than bravery. He will wait for his friends, but we should go at once!"

"Hauptman?" Ryan repeated. It was a name he'd not heard before.

"Yes, Hauptman!" she said. "I will tell you everything, but not here."

Foley gave a shake of her head, eyeing the woman. "Why should we follow you? Who are you to Pfeiffer?"

She threw up her hands. "If you must know, I was here to shoot him in the face! Now, really, we have to go—"

Around the corner, the elevator chimed as the car reached the floor and whirred to a stop.

"Sheisse!" Elke Hauptman cursed. "That KGB fool came up alone!"

Running away went against everything in Jack Ryan's makeup. Rather than risk being shot in the back, he bounded toward the elevator, closing the distance. The chime pinged again. The doors slid open, revealing a startled man whose hand dropped immediately to a holstered Makarov at his belt. Young and farm-boy strong, he outweighed Ryan by at least fifty pounds. The heavy coat made him look like a monster.

The man spat something in Russian, a curse, from the tone of it, and began to draw the pistol.

Ryan sprang through the doors, slamming the Russian into the back wall of the elevator. Ryan trapped the gun arm with both hands, while driving the point of his shoulder into the man's chest. He brought his knee into the Russian's groin over and over, sometimes connecting, but mostly glancing off the man's thighs during the struggle.

Though his gun hand was trapped, the man still had complete use of his left. He began to pummel blows into Ryan's unprotected kidney. Bucking and twisting, he kicked up a leg and used the wall as a platform to throw Ryan off.

Enraged, Ryan fought his way through the nauseating pain. He rolled his shoulder inward toward the Russian's centerline, bringing the man's gun arm with him. He borrowed a page from his opponent and kicked off the wall with his feet, slamming them both against the wood paneling on the opposite side of the elevator.

Only seconds had passed, and the doors hissed closed behind them. The car began to move again. Down.

Ryan drove his forehead upward, slamming into the bridge of the man's nose. The delivery wasn't textbook, and the blow stunned him, too, but at least blood wasn't pouring from a gap in the top of *his* nose.

The Russian staggered sideways, the Makarov slipping from his hand. He was up again in a flash, lunging for the gun on the ground. Ryan kneed him brutally in the face, then kicked the gun away. He reached behind him and blindly started pressing buttons. The Russian's friends were on the way. He had to stop the elevator before it reached the bottom and opened to a bunch of KGB thugs. He was having a tough enough go with this one guy . . .

Foley almost made it through a gap in the elevator doors, but they slid shut when she was just inches away. She spun immediately, sprinting for the stairs, giving Elke Hauptman's shoulders a yank as she ran past.

"Come with me!"

"What . . . Where are you—"

"Elevator's going down," Foley said. "We took it part of the way up and it was pretty damned slow. If we take the stairs now—"

"We can beat them down," Hauptman said, finishing Foley's sentence.

They hit the stairwell at a dead run. The door cracked like a gunshot when Foley flung it open.

"You said you came here to shoot Pfeiffer," she said over her shoulder, bounding down the stairs with Hauptman in tow.

"Yes . . ."

"Good," Foley said. Still running when she reached the landing, she grabbed the metal banister and whipped around, keeping up her speed as she descended the next flight. "Then give me your gun!"

Ryan and the Russian faced each other, panting, hunched forward, both with their backs to their respective walls of the elevator. The gun was on the floor between them, but whichever one of them moved to get it would earn himself a boot to the teeth. Ryan had not been in many fights as an adult, but the ones he had been in were brutal, more than one of them to the death. His old man had been a scrapper, though, and instilled a fighting spirit in his son—at least enough that he could protect himself. Chiefly, the elder Ryan had taught his son to take the fight to his adversary. Most fights, the old man said, were not fights at all, but shoving matches to establish dominance. The way to win a fight was not to joust and parry, but to attack, furiously and without warning—speed, surprise, and violence of action.

So he did . . . and the Russian soaked it up like Ryan was throwing marshmallows at him.

Ryan got what he thought were a couple effective jabs and two good right crosses to the man's jaw. His nose was bent sideways, and his teeth smeared with blood, but apart from his looks, he did not seem any the worse for wear. He didn't slow down, and the liver shots he meted out to Ryan's torso said he still had plenty of power.

Ryan slumped, flailing for the wall to keep his feet.

The Russian chuckled.

Ryan suddenly felt heavier. Cables clanked as the elevator slowed, then whirred to a stop.

Behind him. The chime dinged and the doors opened with a sullen hiss, like it was ready to get rid of these guys.

The Russian's eyes flitted toward the doors for a split second. Ryan roared, shaking off the pain, and pushed forward. He swung wide, cuffing the man hard across the ear.

The Russian tried to shake it off, but Ryan sent a snap kick to the groin. The man moaned in pain, bending at the waist to protect himself and meeting Ryan's knee on the way down. He fell as the doors opened, but, to Ryan's horror, landed directly on top of the gun.

Ryan sprang forward, attempting to trap the Makarov before it came up. The Russian growled and threw him off, rolling him out the open doors and into the bright lights of the fifth-floor hallway. Now on his back, Ryan scrambled crablike around the corner as the Russian got off a shot. The bullet whizzed past his ear like a wasp, the muzzle blast deafening in the narrow confines of the hallway.

The Russian shouted something unintelligible, but almost anything in Russian sounded like a threat. The elevator door started to close, but the toe of an extra-large boot stepped onto the threshold and bumped it back open.

Ryan rolled, scrambling to his feet in the middle of the hall, completely exposed. An apartment door opened behind him, then slammed quickly as the occupant saw what was going on. Ryan was too far away to intercept the Russian when he came off the elevator, but he had to try. There was nowhere else to go.

The Russian did a quick peek, then came out slowly when he saw Ryan's hands were still empty.

Heartbeat thudding in his ears, Ryan was vaguely aware of a noise at the other end of the hall—frantic footsteps, a frenzied shout. The Russian heard it, too. Startled, he shot at Ryan, then spun. The bullet tore a hole through the shoulder of Ryan's coat but missed his arm. He looked up to see Mary Pat Foley stop down the hall, some ten feet away, brace herself, and bring up a revolver in both hands.

Elke Hauptman stood frozen beside her, hands over her ears, anticipating the gunfire.

Foley and the Russian fired simultaneously, Foley pulling the trigger twice in quick succession.

Ryan flinched at the concussive reports. Foley teetered,

took a half-step forward to catch herself, and then staggered sideways to lean against the wall. Her face twisted into a cringing grimace.

The Russian stood rooted in place for what seemed like forever. The Makarov slipped from his hand and clattered to the carpet a split second before he dropped to his knees.

Ryan jumped forward to grab the pistol before the Russian could retrieve it, but it didn't matter. A geyser of blood arced from a hole in the man's neck, painting the floor in front of him. Foley's bullets had both hit home, her first striking him in the abdomen, her second destroying his collarbone and severing his carotid artery.

He gurgled something and pitched forward, landing on his face.

Ryan knelt to scoop up the Makarov.

"Check his pockets," Foley shouted, fading fast. "I'd like to know who shot me . . . who we're dealing with here."

She was wounded, so Ryan started for her.

She shook him off. "Check his pockets!" she insisted.

He found a small cardboard credential folder in the inside breast pocket of the man's coat. The photograph showed him in a green uniform. *Mikhailov, Vladimir* was printed under a wreathed globe with hammer and sickle and the Cyrillic letters for KGB. On the facing page was a green ID card with a slightly newer photo, this one in a suit. The verbiage, written in Roman letters, granted Mikhailov access to facilities of the DDR Ministry for State Security.

"KGB," Ryan said. Beyond the Russian name, a KGB officer might carry Stasi credentials, but not the other way around.

Mikhailov shuddered, gasping agonal breaths, the horrifyingly unnatural sounds that people make during their last moments of life. Ryan's rational brain told him there was nothing he could do. Even so, he gave the Russian's shoulder a firm squeeze, one last bit of comfort. He was so young, just doing his job. If Ryan was going to hold anyone responsible, it would be the boss, the person who'd sent Vladimir out here to begin with.

Elke stood in stunned silence, staring at the massive pool of blood spreading from the dying man's head. Her shoulders lurched as she gagged, and then vomited. "I . . . I have never seen . . ." She shook it off, running her sleeve across her mouth. "We need to go . . ."

Makarov in his right hand, Ryan stuffed the credentials back into the Russian's coat, then gave Elke her own reassuring pat on the shoulder as he moved to check on Foley. Her face had gone pale. Beads of perspiration formed on her lip.

"Shit . . ." she whispered. "I think this is bad."

Ryan's chest rig was vibrating nonstop, so much so he'd grown numb to it.

He stuffed the Makarov into his pocket and took the heavy revolver from Foley before she dropped it. A snap of his fingers got Elke's attention and then he passed the revolver off to her.

Black tights concealed the blood trickling down the

side of Foley's leg, but her boot left tracks on the floor each time she shuffled her feet. Ryan reached inside her coat, running a hand behind her back, searching for wounds.

She pulled away. "No time . . ."

"Can you walk?"

Foley gave him a sardonic side-eye, wincing. "Well, I'm not staying here."

The door on the street side of the hallway yawned open. A little girl of nine or ten poked her head out.

"Sie kommen!" she hissed. They are coming. The door slammed as quickly as it had opened.

"Follow me," Elke said, regaining some of her composure. "There is a way out through the basement."

Ryan looped Foley's arm over his shoulders. "Where are you hit?"

"Not sure," Foley said. "Feels like my spine, but I can still feel my legs, so . . ." She looked up at him. "Did you get that guy's gun?"

"I did," Ryan said. "Just having a gun might get us shot, but I'm thinking—"

"Oh, Jack . . ." Foley cut him off. "They're definitely going to shoot us if they catch us now."

She coughed, grimacing. A single tear ran down her cheek. Ryan feared the Russian's bullet had clipped her lung, but she kept going, as if she were the one dragging Ryan to safety and not the other way around.

Maybe that's exactly what it was, Ryan thought.

Elke walked faster, the only one of them not shot or

battered from a fight, reaching the end of the hall a few steps ahead of Ryan and Foley. She turned and flicked her hand, urging them forward as she flung open the door.

"This way—"

She froze, half in, half out of the doorway, gasping as if she'd just been punched in the stomach.

"Oh, nooooo!"

One arm around Foley to keep her from sliding to the floor, Ryan shot his free hand to his coat pocket, his thumb pushing up the Makarov's safety with a resounding *snick*.

48

Dieter Fuchs stood across the street from the Linde Apartments in the shadow of a yellow phone box—and watched. His name meant *fox*—the smartest and most cunning of all animals—and he had spent the bulk of his life trying to live up to those qualities.

Colonel Schneider's spy had given them complete descriptions and tactics of the CIA team from Helsinki. It had been a straightforward operation to follow them to the place where the American man and woman were supposed to meet CALISTO. They'd gone up earlier, alone, and had yet to come down. Selma and Felix were taking care of the Helsinki team, one by one. Fuchs had planned to follow the couple to their meeting until this man in the brown Lada had arrived and parked himself at the far end of the block.

He recognized the interloper as KGB at once, prompting him to take a step back and meld deeper into the shadows. Fuchs and the rest of the Trinité did frequent work for the Russians, but not today. This time, they'd been sent by Colonel Schneider of the Stasi. The colonel was absolutely clear: He wanted this matter—finding and neutralizing the traitor whom the Stasi referred to as LAVENDEL and the West called CALISTO—to be handled without the knowledge of their Soviet cousins, or anyone else in the Ministry for State Security, for that matter.

Fuchs was fairly certain he'd seen the traitor LAVENDEL slink away from the corner. Just a shadow, there one moment, gone the next. He could not be sure. It was highly possible that the turncoat was still upstairs with the Americans. The Russian at that end of the street hadn't paid any attention to the fleeting shadow—if he'd even seen it. With no way to get word to Selma or Felix, Fuchs decided to stand fast and watch.

This new Russian's arrival, as green and inexperienced as he appeared, was as annoying as it was startling to Fuchs. All of the DDR, but especially East Berlin, was rife with secret police who kept their secrets from one another. Countless task forces, groups, and squads vied to recruit, blackmail, or neutralize this traitor or that diplomat. So many cooks were bound to crash into one another in such a cramped kitchen—more frequently than the fools in the West realized. Under just the right circumstances, the Main Enemy (the U.S.) did not even need to show up for chaos to ensue. All the good socialists would just shoot one another. The Stasi did not advertise it, but two of their most recent on-duty deaths had occurred while stopping dissident escape attempts in tunnels under the Wall. Both had been caused by friendly fire—Stasi bullets killing Stasi boys.

Add the heavy-handed thugs with Soviet military intelligence to the mix and the city, the entire country, really, was a powder keg with fuses lit and burning at every turn. Fuchs had found himself in the cross fire more than once, an exceedingly dangerous place, since he was neither KGB nor Stasi, but a hireling with no sense of patriotism for the socialist cause. None of his employers would shed a tear if he caught an accidental bullet. He and his team were at once necessary, repulsive, and very well paid.

He thought briefly of intercepting the KGB officer, but that would be stirring a nest of hornets. The first one or two could be swatted away and killed with relative ease, but then the others would come, roaring out of their nest in an angry, unstoppable force. The Stasi were just as bad. Worse, even, because they were more refined. More likely to smile as they stung you to death. Beyond that, both organizations were frequent clients. War with any one of them was just plain bad business.

Fuchs looked on from across the street while the agent spoke briefly to a man with a dog at the front doors. Whatever he'd learned took him inside—quickly, with the blind recklessness of youth focused far too intently on a mission. Whether the agent was going after Colonel Schneider's traitor or someone completely different, there was a good chance this would not end well for him.

Fuchs would watch from the shadows. He was comfortable there.

His earliest memories were of dark corners, playing lookout while his old man stole or beat or killed. Postwar Germany had been a mecca for men of the Ringvereine, the Ring Club thugs like his father who preyed on others. Marshall Plan dollars flowed like rain, rebuilding the country—and lining Linus Fuchs's pockets. Construction, garbage, home furnishings, plumbing—money or goods changed hands, and Dieter's father got a slice of everything.

Dieter had no memory of his mother, not her hair, her eyes, nor the sound of her voice. His was a childhood of alcohol, many, many women, and shadows. Every new mistress was to be called Mama. The longest one lasted four months. To Dieter, *Mama* was just a word, with no more significance than "Hey, you." Perhaps even less.

Linus made more than a million dollars before Dieter was ten years old—and lost it all by the time the boy turned eleven.

Beautiful women gave way to not-so-beautiful women, women with souls as scarred as their faces, women who traded their bodies not for Linus's money but for a bowl of soup and a place out of the cold. More often than not, even that came with a dose of the old man's white-hot rage.

Dieter hadn't intended to leave home at fourteen, at least not consciously. He'd simply found the shadows preferable to the rot of whores and the stink of his father's misery. He'd stayed there in the dark and found a way to thrive—killing people for money.

He'd met Selma and Felix by chance at a point in his

life when he needed muscle and an extra set of eyes. They came as a pair, indivisible, and he'd hired them both. He'd intended to kill them after that one contract, to tie up loose ends, but another job had popped up on the heels of the first, and he'd kept them on, always thinking he'd kill them in the end. Job followed job and he began to find them indispensable. After a year, they'd confessed one evening over cognac and cigars that they had planned to murder him as well. After a bit of discussion, they decided to see where their relationship took them . . .

The screech of tires on snowy pavement pulled Fuchs out of his reminiscing. Two Ladas and a sputtering Trabant slid to a stop in front of the apartment building. Four men emerged from the vehicles, the first Lada with a driver and his passenger—the man in charge. The man in the Trabant got out, then after some order from the boss, leaned back inside his open driver's door and spoke into the radio.

Passersby spun on their heels and went the other way. Two women, local housewives from the looks of them, all but ran across the street, going so far as to wade through a river of melting gutter slush to avoid the responding secret police.

Then, as if materializing out of nowhere, a tall figure with a wool cap pulled low over his ears emerged from behind a concrete planter halfway down the building. Fuchs had not noticed the planter or the man until that very moment.

He staggered toward the arriving KGB men, stopping, swaying in place as if to get his bearing or keep from toppling over. Fuchs took a small monocular from his pocket and held it to his eye, hooding the end with his fingers to minimize any reflective flash that might signal his presence. It was too dark to get a clear look at the man's face, but that wouldn't have mattered. The hat was pulled low and his collar buttoned high, concealing all but a thin strip around his eyes. Even that was enough to tell Fuchs what he needed to know. The man moved as if he were intoxicated, but his eyes were stone-cold sober.

Something was wrong.

John Clark felt it in his bones. He'd not seen or heard from any of the Helsinki team in the last hour. They'd kept on the move initially, leapfrogging around the area so as not to become stale to the local population. Strangers passing through were one thing. Strangers who lurked caused people to call the authorities.

People had come and gone from the apartments, most of them looking like residents or someone visiting residents.

Clark had walked to the end of the block when the brown Lada arrived. There were some naked trees with substantial trunks to keep behind and little street lighting to give away his movements. He was able to keep an eye on the apartment lobby while he got a read on the kid behind the wheel.

He'd heard a commotion halfway down the block that ran beside the apartment building—a female voice in distress. Beginning to worry in earnest over the cover team,

Clark eased that way to check out the sound. He found scuff marks in the snow, and something dark on the pavement.

Blood! Someone was taking out the Helsinki team. These guys were Mokriye Dela—the KGB's wet work department.

Hitters.

He was gone only an instant, but by the time he returned to the corner, the Lada driver had crossed the street and gone inside.

Clark cursed at his own stupidity and began working his way along the front of the building, staying low behind a large rectangular flower planter. Three more vehicles arrived, and four men jumped out amid squealing tires and slamming doors, forming up behind the rear of a stubby white Trabant to receive their last-minute orders. Clark stayed low long enough to see who the men deferred to, who was in charge, and then stood up, and staggered directly toward him as he stooped over the trunk of the vehicle, referring to a piece of paper—some kind of operational plan or diagram of the building.

A little late for that, bud, Clark thought as he closed the distance.

Men in charge liked to seem like they were in charge, especially in front of their subordinates. This one couldn't have been much over thirty-five years old, relatively young for a boss, which would make him all the more sensitive about establishing his seniority. The others called him Comrade Major Popov.

The man from the Trabant saw Clark approaching

first and grunted something to the boss. Popov looked up from his ops plan and gave Clark a cursory scan, deemed him a drunk piece of horseshit, and told him as much before ordering him to keep moving. His pathetic German was so bad one of his men repeated it to be certain Clark understood.

Clark raised both hands to show that he wanted no trouble, but continued to stumble toward the group. Popov took it as a personal affront that this drunk asshole was not following his orders. His men moved to confront Clark, but Popov would have none of that. He would take care of this idiot personally. Clark made it to within ten feet. All four men were bunched together shoulder to shoulder—close enough that Clark was able to shoot them without moving his feet.

Every one of these KGB men was armed and a serious threat to Ryan and Foley if they were allowed to get inside—but their guns were buried under sweaters and heavy coats.

Clark drew the Glock before it dawned on any of the men what was going on, interrupting the process whereby human beings made decisions—observe, orient, decide, act. The OODA Loop. In times of great threat, like a terrifying man pointing a black gun at your face, the brain had to reboot—reorient before it could make a new decision and then act on that decision.

While the Russians were thus engaged, their brains frantically attempting to catch up to their present situation and order their muscles to draw pistols and protect themselves, Clark shot each of them twice center mass. It

was an oft-repeated credo among fighting men that anyone worth shooting once was worth shooting many
times. He took the Russian on the left first, so as not to
waste precious time swiveling back and forth.

Clark felt certain that if he'd had more time behind
the Glock, he could have been significantly smoother—
and smooth, as they said, was fast. Even so, the first Russian was still standing by the time Clark took the last
one. For a moment he thought perhaps they were wearing some sort of body armor, but Popov coughed, sending a curtain of blood down his chin, and then fell
sideways, knocking his two compatriots to the ground
like dominoes. Clark shot the last man standing under
the nose. He scanned the area over the top of his sights,
and then turned and walked into the lobby—moving to
contact.

Foley was capable, but Ryan was a wild card, and wild
cards got people killed.

It went against his instinct, but Clark adjusted his
wool hat so it covered less of his face as he entered the
lobby of the apartment building. Looking as though he
wanted to hide would serve only to get him noticed. A
man with a little dog came off the elevator when he was
halfway across the floor.

"He is on floor five!" the man said in broken Russian,
hollow, stunned by something. "Not good . . . not
good . . ." He hurried past, clearly mistaking Clark for a
responding KGB officer.

49

Dieter Fuchs watched in awe at the speed and conviction with which the American had killed the four KGB officers. Oh, he was American. Of that, Fuchs had no doubt. It was customary for the Stasi, KGB, GRU, and the secret police of any number Soviet Bloc states to contract out their killings—a policy that had made Fuchs and his partners a very wealthy threesome. The Americans liked to keep things in-house. They wanted to retain more control. If the United States decided someone needed killing, they did it themselves.

The wind had kicked up, making it feel much colder. Spitting rain turned to driven snow that slapped the face, and then back to rain again. Grays grew grayer and shadows intensified, heaping an added measure of dread to the already supercharged air.

This man was good, as efficient as anyone Fuchs had ever seen, but how in the world did he plan to get away?

A chill ran up Fuchs's spine. Perhaps the man did not intend to get away, not yet at least. He was obviously here to protect the two Americans upstairs. They'd not yet emerged, so it stood to reason that he was still out there, in the dark, doing his job.

Fuchs shot a glance over his shoulder. Cursed himself for being so jumpy, and stepped into the phone box. It was like a deep freeze inside, but at least it was out of the wind.

Fuchs peeled off a glove and held it between his teeth while he fed a twenty-pfennig coin into the phone and listened to it clatter in the cold metal. The glove went back on immediately.

Colonel Schneider answered on the first ring.

"Tell me you have LAVENDEL?"

"We do not," Fuchs said. "Nothing yet. There has been a development . . ." He offered no excuses, but recounted what had happened with the dead KGB officers, describing in as much detail as possible the actions of the assassin in the shadows.

Schneider fell silent, breathing heavily into the phone while he thought.

"There was gunfire," Fuchs continued. "Someone has surely called the police."

"I will take care of them," Schneider said. "You are sure this killer was an American?"

"Yes."

"I want to make sure I understand," Schneider said. "None of the dead are MfS?"

"KGB," Fuchs said. "I have not checked their credential cards, but I feel sure I am correct."

"How did they . . ." Schneider's voice trailed off. He thought for a moment, then said, "Never mind. I will make a call, then come to you. Is your team whole?"

"We are fine," Fuchs said, suddenly realizing he'd not heard from Selma or Felix in more than an hour. Now they were out there with the American killer.

The high-low sirens of at least three Volkspolizei vehicles carried mournfully down the street, sounding even more anemic than usual in the cold.

"I am on my way," Schneider said. "Colonel Zima of the KGB may arrive before I do. Do you know him?"

"He employed us earlier in the year," Fuchs said.

"Ending on good terms?"

"He is still alive," Fuchs said. "As are we. So, yes."

"Good," Schneider said. "Stay out of sight until one of us get there. Those Volkspolizei idiots are liable to shoot you and ask questions later."

"Of course," Fuchs said, agreeing to do exactly what he'd planned to do anyway. He'd been a thief long before he became an assassin and hadn't remained alive this long by rushing blindly into danger. Though the thought did occur to him that it might be safer among the People's Police. The American in the shadows hadn't hesitated to shoot, and he'd hit what he'd aimed at one hundred percent of the time.

50

The man in the stairwell stood blinking at Elke Hauptman with a hangdog look and a quivering chin. Blue eyes flashed between icy anger and pitiful, heartrending sadness.

Ryan took the gun out of his pocket anyway. His father had often told him that in an adult male, tears were often a precursor to violence.

"No, no, no," Elke said. "This is my husband, Uwe."

"Elke!" The man spoke in rapid-fire German. "Why? What is going on? Who are these people?" His eyes fell to Foley and then the concrete floor around her feet. "I heard shooting. You are injured?"

"Elke!" Foley snapped.

"I will explain, my love. I promise." She took him by the hand. "But we are in danger if we stay here."

"I heard shooting . . ."

"Hence the danger," Foley said, in no mood to stand around. "Let's go."

Four flights down, Elke stopped and looked back at Foley, nodding at her foot, chin quivering in fear.

Ryan knew how she felt. The bare concrete and steel of the stairwell seemed like it was closing in around them. Every footfall snapped like a gunshot echoing up and down.

"You are bleeding badly," Elke said.

"I'll be fine," Foley said.

"I am sure," Elke said. "But we will not be if we do not make a change. The partners of the man we killed will conduct a thorough—"

Uwe, who still clutched his wife's hand, spun her toward him. "What do you mean 'killed'?"

She ignored him. "If we leave a trail of blood . . ."

Foley groaned. "I see what you mean . . ."

Ryan dropped the pistol in his pocket and ripped open his shirt, unfastening the elastic band that held the signaling device to his chest.

"Here," he said, gently turning Foley so she faced the wall. "Raise your arms if you can."

Foley understood immediately what he intended to do. She gritted her teeth and nodded for him to go ahead.

Judging from the hole in her coat, she'd been shot in the left side. Elke held back the tail of her coat. Blood soaked the waist of her dress and down the side of her hip.

Foley winced and pounded her forehead softly against the wall. "Where's the entry wound?"

"I can't tell," Ryan said. "Everything is covered in blood."

"Unzip my dress." Foley spoke through clenched teeth. "I'm thinking you won't be able to miss it."

"Got it," Ryan said, more than a little woozy. "It's pretty bad."

"I could have told you that," Foley said.

At first glance, Ryan thought Foley had been shot twice. She'd bladed to the side during the shooting, right leg back, left hip forward. The Russian's bullet entered her back at the crest of her hip, likely chipping the top of the pelvis before tunneling under the skin over her kidney. It tore a wound the size of a quarter as it exited, then jumped the hollow of her spine to lodge under the skin somewhere over her right kidney.

Most of the blood came from the exit wound. Ryan used his folded handkerchief as a dressing and pulled the elastic band as tight as he dared without cutting off Foley's circulation.

Still on his knees, Ryan shrugged off his coat and tapped Foley on the back of her left calf.

"Can you lift your foot? Even a couple inches."

She stifled a sob from the pain, but she did it.

Ryan gently removed her shoe and used his coat to pat away the blood from both her stockinged foot and the shoe.

"Are we done?" she asked through clenched teeth.

"That's the best we can do," Ryan said.

"Lead on," Foley said.

Elke led the way again, dragging her stupefied husband

away from the scene of the crime as an accessory. Ryan's makeshift bandage slowed Foley's bleeding enough that they were able to reach the basement without leaving behind too many errant droplets.

The Linde Apartments were a relatively new construction, but the bones of the building had been around since the 1930s. The basement was a maze of connecting tunnels and hallways that had been enlarged and fortified to use as air-raid shelters during the war. Cobwebs draped the corners and dust covered every surface. A single set of tracks matching Elke's footwear ran the length of the basement. Other than her, apparently no one had been down here in years, possibly decades.

"I came in this way," Elke said. "It was to be my route of escape after I killed Pfeiffer."

Uwe Hauptman put on the brakes. He stomped his foot. "What are you saying? You have murdered someone?"

"No." Elke groaned. "I had planned to, but I did not. Now go . . ."

Foley was shaking uncontrollably by the time they reached the stairs leading up to street level. Ryan was supporting almost all her weight. If he'd kept up with all the turns and twists, they were going to pop out almost a block away on the far side of the building that sat adjacent to the Linde *Plattenbau* monstrosity.

"My scooter is parked outside." Elke looked at her husband. "Where is yours?"

"Around the corner," he said. "Out of sight from the front doors, if that is your worry."

"Good," Elke said. "Get it and come back here." She put a hand on Ryan's arm. "Can you ride?"

"It's been a while," he said. "But sure."

"You take your friend and follow on my Schwalbe. My husband and I will lead the way."

Uwe stomped his foot again. "Lead the way to where?"

"My love," she said, taking his hand. "I will explain all. I promise. But if you do not go and retrieve your scooter, we are all going to be shot."

The intense cold braced Foley awake long enough that they could get her on the little scooter. The snow had been bad enough, but it had now turned to a light drizzle, sending the cold deep into their bones. Ryan's teeth began to chatter. He wasn't one to let nerves affect him, but this was more than a little overwhelming.

Thankfully, the Schwalbe was a straightforward machine—throttle and a brake. The engine was small enough that the kick-start worked with little effort. There was plenty of room to ride two-up on the damp seat, if the pillion rode on the back. Foley could barely sit upright, let alone operate a motorcycle, even one as simple as this. No way she was riding on the back. She'd fall off before they made it half a block. Ryan put her up front, trapping her between his arms and thighs to keep her aboard. He had to scoot forward to reach the handlebars, which put Foley on his lap rather than on the seat in front. Her personality was so large that Ryan found himself startled at how small and frail she was.

Her head lolled to the left, pressing her hair against

his jaw. He held it there as the Hauptmans putted away from the curb, surprisingly fast considering the patches of wet snow and damp cobblestone streets. Ryan rolled on the gas, causing the rear end to get squirrely. He touched the brake, threw an arm around Foley when she pitched forward, cursed, gritted his teeth, and then sped up.

Foley noticed and patted his hand, craning her neck to look up, shivering, nestling in against him. Her eyelashes fluttered sleepily under the spitting rain.

"Thank you, J-j-jack," she muttered. "You're d . . . doin' g . . . gr . . . rreat."

Clark didn't have a scientific explanation for it, but he'd learned long ago that extreme violence left a mark on the atmosphere. You couldn't see it, not with your eyes, but it was palpable enough, charging the air like a kind of low-tone hum of static electricity—a kind of smell. He could tell that something had happened in the elevator the moment he got on. A smear of blood on the floor confirmed his fears.

His right hand was in his coat when he stepped out onto the fifth floor, his fingers gripping the FN .32 pistol. He saw the body's feet first, splayed on the carpeted hall. For a split second he thought it was Ryan. A quick peek confirmed it was the KGB officer who'd come up alone. He drew the pistol and scanned for further threats. This was curious. As far as he knew, neither Foley nor Ryan was armed.

Clark stooped beside the Russian and checked for a pulse. More than one of his acquaintances had been killed by an opponent who was supposed to be dead.

The door of the apartment directly across from the elevator opened and two women in housedresses stepped into the hall. Excited about something, they talked over each other, babbling away until the nearest one saw Clark. They both froze, staring at him as he put his hand to the side of the dead Russian's neck that wasn't shot away.

"Return to your home!" he snarled in Russian, a language to which snarling came easily.

The women were German, but it didn't matter if they spoke Russian or not. They naturally assumed he was KGB, someone with whom they had no desire to associate. They nearly tripped over their own feet trying to unlock the apartment and get inside.

Clark moved quickly now.

Fresh blood soaked the carpet in three distinct spots fifteen feet from the elevator. A lot of blood. Someone else had been shot. He cast his eyes up and down the hallway, looking for any sign of the people he'd been tasked to protect. Clark wasn't the panicking type, but he was worried and not afraid to admit it. A healthy dose of concern could push you forward.

It didn't take him long to find more blood farther down the hall. The tracks grew clearer the farther he went. By the time he reached the stairwell, he had a clear imprint of a woman's shoe. He scrubbed the bloody track with the toe of his boot, anxious to deprive responding

KGB and Stasi authorities of anything that would cause them to focus in on Mary Pat. Of course, her bullet hole would likely be the bigger tell.

The blood tracks led to the stairwell, where they suddenly stopped on the fourth-floor landing.

There was no body there, so Clark took it as a good sign.

Now, instead of looking for blood, he watched for disturbed dust, doors left ajar, anything that suggested someone had recently passed this way. Every now and then he found a dab of blood to let him know he was on the right track.

Cold rain hit him in the face when he popped out in an alley behind a building adjacent to the apartments. It hadn't been raining long and there were still a few telltale tracks in the slushy snow. Two motorcycles—scooters, more than likely—and four different sets of tracks. Four . . .

Sirens wobbled in the distance, getting closer—which meant Clark needed to be farther away. He didn't have a read on Ryan's condition, but Mary Pat Foley was bleeding and Clark had no idea where she was. Without looking back, he walked into the night to find out.

51

Colonel Schneider arrived at the Linde Apartments alone. Evgeni Zima brought an entourage of his KGB minions.

There were other Stasi officers present, of course. The place was crawling with suits by the time Schneider arrived. Four dead KGB agents in the street had prompted the Volkspolizei to contact everyone in their Rolodex.

Zima's men had been murdered, so he was running the show. Schneider stuck close to him. The KGB men on the scene assumed he was Stasi. He had a wife and three children in Potsdam but spent so much time in the West that many of the newer Stasi officers knew him only by reputation. Tonight, they assumed he was a KGB man who spoke excellent German.

Zima paced back and forth on the sidewalk next to the bodies of his comrades. He stopped periodically to toe at a bit of trash or flotsam that turned out to be gravel.

"Members of your squad?" Schneider asked.

"They are," Zima said.

"There's something you need to know," Schneider said. When dealing with the KGB, one had to be extremely careful when holding anything back.

Still facing the dead, Zima looked sideways. "And what is that?"

"I have an asset in the West," Schneider said. "And this asset tells us that we have a traitor in the DDR."

"There are traitors everywhere, Rolfe. My men are dead. I do not have time to guess the rest of what you want to say."

"Of course," Schneider said. "We have not identified the traitor. We only know that he has offered to cooperate with the Americans."

"Cooperate how?"

"My source is not privy to that information. The Americans suspect they have a mole, so they are keeping the information compartmented."

"A mole," Zima mused. "So, someone within the CIA?"

Schneider didn't answer for a time.

Zima's head snapped up, snarling. "What did I tell you about having to guess?"

"Yes," Schneider said. "CIA. I am happy to discuss it with you in great detail in private."

Zima heaved a deep sigh, looked Schneider up and down as if figuring out whether he wanted to gut him or not, and then said, "Very well. Tell me about this traitor of yours."

"We have assigned him the code name LAVENDEL,"

Schneider said. "According to my source, an American team is here to meet him . . . or her . . . We have a small operation under way to follow them and learn LAVEN-DEL's identity."

Still fuming. "And I am only now hearing about this?"

"With due respect, Colonel Zima. This information, too, must remain compartmented. We trust you, of course, but we have kept those with knowledge of the operation very small. Our primary mission is to capture the traitor before he does great harm—"

Zima looked him dead in the eye. "Have you?"

"What?"

"Captured LAVENDEL before he does great harm?"

Zima stuffed his hands into the pockets of his overcoat, breathing in hard through his nose. He dipped his head toward the nearest body.

"I do not think you have."

The poor man lay facedown in the gutter, one arm trailing over the curb, as if he'd been attempting to push himself to his knees. The top of his face had been shot away. Schneider had seen wounds like that before—pistol executions from close range. The smaller Makarovs were not quite so destructive. A nine-millimeter Luger often did this kind of damage. The other three looked to have been shot only in the chest, center mass. The bodies were stacked, as if they'd been standing bunched together when they were murdered.

"That one is Major Popov," Zima whispered. He stared into the darkness at nothing. "It could have easily been me. I was with him not two hours ago. You say the Americans are involved in this?"

"This?" Schneider said. "I do not know. But they are here to discuss a defection."

"Americans!" Zima spat. "We have rules. They know these rules. Traitors are one thing. They can be killed, tortured, whatever. Both sides do it." He pounded his fist against an open palm to punctuate each word. "Officers! Are! Not! Touched! What do you think they would do if I gunned down four employees of the CIA? They would weep and wail and threaten sanctions." He jabbed a fat index finger at Schneider. "I will tell you what they would do. They would PNG every Soviet diplomat in the United States. Well, PNG my ass. I am not a coward. They kill four of ours, I will kill ten of theirs!"

Schneider looked up and down the block for Fuchs, who would be able to shed more light on the shooter. He wasn't to be found. Still, now was not the time to mention his story.

Zima was too incensed to change his mind, so Schneider decided to divert his focus to the present.

"What about upstairs?" he asked.

Zima took a few deep breaths, regaining a semblance of composure. "What do you mean 'upstairs'? What is upstairs? The dead are here."

A graying KGB man stepped closer and spoke to Zima in low tones.

"Okay," Zima said after the man had gone. "Another one of my men was following a physics professor from the university. This man called for assistance." Zima waved an open hand over the four bodies. "I gave him the assignment. Instead of assistance, he also gets slaughtered."

"I have a witness," Schneider said. "He saw everything."

A dreadful growl rumbled out of Zima's barrel chest. "One of your men stood idly by while my people were gunned down?"

Dieter Fuchs's voice startled even Schneider, and he knew to expect the man. The little man had a way of materializing in a way that was extremely off-putting, and, Schneider thought, was likely to get him shot one day.

"I was much too far away, Colonel," Fuchs said. "This man was a professional. It was over before I could cross the street."

"You . . ." Zima said in disgust. "It would not be unreasonable to say that this looked like your particular brand of butchery."

"I admit to that," Fuchs said. "But it is not."

"What are you doing here, anyway?"

Fuchs shot a glance at Schneider.

"Taking care of a small matter for me," Schneider said.

"Ah," Zima said. "Your traitor . . ." He looked up suddenly. "What's this about upstairs?"

"The fifth man you mentioned," Fuchs said. "The one who called for assistance. He took the elevator up over an hour ago, following a fellow who I do not think was aware he was being followed."

Zima pursed his lips, exhaling sharply between the gap in his top teeth, visibly shaken.

"Mikhailov . . ."

He spun on his heels and with a snap of his fingers that echoed through the rainy night summoned five KGB officers to accompany him. Even Schneider, who wielded no small amount of power within the Ministry, was impressed. There was little in the world more frightening than a KGB colonel who felt he had been personally wronged. Five officers fell in around Zima in a trench-coated phalanx. A dozen others remained outside in the rain with the Volkspolizei and processed the homicide scene with photographs and diagrams.

Schneider and Fuchs followed the group into the lobby. Any information on LAVENDEL/CALISTO was sure to be upstairs.

An elderly pensioner wearing a maroon tracksuit met them as they were coming in. He pointed to a small knot of women in everything from dressing gowns to a yellow culotte jumpsuit.

"What you are looking for is on floor number five," the old man said.

Zima snapped his fingers again, growling something in Russian that was much too fast for Schneider to catch. The rearmost man peeled away from the group and ushered the pensioner to the wall, flipping open a little notebook to pick the old man's brain clean of what he'd seen or heard.

The group of women from the fifth floor would also be questioned. In the meantime, they told Colonel Zima and the others what to expect—and it was not good.

The Linde *Plattenbau* was comprised of two hundred fifty-two boxy concrete apartments, a third of them under construction and therefore vacant for the time being. These would be the perfect place for LAVENDEL/CALISTO to meet with the Americans and discuss his treason as well as a spot to hide—if one was foolish enough to stay in place and wait for the KGB hounds to sniff them out.

Evgeni Zima dropped to his knees beside the dead boy. He checked the body for a pulse, but the pallor and huge pool of blood left no doubt.

"His Makarov is gone!" Zima's chest heaved. "I will need to inform his wife. She is to have their first child next month." He wiped a tear from his eye with his knuckle. "I sent this boy here."

Schneider shot a glance at Fuchs. That was something.

"Not here, exactly," the KGB man said. "I assigned him to follow a physicist . . . A Dr. Hauptman. He is German . . . One of yours, doing important research. Sensitive research. A family man." He stood quickly, as if an idea had just occurred to him. Half a head taller than Fuchs, he glared down. "Describe this assassin you witnessed on the street."

"Heavy coat," Fuchs said. "Wool hat pulled down low. Well muscled. Over two meters tall. He has had a lot of training. I will tell you that."

"American?"

"Possibly," Fuchs said, seemingly aware that his next words could well begin a bloody war. "He could have been BND."

Zima shook his head. "The Americans are here. They killed my men." He pointed emphatically at the body with each word. "They murdered this boy."

He wheeled and started for the elevator.

"Should we search the building?" Schneider asked.

"My men will do just that," Zima said. "I am going to see to my dead . . ."

"And then?" Schneider prodded.

"Then I am going to find some Americans and shoot them . . . in the face—so they see it coming."

"Colonel," Schneider said. "Perhaps there is more going on here than meets the eye."

"Nonsense! It is clear as day. Dr. Hauptman has not returned home. The Americans have come across the border and kidnapped him for the precious knowledge in his head."

"Can you tell me about this precious knowledge?" Schneider asked.

"You should know," Zima said. "Your people are watching him as well. We found Stasi hardware while placing devices of our own."

"Were they active?" Schneider asked.

Stasi listening technology could be found in every other dwelling in the DDR, many of them from past investigations. Not a day went by that MfS electronics surveillance specialists placing a device did not cry out in glee because holes had already been drilled or wiring run on a given project.

"If your own command wants to keep you in the dark, then far be it from me to read you in," Zima said, smug, obviously still upset about Schneider not being completely forthcoming about his CIA asset. "Alert the border guards to be extra-vigilant. They will surely try to get him across. These American dogs believe they can come to the East and do this without any repercussions? I will show them where the crawfish go for winter!"

The idiom sounded quaint, but Russians understood it for what it was, something akin to banishment to Siberia.

Fuchs spoke up, the breathy timbre of his voice oddly disconcerting. "Colonel Zima, I believe I know a way to help Colonel Schneider find his mole. I suspect this mole will know exactly who murdered this young man, because I suspect he was there when it happened."

Zima stood and fumed. He looked back and forth between the two men, glancing down at young Mikhailov's body every few seconds as if to top off his rage.

"Go on, then," he said at length. "I need to see to these bodies and inform their families."

Schneider sighed, not quite relieved. "So shooting anyone is off the table . . . for the time being?"

Zima pushed the button to summon the elevator. "Unless I see an American while I am still angry. Then all bets are off."

Schneider turned to Fuchs as soon as the elevator doors closed with Colonel Zima on board on his way to the lobby.

"That was a reach," he said. "It was a lone shooter downstairs. You saw it yourself."

"True," Fuchs said. "A professional, to be sure. But look at this." He hunkered down next to Mikhailov's body. "This guy was in a fight. See the bruising on his face. His disheveled clothing. I would bet the pathologist finds multiple injuries in addition to the bullet wound. And he was shot in the neck. No neat center-mass shots like the ones on the street. The bullet broke his collarbone and clipped an artery, but the flesh around it is still relatively intact. I'd say it was a slightly slower projectile."

"Different caliber, different shooter," Schneider mused.

"That is my guess," Fuchs said. "It is a good bet your traitor either pulled the trigger or was with the ones who did. The KGB shows up while he is meeting with the Americans . . . It is not difficult to imagine things going to shit."

Schneider darkened. "I had hoped you would take care of this problem."

"And we were in the process," Fuchs said. "We have successfully whittled down the surveillance team. Now we only need to find the Americans again. They will lead us to your traitor."

"They are long gone," Schneider said. "How do you propose to find them now?"

"I do not think they are gone." Fuchs took five steps down the hallway and pointed at the floor.

"Blood," Schneider gasped. "Mikhailov wounded one of them!"

"He did," Fuchs said. "We know he followed Dr. Hauptman here, to the two Americans."

"So Dr. Hauptman is the traitor?"

"Perhaps," Fuchs said. "But do not forget, both Stasi and KGB have his home under surveillance. I could be mistaken, but I believe his treachery would have been discovered by now. That said, I would bet he knows who the traitor is. If he is wounded, the Americans will be helping him. If they are wounded, he will be helping them. I am telling you, Hauptman is the key. Hauptman will lead us to the Americans, and I feel sure the Americans will lead us to your traitor."

"Agreed," Schneider said. He found a piece of lumber in the elevator alcove and laid it on top of the blood spatter. "Spies killing spies could easily turn into a blood feud between nations—the worst possible kind of war. The Russians will go home to Moscow once the shooting starts and we in the DDR will be left to live with the mess. I am not sure we would survive it." He took a deep breath. "We need to control this narrative. I will find out which unit has Dr. Hauptman under surveillance. How do you propose to locate him?"

Fuchs shrugged as if it were the simplest thing in the world.

"Hauptman is Ossi," he said. East German. "We will find out who he cares about and hurt them until he tells us what we need to know."

52

Wolfenberger Engine Repair sat in a squat wood-and-tin building off a quiet alley between an overgrown vacant lot—that may have once held cars awaiting service—and the back of a textile factory that Elke explained made pantyhose. The clattering noises coming from inside said the night shift was going strong, but there were no cars out back and a cursory glance at the ground said it was not a place employees used for smoke breaks. Elke assured them no one ever came here, earning a sidelong glare from her husband.

They hid the scooters behind a rusted trash bin. Uwe took back the key from Ryan and stuffed it into his pocket as soon as they parked. He made no secret of the fact that he didn't trust any of them at the moment, least of all his wife.

Elke shrugged it off and found a key hanging behind a metal sign advertising East Germany's Club Cola (*Not for everyone. Just for us!*).

Ryan took off his coat and spread it over a surprisingly clean cot in the corner of the windowless back room of the abandoned repair shop. The scooter ride in the snow and rain had nearly done Foley in, and she collapsed face-down on the cot as soon as they got inside. Ryan thought to reposition the elastic around her wound, but she'd reached out and stopped him like something from a kung fu movie, her grip surprisingly firm as she pushed his hand away.

"Let it be," she said. "I'm afraid it'll start bleeding again."

"Please excuse me a moment." Elke disappeared through a double set of doors, leaving them alone with her husband.

"I'm Jack," Ryan said. "This is my friend, Mary."

"I am not pleased to meet you," Hauptman said in heavily accented English. He didn't look to be an especially powerful man, but he was angry, which made him dangerous. "Elke is too kind for her own good. The woman speaks five languages, much more intelligent than me, but she is prone to recklessness. How dare you involve her in . . . whatever this is."

Foley sighed, catching her breath. She spoke into the pillow without turning her head. "We did not involve your wife in anything, Mr. Hauptman."

"Dr. Hauptman."

"Good. I could use a doctor."

"Not that sort of doctor," Hauptman groused. "I am a research physicist at Humboldt University."

Elke came in with an armful of folded wool blankets and a pillow and made Foley's nest slightly more comfortable.

"This place once belonged to a friend of mine."

"Tell it as it is," her husband snapped. "An old boyfriend."

"He was," Elke said. "That is true. I was at university. Very young. Horst Wolfenberger was full of ideas and unable to keep them to himself. A good man, but I could see from the beginning that he was bound to find himself at odds with the state."

"What did I tell you," Dr. Hauptman said. "She is prone to recklessness, associating with a man like Horst."

"I met and married you and Horst attempted to swim the Spree River to reach the West."

She shook away a memory and put her wrist over Foley's forehead.

"You need—"

The movement jarred Foley out of her stupor.

"Where's the SRAC?"

"I've got it." Ryan patted the communication device in his pocket opposite the Makarov. "I was afraid it would fall out of your coat."

"I have to send that message . . ." Foley rolled onto her side, tried to push herself into a seated position, failed, and then made do with propping herself on the pillow so she could thumb-type on the miniature keypad.

Elke nodded at the device. "A way to communicate with your people?"

Ryan glanced up at her from beside Foley, his fingers curled around the pistol in his coat. It was a hell of a thing to live in a place where you couldn't trust anyone. He shook his head and relaxed his grip on the pistol. This woman was terrified—and she'd risked her life by bringing them to what was apparently her secret safe space.

"I need to tell you something," Elke said.

Foley kept typing. "Go ahead."

"I could hear you speaking to Pfeiffer through the wall," she said.

Uwe erupted. "Who is Pfeiffer?"

"A bad man," Elke said. "I am sorry, my love. I am sorry I lied to you. I am sorry for everything . . ."

Tears streamed down her face as she recounted to her husband how the Stasi officer had forced her to steal notes from Uwe's work, among other horrible things.

Uwe Hauptman slumped in stunned silence.

"Doctor," Ryan said. "You said you're a physicist. What's the emphasis of your study?"

"I . . . That is a sensitive matter—"

"Radar!" Elke blurted. "Pfeiffer was extremely interested in everything to do with radar-avoidance technology. I heard him speak of it with others over the phone many times."

Foley set the SRAC on the cot beside her.

"He thought I was only his plaything," Elke continued. "A brainless singer that would not understand what he was talking about on the telephone. What my own husband does."

"But you did," Ryan said.

"Yes," she said. "When he thought . . ." A sob caught in her throat. "He thought I was asleep."

Uwe Hauptman buried his face in his hands.

Ryan glanced at Foley, then back at Elke, prodding gently. "What was it you heard?"

"You asked him about Nevada," she said. "He has never said it, but I believe they have someone in the United States. I heard him speaking about Nevada to another HVA officer on the telephone."

"What specifically did he say?" Ryan asked.

"He sounded excited, like something very good had happened in Nevada, but he did not say what it was."

"When was this?" Foley asked.

Elke looked at the floor, avoiding the sadness in her husband's eyes. "Yesterday. He whispered and I pretended to be asleep, but I heard him say *eleven seventeen*. I am sure of it."

"That's today's date," Foley whispered.

"Not in Nevada," Ryan said. "Germany is nine hours ahead."

"I believe the operative's code name is ZEPHYR," Elke said.

Foley picked up the SRAC and began typing again. "Anything else?"

"Something about a kind of plant. Mint."

"You're sure it was a plant and not a place to make money?"

"No," Elke said. "I am certain it was a plant."

"Code name: ZEPHYR. November seventeenth," Ryan mused. "And a mint plant . . . Maybe they'll have more pieces of the puzzle on their end." He put a hand on Foley's arm.

She sighed and stopped typing. "What are you thinking?"

"Why do we even need Pfeiffer?"

"Asshole or not, he's got viable intelligence."

"Intelligence of Dr. Hauptman's research." Ryan looked the physicist directly in the eye. "Would you want to leave?"

Elke answered for him.

"Yes!"

"Think about what you are saying!" Uwe paced the room. "They would shoot us."

They reverted to German, but Ryan followed the gist of it.

"The Stasi, the KGB, they bug our home," Elke said. "Put cameras in our bedroom! Our own government that you try so hard to serve. How could you want to stay in such a place?"

"I do not *want* to stay," Uwe said. "But what happens to Hans when we are both in prison . . . or dead?"

"A KGB officer was shot with a gun I purchased! Do you think I am going anywhere but prison if I stay here?"

Uwe clutched his hair, rocking back and forth, on the verge of tears. "Oh, my love, what have you done?"

Ryan kept his voice low and calm, though he was anything but. "Hans is your son?"

Elke nodded, chin quivering. "He's just a little child."

"Would you cooperate with U.S. authorities if we could get you out?"

Uwe glared at him. "You mean the CIA?"

"I do," Ryan said.

"How?" Uwe asked. "I do not think it is so simple to get people out into the West. How would you do it?"

Ryan started to say he didn't know yet, but Foley interrupted him.

"Where is your son right now?"

"Spending the night with a neighbor," Uwe said.

"The address?"

"Why do you want to know the address?"

"The address?" Foley asked again.

Elke gave it to her. "I will go and get him now."

"Does anyone else know where the boy is?" Ryan asked.

"I do not believe so," Uwe said. "I was careful and only spoke to our neighbor in person about the arrangement, away from known listening devices."

Foley glanced up from the SRAC. "But this neighbor lives in your building?"

"Down the hall," Uwe said.

"Wait to pick him up," Foley said. "Just a few hours so I can get you some help . . ." She finished typing an encrypted message, then handed the device to Ryan. "Go outside and hit send. Let's hope the cloud layer is thin enough to get a signal through."

"Wait," Uwe said. His face was twisted into a stricken look, as if he were about to have a heart attack or smelled something particularly nauseating. "They can track such devices."

"Not this one," Foley said.

Elke checked her forehead again. "You need food and water. I know a place nearby that sells *grilletta* all night long—for the factory workers. It is only a block away. I will be back in minutes."

Her husband huffed up. "I am not—"

"Yes," Elke said. "You are. It is a horrible thing that has happened to us, my love, but this woman needs food. I will be back, and then you will go get our son."

She slipped out without another word.

The three of them sat in uncomfortable silence for a time, Foley making pitiful sounds and Ryan expecting KGB or Stasi to burst in and shoot them at any moment. Uwe Hauptman sat on an empty oil can with his arms folded, staring sullenly at the two Americans.

Foley broke into a coughing fit. Ryan lifted the blanket and checked to see if the bleeding had started up again. The elastic was soaked through, but it wasn't gushing—something to be thankful for.

"How come this place is so warm?" she asked, her face buried in the pillow.

"There is a common wall." Hauptman breathed deeply, seeming to calm down a notch now that at least some of the truth was out in the open. "The machinery of the hosiery mill generates much heat."

Ryan looked around the shop. "That makes sense."

Tools lay idle and covered with dust. A calendar hung on the wall behind a metal desk. August 14, 1972, was circled in red marker.

"Horst was a good mechanic," Hauptman offered.

"But he was a fool. The man had no aptitude for business. This place is much too far off the beaten path to put a shop to begin with. Then, when the idiot began to have his little meetings and say things critical of the state . . . the Stasi threatened anyone who brought their vehicle to him for repair." Uwe shrugged. "Once a shop is blacklisted no one will do business with it, even after it changes ownership. It is . . . *verflucht* . . . cursed."

Dr. Hauptman fell silent and stared glassy-eyed at the wall, his eyes wet with tears. Ryan perched on the edge of the cot in the *verflucht* garage and held Mary Pat Foley's hand, because he did not know what else to do.

53

It was almost two hours before Elke returned with two paper bags. One contained the *grilletta*—ground pork sandwiches—the other, first-aid supplies.

She handed Ryan the bag of food and dumped the contents of the second bag on the cot beside Foley.

"There is a veterinarian's office down the street from the *grilletta* shop."

Hauptman looked at his wife and shook his head. "A veterinarian could not have been open at this time of—"

"They were not open, my love," Elke said.

"I do not even know you."

She turned to the supplies again. "I found seven percent iodine. For animals, but it will have to do. Some bandages, and suturing supplies."

"Suturing supplies?" Ryan shook his head. "You know how to do that?"

"I make my living as a singer," Elke said. "You are the spies. I assumed you knew such things."

"Okay," Ryan said. He'd taken field medicine courses in the Marine Corps, but retained little beyond RICE and "put the wet stuff on the red stuff" mnemonics. He could apply a tourniquet, but the closest thing he'd ever done to stitches was darning a sock in high school.

Fifteen minutes and a great deal of cursing later, Foley's wounds were cleaned, sutured, and dressed. The shock of it had invigorated her, and though still weak, she was coherent and wide awake.

"What time were you originally supposed to pick up your son?" she asked.

Uwe slouched against the wall across the room, wringing his hands. "I told the neighbor I would pick him up after breakfast."

"I'll go get him," Elke said.

"No!" Uwe snapped. "You stay here, out of sight."

Ryan nodded. Strategically, Uwe Hauptman was the higher-value asset to the U.S. because of his knowledge on radar deflection and avoidance. But he wasn't going anywhere if anything happened to his wife. As far as any of them knew, Uwe could just go about his business as normal. Elke had been seen in the hallway during the shooting. The authorities surely had sketches of her by now. It might take them a while to figure out who the woman in the sketch was, but it was only a matter of time. Neither the Stasi nor the KGB worried about privacy or human rights in the best of times. If they were attempting to track down a murder suspect, they could cast a wide net awfully fast. They didn't give a damn who got tangled up in it, as long as it scoped out their fugitive in the process.

"You should go, Dr. Hauptman," Foley said. "Do not stop at your house. Don't get clothes, keepsakes, anything. Just get your son and come straight back here."

"How will you get us out?" Elke asked.

Ryan perked up. He was interested in that himself.

"We have friends working on that," Foley said.

"It's just after four," Ryan said. "I suggest we close our eyes for a couple hours. That gives our friends time to set things in motion."

The Hauptmans huddled together under their coats on another mat against the wall. The stocking factory next door had slowed production in the wee hours of the morning and radiated less heat. Snow fell in earnest outside, huge popcorn flakes. The temperature continued to drop, and a bitter chill crept over the garage. There were only two blankets. The Hauptmans shared one and Ryan and Foley shared the other.

"I'm sorry," Elke said. She spoke German, obviously pretending that neither Foley nor Ryan had more than a passable grasp on the language, giving she and her husband the illusion of privacy.

Ryan and Foley huddled together and pretended not to hear.

"I don't want you to be angry with me," Elke said.

Uwe said nothing.

"You know how powerful the Stasi are," Elke said, choking back a sob. "He threatened me. Your job. Hansie's prospects for school. What would you have had me do?"

"He forced you," Uwe said. It wasn't a question, but she answered it like one.

"Yes."

"To sleep with him?"

"Yes."

"How many times did you—"

She put a finger to his lips. "Once was enough to kill me."

Uwe began to weep. "I am not angry with you," he said. "But I will tell you this. I am going to end this Major Pfeiffer. I do not care if he is Stasi!"

Ryan found it easier to lean against the wall and let Foley lean on him. Her injuries made it impossible to lie on her back, but if she rolled onto her right side, she was able to share some of his warmth without it seeming to put her in more agony than she was already in.

"Sorry to grunt and moan so much," she whispered, situating herself against his chest. "I'm not sure my husband would be too keen on this situation."

"I thought about that," Ryan said. "My wife wouldn't, either, but she wouldn't want me to freeze to death."

"Yeah," Foley said. "I'm not so sure about Ed . . ."

She nestled closer, shuddering at some sudden pain, then breathing easier as it subsided.

"You okay?" Ryan asked.

He could feel himself drifting, despite the worry and discomfort. The fight and the massive adrenaline dump of being hunted had taken its toll. His body needed to recuperate and was shutting down to take care of that.

"I'm good," Foley said. Another deep breath. "You

remember when Skip asked us if we wanted to write our spouses a note?"

"I do."

"Well," Foley whispered. "It occurs to me that I could die here tonight."

"Mary Pat—"

"Let me finish. It occurs to me that I could die here tonight, and I want Ed to know that I'm okay with that. I mean, I hate for my son to grow up without me, and Ed to be alone, but . . . You know, men aren't the only ones who can be drawn to this kind of life."

"No doubt."

"Are you?"

"Drawn to it?" Ryan mused. "I haven't really figured that out yet."

She chuckled, guarded so as not to jostle her stitches. "Greer thinks you are. And the evidence would seem to suggest he's right."

"Maybe."

"Anyway . . ." Her voice grew softer, breathier. "Tell Ed . . ."

"That you love him?" Ryan finished her sentence.

Foley twisted around just enough to look up at him, meeting his eye. "Nah," she said. "He already knows that. Tell him I was good at my job, that I was a badass . . . and that I went down smiling."

"You tell him," Ryan said.

"Sorry," Foley said, drifting off. "I get philosophical when I'm shot . . ."

54

Communication, or the lack thereof, could make or break an op. Denied areas like Moscow, East Germany, or any of the Communist Bloc countries were especially problematic. Radios and even car phones worked well, so well in fact that trackers could pinpoint where the calls were coming from down to a few meters.

Pay phones were bugged, traced, and often physically watched, making them methods of last resort. The Short Range Agent Communicator like the one Foley had in her possession was miraculous for getting information to HQ via satellite. Agents—the local people being run as spies by CIA operations officers—relied heavily on the SRAC to send relatively difficult-to-trace messages to their handlers without having to make direct observable contact. Outbound instructions were more of a problem. Dead drops, brush passes, clandestine meetings were often the only way to get a message out to an asset in the field—or an operations officer like Clark, who found himself in the truest definition of out in the cold and in desperate need of information.

From the very beginning of this op, the plan had certain communication redundancies baked into it. In case of a break in contact, Clark was to walk past the ruins of Franziskaner-Klosterkirche, a thirteenth-century Franciscan monastery south of the Alexanderplatz station, every hour on the hour. He would see someone whose face he knew with a copy of the *Financial Times*. The *Times* made for a good signal because the pages were salmon color, so it was easy to spot under pressure, but not so gaudy as to arouse suspicion from authorities who might be passing by.

If the contact held the paper low, down by their leg, he was to follow. A rolled paper protruding from under the arm meant danger, move on. No paper was a signal to come back and try to establish contact again in two hours.

There was a U-Bahn station directly across the street. Coming in clean, Clark popped out there and saw Truly Bishop, an East Berlin Station case officer he'd dealt with on a couple of occasions.

She clutched her copy of the *Times* low, patting it against her thigh.

Clark followed at a distance, walking past the alcove behind the church she went in to come around from the other direction so they were not seen going in together.

The meeting would take just a few seconds. No niceties. Straight to the facts.

Her face barely visible in the shadows, Bishop brought him up to speed on the Helsinki team. Two dead. Two wounded. One untouched and with the wounded in an Agency safe house. Mike was still unaccounted for, but had been whole the last time anyone saw him.

She reported Foley's wound, which Clark suspected, and gave him the location of the Hauptmans' son, along with the garage address. Berlin Station was working out an exit strategy at that moment. If they moved from the garage, they were to send a message of their new location via the SRAC. Bishop ended with a description of both Uwe and Elke Hauptman, since it was unknown which of them would go retrieve the boy.

"Good brief," Clark said. "Anything else?"

"Not from MP," Bishop said. "But the boss says to tell you that any resolution that does not include a prelude to World War III is preferred."

"Noted," Clark said, and walked into the darkness without looking back.

55

"Eleven . . . seventeen . . . mint . . ." Special Agent Betty Harris read the encrypted cable in the FBI's Salt Lake City field office. "Not exactly the Rosetta Stone for cracking this."

There were a total of thirty-six agents from the Salt Lake, Denver, and Las Vegas field offices working this UNSUB case. Most were out running down leads or watching transportation hubs, no matter how seemingly insignificant, but five had come in, including Air Force OSI Special Agent Gillum. All of them hoped to lend their brains for a little blue-sky session after this new information had come in by cable from the CIA.

Everyone in the briefing room looked as blank as Murray felt.

Murray took a long drink of lukewarm coffee and doodled in a well-used Skilcraft government memorandum notebook. The "government green brains" were the perfect size for his pocket and he'd carried one since his first days as a NAT at Quantico.

"Our Agency contacts think ZEPHYR could be a code name," Murray said. "They believe our UNSUB is an East German national, or possibly Russian."

"CIA believes it, that's a good reason to think otherwise," a silver-haired agent in the back said.

The rivalry between the Bureau and the CIA went all the way back to the end of World War II, when J. Edgar Hoover tried to convince Truman there wasn't a need for anyone but his G-men. Hoover, along with the help of the Army, had succeeded in getting rid of the wartime Office of Strategic Services, but William Donovan (and the Soviet threat of the Cold War) eventually convinced Truman of the need for a strong Central Intelligence Agency, though he never got to lead it. Hoover got along with the first director Truman appointed, but he didn't care much for the CIA as an agency. Later, when Dulles was tapped to lead the CIA, Hoover refused to cooperate on many occasions. They'd grown out of that, sort of. Murray got along with the Agency folks he knew just fine—as long as they stayed in their own swim lanes.

"I want us all thinking outside the box," Murray said.

"Eleven seventeen could be a time," an agent named Morino who was sitting near the door said.

"Maybe," Murray said. "But today's November seventeenth. You could drive a truck through that coincidence."

Harris leaned back in her plastic chair and smoothed

her hair. The high desert air had sapped it of some curl, and she kept having to push it out of her face.

"ZEPHYR . . ." She shook her head. "What about the word *mint*? That mean anything to anybody?"

A murmur went around the room.

"So, not a damn thing," Murray said. He fanned the sheets of the little green notebook and thought. "Okay," he said. "Let's say ZEPHYR will be somewhere on the seventeenth—"

"To meet someone named Mint?" Special Agent Gillum offered.

"Or at the mint," the older agent in the back offered.

"Mints are government installations," the agent in front said. His name was Blackwell. "Our UNSUB will want to put as much distance between himself and security as possible."

"Right," Harris said. "So Mint could be a password . . . or the location of the meet."

"Meet at Location: MINT . . ." Murray tried that on for size. He wanted to throw the notebook against the wall. The process was maddening, but it helped to talk it out.

"Mint is green," Morino said.

Harris stood up and paced. "How do you say *mint* in German?"

Blank looks.

"I'll go find a dictionary," the silver-haired agent said. "And some road atlases."

"And a Russian dictionary," Harris said. "The Soviets are in on this, too."

"*Myatnyy*," Morino said.

Blackwell turned and looked at him.

"What?" Morino said. "That's how you say *mint* in Russian."

"I'm just surprised you don't speak Spanish."

The agent grinned to show he was kidding, but said, "Morino's an Italian name, dumbass. My wife speaks Spanish."

"How do you say *mint* in Italian, then?"

"*Menta*."

"Yeah." Murray groaned and threw up his hands. "This isn't getting us anywhere. Let's try this. While Potter's finding our reference books, let's think about what we had before this new intel came in." He pointed to the pencil sketch on the board. "Our UNSUB is patient enough that he sits for days waiting to catch a glimpse of our classified aircraft. We have an empty case in his vehicle that looks like it contained a night-vision device and a large pair of binoculars. He's wanting . . . what? What's a look going to do for him? No way he knows he's going to hit the mother lode and witness a crash." He looked at the agent in the front row. "Blackwell, you were a Navy pilot."

"That's correct," Blackwell said. "Finished up flying F-4 Phantoms."

"Okay," Murray said. "What sort of information could our UNSUB get that justifies sitting on his ass for weeks hoping for a little peek during a flyby? He's essentially hoping for a UFO sighting."

"Flight patterns," Agent Blackwell said, as if it should

have been obvious. "You know. Maneuvers. Tactics. Basic shape of the aircraft could tell him a lot. I mean, these UFO groups describe black triangles. Even knowing the shape of the wings could add to what the Soviets and or the Germans already have and really jump-start their research."

"That makes sense," Murray said. "So, we know he's patient. A hunter."

"We know he will kill anyone who gets in his way," Gillum added.

"True," Murray said. "He's brazen enough to rush in and grab a piece of the wreckage when he has to know it's about to rain military personnel. Then he's smart enough to slip away without getting caught."

"So our UNSUB likely has significant training in espionage," Morino said. "Could be former military."

Gillum said, "Whatever piece of wreckage he grabbed would have to be small enough to carry, but big enough to be important to him intelligence-wise."

"So," Harris said, "this suave, patient, smart, brutal foreign agent is attempting to get a bit of tech the size of a pie pan out of the country. That shouldn't be too difficult."

"Except he'd have to drive," Blackwell said. "We're sitting on all the airports. We've got security people searching luggage. He'd be stupid to try."

"Maybe he's at some little desert airstrip that we're not watching," Harris said. "Or, hell, a wide spot in the road where a plane could land. An asset this important would have some logistical support."

"Maybe." Gillum shook his head. "This guy has the balls to kill and rob and leave a little kid alone in a parking lot, but he's got to know that every time he does something like that, he's risking interaction with the authorities, or some citizen with a pistol. He could have logistical support now, but he didn't have it down south when he took a risk and jacked that lady's car."

"Okay," Murray said. "His last known point was heading north from Nephi, Utah, when Ms. Peterson rolled out of the trunk." He rubbed his face, sifting through the jumble of thoughts rattling around in his head. Everything they were saying had been said before, more than once, but rehashing helped turn over old ground, and every once in a while, that found hidden gems. "Salt Lake is the obvious destination. Big enough to hide, lots of choices for routes out of town."

"He could be running for Canada," Gillum said.

"A trained German agent with the support of a foreign power like the Soviet Union," Harris said. "I'm thinking he'll take a boat out of the country. He'll need to get to the coast."

Potter came in with four Rand McNally road atlases. He gave one each to Murray and Harris. The rest of the agents shared the last two. "The receptionist is running to Deseret Book for some German dictionaries."

Blackwell thumbed through one of the atlases. "Driving would be risky, but with agents at the airports, bus stations, and train stations, it would be difficult for him to do anything else."

"Harris," Murray said. "Jump on the radio and get

with whoever we have at the Amtrak station here in Salt Lake. Find out the departure times for trains going east and west."

"Sure thing, boss." She opened her folio and ran a finger down her assignment list. "Green and Rawlings are there."

"Potter," Murray said. "If you'd do the same at the Greyhound terminal. I want everything on the board. Gillum, you look into the airstrip thing. Make sure we're not leaving out any obvious dirt strips. Enlist local PDs and sheriff's departments to help check any landings and takeoffs. And contact whoever you need to, to ensure we have a military escort ready to intercept if we do find an aircraft."

Morino looked skeptical. "I'm not sure they can do that unless it's over a military range."

"They had gunships patrolling the crash," Murray said.

"That's correct," Gillum said. "We find the stolen piece of debris and we just consider it an extended part of the national disaster site."

Harris, who was in the corner of the conference room talking on a Motorola handheld, snapped her fingers to get Murray's attention. She turned the volume all the way up on her radio, then raised it to her mouth.

"Green, Rawlings, repeat what you just told me."

She held the radio speaker-out so the rest of the room could hear everything.

"The next eastbound train leaves Salt Lake City for Chicago at 3:05 a.m. Today's westbound pulled out of here about ten minutes ago. It arrives in Emeryville, California, at . . . 4:10 p.m. tomorrow."

"Copy that," Harris said. "And what's the name of the train?"

"The name," Green said. "The California Zephyr."

56

The sun was already up, but the November weather was so cold and gray that twilight sagged well into the morning. The good citizens who lived along Auguststrasse were up and about, going to work, sweeping snow off their stoops, or trying to get their buzzy little two-stroke cars to warm up enough to blow the frost off the windshields.

John Clark had arrived at the Hauptmans' block early. A long night of walking in the cold was quickly robbing him of his strength and, when he admitted it to himself, making him a little loopy. He could get by fasting for another meal, as long as he could find somewhere to get warm. He would be fine out in the cold if he could get some food in his stomach. It didn't even have to be good food, just plain calories—stale bread, cold meat of almost any kind, a boiled potato . . . He knew he was in trouble when the thought of a boiled potato made his mouth water.

The trick to going into denied space was to act as if you belonged. In a country where secret police bullied their way into people's lives, bullies could go where they pleased. If he acted like a Stasi officer, people would defer to him as they would a Stasi officer.

He walked past the apartments, paying special attention to the upper floors of the building across the street, a *Plattenbau* almost identical to the ones the Hauptmans lived in, at least from the outside. Knowing the East German utilitarian mindset, Clark doubted the designers had made many changes to one over the other.

On the second floor from the top, four windows were missing any kind of curtains or draperies. Two were ringed in frost, as if the heat was turned off in them completely. Those were the ones Clark focused on. Even with no heat, the surrounding apartments would make them feel extremely comfortable compared to what he was dealing with outside.

He counted the location of the windows, made a mental note, and walked in like he knew that he belonged there. Vacant, the apartment had a dead bolt that had not been turned and the knob lock fell quickly to his tension tool and pick. The water worked, so he made do with a long drink to fill his belly and clear his head. There was no refrigerator, no food in the cupboards, just piles of trash and an overall layer of dust. Clark was so cold and tired he found himself almost giddy that there was a wooden chair for him to rest in, well back from the window, to give him a good vantage point without being spotted, and an old canvas tarpaulin that smelled like mildew but was perfect to wrap up in while he watched.

The life of a spy. Nobody ever warned you about all the cold apartments, wooden chairs, and musty tarpaulins. Clark smiled. If stuff like that ran you off, you didn't belong in this line of work in the first place.

With all his hours of training in Navy Special Warfare, people who worked with Clark often assumed he'd come into the intelligence community fully formed, with no need of further training or curriculum. That could not have been further from the truth.

While it was true that Clark had an innate aptitude for the job, for reading people, he still had a lot to learn. The physical skills were a cinch—running, shooting, fighting . . . even killing. The James Bond stuff was practically nonexistent. Oh, he'd swam out of plenty of submarines as a SEAL, and even smacked a guy with a speargun once, but in all his years as an operations officer in the Clandestine Service, and even the more specialized Special Activities Division, he'd never been called on to land a plane in distress, fly a mini-gyrocopter (damn it), or defuse a nuclear device with an actual ticking clock. The guys that used those were just begging to have their bombs defused.

The truth was no one was born knowing how to pick a lock. Even if you had terrific instincts, someone had to teach you how to run a surveillance-detection route the correct way. Speaking a third or fourth language required the frequent use of flash cards and hours of study to stay proficient. Clark was good because he worked at being good. Constantly in the gym, on the range, or in the classroom—or just reading on his own. Lifelong learners made the best spies . . . and, as far as John Clark was concerned, the best people.

Uwe Hauptman arrived at ten minutes to eight. He walked past his own building all the way to the corner without giving it an obvious glance. Someone had taught this guy to do an SDR. Hauptman disappeared for long enough that Clark began to second-guess himself. Maybe it was someone who looked like the professor. Then Hauptman rounded the far corner and walked down the street again, having circled the entire block. He turned in this time, stopping to stomp the snow off his boots.

Clark waited for him to get inside, scanning up and down the street. No one.

Clark threw off the tarp and, after taking one more drink of water, trotted down the stairs. If no one was following Hauptman, then there was a good chance that the people who were after him—the people who had killed and wounded the members of the Helsinki team— were already inside.

57

As instructed, Uwe Hauptman bypassed his apartment completely. Elke and the Americans had warned him in no uncertain terms. His home, the place with all their photographs, all their memories, was poison, a trap that would get him and, more important, his wife and child killed. Instead, he went straight down the hall to Lorna Shuman's. His goal was to get Hans and get out fast. It was possible there were cameras in the hall as well, but that could not be helped.

It dawned on him as he approached the door that all of this was going to be extremely difficult to explain to his son. Why could he not bring his favorite book? His special blanket . . .

Uwe stopped cold ten feet from Lorna's apartment, eyes wide. Dread and terror washed over him instantly, like he'd walked through a spiderweb in the dark. He wanted to run, to scream, to hit things.

Lorna Shuman's door stood ajar.

Uwe tried to shake it off, steeling himself. Her husband was away at training. Perhaps he'd returned early or she'd gone out to get the paper or milk or . . .

The door yawned open, pushed by a dark man with even darker eyes. His hair was pulled up in a stubby ponytail, high on the back of his head, like he was trying to mimic a Japanese samurai.

A broad smile crossed his face and he rubbed his hands together. "Uwe Hauptman! You are finally here!" the man said.

"What? Who?"

"Shhhh," the man said. "We do not want to alarm the neighbors." That smile again. Sickening, like spoiled milk. "Hans will be so happy to see his daddy!"

The mention of his son's name jolted Hauptman forward. Filled with rage, he rushed blindly, intent on ripping the man to pieces.

Instead of meeting him head-on or fighting at all, the man opened the door and stepped aside, a matador avoiding the oncoming bull.

Hauptman was vaguely aware of the door shutting behind him a moment before something struck him hard in the side of the head. Stunned, he fell to his knees, lashing out at nothing. He'd never been in a fight, even in school, and did not know what to expect.

"Calm down," the ponytailed man said. "We do not want to hurt you."

A hoarse chuckle came from the left.

"Speak for yourself."

Hauptman opened his eyes to a muscular woman, nude but for an open bathrobe, standing beside his son, who wore only his undershorts. The sound of a filling tub hissed from the open bathroom door behind them. At first, Hauptman had thought it was a man. Tall, muscular, defined pectorals and narrow hips. But the lack of clothing left no doubt that this was a woman—albeit with a strong jaw and a neck that flared like an angry cobra.

The sight of a naked body was not startling in the DDR. It was nothing to be ashamed of. Nude resorts, lakes, cabins, while not the norm, were not uncommon, either. But seeing this giant with her hand on his son would have been terrifying whether she had clothes on or not.

She patted a trembling Hans on top of his head, mussing his hair.

"The boy and I grew tired of waiting for his papa," she said. "We decided to have a bath and warm up."

A third person, someone Hauptman hadn't noticed, laughed from the kitchen. "A bath . . ."

His vision cleared slowly, and Hauptman was able to make out the man's features. He was much taller than the one in the ponytail, huskier, closely cropped hair, and a turtleneck sweater with sleeves that were far too long.

To this man's right, Lorna Shuman sat tied to one of her dining room chairs. Her mouth was taped shut. Her shoulders shook. Tears and mucus ran down the front of her face. The cries of an inconsolable baby carried down the hall from a dark room at the back of the apartment.

Hauptman raised both hands.

"I don't know anything," he whispered.

The man with the ponytail looked at his two comrades and shrugged, rolling his eyes.

"Uwe, Uwe, Uwe," he said. "Only people with something to hide blurt out things like that. Besides, who told you that we are interested in something you know?"

"I . . ."

The one in the ponytail put a finger to his lips.

"Shhhh."

The big man in the sweater came around the table to stand next to Ponytail. Lorna's baby continued to cry out for her, sobbing, coughing, choking on its own breath. The heartbroken woman struggled against her bonds. Her face flushed red. The veins bulged purple on the side of her neck until her head lolled.

Hans tried to run, but the cobra-necked woman grabbed him by the arm, lifting him off the ground.

"We're going to have our bath."

"Wait!" Hauptman said, desperate.

Hans looked at him, sobbing.

A pistol lay on top of the television console behind the woman, next to a stack of folded clothing, as if she'd set it there while she undressed for her bath.

She saw him looking at it and laughed. "Oh, look, he wants his papa to save him. Are you going to save him, Papa? If you think you can reach the pistol before I pick it up and blow his brains out, feel free to try."

"What do you want from me?"

Ponytail shook his head. "And there you go again. That makes me think you know exactly what we want."

Lorna's weeping and grunting started up again. The man in the sweater had taken up a spot beside her and now stroked the top of her head as if trying to soothe her.

It was not working.

Ponytail took a carving knife from the butcher block and dragged the point of it down the counter so it made a hissing noise.

"Let me explain to you how this will work," he said. "I do not intend to even ask you any questions. You already know what I need. At the first lie, I will kill this woman's baby—"

Lorna thrashed and jumped, tipping over the chair. The man in the sweater caught her easily and sat her upright, like this had happened before.

". . . and then the woman . . . and then . . ." Ponytail shook his head slowly and pointed the knife at Hans. "But I do not think we will get that far, because your dear boy will not die quickly."

The woman took the boy by his wrist, *tut-tut*ing her friend. "But not before we have our bath."

Hauptman swallowed.

"Hans," he said, quieter now. "I am so very sorry . . ."

Ponytail frowned, brandishing the knife. "As you wish," he said. "I will go and fetch the baby—"

A crack to Uwe's right caused everyone in the room to turn at once. The front door flew open and a tall man flowed into the room, pistol up, eyes wide, searching.

Hauptman had never seen Kurt Pfeiffer, but this had
to be him, come to admire his handiwork.

Clark's only plan was to go in and destroy the threats.
Entering the apartment was like climbing into a car
in the middle of a wreck. A baby screamed. The Hauptman boy wailed in the arms of a naked giant, and a
woman tied to a chair made awful, otherworldly sounds
that chilled even Clark, who thought he'd seen everything.

The man with the knife was an obvious choice.

Hauptman was kneeling, hands up, but he turned as
soon as he saw Clark, roaring at him.

"Pfeiffer!"

"What? No, I'm not Pfeiffer," Clark said. He shot the
ponytailed man with the knife twice above his ear.

But Hauptman was already moving, and Clark, who
was rarely taken off guard, found himself bowled over by
an angry husband out for his pound of flesh.

Clark attempted to shake the man off, tying up his
gun hand.

"I am not Pfeiffer!"

A new threat rushed in from Clark's left, growling and
brandishing a knife. Clark spun, taking Hauptman with
him, narrowly avoiding the blade.

There was really no such thing as a knife fight. There
was knife defense—running away—and knife attack—
best accompanied with a healthy dose of surprise. Clark

surprised his attacker when instead of trying to disen-
gage from the snarling Uwe Hauptman, he drew the
Fairbairn Sykes dagger from his belt and drove it into the
new threat's throat as he turned for another attack. Even
so, the man's blade sliced a neat gash across the shoulder
of Clark's wool coat.

Clark shoved an astonished Hauptman away, freeing
his Glock to dead-check the man he'd just stabbed. He'd
seen people like this do a hell of a lot of damage while
they were bleeding to death.

Two down, Clark pivoted, swinging the barrel past
Hauptman to settle on the snake-hipped woman who
stood naked holding the terrified kid in front of her like
a bulletproof vest. Blood dripped from a ragged bite
wound in her forearm. *Good job, kid,* Clark thought.
She'd locked on now, feigning a smile, but inched backward toward a gun on the TV behind her.

"How many?"

"These three only," Hauptman said, finally figuring
out that Clark was on his side.

A scant fifteen feet away, the woman would have normally been an easy target, but the kid was big, and she
was strong enough to hold him up high so he covered
her face and most of her vitals. Worse yet, he would not
stay still.

The boy writhed and fought like a wounded animal
caught in a trap, adding layers of difficulty. The unnatural way he held his left arm made Clark think the woman
had broken it when she'd hauled him up.

"Lower your weapon or I will break his neck!"

"Listen to me, Freakshow," Clark hissed. "Put him down . . ."

The side of the woman's head presented itself, but the screaming boy jerked that way before Clark could take a shot. The woman gave the boy a violent shake, growling at him to calm down.

Unfortunately for her, he did.

Clark's first shot destroyed her right knee, causing her to list that way. The boy, feeling her grip relax, pushed away. Clark's shots stitched upward, taking more target as it was exposed. First her shoulder, then the top of her chest, and finally one on the point of the chin.

Clark secured the pistol that was on top of the TV, press-checking it quickly to see that there was a round in the chamber in case he had to use it later. With eight rounds gone from his Glock, he swapped out the remaining nine rounds for his last fresh magazine, dropping the partial in his coat pocket. Ten rounds was a lot, but eighteen was better.

Hauptman rushed to his son and tried to embrace him, but the boy was having none of it. He screamed and held his elbow.

Clark considered cutting the woman free, but decided that since she was an unknown, he'd put a pin in that.

Facing the door, he knelt beside the crying kid. This was a problem. He'd been in the apartment for less than two minutes, but the neighbors had surely called the police. They needed to leave, but there was no way this child was going to slip past anyone.

"I'm a friend," Clark said to the boy, taking his arm firmly but gently.

He breathed a shuddering sigh.

"Nursemaid's elbow," Clark said to Hauptman. "The joint's popped out." He pulled the sobbing boy closer, gently bending his arm and turning his wrist so the palm faced upward. The boy began to hyperventilate, squealing from the pain. Clark found the offending radius bone and covered it with his thumb.

"Try to be brave," Hauptman said.

Clark pushed, popping the bone back into place. The boy shuddered again and stopped crying almost immediately.

Clark stood up, turning toward the door, pistol in his hand again.

Three minutes down.

"He is brave," Clark said. "He doesn't have to try." He picked up the carving knife from the floor. Lorna Shuman jumped from her chair as soon as he'd cut her free, stumbling on numb legs to get to her crying baby.

Clark and the Hauptmans were gone before she got there.

58

Jack Ryan sat up at the noise outside the door, jostling Foley awake. It was too early for Dr. Hauptman to have returned with the boy.

Foley groaned, tensing when she realized Ryan was staring at the door.

Across the room, Elke Hauptman shot a worried glance at Ryan, then reached into her bag for the revolver.

"Mary Pat," a voice said from the front room. A female voice. "I'd appreciate it if you didn't shoot me."

"Jen," Foley muttered.

Ryan frowned. "Jen North?"

Foley eased herself into a sitting position.

"How'd you find us?"

"Happy to tell you," North said. "As soon as you promise not to have someone sneak up behind me and cut my throat."

"I'd cut your throat myself, sister," Foley said. "No point in sending someone else. What do you want?"

Silence—for long enough that Elke began to squirm.

Then, "I got your message."

"Wrong," Foley said. "I didn't send you a message."

"Okay," North said. "I got the message you sent to Berlin Station."

Foley sighed, defeated. "You have the codes to the SRAC . . ."

"I do."

Ryan's grip tightened on the Makarov, though he had no target. He whispered, "That means the Stasi have the codes to the SRAC . . ."

"Your new friend's pretty smart," North said. "Not bad to look at, either, for a headquarters puke. But no. I kept that little bit of intel for myself. You know, rainy-day shit."

Foley maneuvered herself up so she was leaning against the wall. She tapped Ryan's hand, opening and closing her fist until he realized she wanted him to hand her the pistol.

He caught her eye, saw that she was far better at this kind of thing than he was, and handed her the gun.

Elke pointed at the door, pantomiming that she was going to move, offering to be a distraction. Foley shook her head.

"What's going on in there?" North said.

She was closer now, just around the corner outside the door, separated from them by a thin waferboard wall.

Foley realized it, too. She kept the little Makarov low, but aimed it where North was standing.

"Just trying to figure out what your play is," Foley said.

"I need you to listen to me, Mary Pat," North said. Remarkably staying put in the same spot, judging from the sound of her voice. "I know you're getting ready to shoot me." A sound like a sob. Was she crying? "Hell, *I* would shoot me if I were you."

Foley lifted the gun a hair, ensuring that the slide was free from her thigh, able to move with the shot and not cause the gun to jam.

"Here," North said. "Maybe this'll convince you."

A soft grunt came from the other side of the door as North stooped down and slid her pistol across the floor.

"Have your boyfriend secure that," North said. "Hell, he can point it at my head if he wants, but I'm coming in to talk."

We'll always have Berlin, sweetheart," North said while Ryan patted her down for other weapons. He found a knife in her belt and passed it off to Elke.

"You're not helping your case by being a smartass," Foley said. "It's cold outside. You wearing tights?"

North smirked. "Kind of you to be concerned, but yeah, I'm wearing long johns."

"Good," Foley said. "Jack, pull her jeans down around her ankles and sit her on that." She motioned to an overturned bucket.

"I'll do it," North said, unbuttoning her pants before Ryan had to. He stepped clear with her H&K in case she had anything else hidden down there. "Pretty smart, hobbling me."

"Yeah, well," Foley said. "I'm not in the mood to fight you."

North's jeans pooled around her feet, revealing a set of snow-white thermals.

"Remember that time in Tbilisi? We were convincing that Azerbaijani gunrunner that he should—"

"Cut to the chase, Jen," Foley said. "What is it you want?"

"I wanted to thank you," North said.

"Thank me?"

"For not rushing to judgment. I told you I had the SRAC codes. I read the message you sent. You warned them about me, but insisted there was no proof. I mean, who does that?" She answered before Foley had a chance to. "I'll tell you who does that, pretty much no one. This Agency will crucify their brightest stars if there is even a whiff of espionage. You don't even have to be a mole, someone just has to accuse you and then you're branded as one for life."

"So you're clean?"

North leaned her head back and laughed at the ceiling. "Hell, no, I am not clean. I sold out my country and my friends a long time ago. But that's the point. I quote, 'CALISTO veracity unsubstantiated. Story re: JN needs confirmation.' I mean, talk about giving me the benefit of the doubt . . ."

"Jen . . ."

"Look," North said. "I want to help you. I can get you out of here, but we need to leave now."

"Go," Elke said. "I am waiting on Uwe."

Ryan shook his head. "We can't go just yet."

"I get it," North said. "You're waiting for the husband and kid. You know there's a good chance they didn't survive the morning. And even if they did, they'll have some very brutal people in tow when they return."

"Maybe so," Foley said. She seemed to have perfect faith in the "insurance" she sent to protect them.

North's shoulders fell. She slumped forward, looking and surely feeling ridiculous, sitting on the bucket with her pants around her ankles.

"I was six weeks along before I realized I was pregnant," she said. "I mean, there I was, a highly educated, globe-trotting spy and I let some guy knock me up. I mean, holy shit, how stupid can you be . . ." She buried her face in her hands like she was going to break down, but caught herself. "It was so innocent in the beginning. Lane Buckley is such a handsy asshole. He just . . . I mean, there I was, doing the best work of my life, turning and then running one of the most valuable assets the Agency has seen in a decade, and that pompous dick treats me like I'm three parts coffee-getter and one part potential piece of ass that he can add to his trophy belt." She looked up, still clutching her hair, and met Foley's eye. "You know how I am. I met this guy at a hotel bar—"

"Jen," Foley said.

"I know, but, Mary Pat, this one actually listened to me. Treated me like I was somebody. And he didn't have some fancy job that he got to brag about all the time, I mean, he told me he was in the trash business. Waste disposal. When Buckley screwed me over and took all the credit for Chernenko . . . I just needed a listening ear, I guess. This guy went back and forth to the DDR with his waste-management job, and it turned out he had access to some decent East German financial documents. I thought I could develop him as an asset. Buckley was still chief of Bonn Station and there was no way I was going to trust him, so I just worked off the books.

"Rolfe gave me the listening ear I needed . . . and as it turned out, a little something extra. You know what it's like, Mary Pat. A male case officer sleeps with a local and the powers that be transfer his ass. The good old boys would have quietly slapped him on the back for his prowess and found him a soft place to land and get back on his feet. Besides, a paid move when he probably wants to get the hell out of Dodge is hardly a punishment. It's different for us and you know it. If anyone in Bonn . . . or Langley . . . had found out I slept with a source, let alone gotten myself pregnant, they would have thrown me in an active volcano if there had been one handy."

She wiped her nose with the back of her forearm.

"Can I please pull my pants up?"

Foley shook her head.

"No."

North sighed, resigned to it.

"The thing is," she said, "Rolfe didn't freak out like I

thought he would. I mean, he was a real gentleman about it. He asked what I wanted to do and then vowed to support me. Remember I thought he was still my source then. When I told him I was worried about what a pregnancy would do to my career, he arranged for it to be taken care of over here . . . Typical German efficiency. I went back to Bonn depressed, but hopeful.

"It took me all of ten seconds to realize that I was now his source . . . I tried, Mary Pat, I really did. I mean, I only gave him shit intel at first, but he pressed and pressed and pressed . . ."

She started to cry in earnest now.

"I thought that girl was onto me . . ."

Ryan frowned. "Ruby Keller?"

North nodded emphatically, racked with sobs. "I heard her singing about dead kids, *Kindertotenlieder* . . ." She covered her face with her hands again. "I swear, I thought she knew . . ."

"Where is she?" Ryan asked.

North sniffed. "In prison. Hohenschönhausen."

"But she's alive?"

North nodded. She wiped her face again. Still jolted by periodic sobs, she composed herself by degree.

Foley cleared her throat, raising the Makarov. "Go ahead and pull up your jeans."

"Thank you," North said, doing just that and then resuming her seat on the bucket. She knew the drill. "Look, I know everything I just told you is not an excuse, but it is a reason."

"I'll give you that," Foley said.

"I'm going to get you out, if you'll let me, no strings attached, but would you do me one little favor?"

"Jen—"

"Hear me out," North said. "One of these days, you're going to transfer, and Moscow will send a cable to your new station informing them of all your exposures. I don't know how many you have . . . but . . ." The sobs started to take over again, but she got the better of them. "But somewhere in that list will be a line that says something like '. . . BETRAYED BY THE TRAITOR, JENNIFER NORTH . . .' People will talk shit about me for years, decades maybe, but if you get the chance and some new kid asks you, just tell 'em there was more to it than that . . . Or don't, I don't give a shit anymore. I would like to get you out of here, if you'll let me."

"How do you propose to do that?" Foley asked. "I'm not sure you're even in such good standing, with everything that's gone down."

North rose to her feet, apparently no longer worried about getting shot.

"A tunnel."

59

Jack Ryan knew the story. Most everyone in the intelligence community heard it at some point early in his or her career.

Operation Gold—1,480 feet of tunnel under the most heavily patrolled and guarded stretches of border in the world. Worried about Soviet nuclear testing in the early 1950s, the CIA and MI6 had decided they needed to devise a way to tie in to communication lines in East Berlin. The Germans were still digging out from the war back then and were a relative footnote compared to the KGB and GRU.

Work on the tunnel began in September of 1954 and was completed in approximately eight months. It remained operational for almost a year, during which time it recorded tens of thousands of Soviet communications, believed by the CIA to be well worth the cost of construction, which was equivalent to the cost of two U-2 spy planes.

Unbeknownst to the Allies, a well-placed Soviet spy in the British MI6 passed the plans of Operation Gold to his handlers, exposing this brilliant intelligence coup from the time of its inception. The Soviets not only allowed construction to continue, but also allowed the tunnel to function for almost a year, not even using it to pass disinformation, apparently fearing that would burn their high-value mole. The mole was eventually transferred, and the Russians were able to "discover" the tunnel.

"So," Ryan said. "You're saying there is a Soviet tunnel?"

"No," North said. "I'm saying there is an East German tunnel. There are only a few in the Stasi who know of its existence. I wouldn't have known, but I followed Rolfe Schneider there a few months ago. We . . . I mean the West . . . don't stop people coming and going, but we do keep a record. They use the tunnel when they want to keep from setting off alarms. It's a way for them to operate in our area without our even knowing they're in the country."

Ryan gave a slow nod. "That's how they got Ruby Keller across."

"That would be my guess," North said. "I doubt your CALISTO is even privy to it. I've never been in the damned thing, but I know where it is. The basement of an abandoned apartment building that runs adjacent to the Wall. There are photos of people trying to jump out of it in the weeks after the Wall first went up. The Stasi cordoned it off immediately and hasn't let anyone in since . . . Except themselves. They call it IRIS. It's small, and you have to get down on your hands and knees in a couple—"

The front door rattled. Everyone froze. Elke tensed and then stood when Uwe called out for her.

"Who wants *grilletta*?"

He'd not taken time to go for sandwiches, but used the agreed-upon pass phrase to keep from getting himself shot.

Elke answered with the *all-clear*.

"Maybe for lunch!"

A moment later, little Hansie burst through the doors and ran for his mother. Uwe followed him in, ashen and drawn.

"Are you alone?" Ryan asked. He'd expected to meet this mysterious protector that Foley had been communicating with, that Jim Greer put so much stock in.

Uwe nodded. "I am. John . . . if that was really his name . . . He said he prefers to keep watch outside. That he will lose his value to us if he comes in."

Foley scooted herself to the edge of the bed, grimacing as she tested her legs.

Ryan swooped in. "Let me—"

She batted him away. "I can do it! Seriously, if we're going to get out of here, I need to see if I can walk. Nothing's broken. It hurts like hell. I'm pretty sure I was so bad last night from blood loss. Feeling . . . some better . . . now."

She pushed off the bed, struggling uneasily to her feet. Then took a breath. Step. Breath. Step. Breath. Until she loosened up. "Okay," she said, moving slowly, but moving forward.

"The rest of you get ready to go. I'll be right back."

"What's the matter with her?" North asked, looking at Ryan.

"She wants to make sure her friend gets out."

"What friend?"

Ryan shrugged. "Honestly, I have no idea. He's just . . . there."

Car theft was rare in a country where all the cars were shitty and there was no place to go anyway. People left them unlocked with the keys in the ignition or, more often, started them with a nail or a screwdriver.

Foley found a likely Trabant 601 at the end of the block, took a peek inside, and found the nail in the ignition as she'd hoped. It would be tight, with barely enough room for two, let alone five adults and a child. But it was better than taking the U-Bahn. The Stasi would be watching every station. Foley checked up and down the street. The untouched snow around the car led her to believe its occupant had come to work for the early shift at the hosiery mill. It was a "Deluxe"—made of Duroplast and recycled trash—and cost a year's salary.

"I hear they do zero to sixty in thirty seconds," John Clark said, crunching up in the snow behind her, hat pulled low over his ears.

She knew he was out there and had expected him to approach if they were clear.

"You okay?"

"Just a little bullet wound," she said. "I lost some blood, but I'm feeling some better today." She rolled her shoulders, felt a stitch tug against her wound, and winced. "That said, I could probably use a doctor. Look, John, we have a way out."

She told him about the tunnel, giving him the general location.

Clark tapped the Trabant. "Not nearly enough room in this thing for all of you," he said. "Not if North comes along . . ." His face grew dark. "Which she should not."

"She has to," Foley said. "She's the only one who knows how to get in."

Clark cast a glance over each shoulder. "You'd better go, then. I'll watch your six."

"John—"

"I'll take the U-Bahn and meet you there," he said. "Don't worry about me."

Ryan, worried that cramming in the little clown car would kill Foley, insisted on staying behind.

"No way, José," Foley said. "We all go."

And she made it work, planning where everyone would sit before they approached the car so they could get moving before anyone in the factory happened to look out and warn Adolf that someone was jacking his ride.

Dr. Hauptman drove; he was tallest. Foley sat in the passenger seat so her wounds wouldn't be crushed. Ryan, North, and Elke all crammed in the backseat together, with Hans on his mother's lap. They didn't worry about having enough seat belts. The car had none anyway.

WEST/EAST BERLIN

Wollankstrasse
Underground Station   ■ ■ Tunnel Entrance

N

WEST BERLIN

Berlin Wall

EAST BERLIN

Elke's Apartment

Checkpoint Charlie   Berlin Wall

© 2022 Jeffrey L. Ward

Ready to go, Foley took out the Makarov and set it in her lap. Ryan understood from the look on her face why. She was too injured to fight, and she wasn't about to let herself get arrested.

Hauptman turned the nail and the car sputtered to life, sounding not quite as powerful as the riding mower Ryan used on his lawn outside Baltimore.

Bursting at the seams, there was a real danger the car would not be able to carry this much weight, at least not at road speeds.

Hauptman checked over his shoulder, as much for the owner as for oncoming traffic, and then pulled into the snowy street. The windows began to fog immediately.

"I have bad news," Hauptman said, deadpan. "Everybody has to hold their breath."

The intense stress of the situation set everyone laughing, even Mary Pat, who held her side and laughed with one eye shut.

Hauptman leaned forward and wiped the windscreen with the cuff of his sleeve as the little Trabant slowly but surely picked up speed.

60

The Amtrak station was just two blocks from Pioneer Park, west of downtown Salt Lake City, not far from the FBI field office. They were open for only a few hours, on either side of arrivals and departures. The staff was eager to go home and provided Special Agents Green and Rawlings with the latest passenger list by the time Murray and the others arrived.

Sixty-four people had gotten off the train in Salt Lake; forty-four had boarded before it departed.

"We put eyes on every one of them," Green said. "He could have gotten on, but—"

"Don't beat yourself up," Murray said. "We're working off a shitty pencil sketch. This guy could have shaved his head or been wearing a wig."

Harris had the passenger list and was ticking down it with a pen, reading off the names.

"Passengers have to show ID?" she asked Peggy, the

Amtrak staffer who'd stayed behind. She was young, a student at the U, and said she needed to get home to study.

"Usually not," Peggy said. "Depends on who's working the ticket desk. The agents had us asking everyone tonight, though."

Harris continued to pore over the passenger list, chatting with the Amtrak staffer.

Murray ran a hand through his hair, thinking, wishing for a cup of coffee, and walked across the ticket station to study a large wall map that depicted the tracks. He couldn't remember the last time he'd slept.

He stood and stared at it for a good five minutes, going stop to stop in his mind, trying to put himself in the UNSUB's shoes.

"Next stop is in Elko, Nevada . . ." he said at length. "Maybe the son of a bitch drove it . . ."

Harris spoke up from across the room. "Or maybe the son of a bitch got on in Provo." She carried the passenger list over to Murray and stood beside him, looking at the wall map. Gillum and the two other agents followed. "Look at this," she said, using her folder to point at the map, following the path of the tracks south. "Provo is, what, a little over an hour south of here. Peterson escaped from the stolen Toyota about forty miles south of there. We don't know when our UNSUB figured out she was gone, or if he even has, for that matter. He may have just dumped the car assuming she was still inside the trunk. But here's the deal. We've been assuming all along that he'd come to the larger city because it would be easier to blend in. I think he just cooled his jets in Provo and boarded there."

Murray looked over her shoulder at the passenger list.

"How many got on there?"

"Seven," Harris said. "Judging from their last names—a family of three, a couple, two singles."

"Okay . . ."

"I think it's this guy. Paul Davis."

Gillum stepped up. "What makes you say that?"

"For one thing, the two families are, well, families. Ninety-nine percent chance that this guy is traveling alone. And the other single is named Jeremiah Washburn. I mean, who makes up an alias like Jeremiah Washburn?"

"Maybe it's his real name?" Agent Green asked.

"It could be," Murray said.

Peggy came out of the ticket booth with a stack of flimsy thermographic facsimile papers and handed them off to Harris.

"Is this what you're looking for?"

Harris thumbed through the stack until she reached the fifth sheet down. Her eyes brightened and a smile spread over her exhausted face. She turned the clipboard around and showed it to Murray. It was Paul Davis's receipt, filled in by hand at the station. He blinked, trying to figure out what she was talking about, like working through a Sunday newspaper brain teaser. Then he saw it.

"The date," he said. "Of course."

Gillum and the others, including the Amtrak staffer, crowded in to see what she'd found.

The OSI agent smiled and shook his head in disbelief. "You were right," he said. "We've got him!"

Almost giddy, Harris pointed it out to Green and Rawlings. "Germans write the day before the month, and customarily use periods instead of lines. Paul Davis, or whatever his name really is, is under a lot of stress. Looks like he went into autopilot after he signed his fake name."

The top portion of the ticket stub had apparently been filled out by the station attendant, but the bottom line bore the passenger's signature and the date.

Paul Davis 17.11.85

"I'll be damned," Agent Green said. "Son of a bitch let a dot and a date trip him up . . ."

Murray wheeled to the wall map. "We don't have him in cuffs yet."

"Next stop is Elko," Harris said.

"The Zephyr pulls out of there at five minutes past three." She checked her watch. "Crap. That's, like, just over two hours from now."

"How long to drive it?" Murray asked the group.

Rawlings, who was stationed in Salt Lake, said, "Three, three and a half hours, but we can do it faster. Vegas has an RA assigned to Elko. Or they did."

"That's perfect," Murray said. "Let's get them on the horn and make a plan. I'll call the SAC in Las Vegas and grease the skids."

Harris carried her folio to the Amtrak ticket desk,

where Peggy showed her the phone. She returned less than a minute later, shaking her head.

"That's not gonna work. Jerry Gonzales, the Elko RA, is detailed to the National Defense Site at Whitney Pocket."

"Of course he is," Murray said.

"So," Rawlings said. "If we're gonna drive it, we better haul ass." He looked at Peggy. "Sorry, hon."

"I don't want to risk losing this guy because one of us has a flat tire or an antelope jumps in front of the Bu-car."

"Elko PD?" Green said.

"Maybe." Murray studied the map, the beginnings of a plan percolating in his tired brain. "How far away is Winnemucca?"

"I'm not sure," Peggy said. "But the Zephyr rolls in at five-forty a.m."

Harris had torn the pertinent map pages out of one of the atlases at the office and now took them out of her folder, unfolding and holding them against the wall. She added up the numbers along Interstate 80.

"Four hundred miles and change," she said. "No way we can get there in time. Can we call the station and have locals pick him up?"

"We could," Murray said. "But I have no idea how big their department is. This guy has killed two and attempted to kill a third. If something goes down, they'll be two hundred miles from anywhere." He drummed his fingers on the map, thinking, rethinking, then said, "We'll take him in Winnemucca. With any luck we'll have a Reno RA that hasn't been assigned to the National Defense Area. They can meet us there."

Harris cocked her head. "Meet us there?"

"It occurs to me that the deputy director of the FBI, or more likely someone above him, picked me up on the firing range in a helicopter and then flew you and me all the way across the country in a Lear 35." Murray shot a glance at Gillum. "I'm thinking we should be able to get permission for the Air Force to fly us where we need to be."

"Already on it," the AFOSI agent said. "You guys gear up and I'll get us a plane and meet you on the flight line at the Hill. The base is about half an hour north, so we should get on the road."

Murray checked his watch. "The Zephyr gets there in five hours," he said. "I'd like to be on the ground and set up in three."

61

Mary Pat Foley sent a burst message to CIA US-BER via the SRAC, advising them to stand by with medics across from the Wollankstrasse subway station, the nearest landmark to where IRIS emerged in West Berlin. She didn't give them the exact address, partially because she didn't trust Jen North, but primarily because she didn't want any USBER personnel tripping any alarms and alerting any sentries in the East if they tried to enter the tunnel.

She didn't explain it, but Ryan suspected that Foley had asked for medics not only because of her injuries, but for any they might incur during the crossing.

He nearly fell on the icy road when the ragtag group of fugitives all but exploded out of the little Trabant. According to North, they were one block from the Bernaustrasse neighborhood apartment that concealed the tunnel's eastern entrance. The air around the group hummed with excitement. Ryan took Foley's arm and matched her gait. She was walking a little better, loosening up from the movement, but he could tell she was still in a great deal of pain.

"Will Major Pfeiffer be here?" Uwe Hauptman asked.

"I hope not," Ryan said.

Hauptman pursed his lips together and nodded. "That is too bad." He'd made it clear that he was prepared to leave the Stasi swine alive if that was what it took to save his family. But if he ever saw the man on the street . . .

North pulled up short half a block from a boarded-up building of gray brick and concrete. It had been partially rebuilt after the war, but the East German government had ordered its occupants out after the Wall went up, ostensibly because it would be too easy to rig an escape, but the real reason was IRIS.

"There will be two guards inside," North said. "They have cameras on the front, so we'll need to go in fast. No huddling up at the door. Just *boom*! In! *Boom. Boom.*"

Ryan understood immediately that the last two booms were someone taking out the two guards.

"The stairs are to the right," North continued. "Straight down to the basement. The tunnel is down a long hall about thirty feet in front of you when you reach the bottom. It's blocked with an old shelving unit, for camouflage more than anything. The door behind that is solid wood, but it's only secured with a simple padlock. Once inside, we'll have about a four-hundred-yard sprint, about fifty yards of it single-file."

"We'll go in fast," Foley said. "North will lead

because she knows the way. Hauptmans in the middle. Ryan and I in the rear."

"Let's put you in front," North said. "I don't want to leave you behind."

"I'll keep up," Foley said. "But I'm in no shape to see to the guards."

Ryan clenched his teeth and nodded at North, knowing exactly what he was signing up for. "I can help you with that."

Elke fell back to take Foley's arm. "I will walk with you."

"All righty," North said. "It's apt to get noisy real fast once we breach that door. Most Stasi don't even know this place exists, but they'll get here PDQ and figure it all out once the shooting starts. I'd like us to be in the tunnel inside of ninety seconds after we breach the door. Ryan and I will peel off and see to the guards, you all just keep trucking downstairs. Shoot the padlock if you have to, but try to keep from shooting anything else. I'm not a hundred percent sure, but knowing our East German brethren like I do, I'm betting they'll have the whole place rigged to explode."

Foley nodded as if she'd expected the same thing. Ryan thought that little fact was something North should have led with, but he kept his thoughts to himself.

North held out her hand to Ryan. "Can I have my gun back?"

Foley groaned. "Go ahead."

"Okay," North said, the pistol under her arm and out of sight from any passersby. "Ready?"

Uwe Hauptman picked up his little boy and nodded.

———

It was over almost before it began. North put her boot to the door, but it didn't budge. A trickle of dust skittered down off the hinges into the snow. The guards inside had surely been alerted by the loud bang.

Rather than kicking it again, North put two rounds through the locking mechanism, severing the bolt. She shouldered her way in, H&K P7 low at her waist, firing point-blank at the sallow-faced guard who had come to check out the noise. The shots took him low in the belly and his finger convulsed around the trigger of the black machine pistol slung around his neck, firing an automatic burst into his own foot. The second guard had been in the restroom and came out slightly behind North. Ryan shot him once, hitting him in the chest. North finished him off and barked at everyone to keep moving.

Having peeled off to take care of the guards, Ryan and North were at the rear of the stack. Foley and the Hauptmans were at the base of the stairs by the time Ryan hit the first step at a dead run. Oddly, they were all stopped at the bottom, bunched together as if they'd hit a barrier. Ryan saw what it was when he reached the last step.

North gasped behind him.

"Rolfe!"

"Let me see your hands!" a tall man with perfect teeth said, motioning with a PM-63 machine pistol identical to the ones the dead guards upstairs had carried. "I do not want to shoot you, but I will."

North gasped again. "How did you—"

"Oh, my sweet Jennifer . . . When I could not locate you today, I knew you would come here. Frankly, I had thought you might try to break your little pet out of Hohenschönhausen and bring her through." He pushed the muzzle of the weapon toward her. "Are you going to introduce me to your friends?"

"Rolfe Schneider," North whispered. "Stasi colonel."

"And?" the German prodded.

"And my control."

Hans Hauptman swayed on his feet, terrified that there was about to be more killing. His father reached for him.

"Hands!" Colonel Schneider barked again.

Hauptman did as he was told. Hans leaned in to his legs for support.

Schneider pointed the machine pistol at Foley's chest. "You, too, little lady."

Her hands had dropped appreciably toward her coat pocket. She complied, wincing visibly.

"Oh," Schneider said. "Are you hurt, my dear? Were you, perhaps, shot by a young KGB officer in the Linde *Plattenbau*?" His face grew darker. "Oh, Jennifer, do you betray everyone you know?"

Ryan watched in horror as Foley's hand dropped toward her coat again. He'd taken the Makarov to deal with the upstairs guards. But she didn't need a pistol. Serious about not being taken alive, she only needed him to think she had a pistol.

Ryan spoke up, hoping to interrupt her plan.

"Colonel," he said. "I'd like to propose a deal."

"Americans . . ." Schneider laughed. "You are in no position to make deals."

Up to this point, Elke Hauptman, partially hidden behind her husband and son, had to Schneider been nothing but an East German housewife. Ryan and the other two women were spies, that much was clear. Dr. Hauptman was a man, so he bore watching. But Elke had been completely invisible, a gnat. She cocked the Nagant revolver in her hand, pointed directly at Schneider's belly.

"This is the gun that killed the KGB pig," she said, remarkably calm. "All we want to do is leave."

Ryan drew the Makarov. North followed suit and aimed her H&K.

"You bastard . . ."

"Don't!" Ryan barked.

Schneider raised his right hand and lowered the machine pistol to the concrete floor with his left.

"I do not know what your name is," he said to Ryan. "But if you think she is not going to shoot me—"

"Seriously, Jen," Ryan said. "I want him alive." Then, to Schneider. "Now, let me tell you what I am thinking . . ."

"If you have the authority to make that happen," Schneider said after Ryan had finished, "then I should keep you here as a prize."

"You should," Ryan said. "Except you have three guns pointed at your lungs, so I think you'd like my plan better."

"Please go," North said. "His men will be here any minute."

"Come with us," Foley said. "I'll tell them what you've done."

North shook her head. "They know what I've done. No, someone needs to stay here and babysit Rolfe, make sure he keeps his end of the deal. He might just decide to blow the tunnel on you."

Foley put a hand on her shoulder. "You know what you are?"

North sobbed.

"A traitor?"

"Well, yeah." Foley sniffed back a tear. "But there's more to it than that . . ."

In October of 1985, East German runner Marita Koch ran four hundred meters in a world record time of 47.6 seconds. Ryan and the others didn't cover the tunnel quite that fast, but they were all panting by the time they popped out in the basement of an office building rented by a West German construction company fronting for the Stasi. The frumpy woman at the desk, who up to now had gotten to live a cushy life in the West and do nothing all day but sit and answer telephones, stood up and screamed when she saw them.

"I am going to use your phone," Foley said to the woman in curt German. "If you get in my way I will shoot you in the ass."

Hans Hauptman giggled.

His parents began to weep.

The woman raised her hands and stepped aside.

Jack Ryan turned and watched the black mouth of the tunnel behind them, wondering what kind of evil might follow them out.

Holy shit," Billy Dunn said when he met the group on the street. He was armed and facing outbound, covering them from any HVA operatives on this side of the Wall. A squad of heavily armed CIA case officers wrapped the Hauptmans in blankets and escorted them to a convoy of waiting vehicles. One of them, on orders from Foley's SRAC message, had brought a plastic train for Hans.

Hulse and Ryan helped Foley to a waiting ambulance.

"Somebody should be helping you, Ryan," Hulse said. "You look like warmed-over shit."

"I'm fine," he said. Then, to Foley, "You notice how good it smells over here?"

"We are literally four hundred yards away from where we just were," Foley said. She stopped, took a deep breath, grimacing from the effort, then said, "You know what . . . It does smell better."

62

Dan Murray took one look at the airplanes and felt his stomach do a flip.

"What in the actual hell . . ."

Two Air Force Security police officers had taken one look at his FBI credentials when he'd arrived at the front gate and requested that he follow them.

Instead of a comfortable Lear 35, he found three Northrop T-38 Talons ready and waiting on the flight line. The sleek two-seat supersonic trainers were ubiquitous across the Air Force and Navy. Virtually every fighter pilot had spent time in a T-38 cockpit at the beginning of their career. By NASA tradition, space shuttle astronauts arrived at Kennedy Space Center before a flight in the little fighter trainer.

A bantam rooster of a man strode up like he owned the place and shook Murray's hand. "Colonel Dave Finn," he said. "My friends call me Huck." He glanced down at a clipboard in his left hand. "I have Special Agents Murray, Harris, and Gillum. Is that correct?"

"Yes," Murray said, dumbfounded.

"Outstanding," Colonel Finn said. "I understand you're in a hurry. Chief Robbins will get y'all into flight suits and we can be on our way." He turned to go, then spun, shaking his head, mouth tight. "You know I've gotta say it . . ."

"Gotta say what?"

Murray was still trying to get his head wrapped around strapping himself into the backseat of a supersonic jet.

"If you're goin' to Winnemucca, man, with me you can ride . . ."

Max is somewhere around seven hundred forty-six knots," Colonel Finn said over the intercom when they were zipping along at thirty thousand feet somewhere over eastern Nevada. "That's eight hundred fifty miles an hour, give or take. I told my guys we'd keep it around six if that's okay with you. That'll get us there in a little over thirty minutes."

"Plenty of time," Murray said, and did not speak again until they touched down in Winnemucca Municipal Airport.

———

That was amazing!" Betty Harris said, a smile permanently affixed to her freckled face.

"Yeah," Murray said, wiping some of the sandwich he'd eaten four hours earlier off the corner of his mouth. "I'd rather not do that again."

Two plainclothes officers from Winnemucca PD met the team in unmarked Ford Crown Victorias and took them to the train station. George Ortiz, resident agent in the Reno FBI office, arrived shortly after they did.

They were two hours early.

Harris spied a stack of dusty suitcases in the corner.

"More passengers?"

"Lost and abandoned bags," the Amtrak agent said. His name was Rodgers, and he looked as tired as Murray felt.

"Mind if we borrow them for a few minutes when we get on the train?"

"Knock yourself out," Rodger said. "Like I said, they're abandoned. I just haven't gotten around to tossing them in the dumpster."

"Coffee?" Murray asked.

"I wish," Rodger said. "There's Cokes in the machine outside and some Fritos, I think, but that's about it."

Murray thought about the combination of Fritos and Coca-Cola on his belly for a minute and decided to stick with the water fountain.

"The life of an FBI agent, eh, boss?" Harris said, still beaming from the flight.

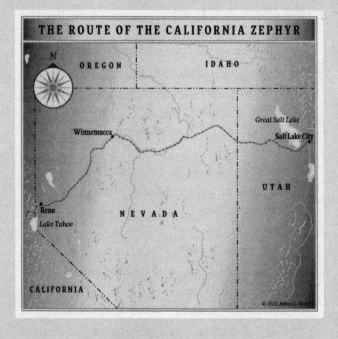

Murray gave a sardonic chuckle. "I was just thinking the same thing, Betty. The exact same thing . . ."

The California Zephyr squealed to a halt in front of the Winnemucca, Nevada, station ten minutes late and an hour before dawn.

Nine other outbound passengers didn't arrive until just before the train, and the three FBI agents and AFOSI agent Gillum were able to board with the group. They carried duffels from the abandoned bag pile in case their UNSUB happened to be looking out the window.

Fast asleep in roomette number 11 on #531, one coach away from the dining car, Garit Richter opened his eyes when the train rolled to a stop. He held his breath and listened for sirens, marching boots, anything else that might suggest authorities. Instead, he heard the grunt of passengers dragging their bags down the narrow corridors, doors sliding open, a child whimpering from fatigue.

Then a woman's voice, trying to locate her room.

"Number fourteen," she whispered, taking special care not to bother her fellow passengers. *"This is us, hon . . ."*

It was a sweet voice, and Richter rolled onto his back in the narrow lower berth, thinking he might like to meet a woman with such a voice.

An instant later, the door of his roomette slid open

with a terrifying *whoosh* and a very angry-looking man shoved a black revolver in his face.

Y ou know," Harris said, after they'd gotten their still-unidentified subject seated in the rear of Special Agent Ortiz's Crown Victoria, "in the Academy every practical exercise where we're going to arrest someone ends up in a bloody gunfight."

"And this could have," Murray said. "If this puke would have had a gun—or been able to reach his knife. Don't forget he murdered two people and nearly did the same to a third."

Harris lifted the burned piece of metal. "All for this," she said.

"Yeah," Murray said. "I was always more concerned with the murders than the top secret aircraft tech. They'll develop something, then we'll develop something better, then they'll top that, and so on and so on . . . This shit that caused us so much grief will be on the cover of *Popular Mechanics* in two years, mark my words."

"Until then . . ." Special Agent Gillum swooped in. "I'll take that." He shot Harris a wink. "Colonel Finn's waiting to take me back to Tonopah. I'm sure his guys could drop you off in SLC if—"

"She can go if she wants," Murray said. "I am good to take a ride to Reno in a subsonic Crown Vic."

"Rain check on that, Gillum." Harris chuckled. "I'd better stay with my wingman and get this asshole to Reno."

Though their UNSUB had been arrested in Winnemucca, he'd be transported to Reno to appear before the nearest federal magistrate for an initial appearance and an identity hearing the following day. Attorneys from Main Justice were flying out the next morning to make certain the hearing was sealed for national security reasons. The local PD was instructed to keep quiet about the arrest. All the news and cable channels were still camped out near Whitney Pocket, hoping for a shot of the super-secret airplane, and had no idea there had been a piece of it in FBI custody in Winnemucca. As secrets went, northern Nevada was a good place to keep one.

"I wonder if he'll tell us what 'mint' had to do with anything?"

Murray shook his head. "This asshole won't even tell us his name."

Special Agent Ortiz came around the Crown Victoria in time to hear the end of the conversation.

"Mint?"

"Part of the coded message," Harris said. "What's *mint* in Spanish?"

"Yerba buena," Ortiz said.

Harris took the folded page out of her folio and smoothed it out on the hood of the Crown Vic. She tapped where the tunnel ran under the Bay Bridge between San Francisco and Oakland with her index finger.

"Yerba Buena."

"Yerba buena means 'mint'?" Murray chuckled. "I always thought that had something to do with marijuana . . . you know, 'good herb' . . . I'm willing to bet you we are victims of over translation. Whoever caught this intel in Germany likely spoke Spanish, translated it into English, thinking they were doing us a favor. Let's get on the phone with San Fran and have them check out Yerba Buena. Good chance our guy's meeting a boat there. They can snatch his contact."

"Will do." Harris gave a long, feline yawn. "This makes my brain hurt. I'm looking forward to a hot bath and a long sleep."

"Me too," Murray said, studying the UNSUB through the window. "But it occurs to me that I have some apology calls to make to that police sketch artist. This guy does look a little bit like Captain Kangaroo."

63

Huge popcorn flakes sifted from a gunmetal sky turning the Grunewald Forest into a snow globe. Kurt Pfeiffer walked purposefully up the wooded path off Clayallee toward the McDonald's. Eyes wide, he enjoyed the feeling of snow kissing his face. He could not help but smile inside that he'd pulled this off.

Thirty feet in front of him, at the edge of a small parking lot, were two faces he recognized, Skip Hulse, the chief of base of Berlin Mission, and William Dunn, a junior clandestine service officer who two of Mielke's Maidens—prostitutes in the employ of the Stasi—had been trying unsuccessfully to recruit for the past four months. So far, the lad would go no further than buying them a drink and showing them how to fold paper cranes.

Hulse was holding a copy of *Der Spiegel*, as he'd said he would if all was well. Pfeiffer was to travel under a pseudonym and he was taken aback when Hulse tucked the magazine in his pocket and called him by his true name.

Four very large military-looking men stepped out of the shadows and surrounded him, pinning his arms. Before he knew it, they'd spun him around and wrenched his hands behind his back, ratcheting on a pair of handcuffs.

"Kurt Pfeiffer," Hulse said. "You are under arrest."

He gasped. "For what?" His throat convulsed, sending his voice up an octave. "We had an agreement!" He struggled against the cruel metal cuffs. "I am telling you we had an agreement. Talk to the woman. She will tell you!"

Hulse scoffed and glanced to his left toward the forest. "You mean *that* woman?"

Pfeiffer turned to look through the falling snow and found none other than Elke Hauptman standing at the base of a large linden tree.

She smiled and blew him a kiss as the military men led him away and shoved him into the back of a waiting Mercedes sedan.

He had to hunch over to keep from hurting his hands on the cuffs.

He leaned forward to get the driver's attention. "Where are we going?"

Hulse sat down beside him, but said nothing.

"Are we going to see a judge? What is the meaning of all this? I demand to know where you are taking me!"

Hulse looked sideways without moving his head, as if deciding whether or not to waste any words.

"Well . . . since you demand," he finally said,

mocking. He let his head fall to the side, meeting Pfeiffer's eye. "We're taking you home, Kurt. You're officially PNG'd in the West."

Pfeiffer released a sputtering gasp. "Persona non grata? What are you talking about? I thought you said I was under arrest."

"Aw," Hulse said. "That's just for the gun charge. Pretty sure we can make that go away."

"I do not have a gun!"

Hulse produced a clear plastic bag containing a Makarov pistol and an empty magazine. "You mean this isn't your gun?"

"No! Where did you get that?"

"Hmm," Hulse said. "It might belong to a recently murdered KGB agent . . . but I could have sworn we got it off of you." He shrugged. "Doesn't matter. I'm sure you guys will work it all out once you tell them about the mix-up."

"You are turning me over to them?"

"Yep," Hulse said. "With your gun."

"You can't be serious! Do you realize what you are giving up?"

"I don't know, Kurt," Hulse said. "A very frightened young woman who works for our State Department gets to come home. You seem like a pretty good trade."

Admiral Greer and Lane Buckley arrived in Berlin before lunch and accompanied Ryan to the base hospital to look in on Foley.

Her heart monitor sped up momentarily to match her glare when the ADDO walked into the room.

"Lane," she said, stone-faced, before smiling at Greer and Ryan.

The admiral closed the hospital room door and shut the blinds. "This isn't exactly a SCIF," he said. "But I think it's secure enough that I can tell you two what an outstanding job you've done."

Buckley, who looked like he'd been spoiling for a fight since he arrived, walked to the window and peered around the miniblinds.

"I don't get it, Admiral," he said. "You talk like we should give these guys an award when I came over here with the full intention of chewing them new assholes. Because of them, we just lost one of the best intelligence sources we've had in years."

"Is that so?" Greer said.

"Yes, Admiral," Buckley said. "I believe it is."

Ryan took a deep breath, forcing himself not to punch this arrogant asshole in the throat.

"Are you telling me you'd be okay trading an innocent kid's life for a thimble of information that will be stale before we get it into a report? What the hell do we gather intelligence for if not to protect people like Ruby Keller?"

"No one expects you to understand an operational mindset, Ryan," Buckley said. "You stick to analysis. Let ops handle the heavy lifting."

Foley's lips pulled back in a snarl. "How about I grab you by the balls and do a little heavy lifting, you sanctimonious—"

Greer gave a quiet nod and she backed off.

Buckley wagged his head. "Listen. I understand you guys are spun up by all this."

Foley's heart rate began to accelerate again and she very nearly came out of the bed. "You listen, dickhead! You have no idea how—"

Another look from Greer.

Foley raised an open hand. "Okay . . . okay . . ." She inhaled deeply, then blew it out slowly through her mouth, regaining some semblance of control.

"It helps not to look at him," Ryan said. He was every bit as mad as Foley, but if he bowed up, Buckley would take it as a threat to his manhood and things were sure to get physical. It was an option that Ryan had yet to rule out. As Cathy often reminded him, his fuse was very difficult to light, but it was incredibly short, burning down instantly if someone managed to touch it off.

"I'm trying to tell you I do understand," Buckley continued. "I didn't make it to assistant deputy director without seeing some things. You've been in some shit, I get it. But sometimes, a thimbleful of intel is worth a half-dozen lives . . . or more."

"Maybe sometimes." Ryan looked Buckley directly in the eye. "But not this time." He gave a determined nod, realizing that he'd reached a firm conclusion. "You know, I wasn't sure before about this new job at Langley. But you've made the decision for me."

"Sorry you feel that—"

Ryan cut him off. "If this is the way you do business,

then I will gladly come and work on the seventh floor, just so I can counter every program you have going."

"Oh," Buckley said. "You're not working in any office near me. Not with that attitude, mister. Ritter will make sure of that."

"He's right, Jack," Greer said. "Sometimes things don't work out with the sort of equity that we'd like for them to. Ruby Keller was treated like shit by that female Stasi guard. But . . . so goes the war. There is little we can do about Mitzi Graff. And sadly, as much as I'd love to see you working on the same floor as Lane, I'm afraid that's not going to work out."

Buckley twirled his Montblanc pen in his fingers and beamed.

Greer put a hand on Ryan's shoulder. "I'm sorry, Jack, but in light of everything that has occurred, Ritter, Judge Moore, and I all feel it would be better for Buckley to head up the CIA's Office of Congressional Affairs . . ."

Greer didn't say it, but of all Lane Buckley's traits, his ability to kiss ass was stellar. He'd be fantastic in Congressional Affairs, and was just self-important enough to think of the move as a promotion.

"Are you going to be all right?" Greer asked Foley after Buckley left her hospital room.

"I'm fine."

"Jen North?" Ryan asked.

Greer nodded grimly. "Sources say Colonel Schneider shot her about the same time you came out the west end of the tunnel—which they have filled with concrete on their end, by the way."

From Foley: "The East Germans will use this to embarrass us."

Greer gave a knowing nod. "I'm sure. It's what they do."

"Well," Foley said, "I think we can handle it. Not too many of our people fleeing to the East to escape democracy and a free press."

"Too bad about Jen North," Ryan said.

"It's a sad deal, for sure," Foley said. "But I'm not shedding too many tears. She helped us escape, but let's not forget she betrayed the Helsinki team." She looked at Greer. "Any word from Mike?"

"Two confirmed dead," Greer said. "Mike joined the others from the safe house and they hitched a ride north to the Baltic. They should be in Copenhagen by nightfall."

"What about the two bodies?" Ryan asked.

Foley closed her eyes and pounded her head softly against the pillow.

"Stars on a wall, Jack. Stars on a wall . . ."

They sat in silence for a time, each of them knowing that if they were to die in some enemy land, they would be buried there, likely in an unmarked ditch, their family fed some fiction as to the cause of their death. At some point, the stonecutter would carve another memorial star on the wall at Langley. No name, no date, just one of many simple stars to mark the newest sacrifice.

"It's all so tragic," Ryan whispered. "Even Jen. I know she was your friend once."

"No." Foley sighed, coming to terms with it all. "We

worked together. That's all." She gave Ryan a wan smile. "It's not like she ever stitched up my bullet wounds or anything . . ."

Greer raised an eyebrow at that.

Ryan said, "You'll be happy to hear Ruby Keller made it back."

"I heard," Foley said. "Missing her thumb and pretty shaken up. And Pfeiffer?"

"He's back in the East," Ryan said. "With his Makarov."

"Good," Foley said. "I know it's the way things are, but it pisses me off that nothing can be done about that Stasi guard."

"Oh," Greer said. "I didn't say nothing could be done. I said there wasn't much *we* could do."

Greer nodded to Ryan and they both turned to go. Greer opened the door, and then went back to Foley's bedside and put his hand on her shoulder. "That friend of ours." He gave her a smiling nod. "He's home, too."

EPILOGUE

One week after the powers that be had let the little American bitch go free, Mitzi Graff put on her tracksuit and wool hat and went for a five-kilometer run through Prenzlauer Berg People's Park, as she did every Tuesday and Thursday night to work off steam from the rigors of her job. They'd brought in a new one for her, a former Stasi major who had decided to blab to the West. Fortunately, he'd been caught before he could give up any secrets. Unfortunately for him, he'd been captured with a dead KGB officer's pistol, that officer being a favorite of KGB Colonel Evgeni Zima. Graff did not expect the miserable slob to last a week. Even if he did, Zima would see that he was taken to Moscow—and then . . .

Graff slowed to a trot. It was awfully cold and awfully dark for old folks to be out walking.

The old woman was woefully thin, not nearly enough

meat on her bones to be out in this weather. At least she was smart enough to get out of the way. The old man was a different story. He stumbled a little, then stopped in the middle of the trail, frozen like a stag in oncoming headlights.

"Clear the trail, Grandpa!" Graff shouted, slowing to spit.

"Mitzi Graff," the old woman whispered as she went past.

Graff slowed, puffing great blossoms of vapor, running in place so she did not waste her workout. "How do you know my name, Grannie?"

"Ruby Keller told me," the old woman said as she shot her four times in the chest with a suppressed pistol.

"Come, Lotte," Graff heard the old man say as they walked away, leaving the freckled guard writhing in the snow.

Cathy Ryan made it her habit to unpack for her husband. Not because she didn't trust him, but because he would leave his suitcase full of dirty clothes sitting in the closet for a week. And sometimes he left little presents for her and the kids to find.

Jack Junior sat on the edge of the bed, bouncing, singing a little song, and "helping," which usually meant throwing things on the floor. At the moment, he'd draped his father's huge wool coat over himself like a tent. A dry cleaner's tag on the lapel relieved her of worry that the coat might be covered in who knew what . . .

She sorted through the bag, tossing dirty skivvies in a basket, folding a pair of slacks that it looked like he'd never worn, thinking of all the things she had to do to get ready for the move back to the States for Jack's new position at Langley . . . and her new job at Johns Hopkins . . . Jack Junior brought her back to the present with one of his maniacal giggles. When she looked up to check on him, she saw his little finger sticking out of a hole in the shoulder of her husband's coat.

"Just a minute, buddy," she said. "Let Mommy see that."

She took the coat and lifted it up, putting her own index finger through not one, but two holes . . . an entry and an exit. Bullet holes.

"Jack!"

Coat in hand, she spun to march downstairs, but he was already there, standing with his hand in the doorway, looking handsome and important and worthy.

She held up the coat. "Some secrets?"

He sighed, soft and exhausted, the kind of sigh that said he was happy to be home and safe with his little family.

"Afraid so . . ."